BLACK ICE

BLACK ICE

CARIN GERHARDSEN

TRANSLATED FROM THE SWEDISH
BY IAN GILES

SCARLET
NEW YORK

BLACK ICE
(DET SOM GÖMS I SNÖ)

Scarlet
An Imprint of Penzler Publishers
58 Warren Street
New York, N.Y. 10007

Text © 2018 Carin Gerhardsen
First published by Bookmark Förlag, Sweden
Translation © 2021 by Ian Giles
Translated into the English language by Ian Giles
Published by arrangement with Nordin Agency AB, Sweden

First paperback edition: May 2022

Interior design by Maria Fernandez

Library of Congress Control Number: 2021907089

ISBN: 978-1-61316-308-5

eBook ISBN: 978-1-61316-223-1

10 9 8 7 6 5 4 3 2 1

Printed in the United States of America
Distributed by W. W. Norton & Company

A lie is like a snowball:
the further you roll it the bigger it becomes.

—Martin Luther

41-YEAR-OLD MAN MISSING WITHOUT TRACE

The alarm was raised when police were contacted by a relative on Tuesday evening. The man reportedly drove his car to work in Visby at around eight o'clock in the morning. After remaining at his place of work for the duration of the morning, he left around lunchtime. When he failed to attend a meeting scheduled for the afternoon, his employer contacted his wife, and she later reported him missing.

The police have worked together with his family and colleagues to identify places that he may have gone to. They have also searched the surrounding area but say that it is not possible to carry out a more extensive search as they currently have nothing to go on. The man's mobile phone was last active in the vicinity of his workplace.

When he was last seen, the 41-year-old was wearing a black jacket, light shirt, and a pair of dark trousers. He is described as being of normal build, 5ft10, with short dark hair and brown eyes.

The police have encouraged the public to get in touch if they know anything about the disappearance.

GOTLANDS ALLEHANDA

JANUARY
2014

1

Jeanette

IT WAS ONLY once they left the busy roads around Visby and got out into the countryside that she was able to relax. There was always the same stress, the same fear that someone would recognise her sitting in the wrong car beside the wrong person. The lies at work: an errand to run, a dentist's appointment, late lunch with a girlfriend.

You had to be inventive when pursuing forbidden love, and a good actor to boot.

Jeanette did not consider herself to possess either of these qualities. Yet here she was, her heart thumping and her cheeks crimson, using every ounce of calm she had.

What exactly was she playing at? Was it worth it?

She studied her lover discreetly from the side. The way he held the wheel with one of his coarse hands while the other hung loosely by one thumb. The superficial veins crisscrossing the back of his hand. The vigilant eyes taking note of everything happening on the road and around them. His chest rising inside the unbuttoned jacket as he breathed.

"Was everything okay?" he asked. "Did anyone say anything?"

"I said I needed to pick out new tiles for the bathroom."

"And no one questioned that?"

She shook her head.

"Are you doing up your bathroom?"

"Don't know," she replied. "Seems like it."

What did they need a new bathroom for? Her husband thought a new bathroom would change their lives for the better, but she needed something else. Clearly—since she was sitting here risking the entire world that she knew for a moment of love with someone else's husband.

"I don't like lying to my workmates either," he said. "Leaving early under false pretences. But it is what it is."

The relationship was a month or so old. They could no longer dismiss it as a passing whim. They had been sneaking off like this a couple of times a week, and it dominated every part of her mind.

She didn't really know him all that well. Their workplaces were next to each other but had nothing to do with the other. She worked in a furniture shop; he ran a garage. They were never seen together, never called each other, never exchanged any secret messages in the car park. Anything that needed to be said was dealt with here in his car, always during the day, and compensated for with overtime on other occasions. No one ought to suspect anything, so they really had nothing to fear. They could simply let themselves be possessed by each other's lust, the lingering warmth in their bodies and the desire for the next meeting.

"It is how it is," she repeated. "Is that how it's going to be?"

He smiled.

"What would you prefer? Is this enough for you, or would you dare to throw yourself into something new?"

She didn't know what to say. Would *he* dare to take that step and leave behind the old? Her answer was dependent on his. She didn't want to give him the satisfaction of knowing exactly where he had her if he didn't give her anything to hang on to.

Their love was passionate right now. She was in a state of sickness—she couldn't sleep at night or concentrate in the day. But would it last if she was honest with her husband, asked for a divorce, and turned their shared home into a war zone? Would this new irrepressible love cope with that? And for how long?

Perhaps it was the validation she needed. The reassurance that she was still worth loving, still worth making love to. Now she had that, and perhaps it was enough. This man had given her so much energy and joie de vivre that it had shaken new life into her deeply soporific existence. But that wasn't necessarily the same thing as her giving up her home and her finances, turning her back on the man that she had sworn to love. She was conscious that it was novelty's charm that appealed. It wasn't impossible to leave it behind, go home and be a good wife instead.

She tried to persuade herself, but she could already sense the scent of her lover's naked body, the warmth of his breath and the passionate sounds that would soon fill the car.

Even so, she was still of two minds. She felt rather pathetic sitting there like a schoolgirl and dreaming of a future that almost certainly didn't exist. Pathetic, and somehow dirty. She was lying and deceiving for just a few transient moments of devotion each week. Her lover was the direct opposite. He took life in his stride, a smile always on his lips. If she were to end the relationship, he would find a new cause for rejoicing and continue smiling.

They were getting close to the location of their rendezvous and heartbeats in the car quickened. He put his hand on her thigh and she could barely contain herself. She wanted to pull off her clothes and throw herself onto him, press her lips to his, and let herself be embraced, a wave of heat flooding over her.

The sky was getting dark and it began to snow gently. The weather forecast said it wouldn't freeze until night, but the road already looked slippery. They approached the old limestone quarry by Madvar. For a moment, the tires lost their grip and the car skidded precariously.

2

Sandra

HER ARMS FILLED with odds and ends, she stood in the car park outside the XL-Bygg DIY store cursing her stupidity. Today she had finally made it to the store to find some bargain Christmas decorations and outdoor lighting on sale. Of course, she hadn't considered for a moment that she would, as usual, buy too much, all while her car was at the repair shop and her father couldn't help her. She hadn't meant to buy more than she could take on the bus, but here she was loaded up like a packhorse.

The ground was wet and dirty, making her reluctant to put down her boxes and paper bags. She didn't have any gloves—it had been far warmer when she had left home in the morning.

She had called for a taxi twice and on both occasions she had been promised a car within a few minutes. Forty minutes had elapsed so she now put down her purchases to call again.

"This is ridiculous," she said, making an effort to sound angry when she was really just irritated. "I live in the country and can't very well walk all the way to Vejdhem."

"How strange," said the voice on the other end of the line. "There must have been a misunderstanding somewhere down the line. I'll prioritise your booking and send a car immediately."

Yes, that was certainly the case, and at that point Sandra should probably have made an acerbic comment. But she wasn't especially ready for battle—more timid than anything—so instead she politely offered her thanks and ended the call. She sighed heavily, glancing resignedly at the mountain of shopping, and tapped at her phone, her chubby fingers frozen stiff, looking for an entertaining YouTube video to pass the time.

Before she had time to start watching, a man appeared in front of her. She had noticed him a little while ago when he had passed her with rapid steps on the road between the store and his car. Apparently he had changed his mind and turned around.

"Vejdhem," he said. "Is that where you're going?"

He looked pleasant; his thick dark hair, greying at the temples, reminded her of a younger version of her father.

"Yes," Sandra replied. "I've been waiting for the past forty minutes for a taxi that is apparently never coming."

"We can sort that," said the man. "I'm going that way, so you can get a lift with me."

Then he bent down and picked up her things, managing to get everything before walking towards the car.

"Thanks," said Sandra in relief, following. "That's really nice. I should probably cancel the taxi."

"Do you feel they've done anything to deserve that?" he said with a smile.

Sandra didn't disagree; she didn't owe the taxi company anything.

He put the shopping in the boot and held open the passenger door. She got in and tried to blow life into her chilly fingers.

"It seems to have got really cold suddenly," she said as they pulled away.

"It's the 'Siberian chill' on its way," he said, referring ironically to the alarming headlines in the evening papers.

He had a sense of humour, which made any conversation easier. After all, they were going to spend some time together.

"Do you live near Vejdhem?" Sandra asked.

"No, but I have an errand to run in your neck of the woods, so it isn't even out of my way."

Conversation flowed. Sandra didn't get in many words, but she didn't need to either. She listened with some interest as the man told her about his passion for Gotland's history, as he summarised the ice hockey league standings, and when he told her about his efforts on behalf of human rights and against hunger and war and environmental destruction and everything else. He ensured there were no awkward silences in the car, and Sandra was grateful for that.

However, she thought he was driving a little carelessly. He wasn't attentive enough when passing or at crossroads, and he was often looking at her rather than the road while talking. After a while it occurred to her that the loquaciousness and lack of concentration in driving might both be because he was not altogether sober, even though it was only a little before three o'clock in the afternoon. On reflection, wasn't there a whiff of spirits in the car? Fortunately there wasn't much traffic on the roads and she would soon be home.

They drove past the old limestone quarry at Madvar. The road was suddenly covered in black ice, and instead of slowing down the man accelerated into the corner.

3

Jan

HE ZIPPED UP his fly, did up the button, and tightened his belt. He bent forward and kissed her softly on the mouth and both her cheeks. She was steaming with warmth and had the diffuse scent of woman. Shampoo, lotion, soap, or a mild perfume—something attractive that tempted him to stay in the warmth around her body. But he restrained himself and a moment later he was in the driver's seat, in an excellent mood in spite of everything.

Putting the key in the ignition made the music come on. He turned up the volume and tore away. Even if tires hardly ever screeched these days, he still loved the powerful forward motion of the car, the feeling of being pushed back into the seat. His fingers drumming the wheel in time with the bass, he pulled onto the main road.

It appeared out of nowhere without a moment's warning. Just as he was exiting the corner by the ravine, the oncoming car appeared in his field of vision. It was rushing straight towards him at high speed across the black ice.

At the same moment he caught sight of it, he knew it was all over. For one or both of them. He had snow tires and wouldn't be able to dodge the car, wouldn't be able to stop even if he slammed on the brakes. He just wanted it to be over. Quickly.

4

Jeanette

HER HANDS TREMBLING, she brushed off the worst of it. Earth, clay, twigs, rotting leaves. There was broken glass strewn all over the ground. All this glass and dented metal looked unreal when contrasted against nature. She was so shaken up that her body wouldn't obey her, fits of shivering taking hold of her, her teeth chattering. She still had enough presence of mind to get out her mobile. To immortalise what seemed most unreal about the picture.

The blood everywhere inside the car. The man stuck in the driver's seat with a large piece of glass in his throat.

Once again, she noted that he was presumably already dead. The large shard of glass was like the blade of a knife between cartilage and tendons, and surely made it impossible to breathe. He had an open wound on his forehead, and judging by the angle, his neck might very well be broken.

Jeanette debated with herself once again. What was the point of calling emergency services if the man was already dead? She would be obliged to disclose who she was, as well as having to explain under police questioning why she had been in this out-of-the-way location in the middle of winter. It would all come out, her husband would find out—everyone else too. The affair really wouldn't stand up to scrutiny in the light of day, her reputation would be damaged and her future . . . No, you made your own luck, and she had a crucial decision to make here and now.

She did it. She laboriously pulled herself to the boot—the door was wide open after the passage through the air. She picked up the bag and forced the strap over her shoulder. She threw a regretful glance at the smashed-up car and its driver. But the decision had been made. She started to climb out of the ravine.

Darkness was falling quickly now, and it began to snow heavily.

5

Sandra

AT FIRST, she was more or less paralysed and didn't know what to do. She was overwhelmed by a feeling of unreality—that she wasn't present in her own life. Was it just a bad dream? She knew the answer, but couldn't take it in.

Things like this didn't happen to Sandra. She was too respectable, too grey and boring. Her upbringing had been sheltered: an only child pampered by her parents and poorly equipped for adversity. As a result, she lacked the experience required to respond sensibly when life deviated from its usual path.

Naturally, she ought to contact the police. Criminals couldn't be allowed to get off simply because people didn't dare to or have the energy to report them. But she sat at the kitchen table with the phone in front of her and couldn't bring herself to call. Not the police, not her parents, not anyone else.

She couldn't think clearly, let alone express herself in a composed and comprehensible manner. So what should she do? What would tomorrow be like if she didn't do the right thing today?

Her body was throbbing and aching—should she at least seek care?

No, not today. Her body and soul were too lacerated. She didn't have it in her to be examined or patched up, let alone explain herself, accounting for what had happened. Because that would certainly mean the police would be brought in, and she would be called to account: Why hadn't she raised the alarm sooner? Why hadn't she done anything? How could she let it happen? The smell of alcohol in the car should surely have been some kind of red flag?

Sandra knew she lacked the ability to make wise decisions and take control of her life. Not just today, but every day. So how was she supposed to change that right now when life was showing its very worst side?

Outside it was already dark. The snow was whirling down in huge flakes, and the thermometer in the window was showing several degrees below zero. Her gaze moved to the kitchen counter and lingered on the whisky bottle.

She eventually mastered her listlessness and got up. Then she stumbled to the kitchen counter, grabbed hold of the bottle and raised it to her mouth. She tipped back a considerable amount of what was left in the bottle and wiped her mouth with the back of her hand before putting the bottle in the larder. Then she went to the bathroom and got into the shower.

6

Jeanette

SHE REPEATED the same thing in her head over and over again: "it wouldn't have made any difference, because he was already dead." Occasionally with the addition of "or as good as." Because she couldn't be one hundred percent certain what condition he had been in when she had made her decision. Her *selfish* decision. When she had decided to leave him down there in the ravine to meet her new—and hopefully lighter—fate.

When she got home, she had pretended nothing had happened, which was easier said than done with a torn coat and muddy shoes. But her husband accepted her vague references to changeable weather and slippery pavements, and she babbled about the bathroom renovation, largely because the last normal, everyday conversation she had had before the accident had been about those bloody tiles.

He might have perceived her as unusually emotional, with an unexpectedly positive attitude towards the refurbishment in which she had previously been barely interested. But he didn't ask any questions, talking on and seeming more content than he had for a long time.

His enthusiasm made her feel calmer for the moment but did nothing to alter her thoughts once silence fell. She went over what had happened from all angles, clumsily trying to shake the feeling of guilt.

In her head was a constant dialogue between herself and some kind of superior moral entity:

Why should a dead man be allowed to drag me through the mud?
Because he might not have been dead.
After that crash and with those injuries, he must have been dead—he wouldn't have survived until the paramedics arrived.
How do you know? Do you have any medical training?
Anyone could see that he was dead or almost dead. His life would have been intolerable had he been saved.
Who are you to decide what constitutes tolerable?
True.
If he had been saved, you said? So there was a tiny chance he could have been saved?
No. No, there wasn't. Not even one in a million.
But still. Just leaving him there? Bleeding to death. Not able to breathe. Is that humane?
There was nothing to be done.
I'm not the first person to have a little something on the side.
Nor the last person to be seen as a whore on those grounds either. I have my life ahead of me—he was dead or dying. What does it matter?
It matters to someone. Wife, children, siblings, and parents who will miss him. Who have a right to know.
I acted in a way that benefitted me. Most of what I do is for others' benefit, but I helped myself and my future. I did what was reasonable in the situation.

Jeanette fought with her internal demons, struggling to convince herself that her actions had been rational. To persuade herself of the long-term positive effects. But her conscience gnawed at her, eating into every single one of her thoughts and dreams.

She had to do something to avoid succumbing to the burden of guilt.

7

Sandra

"YOU'RE WASTING AWAY, sweetheart," said Dad, placing a hand on her shoulder.

Sandra jumped hard, which is what she did in response to any unpredicted touch nowadays. It wasn't the first time that her parents—whom she often ate with but was not currently confiding in—had remarked that she had lost weight. The fact that her appetite had been blown away was a welcome side effect of that awful thing that she would have preferred to forget but couldn't.

"Gosh, you frightened me," said Sandra with a small laugh that was intended to trivialise her reaction.

Her father didn't look especially convinced.

"I didn't mean to," he said with a concerned frown between his eyes. "Sorry."

Both he and her mother had almost certainly noticed that something was off, but they maintained discretion and gave her the room she needed without expressing excessive curiosity. She was particularly unappreciative of unexpected sounds. She would glance constantly over her shoulder, semi-neurotically ensuring that no one was watching her from a distance. She struggled to fall asleep at night and found it hard to focus on work during the day. Of course, it wasn't all that intellectually demanding, but she had to pay attention to customers' expectations, perceive their needs as they wandered around the shop, and accompany them to the shelf they were looking for. And her distance learning course on which she normally spent her evenings was on hold for the time being. Her thoughts were elsewhere.

Her car had been fixed, but it was Sandra herself who felt like she wasn't roadworthy. She was afraid of the cold, potential slipperiness, unpredictable manoeuvres by fellow motorists, and driving in the dark. She was highly strung and low spirited—far from her usual easygoing, good-natured self.

The thought of contacting the police was gnawing away at the back of her mind. Sandra wondered whether doing it would make her feel better or have the opposite effect. Of course, she ought to do her duty as a responsible member of society. Ensure that that man was stopped and punished, and that no one else was affected. At the same time, if the police managed—against all probability—to find him based on her vague description, then she would have to come face-to-face with him. That was something that horrified her rather than tempted her, even though it ought to be the other way around. She would have to testify against him in court, unless the case was dropped—which in all truth was the likely outcome. Because she had no idea what his name was, what car he drove, where he worked, or where he lived. And it was doubtful whether she would even be able to pick him out in a lineup with any certainty.

And what would the point be of using up police resources and taxpayers' money, if any investigation would eventually be discontinued?

This was why Sandra came to leave such thoughts where they were. She pushed herself onwards in order to return, as far as possible, to an ordinary life. And the days passed.

8

Jeanette

IT WAS MORE than two weeks later when the missing man's photo was published and he was named in the local press. At first, Jeanette couldn't believe her eyes, rereading the article several times before putting the newspaper down and putting her hands to her head.

Missing? What did that mean?

Investigations had met a dead end, according to the journalist—there was apparently nothing to go on.

In one way this was a good thing, but it was a bad thing in many other ways.

"Headache?" her husband asked from across the breakfast table.

She was so dazed by the traumatic news that she wasn't aware of his presence, so lonely in this that she had forgotten she wasn't alone in the room.

She said yes, excused herself, and went to the bathroom where the medicine cabinet was. She quickly gulped down a couple of painkillers, double the dose set out in the printed instructions on the box. Then she sat on the toilet seat lid with her head in her hands and tried to structure her thoughts.

In one stroke her entire already turbulent existence had been turned upside down. The police were asking for help; family and friends knew nothing. No one knew anything.

Except her. Jeanette had the answer to everyone's questions; she was sitting on the opportunity to untangle all the knots and give the chief mourners some peace of mind.

But at what price?

Far too great a price, without doubt. She knew that she had committed a criminal act, even if she had no idea what classification it had. Jeanette was not willing to give up her own well-being for the sake of a group of strangers. She didn't owe them anything, she really didn't. And even if her well-being wasn't great at the moment, she had made her choice down there in the ravine, and she couldn't change that. It was too late to fix this. She didn't want to spend years in prison for it—she wouldn't survive that.

No one would feel better for knowing that she'd had a relationship with the missing man. It would merely add salt to the wound.

JEANETTE BARELY SLEPT at night. Despite her entire being downright screaming for rest, her brain refused to relax. Instead, it would paint ghastly pictures on the inside of her eyelids that made her heart pound and her skin sweat so much her sheets darkened with perspiration.

In a feverish half-torpor, she saw the man in the metal wreckage deep within the inaccessible ravine. The face damaged beyond recognition, covered in wounds and bruises. The shard of glass like a spike in his throat, and eyes that would open without warning and plead for help that never came. The rib cage that rose to permit a solitary, rasping breath, blood pulsing through the open wound on the forehead.

Fantasy and reality merged into one, and she lay there tossing and turning through the nights, unable to reason her way to relief in her conscience-stricken state.

It was only during the day that some sense took hold, when her rational inner voice had a little room to manoeuvre. But the restless nights took their toll and the lack of sleep led to something that began to seem like depression.

And the days passed.

Our beloved
Charlotte
Wretberg
Born 3 July 2003
Loved and missed
16 September 2009
MUM and DAD
Granny
Grandma and Grandpa
Friends and family

———

No longer can I caress
your cheek
No longer can I squeeze
your hand
You have reached
another land
Where nothing can hurt you

———

Funeral service
at Västerhejde Church
Friday, 2 October
11:00
The ceremony ends
after saying farewell
at the church.
Please remember
Charlotte
by donating to
the Childhood Cancer Foundation.

MAY
2018

9

Sandra

IT WAS A slightly chilly but beautiful spring evening, and the blackbirds and willow wrens were competing in the auditorium that was her parents' garden. It hadn't rained for some time, so Erik and his grandfather were keeping busy by watering the shrubs. Sandra could hear her father explaining in full detail to his grandchild how important it was to water in the evening. Erik listened to everything his grandfather said with great interest. He adored his grandparents and the love was undeniably mutual. Erik was at least as spoilt as she had been during her own childhood. But you could hardly be loved too much, she told herself.

The meal was finished and Sandra helped her mother to clear the table. She probably didn't want help, but Sandra felt she exploited her parents enough as it was, and at least tried to do her share. Coming here and eating so many nights a week seemed immature, but that was how all the other involved parties wanted it. She didn't want to take that joy away from them, even if it didn't exactly score her any adult brownie points.

"Volunteer work again this evening?" her mother asked.

"Of course. If I've got nothing better on, then I give my time to Friends-on-call."

"Isn't it hard work? Doesn't it clash with your actual job? Surely you need to rest just like everyone else."

"It's not all that onerous," Sandra reassured her. "I feel like I'm making a difference and that's important to me. Almost therapeutic."

"If you need therapy you can always come to me, dear."

"I know that, Mum, and I have all the support I need from you two. But it feels good to help others. To comfort and care."

"Isn't it just a load of mucky old so-and-sos who call?"

"Mucky old so-and-sos?" Sandra laughed, putting the frying pan down in the sink. "No, definitely not. It's mostly sad people who call. Lonely, perhaps frightened people who don't feel they have anyone else to turn to with their thoughts and worries."

"Isn't it a great drain acting as a sponge for other people's misery?"

"No, Mum. Quite the opposite. Your own troubles often seem trivial when you hear other people's stories."

"Troubles?" said her mother, frowning. "Aren't things going your way?"

"Less and less," said Sandra truthfully. "Almost never. But I have you and I have Erik. I have a varied job and colleagues I like. What more can I expect?"

"Well, if you say so," her mother sighed, without sounding altogether convinced.

It wouldn't be long before the question of whether Erik could stay the night with his grandparents came up. Sandra put the final bits and pieces in the dishwasher and wiped the kitchen counter.

"You know that we're more than happy for Erik to spend the night here? To give you a little alone time."

Sandra vaguely grasped that "alone time" had something to do with blokes and, by extension, wedding bells. That kind of pressure got a little tiring in the long run, but it was nothing she couldn't put up with.

"I know, Mum," she replied. "But I also love having Erik around me. Bathing him, brushing his teeth, and reading him a bedtime story. I like to know he is sleeping in his room as I do grown-up stuff. Thanks all the same—but not tonight."

AN ELDERLY MAN whose dog had been run over was the evening's first caller to Friends-on-call. He talked freely, not afraid to lay bare his feelings. He just needed someone to listen, and Sandra did. Occasionally, she would insert the odd encouraging rejoinder, and after around twenty minutes the man had talked it out.

He was followed by a young woman named Ellen who would call almost every evening when Sandra was on duty. She had learning difficulties and seemed rather happy-go-lucky—she just wanted someone to share her day with. Sandra asked questions with interest and listened to the amusing replies. It was an honour being someone's confidant like this, sharing the daily life of someone whom she would otherwise never have met.

She then quickly dealt with a call from an unhappy mother who was having difficulties with her child who had ended up in a bad crowd.

Then the phone fell silent. That was to be expected. Three calls per shift was usually more than enough to cover the needs of fifty-seven thousand Gotlanders for an evening. Sandra went to get ready for bed. But just as she was about to set the phone to airplane mode it rang, even though it was almost midnight and her shift was due to end.

The conversation fumbled into life.

"Kerstin," the woman replied with some hesitation. "My name's Kerstin."

Her voice was a little raspy; perhaps she'd had a tough life. But it might just be that she smoked a little more than her voice could cope with, or that she was suffering the aftereffects of a cold.

"I'm glad you've turned to Friends-on-call, Kerstin. Before we get started, I just have to inform you that if anything you say makes me suspect that you or someone else has committed or is planning to commit a serious crime, I will contact the police. Are you okay with that?"

"Of course."

"Beyond that, you can be sure that what you say will stay between you and me. Does that sound okay?"

"That sounds good."

"Great. Was there anything in particular you wanted to talk about?"

"Anything in particular? No, I'm not sure . . ."

"We can talk about anything. I'm here to listen, but the conversation is entirely on your own terms."

"I'm also a listener," said Kerstin. "Normally."

Then she went quiet, and Sandra had to make an effort to keep the conversation going. It was unusual for callers not to have something specific they wanted to discuss.

"You step back and watch? Or do you mean that people come to you with their problems?"

"A bit of both," Kerstin replied, without developing her answer further.

"Do you find it too much?" Sandra attempted.

"It's okay."

"Because it can be all too easy to become the shoulder that everyone wants to cry on."

"Not for you, apparently."

"You and I are anonymous to each other," said Sandra. "That's the difference. I can't help you in any way except by listening and trying to cheer you up. If you're there with a living, breathing person, then there are greater demands on what you do and how you follow up. It can be a tough job to be the one who has to put the pieces back together when someone around you doesn't feel good."

"It's okay," Kerstin repeated.

Sandra struggled to find a way to keep the conversation going.

"So you're a listener. Does that mean you don't talk much yourself?"

"Exactly."

"Why is that? Perhaps you're shy?"

"No, I wouldn't say that. Just don't have anything to say."

The conversation continued hesitantly without anything really being said. The receiver was silent for long stretches. But there was something about this woman that awoke Sandra's interest more than usual. The sad, restrained tone in her voice. Her unwillingness to talk at all and the courage it must have taken for her to do so anyway.

"I notice that you find it difficult to talk about yourself," said Sandra. "So I have to say it's great that you are doing it anyway."

"I've barely said anything," said Kerstin, with what might be a small laugh in her voice.

"You will," said Sandra encouragingly. "We're getting to know each other. Creating mutual trust. That takes time. It'll be easier next time you call."

"You think I should call again?"

"I definitely think so. Sometimes you need to be the person in focus. Particularly in your own life. If you don't think it's working well with me you can request to speak to someone else."

"It's okay. I might call again then."

"Do. Take care for now."

"Thanks for taking my call," said Kerstin.

Then it was over. It had been a bit of an ordeal, mostly because Sandra herself wasn't especially inventive when it came to topics of conversation. That yoke didn't normally rest on her shoulders. Strictly speaking, they hadn't talked about anything, yet strangely enough Sandra was looking forward to a potential next time. She assumed there was a tragedy behind the sadness in Kerstin's voice, something weighing her down that would soon enough bubble up to the surface. It awoke Sandra's curiosity, and she hoped she would be a part of it when it happened.

10

Jeanette

IT WAS A rowdy afternoon by the East Gate in Visby. Some lads were being loud and the police had been by several times to try and make them see reason. They rarely detained anyone—the gang that hung out there by the benches was mostly harmless. But sometimes things got heated, and this was one of those occasions.

Jeanette was having one of her worse days. The anxiety was like a cancer in her stomach, and she knew that she had been irresponsible to mix sedatives with alcohol. Now she was dizzy and felt bad. She sat swaying on the bench with her hands over her ears. She simply hoped the racket would stop so that they could all have some peace and quiet in the spring sunshine.

It seemed she was the only one who thought that. The two at loggerheads with each other—about a negligible sum of money, which was what it was almost always about—had their fists clenched, ready to fight. The others—two women and around ten men—were trying to talk sense into them and keep them apart. Jeanette kept to herself, and didn't have the energy to engage with them—she didn't really feel that she belonged there.

Yet it was here she had ended up, here that she spent much of her long, meaningless days. She had come down a long way in the world, and it had happened so quickly. After living a well-ordered life with financial security, one day she had dropped it all to indulge in various chemical substances on a full-time basis. One thing led to another, and one day the benches frequented by the lushes by the East Gate had simply seemed like a better place to waste her life than the solitude of a one-bedroom flat in Gråbo.

They were almost coming to blows, and the profanities were coming thick and fast. Everyone was involved in some way, except for Jeanette. Curious passersby stopped to see how it would pan out, while the police were conspicuous by their absence at the very moment they were most needed. The volume was becoming unbearable and Jeanette decided to go. Not far, just towards the Money Box and Dalman Gate tower, where she would be able to slump down on the grassy slope until everything had calmed down.

The very moment she got up, she was floored by an elbow gone astray. When she came to, she was lying on her back on the asphalt path, her nose bleeding. The dispute had ceased and everyone's attention was directed at Jeanette.

Both combatants were repentant and helped to move her into a semi-upright position on the bench. One of them, Lubbi, sat down with his arm around her neck and tilted her head back.

"Nanna is fetching ice from the Indian corner shop," he said. "Sorry. We really didn't mean it."

"I know," said Jeanette. "But there's no bloody need to carry on like that at all."

"Want some refreshment?" Lubbi asked in a transparent ploy to change the subject.

"Aren't there lots of people standing around watching?"

"Who cares? Anyway, they've gone. The ambulance is on the way."

"You're joking?"

"I'm joking," Lubbi confirmed with a hearty roar of laughter. "Here you go."

Then he gently lifted her head and gave her a slug of vodka straight from the bottle. It might not have been exactly what she needed, but she didn't decline it. It felt good to be fussed over; for once she was the focus of everyone's attention. She leaned back again to stop the flow of blood.

"Here she comes, our very own Barbamama," said Lubbi.

Nanna sat down on the bench on her other side. She had managed to procure a plastic bag of ice that she now applied to Jeanette's nose.

"How does it feel?" she asked. "Does it hurt?"

"It's working," said Jeanette.

"Thank you for making peace between those two tearaways."

"Did I?"

"You must have noticed," said Nanna with a sneer at Lubbi. "Now they're being nothing but doves of peace."

Yet another guffaw from Lubbi. Jeanette laughed too and straightened herself on the bench.

"I think it's stopped bleeding," she said putting the ice pack down on the ground in front of her.

She looked around. Everything was back to normal. On the other benches they were sneaking swigs while bickering with each other. The spring flowers in the planters between the benches were resplendent in the hot sunshine. The birds sang and the air was finally warm. The perfect conditions for the life she was now leading.

People walked by with deliberate steps and airs of importance. Just a few years ago she had been one of them, someone who went to work every morning and came home with a bag of groceries in the evening. Someone who went to the gym and yoga, who took care of her health, her appearance, and other things like makeup and accessories. The bathroom tiles.

The anxiety that had temporarily left her in conjunction with the blow to her face returned. It couldn't be cured, but there were two ways to deal with it in the short-term: tablets and alcohol. Both options were devastating in the long run. Her stomach was turning, her head spinning. She couldn't take more right now; she would have to withstand the pain some other way.

"How are you, babe?" said Lubbi, putting a hand on her knee. "You're ghastly pale."

"I'm fine," Jeanette lied.

"Perhaps we should have called an ambulance? You might have a concussion."

"It's not that, I promise. I'm just having a really shit day. In here," she added, gesturing at her head.

And then the tears came. She felt stupid crying in front of all these people who really didn't have it good either. But the tears welling up inside her couldn't be stopped. It wasn't a dramatic show, no sobbing, just a small and silent trickle of tears running down her cheeks.

But Lubbi saw. He put his arm around Jeanette again and pulled her close.

"What's weighing heavy on your heart?" he asked pompously in an attempt to play down the situation.

"I miss home," said Jeanette. "Miss everything I used to have before I became like this."

"Like this?" said Lubbi. "You're a good-looking girl, Jen. There's nothing that needs changing about you."

"I miss my daughter and my husband and our home and all our stuff. Not so much my job and . . ."

"Daughter?" Nanna interrupted. "You have a daughter?"

"You've never mentioned it before," Lubbi agreed.

"Had," said Jeanette in despair. "She died."

"That's shit," said Nanna, putting her hand on Jeanette's.

"I'm sorry," said Lubbi.

He was quiet for a while before returning to the subject.

"I don't want to dig around and open old wounds and all that, but if you want to talk then you're welcome to. You might feel better?"

Jeanette wanted to talk, but hadn't touched on the subject for a long time. She didn't quite know where to start.

"She was called Charlotte," she said simply.

"Beautiful," said Nanna. "Beautiful name."

"How old . . . was she?" Lubbi asked.

"She was four when it was diagnosed," said Jeanette, wiping her nose with her sleeve. "Acute myelogenous leukaemia."

"Leukaemia," Lubbi repeated. "Fuck."

"She was in pain, had bruises everywhere, infections that never went away, and she was always tired. She had treatment for almost two years. Chemotherapy. And then she had a bone marrow transplant. Nothing helped. Her kidneys stopped working and eventually she couldn't cope any longer. She was six when she gave up. Almost nine years ago. She would have turned fifteen this year."

No one said anything for a while. Lubbi held her tight and Nanna squeezed her hand. It felt a little better now that someone actually cared. It didn't change what had happened, but in that moment she felt warmth from these people, of a kind she rarely experienced any longer.

"She suffered so much during those years," said Jeanette when she had collected herself. "We suffered too—my husband and I. It was horrible standing by and being unable to do anything except be there for Charlotte. And eventually having to part from our child, to bury her . . . It's indescribable."

"How did he take it?" Nanna asked. "Your husband?"

"While Charlotte was still alive, we were strong together. Incomprehensibly strong, on reflection. One or both of us were always with her. We were united against the rest of the world, against disinterested healthcare workers and unsympathetic authorities. But when we lost Charlotte, everything that had kept us together vanished."

"You got divorced?" said Lubbi.

"Not at once. We wore each other down for another five years. He struggled on, pretending everything was normal. I became increasingly blasé, got tired of our empty lives and our boring conversations. I long for those now. But at least we shared our grief after Charlotte died. We could have talked about it. I wanted to, but he kept all that difficult stuff at arm's length and wanted to move on with his life, as he said. He was probably right—I'm a much weaker person."

The tears began to flow more heavily. Jeanette snuffled and wiped the tears on the arm of her jacket. Lubbi and Nanna sat quietly, waiting for more.

"I met a guy at work," Jeanette continued. "He was married with kids, but we started having an affair. We used to sneak off in his car in the afternoons. For a rendezvous. It felt grubby and deceitful, but you have to start somewhere. You can't leave your old relationship headlong before you've at least tasted the new one."

Lubbi opened a can of beer and passed it to Jeanette. She knew she shouldn't, but she still drank from it. She offered it to Nanna too, but she declined, so Jeanette handed the can back to Lubbi and carried on with her tale.

"We talked about a future together. I was head over heels in love with him, ready to give up everything I still had. It didn't seem like much then, but looking back . . . And it went to hell with the new guy. A complete disaster. I got depressed and had panic attacks. I was on sick leave and started taking tranquilisers. Drinking box wine. I stopped working out, stopped socialising with people, stopped talking to my husband. He didn't know about the affair, but after six months or so he'd had enough of me and the awful state I was in. Completely understandable, but I didn't care. To begin with. Until reality caught up and I saw this worn-out, skinny pisshead looking back at me in the bathroom mirror. It didn't exactly relieve the fear of going back to work and normal everyday life."

Both Nanna and Lubbi cast their gazes down, probably because they associated that more with their own dreadful existences than with hers. Neither of them disagreed, so they were backing her up in a way.

"What did I do then?" said Jeanette. "Did I pull myself together and stop using? No, I sank even lower. I'm useless and my life is one huge fiasco."

The conversation was over. The others came over and the mood was broken, perhaps partly because Jeanette's final words could be taken to apply to any one of them. Lubbi and Nanna were free to ignore their own failures, so what was it that drove Jeanette to brandish the truth in their faces? Did she feel deep down that she was superior to them?

She decided to express herself differently in future. Not to say disparaging things about herself that essentially encompassed the whole wretched gang on the benches by the East Gate.

11

Sandra

"MUM, WHY DON'T you want me to fight?"

Sandra was sitting in the armchair in her son's room trying to read while Erik fell asleep. Not because he was afraid of being alone or the dark or needed company, but for her own sake. Sometimes it took a while for him to relax, in which case they would talk. About the book they had just read, or about something that had happened during the day. Sometimes about bigger things like outer space, the sea, and poverty, and often about everyday but equally fascinating things like buses, scarecrows, and electricity. Now it was apparently crime and punishment.

"Because hurting other people isn't allowed," Sandra replied. "It's a crime that you go to prison for."

"Igor isn't in prison," Erik retorted.

"We don't put children in prison in Sweden."

There was silence for a while before Erik continued.

"I don't think it would be that bad to be in prison."

Sandra had to stifle the laughter about to erupt within her. Goodness—where on earth had he gotten that idea from?

"It's probably best if you avoid ending up in prison," she said with a smile, pinching his cheek fondly. "Sleep tight, darling."

Erik had a lot of thoughts and was good at expressing himself. He was early in many ways: he had already been walking by nine months and started talking at thirteen months. And he liked to talk a lot, bubbling with enthusiasm to say everything he thought and felt.

What a joy to have a son like this, Sandra often thought to herself. Reflective and empathetic, free-spirited and expressive. Rather a long way from her own personality, fortunately. She was uptight and scared. Didn't look like much to the outside world: fat and clumsy, dull mousy hair and protruding teeth. The boys weren't exactly queuing up, and it was something her parents refused to see and understand, whilst at the same time it disappointed them.

She didn't get much reading done. Her thoughts wanted to stay in the real world with its many drawbacks as well as its bright sides. Erik was one of the best of these, and without him life would be barely worth living. She closed the book and studied him by the light of the reading lamp. What had she really given him? Apart from love and care? His colouring wasn't hers, nor the body shape or the extrovert nature. But he's good-natured, she thought, taking each day as it comes. And he wants the best for people.

Erik had fallen asleep now, so Sandra turned off the light and left the room. She tidied a little in the hall and the living room, having cleaned up in the kitchen after dinner. Then she sat down at the kitchen table with a cup of tea and a magazine, expecting her mobile to ring.

She was completely different on the phone. There she pretended she was someone other than who she was. First and foremost, she dared to think aloud and talk. She might not be that talented at keeping a conversation going, but periods of silence were also permitted. For most people, it was her ear that was most important, her patience and the brief comments. No one knew who she was or what she looked like; she hid behind a voice that sounded empathetic and experienced all at the same time. Or perhaps it was the opposite, that she didn't need to hide behind that voice because it was her own.

This was something she often thought about. Whether, with a little mental effort, she could disregard her appearance and take the sting out of her anxiety when around people, instead playing the role of a woman standing on a cliff in the wind. She cared and supported, with mild admonishment recalibrating people who had ended up in spiritual imbalance.

But no—no one could consciously suppress their fears and the knowledge of their own weaknesses.

Her mobile vibrated. Ellen was first up. Wonderful, cheerful Ellen, who most often saw the bright side of life. It was the same today, and her mood was infectious. There was a long account of a visit to the swimming baths followed by a request that Sandra talk about her day. She did—albeit taking care to maintain her privacy and being careful to avoid disclosing any identifying details about where she worked or lived. In Ellen she had nothing to fear, but sooner or later she was bound to be saddled with a psycho.

Then there were two calls from the same person about an hour apart. He introduced himself using different names and talked about completely different issues, however. Sandra pretended not to notice, approaching the problems with enthusiasm. The first was to do with a cancer diagnosis and the crisis that had followed it, the second about anxiety relating to something he feared might be considered domestic violence in the eyes of the law, but which was really just physical contact of the rougher kind.

Sandra thought she dealt with all of it well, particularly the second call when she strove not to judge but simply to get the man's feelings about the whole thing straight. Strengthened by faith in her own objective therapeutic abilities, she took her second call from Kerstin just before midnight.

"I'm glad you've called again," said Sandra.

She really did mean it; she had been looking forward to this call since their last one had ended. Kerstin said nothing.

"How are you?" said Sandra.

"So so," said Kerstin with some hesitation.

"Do you know why?"

"What do you mean 'why'?"

"Why don't you feel all that good?"

"I have a sore throat," said Kerstin.

"That sounds annoying. But it will pass," said Sandra, who didn't believe that Kerstin was calling Friends-on-call to discuss streptococcal infections.

"I cry a lot," said Kerstin unexpectedly. "My husband died."

"That's very sad. Did it happen recently?"

"No, but it comes in waves. I think about how old I'm getting and how empty it will always be here in the house."

How to answer this kind of statement? Loneliness was what callers to Friends-on-call had in common. But loneliness took on many different guises. Some felt lonely in a bad relationship, others were frozen out at school or work. Then there were those who were lonely in all ways—those who had no one to share their life with, no work to go to, no children or grandchildren. Some perceived themselves as lonely because they couldn't think straight, or were unable to open up and let other people in.

"I could say things like 'you're no older than you feel' or 'there's plenty more fish in the sea,'" said Sandra. "But I don't know anything about you and your situation, so they would just be empty words. But perhaps you would like to tell me something about your husband. What was he like?"

"You still wouldn't understand," said Kerstin.

"When did he die?" Sandra asked instead.

"Four years ago. I waited and waited, but he never came back. I knew he was in the car, knew something had happened. I had spoken to him just before the accident, and he was supposed to be home soon."

"A car accident? How terribly tragic."

Indeed it was. But Kerstin was talking. She had uttered several sentences in a row of her own volition, talking about something that was surely the worst thing she had experienced. Just as Sandra had guessed, painful tragedy lay behind Kerstin's broken voice and inability to share her thoughts. However, Kerstin was not alone in having lost a loved one, her life partner, in dramatic circumstances. She was one of many, and ought to be able to find support and comfort from people with similar experiences. But she had turned to Sandra—Sandra who had no comparable experiences of her own. Absurdly, she felt honoured, and was overcome with inexplicable tenderness towards Kerstin.

"He was missing for four days," said Kerstin. "Do you understand?—for four days."

"Missing?" said Sandra, who didn't quite follow this.

"There was black ice and the car crashed into a ravine. He was stuck there for four days before someone found him."

Now Sandra didn't know what to think. If Kerstin had spoken to him just before the accident then the police with all their resources must surely have been able to locate him. What was more, surely the smashed-up car must have been visible from the road—another motorist must have asked themselves why there was a car down in the ravine.

"It took several hours for him to die," said Kerstin, and Sandra now heard her voice cracking.

"How awful," was all she could bring herself to say.

"According to the police, he was stuck there with a cracked skull and difficulty breathing for more than two hours before he died. And it was four days before they found his body."

"Despite them searching?" said Sandra, who was beginning to feel physically sick as the picture of the horrible accident emerged with increasing clarity before her.

The receiver fell silent. The only thing audible were stifled snuffles.

"Despite them searching?" Sandra repeated, who really couldn't believe the four days being mentioned.

"The car was quickly covered in snow," said Kerstin. "It wasn't visible from the road until it thawed four days later."

"But still," Sandra couldn't stop herself from persisting. "You must have had some idea about roughly where he was, and the police have dogs and thermal cameras. I don't understand why it took four . . ."

But Kerstin was gone. And Sandra was sat there with the mobile in her hand, staring blankly into space.

12

Jeanette

A NEW DAY and different but still familiar emotions were governing her. Jeanette felt better, but not well—she never did. But today the booze was like a peaked cap surrounding the brain with cotton, wrapping the body in a sense of well-being that was reminiscent of a soft and warm fleece blanket in front of a roaring fire. Here and now she was safe, surrounded by people who wanted the best for her and whom she cared about in return, screened off from all those people walking past with their vague outlines, their gazes neutral or contemptuous.

On days like this she didn't care about them, all those people who lived real lives and hurried from work to the bank to home to kindergarten to the shops—from life to death. She couldn't care less about their welfare, and even though she occasionally recognised some of them from her former life, she never let herself be depressed. Life was here and now, amongst those people who shared her daily existence, her joys and hardships.

She was still getting over the blow to the nose that had floored her the other day, the black eye that had now gone a shade of poisonous green. Her fellow companions in misfortune were treating her gently, showing a tenderness that she had not experienced for a long time, with gentle physical touches and soft words. She responded to the friendliness with heartfelt words and laughter that was infectious.

A day on the bench could be like that—and that was presumably what they all hoped for every day. The noisy but friendly atmosphere prevailed while the merciless reality remained at a safe distance and didn't make any immediate or heavy demands.

This was the atmosphere Jeanette found herself in when a person—flesh and blood—took shape amongst the passersby on the asphalt path. Out of the fog of alcohol stepped a figure with a more distinct outline and something markedly recognisable about her. A woman of her own age, but not someone she knew from school or her job. Since she was unable to work out who the familiar face belonged to straight away, she tried to shake it all off, but something stopped her.

The woman was tall and slender with her blond hair tied in a long, loose ponytail that rested on one shoulder. She was wearing a skirt and blouse—office wear—but was relaxed, wearing comfortable shoes and not excessively elegant. She looked nice, Jeanette thought, with her old and rarely utilised eye for looks.

But who was she? For some reason, that woman who was now disappearing behind a car by the School Gate in the city wall meant something to Jeanette—she could feel it. But in what way?

She reappeared momentarily, before turning right to go through the gate onto Södra Murgatan, and shortly after that she was gone for good. Jeanette let her gaze rest on the point where the woman had disappeared, while her brain worked to get to the bottom of who she was.

"You're a long way away, Jen," said Lubbi, who seemed to have kept her under constant watch since the accident a few days before.

It was in that moment that she realised who the woman was. Of course—how could she have forgotten? Granted, she was more out of it than she had thought, which explained her relatively good mood, and the fact that it didn't leave her now that she was thinking about things that she had been making an effort to forget.

"Did you see someone you knew?" Nanna asked as she paced back and forth just behind the bench on which Jeanette, Lubbi, and the brawler, Micki, were sitting.

"Not exactly," Jeanette replied, still unable to draw her gaze away.

"An old lover?" Lubbi suggested.

Jeanette returned to the constricting reality around her and saw Nanna slap him on the shoulder and give him a stern look. But for some reason Lubbi's question didn't bother her. The sense of unease didn't take hold of her conscience, and the blond woman's appearance didn't hurt either. Jeanette refused to let go of this exhilaration she felt in her body—she wanted to continue being at the centre of her friends' attention and being watched by devoted eyes. And hearing her own voice.

Yes, that was exactly how it was. She wanted to talk and be taken seriously, in the same way as she had been when she had collapsed on the path after being hit in the face by a pointy elbow. When she had lost herself in bittersweet memories and felt the combined support of her friends in her new life. This was why she replied honestly to Lubbi's coarse question:

"My old lover's wife."

Maybe it wasn't such a good idea to talk about these things while so inebriated, but there were greater forces within her encouraging her to go the other way.

"The one you gave everything . . . up for?" Lubbi guessed with a degree of sensitivity in his voice that hadn't been there a moment before.

"You remember?" Jeanette smiled at him.

"Of course." Lubbi smiled back. "You loved him and I love love. So was that his wife? You don't really know her?"

"I don't know her at all, but I recognise her," Jeanette replied, pulling out a bottle of cheap, sweet wine from the backpack on the ground in front of her.

"Why did it end between you?" asked Micki, who had missed the whole introduction a few days earlier.

"Because it went to hell, Micki," Lubbi said helpfully. "Like relationships often do."

And that was as true as could be, but Jeanette was ready to give them some more.

"He disappeared," she said, twisting the cap and taking a swig from the bottle. "One day he was suddenly gone."

The others didn't appear to know whether to interpret the information literally or whether she was paraphrasing the sad end to a relationship, but Kat—one of the more boisterous people in the group—squeezed herself onto the bench between Micki and Lubbi and began asking questions.

"Poof!" she said, snapping her fingers. "Magic!"

"You're joking, Kat," said Jeanette, who wasn't in the mood to bandy words about. "But he really disappeared. It was in the papers with big headlines. His family appealed for help."

"But you didn't, because you knew where he was," Kat laughed.

Kat didn't know how right she was, but Jeanette wasn't willing to go that far with her story.

"You finished the bloke off and dumped him in the sea," Kat said. "And I'm sure he deserved it!"

"Stop it, girl," Lubbi warned. "Let Jen tell those of us who are interested what happened next."

Jeanette passed her the bottle. Kat wasn't hard to please.

"There is no what happened next," Jeanette observed. "There's still no trace of him."

She lit a cigarette and took a long first drag on it.

"So the chick who passed by here a while ago," said Lubbi, "is she still married to the guy even though no one has heard from him in—what did you say? Five years?"

"Four years. And four months."

"And the kids must be getting big because you did say there were kids in the mix, didn't you?"

"Yes, two."

"That he won't see grow up. Or is choosing not to. What do the police think? Is he alive or is he dead?"

"They obviously think he's dead," said Jeanette, blowing smoke from the corner of her mouth. "He hasn't left a trace. He went to work as usual one day and disappeared at lunchtime. No one has seen him since then."

"And what do you think?" Micki asked.

"I don't think anything," Jeanette lied. "Life goes on. For me and for her, who just passed by."

"But you seem to have taken it harder," croaked Kat, handing back the bottle. "What with you sitting here on the bench with a bottle of fucking Rosita!"

Then she laughed hoarsely, making her stomach bob and shaking the whole bench. But Jeanette wasn't prepared to let this moment of togetherness slip through her fingers. That loudmouth wasn't going to ruin a day that had begun so well.

"She has the children to live for," she said seriously. "I have nothing."

"Then you'll just have to have kids," Kat clucked cluelessly. "It's not too late."

At this, Lubbi heaved himself up from the bench to drag away an unsympathetic Kat, snarling under his breath.

"Is that how you feel?" Micki asked, taking a step closer to Jeanette. "That your life was over when that slouch headed for the hills? Or snuffed it—whatever it was he did."

"Jen lost her daughter before that," Nanna clarified in a soft voice behind Jeanette's head.

"Oh bloody hell," said Micki. "Now I understand what just happened. Sorry, Jen. Really."

"Thanks," said Jeanette, taking a final drag and stubbing the cigarette out under her shoe. "Sometimes I feel like that, but not today. It partly depends how it settles in your brain—the booze, I mean."

She took another swig from the wine bottle and put it back in her bag. Lubbi returned, pushing Kat in front of him.

"Sorry Jen," she said dismally, gently touching Jeanette's shoulder. "I didn't know . . . You know I didn't mean anything by it?"

Jeanette nodded.

"It's fine," she reassured her, whereupon Kat dejectedly slunk away and Lubbi sat back down on the bench.

"Your old man," he said, leaning forward with his hands clasped between his knees so that he could look her in the eyes. "Your ex-husband, I mean. Are you still in touch?"

"No, we're not. We text each other on Charlotte's birthday, that's all. And on her death day too," she added more quietly, although she didn't really want to think about it.

"You were married," Lubbi argued. "You went through a tough time together. I don't understand how he could let you go so completely. Why didn't he try to help you get back on the right track, if you see what I mean. Does it upset you—me saying that? Should I shut up?"

Jeanette smiled at him. No, she wasn't upset, and she didn't want Lubbi to shut up. But his questions weren't the easiest to answer.

"It was a mutual decision to go our separate ways," she said in defence of her husband. "He couldn't put up with me—seeing me in the state I was in—nor could I. It was me who was lying and deceitful and betraying and couldn't look myself in the mirror. Or him in the eyes. He didn't do anything wrong."

"You can't be sure of that," said Lubbi without a hint of irony. "Perhaps it was your old man who got rid of him. Your lover, I mean."

At first, Jeanette thought he was joking, but she saw from his serious expression that this wasn't the case. Laughter bubbled up inside her, but she didn't want to hurt Lubbi. Instead she looked down at her tightly clenched hands and took a couple of deep breaths.

"He's a good person—my ex-husband," she clarified. "I want nothing except for him to be happy. I set him free because he deserved that, because he deserved a new chance."

Lubbi reached across Micki and put his hand on her knee. The warmth spread through the denim and into her tepid body.

"You do too, sweetheart," he said. "Give yourself a second chance. Leave this life. Stop boozing. See a counsellor. Do something."

And of course she could have done all that, but the rot within her had reached the point of no return. The putrid and tainted thing that was her soul could not be saved either by self-help or therapy.

13

Sandra

ERIK WAS ALREADY ASLEEP and Sandra was also tempted to go to bed. It had been a long day, and after the health and development review at preschool all she had wanted to do was cry. "Erik is certainly advanced verbally, but that doesn't mean he can dominate the other children however he likes. Little Igor, who is not as advanced in his development, felt crushed and that he needed to be seen and heard too. Biting is naturally not a good way to resolve conflicts, but nor is Erik's bullying, and as for a bite mark here or there—what does it matter, when a mental sucker punch so easily leaves its marks on the spirit and brain? The bruise will fade and disappear, but little Igor's self-confidence isn't as resilient—Erik's verbal terrorising might leave its mark for life. More physical emotional behaviour can be dealt with—it leaves visible traces and is more honest. The psychological violence that Erik uses is far more refined, and harder both to discover and to deal with."

Bullying and psychological violence? Erik was a friendly soul who liked to talk. He would never resort to physical violence, but if someone jumped on him, if someone hit or bit him, then of course he would respond. With words. Sandra knew that "little Igor" was in Erik's face all the time, and that Erik was trying to defend himself. She also knew that the principal, who had a grandchild rather like Igor and of a similar age to the boys, struggled to tolerate Erik's "advanced" nature, as she described it when she was at her friendliest. Mostly, she referred to him as being "little but old," which sounded disparaging without being an actual insult that anyone could criticise her for using.

Igor was used to getting his way and used his fists if he didn't, and his parents were idiots. (Who even called their child Igor? Someone cheerfully looking forward to the impending Russian invasion of the island?) The head of school was a manipulative cow. Nevertheless—or perhaps precisely because of that—Sandra had, as usual, simply sat there and listened without making any objections. Of course she would speak to Erik and of course she would try to tone down his "cockiness" and remove those so-called bullying tendencies. That was what she had said, but not what she was planning to do. Erik was no bully; he was empathetic and considerate, and she would never dream of imprinting on him those characteristics that she most hated about herself.

She was ashamed. Sandra didn't want to be a weak parent who couldn't stand up for her child. It would have been wonderful to share parenthood with someone, but things were the way they were, and she couldn't very well bring her father to parents' meetings at preschool. Or her mother, which would make no difference anyway since her mother was almost as compliant as she was.

She took off her trousers, which despite being elastic had sat so tightly on her waist that they had left a deep mark. Then she took off her tunic, which wasn't too tight but concealed a bodysuit that at best redistributed the rolls of fat. It fit so tightly that she could barely take a deep breath, so it came off too. Then she put on her tracksuit bottoms and a gigantic t-shirt which she felt free in. She did all of this in front of the full-length mirror in the bedroom without casting so much as a glance at her reflection. She rarely did.

Then she collapsed on the sofa in front of the TV—she was too tired even to make tea. She channel hopped to a program about people with a limited survival instinct—they had gambled everything away or bought fizzy drinks and fags with all their savings and then some—until the ad break began. She zapped around other channels where there were ad breaks too and eventually ended up on a fairly decent documentary about Japanese fetishes on one of the channels. She fired off a few text messages to a couple of friends, but both seemed to be otherwise occupied, so she didn't get any replies. Whenever this happened, it always made her think that they probably spent time with her sporadically out of decency, and that none of them took any pleasure from spending time with her.

At work, she had the respect of colleagues and a responsible role for which she had qualified through expertise and hard work. Despite her shy image, there was no one there who questioned her. But as soon as she was no longer hiding behind her professional role, her self-confidence came tumbling down. Socially, she was a total zero. *These kinds of thoughts pull me down*, she thought to herself. *Don't send messages if you're afraid of not hearing back. Dump the bedroom mirror if it makes you unhappy. Wear clothes you can breathe and move in. Go out on the town and get hammered. Get a hobby and meet new people. Build ships in bottles or paint watercolours, take tennis lessons, learn to tango or speak German. Don't just sit here being depressed—do something useful with your spare time.*

Her mobile rang, and she was reminded that she was in any case doing *something* useful, even if it was beginning to dawn on her that she mostly did it for her own sake so that she had someone to talk to in the evenings.

It was Kerstin, and Sandra felt herself getting psyched up, as was so often the case—but unfortunately only then—when something in her life required an extraordinary input from her.

"Are you well?" she asked, an uncontroversial opening to their conversation.

"Hmm, well, things are the same as usual."

"Has the sore throat sorted itself out?"

"More or less. Do you have children?"

It might not have been such an unusual question, but the way it was asked—completely out of context—was surprising.

"Why do you ask?" Sandra asked.

"It's something I've been thinking about a lot over the last few days. I think children redefine you as a person. You become someone else. Someone's mother, instead of being just any old woman."

"Of course, you're special to the child, otherwise there's not really anyone who cares whether you have children or not," Sandra expounded. "Are you thinking about yourself, or your mother?"

Kerstin was silent for a few seconds and then replied with another question.

"Are you a good mother?"

It went against Sandra's principles to talk about her own private life, but to get closer to Kerstin, to give something back, she decided to make an exception on this occasion.

"I'm not exactly someone who fights wars on behalf of my child," she admitted with shame. "I'm probably a pretty weak parent, but I'm loving and have good intentions. So in that regard I think I'm a pretty good mother, actually. Otherwise I'm not especially good at anything much."

The last remark snuck out of her. Was that how she saw herself? Bad at everything? She couldn't go around thinking like that about herself without doing something about it. She ought to take her least worst part and do something with it. Even if she wasn't good, she had to be able to train and improve, get into shape and develop.

"Son or daughter?" Kerstin asked.

"A three-year-old son," Sandra heard herself say.

But that was enough. No more disclosures about her own private life; the conversation was meant to be about Kerstin. Sandra was curious whether *she* had children, but the question might be sensitive so she left it open to interpretation.

"Do you have any causes for joy in your life?" she asked.

"No, not any longer. Not since my husband was taken from me."

Sandra heard the crisp sound of a lighter, followed by a deep breath. She took the opportunity to lead the conversation where she wanted it.

"You say he was taken from you. Your way of expressing it sounds . . . Are you saying that death took him? That God took him?"

"No," Kerstin replied harshly. "I'm not."

They were there again, nudging against it. So near, and yet so far. Sandra was convinced that it was the death of the husband and the circumstances around it that was affecting Kerstin more than anything else, yet she never quite got there.

"Our last conversation ended very abruptly," Sandra said. "Did we get cut off, or did you feel unable to keep talking?"

"I don't remember," said Kerstin expressionlessly.

Sandra had a feeling that she probably did, and that the same thing might happen now. Smoke was drawn in and exhaled, and Sandra thought the conversation might end at any moment. But it didn't. Instead something very unexpected happened. After another drag on the cigarette, Kerstin spoke again with what Sandra could have sworn was suppressed rage in her voice.

"It was an absolute ice rink out on the road," she said. "It had just frozen and wasn't gritted. He encountered a car that forced him off the road. Do you understand? He was forced off the road. The barrier that used to be at the edge of the road above the old limestone quarry wasn't there anymore for some reason, and the other driver did nothing to avoid the accident. He cut the corner and didn't even brake or swerve, just drove straight towards the car. Left it all up to my husband. Who slid off the road and crashed into the ravine."

"And he was there until they found him four days later," Sandra added in a low voice.

"Four days. After suffering horribly for the final hours of his life. Stuck with a cracked skull and difficulty breathing, smashed to pieces and frozen. I wish that it had at least been quick."

Kerstin's voice failed, and Sandra heard her crying. She thought it was good for her and badly needed, and hoped that her own presence on the line was of some comfort. But there was something strange about this story, it occurred to her—she was just unable to form the thought clearly.

"I'm sorry," said Kerstin, swallowing. "I don't want to saddle someone else with this. You."

"But that's why I'm here," said Sandra softly. "You *can* cry. I'm here holding your hand, if you see what I mean."

"Thank you," said Kerstin. "And sorry."

"Don't apologise," Sandra insisted. "I understand how you feel and I'm suffering with you, if that's of any comfort."

"Thank you," said Kerstin again, and Sandra heard her putting her hand over the phone to blow her nose in the background.

"Did they catch him?" Sandra asked. "The hit-and-run driver?"

"The police wrote it off as an accident only involving one car. And after such a long time, there was nothing to suggest otherwise."

"But . . . Where have you . . . ? How do you know that it's a hit-and-run? That he was forced off the road by someone who didn't swerve, who saw him fly into the abyss and left him to die?"

After a few seconds' contemplation, Kerstin replied in a low, heavy-hearted voice, "There's photographic evidence."

She spoke doubtfully, with a brief pause after each word, as if she might at any moment change her mind and take the words back. But she didn't. Instead, she repeated them, more clearly and with greater emphasis this time.

"There was photographic evidence, you see, Sandra. That I've seen with my own eyes."

"But then there must have been every opportunity for the police to catch the other driver," Sandra replied.

She was becoming more and more concerned by this story.

"You make it sound so uncomplicated," said Kerstin. "But things rarely are. I have to go."

And then the receiver went silent, and Kerstin was gone.

Sandra stayed on the sofa with her gaze fixed on something in a dimension far beyond the black TV screen. Why didn't you share any evidence with the police, was what she wanted to ask. And where did the photos come from?

There were so many things about this accident that were unclear, and she really wanted to help somehow. Help Kerstin to set her feelings straight about all of this, encourage her to share what she knew so that she received legal redress and could finally have peace of mind.

She handled the subsequent calls that evening feeling preoccupied, but she did what she could to ensure it didn't show.

14

Jeanette

"NOT BLOODY LIKELY," said Jeanette, rejecting Lubbi's offer to sit down with her on the bench.

"Are you in a bit of a mood today, Jen?"

"You stink," she hissed. "I can't bear the stench."

"Why thank you," said Lubbi staring further into the vodka bottle.

"Got out of bed on the wrong side?" asked Micki.

"Stop asking fucking questions and you'll live longer."

"You should sit down and rest a while dear," Nanna said cautiously. "You aren't well."

"You're not my mother."

Her friends' care was missing the mark; just as pain causes more pain so anger causes more anger. But it was only when Kat opened her mouth that it truly backfired.

"Delirium tremens," she said, attempting to make eye contact with the other woman.

Kat said it quietly, in a way that meant everyone could hear her, but not as loudly as if she had been directing it at anyone in particular. She wasn't speaking *to* Jeanette but *about* her, and it sparked

Jeanette into firing on all cylinders. She spat out insolent invectives that belonged to a vocabulary she didn't normally use. Puffed out her chest and made a brutal gesture towards Kat, who involuntarily pulled herself back.

Jeanette then moved around the benches in agitation, muttering long tirades to herself. It was as if the thoughts bubbling up in her head weren't fully thought through until they were spoken out loud. Not because they were especially meaningful—even she realised that—but she had to get rid of them somehow, they had to get out. That was why she was babbling away, stalking from bench to bin to planter. Occasionally, she would bump into someone, and shout and harry them even though they backed away without protest. This aggression was foreign to her—but right now she was in no position to stem the stream of emotions that she barely recognised as her own.

They were all on to her: Micki, Lubbi, Nanna, a young, shy lad called Jimmy, some older worn-out blokes, and even Kat. Everyone was trying to get her to sit down, to cool off, but she waved them away, whirling her arms and answering with abuse. Something got in the way—someone, because she felt the back of her hand touch a face, and she heard the shout. But she rushed on, trying to run away from the ten thousand thoughts that were tearing her head apart and gushing out of her mouth in a long and garbled flood.

Suddenly she was surrounded. They were coming at her from every direction. They looked threatening as they towered above her, and this made her even more angry. She prattled on, swearing, gesticulating, and dashing about in smaller and smaller circles. Then they got hold of her, capturing her, bending her arms against her back so that she couldn't move and get free.

They must have planned her capture without her noticing, because right beside her was a taxi with its back doors open. She screamed and raged, tried to resist but didn't succeed. They pushed her into the back seat—a burly bloke on either side—and slammed the doors before the car pulled away.

She couldn't remember what happened next, but when she came to her senses she was lying on her own bed wearing her shoes and all her clothes. Jimmy was sitting at the foot of the bed and Lubbi adjacent to her head. He carefully brushed the hair from her forehead and held out a glass of water. She took it, and realised at the same moment to her despair that all the evil thoughts that had been chasing her were still there. She lifted her head and tried to drink the water, but her hand shook so much that most of it ended up on her.

Lubbi took the glass and put it down, put his arm around her neck and lay down next to her, holding her hand and trying to calm her down. But it was no good. Her breathing was shallow and very fast, and all the while words were once again tumbling from her mouth. But these were not hurtful words any longer, just a long torrent of emotions—emotions that were actually her own.

It was about the joy of having a child, the spiritual torment as you cared for it, the pain of losing the most important thing in life, the eternal grief afterwards, the betrayal of the person you had promised to love, the shame of letting oneself go and leaving, the feelings of guilt, the rash and fateful decisions, the suffering of living on after everything that had happened and everything she had done, the tragedy that she was still alive even though she didn't want or deserve to be.

It was incohesive and probably incomprehensible, but they listened without interrupting. Jeanette knew there were things she shouldn't talk about, shouldn't even touch on, and she tried to stop herself on several occasions, but she couldn't. Throughout the monologue she lay there coiled like a spring, but Lubbi never relaxed his grip on her. It warmed her and stopped her from shaking, and after a long time—hours perhaps—the words ran out and Jeanette's body relaxed. Only then did Lubbi change position, but still with his arms around her.

"You smell good, Lubbi," she said, her nose in his hair. "Sorry."

"So you remember?" said Lubbi, and she could feel him laughing.

"I'm so sorry," said Jeanette.

"Don't be. We've all been in that state of panic and despair."

"I don't know what happened."

"Delirium tremens, as Kat quite rightly said."

"I was awful. I didn't mean any of what I said."

"No one believes you did."

"You sure?"

"Absolutely sure. But the most recent stuff was perhaps more relevant? Since we got back?"

"Yes," Jeanette admitted. "But you've heard it before."

"Not all of it. Can I ask you something?"

"Of course," said Jeanette without feeling convinced she was ready for it.

"I get the feeling that there's something that you're especially ashamed of, something that you regret enormously. Shame and guilt are the worst emotions to carry around—worse than grief and longing, hate and anger and unhappy love. Do you agree?"

Jeanette nodded hesitantly, sensing that something unwelcome was about to follow.

"Based on what you've said," Lubbi continued, "there's nothing in your life that is in proportion to your self-contempt."

Jeanette didn't say anything, holding her breath and waiting for him to continue.

"You can't just carry around those feelings of guilt. It destroys you. You say you don't deserve to be alive, and that you don't want to be. You can't feel like that. It makes your friends sad and worried."

It was nicely put, and perhaps he would stop there. But Lubbi wasn't done.

"You had an affair, betrayed your husband. That's okay—you know that? You're *allowed* to be unfaithful without going to jail. Or being pilloried. You might not feel great about it, but it's hardly a reason to commit suicide."

Jeanette exhaled. But then the clincher came, the thing she had been worried the conversation would lead to.

"It makes me think," said Lubbi seriously, "that there's something worse. Something you really don't want to come out. And I dare say that's why you're in the position you are now. That it's the reason why you can't bear to go on, that you have panic attacks like the one today. Am I on the right track here?"

Jeanette nodded. Reluctantly, but she had to give him his due.

"In that case I suggest you say what it is. No matter what it is, you'll feel better if you tell us. And it goes without saying that we won't tell anyone else."

Jeanette lifted her head and glanced at Jimmy, who was still sitting on the foot of the bed. He shook his head intensely. Jeanette lay down again and sighed.

"Okay," she said. "You're probably right. It might be a relief to be rid of this burden. But you'll hate me."

"I doubt that," said Lubbi pacifyingly. "We've all done things we regret, things we're ashamed of and would prefer not to talk about. Things we should be inside for."

"I hate myself," Jeanette said with a sigh. "What I've done is so awful, so selfish and cynical and totally fucking dumb. Unforgivable."

Then she took a deep breath and began to tell them.

"It was four years ago, in winter. During the brief period that I was seeing that man I told you about. The one who went missing."

She didn't get further before the doorbell rang. A long, peremptory sound—she couldn't guess who it might be. She closed her eyes and breathed out, grateful to have been saved by the bell.

She heard steps going along the hall, the front door opening, and a voice asking for her. Robust shoes approaching and entering the bedroom. She opened her eyes and saw two uniforms.

"Jeanette Wretberg? You're under arrest in relation to a fight at the East Gate earlier today."

15
Sandra

IT HAD BEEN a long time since it had rained, so Sandra did a lap with the watering can outside her small house. Everything around her was in bloom, and the beauty of nature in the soft light was overwhelming. The tender greenery in its many nuances had a calming effect on the senses, and it was a strong reason why she preferred to live in solitude out here rather than in Visby or another town.

Self-determined solitude had its downsides, but Friends-on-call offset them, even if it didn't fulfil all her social needs. She glanced at the time and noted that it was time to head inside and prepare for the evening's calls. She was hoping to hear from Kerstin, but it had been almost a week since they had spoken, and Sandra had more or less given up hope that she would call again.

Just as she had feared, she had scared Kerstin off with all her curious questions and her eagerness to understand the ins and outs of the terrible fatal accident. The questions would remain unanswered, so Sandra tried to fill in the gaps herself for her own peace of mind. But no matter which angle she looked at it from, she couldn't come up with a plausible explanation for why Kerstin had chosen not to show the incriminating pictures to the police so they could arrest the hit-and-run driver.

Did she have something to hide? Did her husband? Surely that would have come out when the body was found—so what did it matter?

Could it have been a police officer who had forced Kerstin's husband off the road? And if so, did it make any difference? One police officer could hardly hide all the evidence in order to get an investigation closed, and it seemed even less likely he would have the force behind him if he did so.

The so-called photo evidence also demanded an explanation. If there was a speed camera adjacent to the crime scene—for it surely was a crime if the other driver had left the scene—then the police must have examined the images from it, even if there was no suspicion that a crime had taken place. But why would there have been a camera just there? You didn't generally catch people speeding on sharp bends.

It followed that someone else must have taken the photos at the scene of the accident and sent them to Kerstin. The clichéd dog walker, who seemingly didn't have a mobile phone or any other form of contact with the outside world, since they hadn't called the police or ambulance when the accident happened or later? The perpetrator themselves, after being struck down by a guilty conscience? A passing motorist who had initially misunderstood the situation and continued on their way?

Nevertheless, all these theories about this photographic evidence pointed to the same conclusion: Kerstin had *chosen* not to inform the police of its existence.

The thought crossed her mind that Kerstin might have been there herself taking the photos. A completely implausible theory since she would have been able to call the ambulance herself, if the police, for some reason, struck terror into her. That hypothesis was rapidly brushed aside by Sandra, just like the others. The whole thing was and would remain a mystery.

She noted that the grass already needed cutting, but it would have to keep for tomorrow. Erik was asleep, and she didn't want to disturb the peace. It felt like only yesterday that it had been dark when she was collecting him from preschool, but now he was going to bed while it was still practically daylight.

Sandra splashed some water on the bulbs in the pots on the porch, put down the watering can, and went inside. She switched on the kettle, and while waiting for it to boil she sat down on the sofa in the living room to check her mobile.

That was when Kerstin called. After six days of silence.

"How are you?" Sandra asked. "Do you feel better now? You were very upset last time."

"I'm always upset," Kerstin said without beating about the bush.

"I'm glad you've called anyway. I've been worried about you."

"You don't have to worry about me. I'll be all right."

"I was afraid you wouldn't call me again," Sandra said truthfully. "That I was too forward and asked too many personal questions. That I talk about things that are too sensitive."

Kerstin was quiet for a while and then said, "I suppose I do think that."

"You know that it's all on your own terms . . ."

"But I've decided that I need to talk about this stuff," Kerstin interrupted. "That it's good for me."

Sandra sighed with relief.

"It's up to you what you want to tell me," she said. "If I ask questions that you don't like, just say so. Okay?"

"That works," said Kerstin, before falling silent for a while.

Sandra tried waiting her out, but nothing happened. She didn't want to seem too pushy and decided to take a wide path around the subject that had been burning inside her for six long days.

"Can I ask what you do with your time, Kerstin?"

"Nothing much."

"You don't work?"

"I was on sick leave for a long time after I lost my husband, totally lost my spark of life. Then I took early retirement. But I sometimes step in and do supply work in various preschools."

"Was that what you used to do?"

"Yes, but it's more fun now that I don't have to spend every week doing it."

"And when you're not at work, what do you do?"

"I read a lot."

"That makes me happy," said Sandra, and it really did.

"Why?"

"Because people who read have richer lives. Are never idle. And are generally more empathetic."

"I don't feel especially empathetic," said Kerstin.

"How do you mean?"

"There are people I hate."

When Kerstin had been talking about her daily life, her voice had sounded a little dull and powerless. Now there was an edge that was new—they were getting close.

"Hate is a heavy burden to carry," Sandra said. "It drains you."

"And I'm very tired," Kerstin admitted.

"Hate usually dissipates with time," Sandra said tentatively. "I think you would feel better if you let it go."

"I have no intention of doing that. Quite the opposite—I'm nurturing it. Out of respect for my late husband."

"Are you brooding over some kind of revenge?" It suddenly struck Sandra. "Are you planning to take the law into your own hands?"

Kerstin laughed, a joyless laugh that was so sharp it sliced into Sandra's ear.

"Even if that was the case, I wouldn't admit it to you, would I Sandra? If anything I say makes you suspect that I'm planning to commit a serious crime you'll contact the police."

"You know, I'm not sure I would in this case," Sandra said softly.

This was mostly for herself and in some sort of half-hearted hope that Kerstin wouldn't hear it. Or perhaps, on consideration, it was the other way around. Once again she was deviating from the few guidelines she had to follow as part of Friends-on-call. Once again it was Kerstin who had conjured up this disobedience. And for some peculiar reason, this insight disturbed Sandra—she didn't let anyone else control her, no one *had* to do anything. It also gave her the courage to ask one of the questions that she had wanted an answer to for so long.

"Photo evidence, you said. Tell me about this so-called photo evidence."

"I heard what you said," said Kerstin with a smile in her voice.

Sandra pretended to be nonchalant about Kerstin's comment, but a smile crossed her lips too. Tempting a smile out of gloomy Kerstin was a victory in itself.

"How is that you know more about this accident than the police?" Sandra said, developing her question.

Straight away, the natural seriousness in Kerstin's voice became palpable.

"I received a letter," she said. "A few days after they found him, I got a letter. Well, actually, just an envelope with a few photographs inside. Without any comment."

"And what did the photographs show . . . ?"

"The wrecked car seen from a couple of angles from above. On one of the photos you can see his upper torso through the side window. Awful photos."

"Including the head?" Sandra dared to ask. "The face?"

"Yes, unfortunately," said Kerstin mournfully. "At a distance, so it's a little fuzzy, but when I looked with a magnifying glass I could see well enough. I can't erase that picture from my memory."

"I understand how you feel," said Sandra. "At the same time, you don't have to speculate. You know what state he was in, what circumstances. Sometimes it's better knowing, even if the knowledge is almost unbearable."

"I suppose so."

"Was he dead when the photo was taken? Your husband?"

"It's hard to say, but presumably not."

"What makes you think that?"

"The third photo," Kerstin replied. "There was another photo in that envelope."

"That showed . . . ?"

"The other car leaving the scene. A blue Audi."

"Of course," said Sandra, who was beginning to put the pieces of the puzzle together. "But how do you know that it was a hit-and-run? How do you know that your husband was forced off the road?"

"I think the person who sent those photographs thought I deserved to see the full picture. The other car was standing still on the road above the ravine—on the left-hand side of the road, but not in the ditch, not at an angle, and seemingly undamaged. The driver was down by the wreckage, saw that there was a seriously injured person in the car, but he chose not to call the emergency services."

"How do you know that he went down into the ravine?" Sandra asked.

"On one of the pictures of the wreck there's a shadow visible beside the car. A shadow that wasn't there in the other picture, so it must therefore have moved. I'm pretty certain that the shadow is of a person."

"You think the photographer took the opportunity to photograph the hit-and-run driver's car while he was down in the ravine?" Sandra said thoughtfully.

"Exactly."

"It could simply be a fellow passenger. Someone else in the car?"

"Precisely," said Kerstin. "Or someone who happened to be passing."

"But who still didn't take the time to call emergency services?"

"Naturally, it suggests a fellow passenger," Kerstin agreed. "For that reason."

Sandra thought for a while, digesting the information.

"That letter," she said. "Was it postmarked?"

"Yes, in Visby."

"That's not much of a clue," Sandra remarked. "But the photographer was there when it happened and was sufficiently clearheaded to document the accident. The person in question felt obliged to inform you about what had happened."

"But not to call an ambulance," Kerstin added, her voice bitter.

"Someone with a conscience but no backbone?" Sandra reasoned.

"Their conscience only seems to have come to life when it was too late," said Kerstin.

"When did you receive that letter?"

"The day after the death notice had been in the paper. I think the photographer saw that I was the next of kin and thought I had a right to know."

Sandra considered this for a while. That was probably what had happened. But both the photographer and the victim's wife, who had each had crucial evidence against the hit-and-run driver in their possession, had neglected to contact the police, and that was a mystery in itself. The photographer's behaviour perhaps less so, if he or she was closely related to the driver, but Kerstin's passiveness was and remained a riddle.

"Why did it take so long for them to find your husband?" Sandra dared to ask. "I get the impression that the police didn't take your report very . . ."

"The police weren't informed," Kerstin interrupted.

"What did you say?" said Sandra, who thought she must have been mistaken.

"I never reported him as missing."

Sandra checked her impulses and swallowed the questions that were rising to her lips. Kerstin's unwillingness to involve the police had become even more apparent, but her motives were shrouded in darkness. She sat quietly at the other end of the line and Sandra didn't want to push too hard.

"As you may have noticed, I'm avoiding asking the natural follow-up questions," Sandra said.

"I've noticed," Kerstin replied. "But there are several, more important follow-up questions to ask."

"Help me out."

"The perpetrator's registration number was visible in the picture. With a little enlargement I managed to read the number, so I tracked down the owner of the Audi."

"And . . . ?"

"Hallin, he's called. Works as an expert in environmental issues at an international company with an office in Visby. He's also on the local board for a human rights organisation."

Sandra didn't recognise the name, but there was something about the environment and human rights that touched on something in her consciousness.

"When and where exactly did this accident happen?" she forced herself to ask, despite something telling her that she didn't want to hear the answer.

"At Madvar, in January 2014," Kerstin replied. "On the twenty-third, to be exact. Between half past three and four in the afternoon."

Sandra instinctively grabbed hold of the armrest on the sofa as it swam before her eyes. A violent wave of emotions flooded through her, beginning in her stomach and welling upwards until her heart was pounding at double speed and her cheeks were flaming red. She was sweating uncontrollably, desperate to end the call and lie down, to wait for the feeling to die down.

"The hit-and-run driver didn't have any passengers who took the photos," she heard herself say. "They must have been taken by someone else."

"How can you know that?" Kerstin asked in bafflement.

"It doesn't matter, Kerstin—but that's how it is. Take care, I have to go now."

Then she ended the call and lay down on the sofa. The sweat poured down her face and blood pulsed through her at a rate that seemed hazardous. She tried taking long, deep breaths, but it didn't work. Over and over, her lips formed the name of the hit-and-run driver, but her brain was working on just one question:

What should she do with the knowledge?

CAR ACCIDENT AT MADVAR:
MALE VICTIM FOUND AFTER FOUR DAYS

A motorist driving along route 145 close to Vejdhem spotted a car deep in the ravine beside the road just before eleven o'clock on Monday morning. The fire brigade, police, and ambulance service responded on site and found a deceased person stuck in the driver's seat.

The victim was a male in his late forties, and the accident is thought to have happened on Thursday last week. Heavy snowfall is thought to have prevented the car from being found sooner.

There are no witnesses, and it remains unclear what happened, but the roads in the area were treacherously icy at the time in question.

The deceased's next of kin have been informed.

GOTLANDS ALLEHANDA

JANUARY–
FEBRUARY
2014

16
Jan

HE HAD BEEN in a meeting with a customer all morning, and there was nothing new under the sun. They went over same questions again and again, concerning financial and environmental sustainability and green resource efficient finance. Subjects that were certainly close to his heart, but which—despite seeming like buzzwords of the year to the customer's ear—were frankly hackneyed to him. In his role as an adviser and mentor to the still-fairly-unknowledgeable public, he was always a step ahead.

But you had to take the good with the bad, and the good thing was the long lunch afterwards at the elegant Lindgården Inn. Today lunch was on him, since you could hardly expect the customer to pay, even if the customer was called PayEx and was as rich as Croesus. What was more, there weren't many people like him who reckoned that if Wednesday was Little Saturday then Thursday was Little Sunday, and what was Sunday without a long, leisurely lunch?

It was over now, but after three courses, a couple of cold beers, and a digestif he felt sleepy. This could have been easily resolved with a nap in the break room at the office, but since Britt-Inger from HR was ninety percent certain to be lying there in the throes of a migraine, he considered it more resource efficient to swing by the house and close his eyes for twenty minutes before heading back to work.

So he took the car from Stora Torget and eased his way through the narrow streets without scratching his paintwork or rims. Granted, this had never happened before, but it could happen at any moment given he was unfortunately not the only motorist in this town. Then he realised that he might as well stop by the branch of XL-Bygg up at Skarphäll retail park. He could pick up the fittings he had ordered as part of the project to give the family room at home a facelift.

He did that. Just as he had chucked the bag of fixtures into the back seat he noticed a woman in distress standing nearby. A young girl who had—as women do—bought too much, her face wearing an expression of semi-desperation as she tried to call for a taxi. Clearly without success.

He heard where she was going, and it was some distance. But it was cold as hell and she had been waiting for a long time. He felt sorry for her, and also thought that a chat with a young lady would probably have the same energising effect as a siesta at home.

She was delighted by his offer. Happy people made Jan happy, so he had made the right decision, despite it being enormously out of his way and costing him a fair bit in petrol, wear to the car, and loss of income. She was a bit dull and didn't have much to say. Jan talked about the kinds of things that might interest a girl of twenty-five to thirty, which seemed to be nothing much. Then he switched to talking about what interested him, of which there was a lot.

Occasionally, he would try to make eye contact to get some sort of confirmation that he wasn't alone in the car, but she was shy and was mostly watching the road. She was probably a little timid too, because despite her quiet and compliant manner she was playing the role of backseat driver. Not that she commented on his driving, but he could see how she was mentally slamming on the brakes and leaning into corners. On a couple of occasions, she pointed out that it was icy, or that someone was emerging from the right that he might not be able to see.

Jan wasn't easily annoyed, so he was indulgent towards the girl. He studied her discreetly and noted that she didn't look so bad despite her horsey mouth and the fact that she was overweight. All young people were these days—the American epidemic had made it to Sweden. But the freshness of youth forgave most things.

Despite the girl lacking the power of speech he had perked up. He didn't regret for a moment sacrificing his nap for a trip to Vejdhem. He accelerated, making the car tilt on corners, and saw with amusement how she clasped the handle on the inside of the door with both hands.

17

Sandra

HE WAS CHIVALROUS and didn't let her carry a single thing herself. Sandra didn't object, even if she would have preferred not to have to offer him a cup of coffee, given how exhausted she was after the breakneck ride in the car. But it had gone fine in the end, and she really was grateful that he had—for no particular reason—been her knight in shining armour.

"Thank you so much for your help," she said when they reached the hall. "You've been far too generous—you could have dropped me off on the main road."

"With all this?" he laughed, glancing at all the bags and boxes.

She smiled back and held her hands out apologetically.

"At least let me cover your costs."

She said this as she got her wallet out of her handbag, even though she was convinced he would refuse. Adults rarely accepted payment for favours.

"Out of the question," he said, as she expected.

"Then let me at least make you a cup of coffee. Do you have time?"

"I'm sure I have time for a cup of coffee."

Sandra hung her coat on a hanger in the wardrobe and put his on a hook on the wall. She took off her shoes on the hall floor, but didn't want to ask him to do the same. It would somehow be too pedantic, whilst also acting as an invitation to the man to make himself more at home.

She switched on the coffee maker and got two mugs out of the cupboard. That was all she had time to do before he changed his mind.

"I don't suppose I could have a whisky instead?" he asked nonchalantly.

She looked at him for a moment.

"Aren't you driving?" she said hesitantly.

"A wee dram won't do any harm," he said with broad smile.

As if she ought to have known that big, strong men could handle a whisky before getting behind the wheel. He made her feel unsure—was she even allowed to offer him alcohol before he got into the car? But she didn't want to make a fuss, and he probably knew his limits. So she got what she had out of the larder—an almost-full bottle that had been in there for at least a year.

He grabbed hold of it and turned it in his hand. He studied the label and nodded in approval.

"That's more like it," he said, pouring himself a shot in one of the mugs.

Sandra turned her back to him and continued to make the coffee. She heard him drinking, and the cork being removed and replaced once again. She remembered how it had occurred to her in the car that he might be inebriated, that his breath smelled of booze, and that his careless driving might be because he was under the influence of alcohol.

This didn't feel good. She couldn't very well let him loose on the roads while under the influence. It wasn't just about him. She plucked up courage and turned around to face the man.

"Happy?" she said in a forcedly pleasant tone of voice, taking the bottle from the counter where he had put it without waiting for a reply.

Then she took the few paces to the larder and noted that he must have filled his mug generously on both occasions, because almost a third of the bottle's contents was missing.

"Not quite," he said in a voice that didn't sound as friendly anymore. "I don't think you've thanked me properly."

And then she felt him place his hands on her hips and press himself against her. That the situation might develop like this hadn't crossed her mind, and suddenly sweat broke out on her brow. She had to try and get out of this without causing an unnecessary scene. She still had the bottle in her hand—she shouldn't have provoked him by questioning his driving.

"Perhaps you'd like more whisky?" she said in an overly cheerful voice.

She tried to turn away from him while at the same time attempting to escape his unwelcome embrace. She thought that she would wordlessly, without insulting him, let him know that she wasn't interested, and that he should go home or to work or wherever it was he was going. Right now she didn't care that he was too drunk to drive. He needed to leave straight away. She would call the police and ask them to stop him somewhere on the roads, which wasn't much of a thank you for the lift—but he was an adult who made his own decisions, after all.

But his grip tightened. She didn't manage to get free and didn't succeed in turning around. If she were to tell him off, he would feel wronged and probably turn angry, and angry drunk men who took what they wanted like this weren't the kind of people you should toy with. Everything was going wrong and she had to make him understand that he should stop without offending him.

She put the bottle on the counter, took hold of his hands and tried to force them away while slipping out of his grip. But it didn't work—and wouldn't if she didn't take really drastic measures, and she wanted to avoid that.

"Surely you're not playing hard to get?" he said in a darker, more drawling voice than before, speaking into her neck just below her ear.

His breath was warm and moist, his lips wet, and the fumes of alcohol reached her nose when he spoke.

"A little gratitude would surely be appropriate?"

A big, sweaty paw fumbled under her top while the other maintained a firm grip on her waist. Sandra was really getting scared now, and realised there was a risk she wouldn't get out of this. She made a serious effort to free herself, a very definite one, but without words, so that he wouldn't feel trampled on. Anything that wasn't said would never happen—she gave him every opportunity to back out of the situation.

But he merely chuckled quietly and leaned his head back a little, actually seeming to enjoy encountering resistance.

"Hey girl," he grinned, unperturbed. "Take it easy."

Then he manoeuvred his left arm rapidly: got it above hers, bent it, and established a rock-solid grip around her throat. And then he threw her down on the floor. She could hardly breathe, and it struck her that he really was going to strangle her.

That was when she realised it was over. He wasn't going to let her get away.

18

Jan

HE FELT REALLY PLEASED with himself, almost elated to have been able to help. The girl's gratitude was his reward, but it was no big deal—she had been freezing her arse off in the car park with her heap of shopping.

When they arrived, he carried all the bits and pieces inside even though he was already late and needed to go back to work.

"Thank you so much for your help. You've been far too generous—you could have dropped me off on the main road."

"With all this?" he laughed, making a gesture at the mountain of stuff.

She held out her hands and apologised with a smile.

"At least let me cover your costs," she said, pulling her wallet out.

The fact that she was attempting to pay for his petrol was endearing in some childish way, as if he needed financial compensation for taking a small diversion into the country to help a fellow human being. Naturally, he declined.

"Then let me at least make you a cup of coffee," she insisted. "Do you have time?"

Jan resigned himself to it—if she wanted to do the right thing then he would have to let her.

"I'm sure I have time for a cup of coffee," he said amenably.

A cup of coffee would hit the spot, given he had to drive all the way back into town. But as soon as he got into the kitchen, he had other ideas. The subdued light cast by the spots on the ceiling revealed a smart new interior following traditional designs. It smelled of soap and winter apples, while there were pots of coriander and basil standing on the windowsill. New and old, light and dark. The cosy kitchen was an invitation for company, and the devil got into him. That was how it went sometimes—for better or worse—but there was something about the day that felt different and a little festive. He didn't really need to go back to work either—it was mostly Luther who was on his back.

"I don't suppose I could have a whisky instead?" he asked.

That would definitely perk him up, but she seemed hesitant.

"Aren't you driving?" she replied, but he waved away her concerns.

He could handle his drink, and moderate quantities of alcohol made him sharper rather than tired and unfocused. She conceded and got out the bottle.

While she fiddled with her coffee, he drained the first glass—or mug, as it was. And since she had her back turned and probably wasn't paying attention to what he was doing, he poured another snifter. Two drams before going home was just right: it would revive his spirits and eliminate the risk that he would fall asleep behind the wheel.

But he had been mistaken. She wasn't as dozy as he had thought, and suddenly she turned around and took the bottle from him. It didn't really matter since he hadn't been intending to drink more. But that overbearing manner—her *opinions* about what he should and shouldn't do—got to him. Who the fuck was she—a mere slip of a girl—to put him in his place, to mother a middle-aged man? Not least after what he had done for her?

He flipped. He really didn't like that arrogant style, and she looked a little tempting there with her ample rear pointing straight at him.

He crept up behind her and put his hands on her hips, kissing her on the neck. She was a little reluctant there and then, but she needed to know who was boss. He was still angry, and she smelled so good. She was warm and feminine and wonderful—he couldn't help himself.

In his excitement, he pulled her down onto the floor. And not long after, when they had romped around for a bit, she capitulated and gave way to pleasure. Mutual pleasure. Because when they did it the second time she was completely relaxed and there wasn't a shred of resistance. The friction there had been to begin with was nothing more than exciting foreplay.

Afterwards they spooned, and he nuzzled her neck and hair and caressed her gently. She quite simply liked it—he was pretty sure about that. Even if she wasn't exactly standing in the door waving him off as he left.

19

Sandra

FINALLY, IT WAS OVER. She lay on her side while he stood up, so she could see him zip up his fly, button his trousers, and tighten his belt. The last thing he did before leaving was to lean over and kiss her on the mouth and both cheeks. Softly and gently, as if he was thanking her for a lovely time. As if she were his woman and he had to go to work.

As if he would soon be back.

She heard him turn on music in the car and rev the engine. Playful. Happy. She heard him finally drive off, leaving her alone in a silence broken only by the hum of the fridge going on and off close to her ear.

She lay there. She couldn't bring herself to get up, even though there was a cold draught on the kitchen floor and she was half-naked. She would catch cold. She managed to think that but couldn't bring herself to think about anything other than snotty noses, coughs, and sore throats.

Then she cried. Quietly, without moving, for a long time—without forming any particular reason in her mind. She curled up with her arms around herself.

She must have slept too. She came to because her mobile was ringing, but she was incapable of getting up—let alone speaking to anyone. She cried more—empty, meaningless tears that eventually petered out.

That was enough. She hauled herself up and fumbled in the dark for the clothes scattered across the floor. With small, cautious movements she pulled them on—pain making itself known in different places in time with the beating of her heart.

Then she turned on the light in the window, sat down in the half-darkness at the kitchen table, and pushed all her thoughts to one side.

20

Jan

HE BRAKED WITH RESTRAINT. He couldn't slam on the brakes; if he did, he would lose control of the car. He also couldn't swerve. He didn't want to be close to that ravine on the icy road, so it was a conscious choice to keep left on the corner. How was he supposed to predict an encounter on this quiet road in the middle of the forest? The oncoming car was going far too fast—he based his assessment on how fast it was approaching—and it was something he was unhappily unable to do anything about.

He gently braked to mitigate the blow without spinning the car. Better to have a head-on crash than to be hit in the side by the oncoming car, he reasoned. Or to fly into the abyss.

But the idiot in the other car moved to the side and slammed on the brakes. He seemed to have the synapses of a reptile. So instead of the expected head-to-head collision, Jan watched with consternation as the oncoming car avoided him by a hair's breadth and, travelling sideways at high speed, slid across the road and practically flew off the edge. He also managed to see the way it plummeted down the slope rear first before it vanished behind the crest and he had to concentrate on his own driving.

He brought the Audi to a halt about thirty metres beyond the scene of the accident and caught his breath for a few seconds. Then he reversed back to where the other car had disappeared, turned off the music, and hopped over to the passenger seat for a better view. He wasn't sure whether to get out of the car or not—he was in shock and couldn't think straight.

It looked bad. The other car had done a whole somersault before ending up at the bottom of the ravine with its nose facing the road. There was smoke coming from the car, but the engine was quiet. There was no movement inside: no signs of life from the driver or any passengers. And given how the wreckage looked, it would have surprised him if anyone had managed to survive the crash.

So what was he meant to do?

Should he climb down into the ravine and see whether there was anything he or anyone else could do? In these slippery, cold conditions and with ordinary shoes in this rugged terrain? Hardly.

Should he contact emergency services? Then the police would come—that wasn't a great idea. Even though Jan was sober, he would definitely test positive on a breathalyser. Suspicion would be directed at him that would generate an unpleasant ripple effect, and that would be most unfortunate.

When all was said and done, that stupid driver had caused this and had only himself to blame. Someone else would have to find him and call an ambulance. If it was needed, which seemed rather unlikely given how things looked down there—how quiet and still things were.

So Jan climbed into the driver's seat again and drove away. He used side roads to avoid meeting too much traffic. He drove calmly and carefully to avoid drawing attention to himself or risking anything else happening. And without music—the party atmosphere was well and truly gone.

21

Sandra

AFTER DOWNING a large amount of the remaining contents from the offending whisky bottle and lining up the pros and cons of reporting what had happened to the police, she deferred her decision. Instead, she did what so many others had done before her. She showered and scrubbed herself, cleaned and dusted, vacuumed and mopped. Everything that had to be done to eradicate every trace of that abominable man from her body and her home. All that lingered on was the loathing.

She never wanted to think about him again—she didn't want to see anything that reminded her of him. She threw out the clothes she had been wearing that day, as well as the mugs even though only one of them had been used by him to knock back whisky.

She even got a new haircut, getting blonde highlights in her hair, and changed her glasses' frame so that he wouldn't recognise her if they bumped into each other anywhere. Gotland wasn't a big place. The only thing she didn't get rid of was the house itself—she couldn't. She loved her little cottage in the country and wanted never to live anywhere else, so she wasn't going to let him take that from her. The risk was that he could appear again—a fear that was ever present. On the other hand, he could turn up anywhere. If her identity was of any interest to him, he probably already knew who she was.

It was with some effort that Sandra adjusted to her new reality, but after a few weeks in isolation she was ready to meet the world again. Work colleagues, customers, friends, and family—she didn't let on to any of them that the protracted bout of flu had been anything else.

In the end, so many days had passed since the rape that it would have felt stupid to report it. Intentionally eradicating all traces of the perpetrator before then demanding that the police conduct a serious investigation would be pathetic, she told herself.

It wasn't long before she became accustomed to the idea that he would get away with it. That he might do something like that again, as well as having the memory of Sandra to build his perverse fantasies around. And that there was nothing she could do about it.

22
Jan

JUST A FEW MINUTES after leaving the scene of the accident, his hands began to shake violently, then his arms. For the majority of the drive home he was quaking. He was in some sort of shock, perhaps not medically, but it had hit him hard and he didn't feel well.

It could just as well have been him who had ended up over the edge bleeding or stiffening or whatever the hell that road hog was doing right now. Before too long it would be pitch dark and the snow was coming down heavily. The car would soon be covered, and then there would be no chance of it being found until the snow melted, which would take at least a week according to the latest forecast.

So long as he didn't call emergency services, anyway. But however he looked at it, he couldn't see how it would work for him personally. He couldn't call from his own phone; the call would be traced. There were no phone boxes these days, so that was out. And even if he borrowed a phone from someone, they would remember him and be able to give a description later. All calls to the emergency services were recorded, and if the recording ended up on TV then about four hundred people would call in because they recognised Jan's voice.

Granted, it was unlikely that a call like this would end up as part of a TV appeal, but if the police had any sense they would think it a bit odd that someone had called anonymously to raise the alarm about what was meant to be a one-car accident.

And then there was the other thing too, he thought as he miraculously avoided making mincemeat of a rabbit that had hopped into the path of his headlights. There was a minimal chance that that chick—whom he had almost forgotten in the rush of this more shocking incident—hadn't been completely on board. And that she might have contacted the fuzz, or at least called a relative who might have done it for her. She would be able to claim that Jan had drunk a load of booze and that he had left her at this or that time and had passed the scene of the accident at the exact same bloody time as the accident had happened. That wouldn't look at all good to the police.

He had to admit he had been a shade intemperate this afternoon, having put himself at risk of being charged with no fewer than three fairly serious crimes. In the eyes of the law, of course—not his own. The first was no crime at all—just a bit of mutual fun. And the second was no crime either—just an accident, given that Jan was driving with so much care and hadn't been affected by the small amount of alcohol he had drunk. The other madman had been driving too fast and had made bad choices on a treacherous road.

What really bothered him was that the crime he had *not* committed in relation to the accident by the ravine suddenly *became* a crime simply because he didn't want to stick around to see the results of the whole mess. It made him so angry that now that he came to think about it he thumped his fists on the wheel, sending shockwaves all the way up to his elbow.

He began to head for work. So that he could *say* he had been at work that afternoon to anyone who might want to know. He felt so bad and he was anxious too, as he knew full well that he would be unable to produce much during what little remained of the working day. But it was enough for him to show his face a few times to give his colleagues the impression he had been there. The rest of the time he could stay in his office with the door shut.

It would have to be that way. He parked the car in a space on Stora Torget and walked on shaky legs to his office. It was snowing heavily, and he pulled up his hood to avoid getting wet hair.

He told the receptionist he had been for lunch with PayEx and then walked over to XL-Bygg and back to pick up a few things. Then he snuck into his office without anyone else noticing. He sat there, staring into space for the rest of the day—apart from a few interruptions to fetch coffee when voices were audible in the kitchenette. He took care to keep his distance and not breathe in a way that would suggest associations with alcohol to anyone. He coughed into the crook of his arm and encouraged the suggestion that he might have caught a cold.

IT WAS ALMOST a week after that fateful day that he sat at the breakfast table reading about the accident in the newspaper. It said there had only been one car, which was a big relief. If the police had suspected anything else, it wouldn't have said there was only one car. And the poor devil driving had, as expected, died. But who would have thought otherwise? Apparently he had been there for four days, which was a little tragic, even if he had been dead at the time. He must have been, given the long flight through the air and how the wreck had looked.

That reflection in particular put him ill at ease. The fact that the driver in the other car hadn't with one hundred percent certainty died at the moment of impact. Jan had been struggling with that uncertainty for a week now. But he would still couldn't have acted differently, he just couldn't. And it must have gone without saying that the bloke had departed this life in the same moment the car hit the ground and was crushed like that. Jan playing mountain climber in his loafers wouldn't have changed a thing.

His liver pâté sandwich tasted of nothing. He swallowed what was left in his mouth, but put the remaining sandwich to one side under a paper napkin. Perhaps the jar of pickled gherkins had been open in the fridge for too long, even if his wife ate from it perfectly happily. Gunilla, who had no idea how close she had come to being a widow just a few days earlier.

Jan had to make an effort not to be gloomy about everything. He thought that what was really positive was that the victim had been alone in the car: there hadn't been a baby or a wife in the back seat or anything like that. *That* would have been really difficult. Only the driver had left this earth, and that could happen to anyone who was a little careless while driving.

On the other hand, that wife who had been lucky not to be in the car had the misfortune of losing her husband, according to the local paper. But that was a forgone conclusion from the very start, really. Her old man wasn't exactly a rally car champion.

23

Sandra

THE DAYS PASSED and got lighter. Sandra didn't know where she found the strength, but despite the nightmare she had been thrown into, and her new fears, she was on the road to recovery.

During the first weeks after the catastrophe, she had craved solitude and hadn't received any visitors. In the time after that—after she returned to work—she had refused to be alone and had spent every night at her parents'. As part of her recovery from flu, supposedly. There was nothing they liked better, so they happily let her stay with them for several weeks, just like in the good old days.

Five weeks to the day after the attack, she moved back home, standing on the porch with her bag, putting the key into the lock while a strong breeze whistled around the corners of the house. She felt like she had been away on a long journey, which in a way she had. When she crossed the threshold, she was overcome by a feeling of happiness to be home again, of having a place on earth that was hers alone and where she could be herself without any outside demands.

I need to have this attitude, she told herself—*I need to preserve this feeling. I need to take possession of my home and regain mastery of my own life and push the destructive thoughts to one side as best I can.*

Once she had unpacked, she prepared a meal, ate, washed the dishes, and put everything away. Then she lit candles and snuggled up under a blanket on the sofa and relaxed—admittedly with the curtains drawn, but she was able to cope with being alone. Then she began to catch up on what she had missed in her distance learning course, working more frenetically than before; she *would* pass this course and get an intellectually challenging job—that was just how it was. Even if . . . no, thoughts about that would have to wait for tomorrow. The big challenge for the evening was to fall asleep without other adults in the house.

It took several hours, and that was when that dreadful afternoon was at its most prominent place in her thoughts. She lay listening for sounds in the darkness, and heard a multitude. The floorboards creaked, snow tumbled from the roof, and animals ambled around the paddock to the rear of the house. She was waiting for the sound of breaking glass, a lock being broken, or a door forced open. But she didn't turn on the lights, refusing to give in to the irrational fear that that hateful man had forced upon her. Letting him win would be surrender, and she had no intention of doing that.

WHEN SANDRA WOKE the morning after, it was with satisfaction and a purposefulness that was unusual for her. She hadn't given way; she had managed to live her daily life on her own and sleep too. She had taken the first step to establishing routines that were a blend of the old and new, and she was surprised at how quickly she had pulled herself out of her wretched situation. She was scarred, upset and anxious, but she had unforeseen strength. She had glimpsed this side of herself a few times before. When she was four years old and alone at home with Dad, who had collapsed unconscious with a ruptured appendix, and she had called for an ambulance. When she had been in the Lucia procession during high school and Lucia's hair had caught fire; Sandra had been the only one not to take fright and had pulled off her gown and stood there on the stage in front of the whole school in her bra and pants while she extinguished the fire. She was usually mild-mannered—phlegmatic—but when it really mattered, it seemed she had an extra gear, a completely separate superego that stepped in and took command. Something like that was happening now.

Or so she hoped. Because there was something other than fear of a vague external threat to deal with right now. Certain bodily symptoms required her attention, and she was no longer sure she could just dismiss them as irregularity on the grounds of stress and misery.

Sandra took a deep breath as she sat down on the toilet. She was so nervous that her hand shook, although she was surprisingly relaxed given the situation. Things were the way they were, she reasoned, and the important thing was to find out what was going on. Only then could she could think over the possible consequences.

She stopped shaking at the very moment that the blue line appeared in the window on the piece of white plastic. She sighed as she threw the life-changing gadget into the bin, but that was all. She had to keep her head on, be objective and honest with herself and not act rashly.

She made a cup of tea, sat down at the kitchen table, and reviewed all the possible options. She soberly noted that she was almost thirty and wanted a child, that she had never had a long-term relationship and wasn't becoming a hotter commodity on the market with the passing of time. She noted that the father of the tiny life growing inside her looked good and was self-confident. He was socially able and unafraid, and seemed intelligent, educated, and curious. But he also lacked a sense of what was right and wrong, which was no doubt to do with his upbringing. As a result of that, he committed criminal acts, which was his own choice. He lacked empathy and might even be a psychopath, but those qualities weren't hereditary.

Sandra questioned what life would be like for a child born as the result of rape and concluded that the things you don't know don't hurt you. If the truth ever did come out, then her decision to keep the child in spite of the manner of its conception was proof of how welcome and loved the child was.

Sandra had made up her mind. Amongst the overwhelming joy that flooded through her once the decision was made there was also a dash of schadenfreude. That man was going to be the father of her child: a completely wonderful little person who would take on everything he or she encountered. And he wouldn't have a clue about it. He would miss out on this wonderful thing, stuck staring at his reflection in the water lily pond until his pathetic, loveless life came to an end, without ever getting to meet his child.

That was how she intended to thank him for the lift.

My beloved
husband and friend.
Karl-Erik
Barbenius
Born 14 August 1965
has left me with
great sorrow and longing
Gotland
23 January 2014
KERSTIN

———

Memory tends to what in life
was possessed,
Loss tends to what was taken
by death

———

Private funeral.
Donations to
Läkarmissionen
appreciated

MAY
2018

24

Sandra

"IF ANYTHING YOU SAY makes me suspect that you or someone else has committed or is planning to commit a serious crime, I will contact the police." The phrase echoed in her head and had more meaning for her than ever before. Suddenly, she was in possession of information that might put her rapist behind bars. A man she had hated for more than four years.

Granted, he had given her the most beautiful gift: Erik, who in many respects reminded her, in a positive way, of his unmentionable father. But that was unintentional, and the man had also caused her physical pain, grief, insomnia, anxiety, and a vigilance she was not comfortable with.

She had confirmed the fact that it was Hallin through a quick search online. And Hallin wasn't just a rapist, he was also a drunk driver and a hit-and-run driver. Guilty of manslaughter. Of course he had to be punished in some way—the question was how.

If Sandra went to the police now, her credibility wouldn't have improved over the years. Paternity could be easily determined but proving that a rape had occurred four years earlier was practically impossible. It would be his word against hers and that would be the end of it—with the outcome that Erik would be labelled in the eyes of the world as the result of rape, while the perpetrator would be able to thoughtlessly dismiss it all without any legal or social consequences.

On the other hand, if evidence was presented that he had been at the scene of the accident—suggesting he was involved but that he had failed to contact emergency services—the case would take on a different light. Sandra's account of the rape and drinking just minutes earlier and a few hundred meters away would be taken more seriously.

The catch was that Kerstin refused to involve the police, and that Sandra had promised her silence. While this had been with certain reservations, her loyalty lay primarily with Kerstin, and when it came to the punch Kerstin was the victim here.

One of them. This required consideration.

"SORRY ABOUT THE abrupt end to our call last time," Sandra apologised when Kerstin called the next time. "I didn't feel well."

It was true, but her conscience was not altogether clear, since Kerstin was unaware that as of now Sandra was just as interested—or perhaps more so—in Kerstin's case for her own sake. On the other hand, Sandra didn't have to share anything about herself—that wasn't how it worked. Their nightly relationship had grown stronger, their conversations had moved from uncertainty and fumbling about to being frank. And with great engagement she had pushed Kerstin in the right direction, helped her to at least dare to talk about her concerns, which had been the whole idea in the first place.

"Don't worry," said Kerstin.

She really ought to have been wondering how Sandra knew that Hallin hadn't had any passengers.

"Can we pick up where we left off?" Sandra said to her.

This seemed to be exactly what Kerstin had been hoping for.

"You didn't go to the police with the photographs—that much I know," said Sandra. "Was it enough for you to know who had caused the accident? Did that make you feel better?"

"No," said Kerstin.

"You didn't feel better?"

"No. And it wasn't enough, either."

"It sounds like there's more to tell here . . ."

"I'm gathering my thoughts," said Kerstin. "You're not going to report me?"

Sandra wondered what was coming next, and deliberated for a moment.

"No," she then said. "I'm not going to. Whatever you did, I won't instigate any legal proceedings against you. You have my word."

"Thank you," said Kerstin.

"Tell me what you did with the information."

Kerstin lit a cigarette in the background and took a long drag.

"I blackmailed him," she said eventually.

"You blackmailed him?" Sandra said in surprise.

She would never have guessed. Blackmail felt like a crime that rarely happened, and which—for whatever reasons—had passed its best-before date.

"I actually did," said Kerstin, unmoved. "It seemed like a good idea at the time."

"But how? What did you threaten him with?"

"I sent the photos to him."

"I understand that—but what did you want in return? You wanted him to hand himself in, I suppose?"

"No," said Kerstin, audibly blowing out a cloud of smoke. "Well, he was obviously welcome to. But I didn't demand it. I also enclosed a key to a locker down at the ferry terminal with a brief instruction."

"You wanted money?" Sandra said doubtfully.

She had difficulty seeing this grieving person as an old-school blackmailer.

"Yes," said Kerstin, breathing in.

"How much?"

"Six million."

"Six million? What made you think he would be able to pay?"

Kerstin took a while to answer—perhaps thinking Sandra naïve.

"He has an expensive car and a beautiful house," she said. "A well-paid job and a well-dressed wife with diamond earrings. I reckoned he'd find a way."

"Or what?"

"It was implied I would go to the police with the photographs if he didn't do as I said."

"Did he?"

"No," Kerstin sighed. "He didn't."

"And you didn't follow through on your threat either, I take it?"

"No," Kerstin admitted, taking another drag on her cigarette. "And I didn't have it in me to blackmail him anymore."

"But why didn't you go to the police?" Sandra persevered.

"I had blown my chance—don't you get that? If I had gone to the police, they would have done me for blackmail. I might have ended up in prison while he got off due to lack of evidence. I couldn't be sure, and still don't know, how good those photos are as evidence. But I do know one thing—and that is that *I* have no wish to go to prison."

"I understand," said Sandra. "But you must realise how dangerous it is to go up against people like this? To threaten them? He could have watched the locker, waiting for you, before . . . Well, use your imagination. We know he doesn't put much value on human life."

"Yes, I realised that soon enough. But the damage was already done. I didn't dare or have it in me to keep on trying. And perhaps that was fortunate—the first time I got away with it."

"Status quo," said Sandra thoughtfully.

"Can I ask you a question?" Kerstin asked.

"Of course, but I'm not sure I'll answer," said Sandra, who thought she might have an idea of what the question was going to be.

"The thing you said about there being no passengers in Hallin's car—how can you be so sure?"

"I might tell you the day you explain to me why you didn't report your husband missing," Sandra replied slyly.

In reality she had no plans to ever induct Kerstin into her own secrets. To date, no one had been granted access to *that* dark room, and Kerstin, who was weighed down by her own troubles, was hardly going to be the exception.

25

Jeanette

LUBBI HAD MADE an effort and it had paid dividends. He had plucked up the courage—and stayed sober enough—to explain the situation to both the police and the social services employee, not to mention the woman in her late middle age who had been struck in the face by Jeanette's hand. Jeanette had been present, but was in no shape to do anything other than shake or nod her head. After Lubbi's account of her long-term depression following the loss of her daughter and subsequent divorce, everyone involved had become more understanding. It had already been noted that no real injuries had been caused, and when Jeanette became remorseful and apologised the matter had been resolved amicably, the investigation discontinued and Jeanette released.

Since then, Jeanette had stopped taking tablets and settled for the intoxication provided by alcohol. If she knew herself at all, it was probably only temporary, but right now it was enough. She noted with some ambivalence how the others kept an eye on her, ready to step in at any moment and protect her from herself. She liked their caring attitudes, but at the same time she felt constantly under surveillance and thus captive.

To make sure she didn't worry anyone, she maintained a low profile and only spoke in a low voice with whomever happened to be closest. With that approach to the generally high-spirited crowd outside the East Gate, she often ended up on one of the outermost benches together with Nanna.

Nanna was certainly no ray of sunshine, but she was good. She didn't run off at the mouth like most of the others, including Jeanette, although what she did say was generally irrelevant. Jeanette liked her company, even though big-hearted Lubbi was the one for whom she had made the most space in her life.

"Tell me about your lover," Nanna said one day.

If Lubbi had initiated the same conversation, he would have done so apologetically, while offering Jeanette a free pass to change the subject if she preferred. But Nanna was issuing a challenge—although it included all the other elements too. It was in her tone, her eyes, and her body language. Jeanette knew that she was free to decline the invitation, that Nanna didn't want to hurt her or open up old wounds, that she was offering a shoulder to cry on even if Jeanette would never do the same.

After some consideration she decided to talk about him, even though it hurt. She had to try and normalise the memories of her former life, her life experience, even if it brought up old emotions that she had done her best to numb. And the moment felt right. The hubbub was some way off and they were alone on the bench.

Jeanette remembered how close they had been to the most forbidden topic when the police had come and hammered on the door. She didn't intend to go that far again—it must have been a higher power that had saved her that time. But there were other things she could talk about.

"We met at the Lucia celebrations at work," she began. "It was early in the morning before the store opened. The kids from the local primary school came and sang to us. We were sitting on temporary benches in the shop and watching. I got teary-eyed—I always do during any festivities where there's singing that you associate with your childhood. And Charlotte's. I suppose it was thoughts about Charlotte that made the tears start flowing."

Nanna didn't say anything, instead taking her hand and squeezing it.

"He was next to me on the bench," Jeanette continued. "He didn't work for us but in a workshop next door—but he and his colleagues were also invited. He did exactly what you're doing now—held my hand. I'm sure plenty of people were dewy-eyed, but he must have noticed that it was more than that for me. We didn't really know each other—at most we might have greeted each other a few times and exchanged a few words. But it felt good somehow—natural. A stranger just being there and catching you when you fell. When the kids started to file out, he let go. And when the lights came on we nodded at each other and said hi. Then went our separate ways."

Jeanette paused and pulled two beers out of her backpack. She handed one to Nanna and opened the other for herself. Nanna offered her a cigarette by way of thanks.

"And then?"

"Two days passed. I hadn't been able to get him out of my head—I thought about him when I went to sleep, when I woke up, when I was at work, when I was eating dinner with my husband. The gesture affected me deeply—I wanted to hold that hand again. Then we bumped into each other in the car park. He brightened up when he spotted me and asked whether he could give me a lift anywhere. And I said yes even though I had my own car and had been planning to go straight home. Then we drove off together. We talked—about everything in heaven and earth. Apart from my reaction during the Lucia celebrations. Or his. He was tactful."

Both women drank and smoked for a while in silence. The usual hubbub continued around them, Lubbi's laugh drowning out everyone else's. The sun shone in a clear blue sky, the breeze was strong but warm and the many flags on the city wall fluttered in the west wind. People were dressed for the warmth and feeling hopeful—a long and wonderful summer lay ahead of them.

"We had so much to talk about, so much we wanted to know about each other. I barely noticed that we were going the long way around, that we were miles outside of town. Finally he pulled over and turned off the engine. At first we just looked at each other without saying anything, then we both burst into laughter. I was suddenly self-conscious and couldn't think of anything to say. He touched me the same way again, and I let him do it. I wanted to feel his safe, warm hand one more time. I remember wondering where it would lead. But it didn't scare me—it was as if I was watching myself from outside. All my defence mechanisms were down and I let it happen—what happened next."

A young mother with an empty stroller stopped on the path in front of them. A little girl wandered around on the asphalt path before falling over and getting up. She then came toddling at full tilt towards Jeanette, who received her with open arms to stop her from falling over. The child laughed, as did Jeanette, but the mother didn't look happy. She brusquely picked up the girl, put her in the stroller and hurried off. The child protested loudly, and Jeanette followed the stroller with her gaze. Once they reached Skolportsgatan the wet wipes came out—that was how low she had sunk: people had to wash once they had touched her.

She took a swig of beer and lit a new cigarette using the last one, before continuing.

"We continued seeing each other two or three times a week. The time between our encounters felt unbearable. For both of us—at least he had me believe that. The Christmas holidays got in the way, but I worked as many of the days in between as I could in order to have the chance to see him. He did the same."

Jeanette took a long drag from the cigarette and looked at Nanna discreetly to see whether she had lost interest. Nanna caught her looking and gave her one of her rare smiles.

"I'm listening," she said, draining what was left in the can.

"Okay," said Jeanette, drawing breath. "Then it was back to normal—grey and sad and January. I started thinking about what I wanted from the relationship. But there wasn't much to ponder over—I was prepared to leave my husband and all of the worn-out, done to death conversations that our life had become after Charlotte. But I didn't dare take the first step, I wanted to hear him—Peter—say it. He did too, but not straight out. It was wrapped up in questions and assumptions about how our life together might look. I was on my guard: he had a wife and children, and I could imagine how hard and trying it would be, to break away from a life like that. But not how it would reflect on our life together. Would our love overcome all those obstacles, spiteful ex-spouses and sad and perhaps angry children? Neither of us earned much—would we be able to afford to live in acceptable conditions? Especially with two shared kids on top, which required at least one extra room and costs that went up every year. Was the thing that had emerged between us merely the result of curiosity or would it last the course through all the setbacks and disappointments that the future was guaranteed to bring? But we were pushing in the same direction—I was convinced of it. Despite having only known him for a little more than a month, I was prepared to give up everything I had for him. If only he said the right words—first."

Jeanette paused in her account, assessing how to navigate the upcoming rocks. But it didn't matter, not this time. Kat and Roffi, one of the older men, appeared with a couple of disposable barbecues and a clutch of supermarket shopping bags.

"It's Lubbi's birthday!" Kat shouted in her customary manner, making complete strangers standing by the hot dog van in Östertorg turn around and look at them.

"We're celebrating with a barbecue down at Gustavsvik! Bring your own bottle . . ."

A nice idea. It stung a little that it hadn't been Jeanette's. She had completely forgotten about Lubbi's birthday. She had been completely self-absorbed, as usual, forgetting that there were other people who also had needs and deserved attention.

She smiled in a forced manner while the two companions, guilt and shame, took hold of her.

26

Sandra

ERIK FELL ASLEEP in the middle of his bedtime story, completely exhausted by a day of outdoor play in the beautiful but windy weather. Sandra remained sitting on the edge of his bed for a while, stroking his cheek and smelling his newly washed hair. Sometimes she couldn't get enough of this small person who played such a big role in her life.

But everything grew so uncontrollably at this time of year, and it was due to rain tomorrow. The grass needed cutting before it got soaked, because by the time it dried out again it would be more meadow than lawn, and she didn't want that. In other words, it needed doing now because soon the Friends-on-call calls would start coming in on her mobile. She ran her hand through her son's shock of hair, straightened the duvet one last time and left the room, closing the door behind her.

She put on her boots and stepped outside into the unusually balmy spring evening. Apart from the singing of the birds, the garden was silent—not many cars passed here. It was a shame to break the silence with the sound of the petrol lawn mower, but that was how it had to be. In recompense, she could draw comfort from the smell of freshly cut grass and the satisfaction of working with her body while her thoughts kept turning in her head.

The newly discovered knowledge of who the rapist was brought her no peace. Despite the fact that she didn't believe in any higher powers, it felt like the information had landed in her lap for a reason. She had been given an opportunity to influence that man's future—hopefully for the worse—and she truly wanted to take that opportunity.

Gossip was a tried and tested way of destroying a person's reputation, but the question was whether talking crap about Hallin would have any impact on him, given the type of person he was. Sandra's network was limited; his was probably enormous. It would likely come back to bite her with double the force and he would be unaffected by any of it.

In terms of the other crimes he had committed, she couldn't do anything. Sandra didn't have any photographs and as far as the police were concerned no crime had taken place. It would be impossible to prove there had been any alcohol in his bloodstream, nor that Hallin's car had been in the accident, since it didn't bear any trace of it. The photographs were the only thing that existed, and she didn't have access to those.

Today she bitterly regretted that she hadn't immediately reported the rape. If only she had brought herself to pick up the phone, everything would have been different. An investigation of the crime scene would have proven that Hallin had been there, that he had drunk whisky from one of her mugs and that his car had been parked on the gravel outside the house. A medical examination of Sandra's body would have uncovered signs of violence, traces of nonconsensual sexual intercourse. They would also have been able to prove that Hallin was the father of the child born nine months later, and forced him to take financial responsibility.

And even if Sandra, in her self-determined isolation following the rape, hadn't had a clue that a serious car accident had happened just a few hundred metres away, the police would almost certainly have made the connection. They might not have been able to prove his involvement, but Hallin would have compromised himself. They would have tracked his movements that day and probably found out when and what he had drunk before driving to the DIY store. Perhaps that would have been enough to put him behind bars for drunk driving, and there was always the possibility that he would have eaten humble pie and confessed to everything.

Those were Sandra's thoughts as the sun sank below the treetops in the west, while the cut grass spread its sweet scent. Once the job was done, she put the mower in the shed, checked the pot plants and the other plants farther from the house. She decided nature would have to deal with watering them the next day and went inside to take off her boots. She quickly checked on Erik and then padded outside barefoot to the terrace and put her feet up on the table. She continued to blame herself for what had happened as she waited for the first call of the evening.

If only she had shown a little drive when it had been called for, life might have taken a different path. Sandra cursed her weakness at that moment. Not only for her own sake but also Kerstin's. They had to struggle on with their burdens while that swine—who against all odds now had a name—carried on as if nothing had happened. All things considered, it might have been better not to find out who he was.

Sandra was dwelling on that thought when Kerstin called—the first caller of the evening.

"Something occurred to me after our last call," said Kerstin. "You said you were sure that Hallin was alone in the car."

Sandra waited.

"Didn't you?" said Kerstin. "Do you stand by that?"

"I do," said Sandra, without any further comment.

"Okay," said Kerstin with a smile in her voice. "I know you're trying to squeeze me, but that's just silly."

"I don't think you would think so if you knew the reason why," said Sandra seriously. "But I maintain that he didn't have any passengers in the car."

Kerstin evaluated what Sandra had said—perhaps the tone of it frightened her. But soon enough she collected her thoughts.

"If the photographer didn't have anything to do with Hallin, he or she was probably just as much to blame for my husband's prolonged suffering. And even his death. It might have been possible to save him if he had received medical attention in time. The photographer documented the scene of the accident but didn't call emergency services."

"Another person to hate then," Sandra noted quietly.

"But it might be worse than that," said Kerstin. "As you've noticed, I've thought a lot about this since we last spoke. There's another possibility. What if the photographer was involved in the accident?"

"Then why document the fallout?" Sandra responded.

"To direct suspicion elsewhere? Hallin might just have been passing. Stopped and taken in the situation, but concluded there was nothing he could do, that the situation appeared to be under control. He may have assumed that someone—the photographer—had already raised the alarm. The photographer took a photo of the Audi above the ravine, and then implied that it was the car that had caused the accident and then left the scene."

"Shouldn't Hallin have contacted the police later on then, when the newspapers reported it as a single-car crash that was only discovered after four days?" Sandra queried.

She *wanted* Hallin to be guilty. At the same time, the scenario set out by Kerstin was completely plausible. And the fact that Hallin hadn't contacted the police immediately was hardly surprising: he had been driving while drunk and had just raped a woman. The fact that he didn't contact them later on was because he didn't want to admit to having been in the area at that time if the woman—Sandra—had unexpectedly reported the rape.

"Perhaps he doesn't read the papers," Kerstin speculated without conviction.

"That may be the case," said Sandra, whose thoughts were heading in a different direction.

"It would explain why he didn't take the blackmail attempt seriously," said Kerstin. "He wasn't involved in the car accident, so he ignored the whole thing."

"That's true," said Sandra, who really didn't want it to be that way. "But then surely he would have reported the blackmail attempt to the police?"

"He probably thought it was just a joke," said Kerstin, with a laugh. "When you think about it, six million is a pretty daft sum to demand."

Sandra grinned too. They had come so far in their conversation that they could laugh at it all. It was a big step forward for Kerstin—for both of them. Even if Kerstin wasn't aware that this therapy was operating in both directions.

When the call was over, Sandra lost herself in her thoughts once again. Hallin could be innocent in relation to the tragic accident. It bothered her very badly, but the possibility was there. But what other reasonable explanation could there be for the photographer handing over their evidence—which implicitly implicated Hallin as the guilty party—to the widow without calling 112?

There wasn't one. Hallin was certainly a rapist, but there was nothing to suggest that he made light of life and death in the same way. He had let Sandra live even though she could report him. He hadn't bothered to threaten or punish the blackmailer. And not raising the alarm when passing the scene of an accident wasn't punishable, especially not if you were acting in good faith.

Kerstin's subdued rage would probably be directed in a different, unknown direction, while Sandra was henceforth alone in her aversion towards Hallin. His only crime was a rape almost four and half years ago, of which no trace remained. Except for her son, who no one except Sandra could claim had been conceived in circumstances that weren't consensual.

She shivered when she thought about that afternoon and about that dreadful wretch who had taken the liberty of turning her body and integrity into his temporary plaything. She wanted to torture him, crush him—a feeling that had grown stronger than the unwillingness to hear his voice, perhaps even meet him. She hadn't felt that way before she had known who he was, when she had stoically plodded on in resigned ignorance.

And she could do something small to Hallin, it occurred to her. Even if it was out of proportion to the crime he had committed. She could shake him up, drive a wedge into the idyll of family life.

She could demand child support.

That ought to be straightforward and painless. All he had to do was cough up a one-off fee to cover the years that had passed and what remained of Erik's school years. Without getting the authorities involved, of course, which he would probably want to avoid—as would Sandra, on reflection. She had no other intentions other than claiming what was rightly hers. It would be a welcome addition to her limited funds, while also functioning as an acknowledgment from Hallin. And it was definitely better than nothing.

But did she dare?

Sandra remembered how during a previous call she had told Kerstin off for putting herself in danger by attempting blackmail against a man with a lack of respect for human life. But now there was no longer anything to suggest that Hallin had such a careless disregard for life. And a demand for a sum equal to the state-regulated child support levels wasn't extortion.

SHE WAS IN such turmoil that she had felt like she needed beta blockers ahead of this conversation. But she didn't really understand what those were—she suspected they were some sort of prescription drug that was difficult to obtain unless you had some kind of heart problem. Instead, she helped herself to two glasses of red wine to dampen her anxiety, and it helped a little.

It's just one phone call, Sandra, she told herself. Show your best side. He can't see you—don't show your uncertainty.

She was carefully prepared, had written down all the points that were to be ticked off, and had gone over the list several times so that she knew it by heart. She had practiced her tempo and tone and tried out various phrases, but her mind still went blank when he picked up.

"My name is Sandra," she began. "I'm the mother of a three-and-a-half-year-old boy who was conceived through rape in January 2014."

There was silence for several eternally long seconds, then he said, "That's an interesting conversation starter. Would you like me to congratulate you or commiserate? Never mind—how can I help?"

"It just so happens that you are the father of the child. Do you remember?"

Why the hell had she said that? Talking over old memories with the rapist was not what she had planned. Now there was an even longer silence.

"Now I definitely think you're mistaken, Sandra," he said, finally. "Perhaps you've dialled the wrong number?"

"I'm sure I haven't," Sandra said. "And you know that too."

"You know, this is a startling conversation at this time of evening—even if I do say so myself. Are you sober?"

"Let's skip the bullshit and get to the point."

"Oh right—there's a point to this. Exciting."

Not a trace of worry in Hallin's voice. All comments so far had been condescending—in an almost amused tone. What exactly had she been expecting? That he would break down and beg for forgiveness?

"I'm offering you the opportunity to make things right."

"I'm afraid I'll have to decline. I suggest you contact the child's father instead—he'll probably pay up."

"That's exactly what I'm doing. I thought you might be more inclined to take responsibility if we talked about this tête-à-tête, as it were. But if you would rather involve the authorities and so on, we can do it like that."

"You've come to the wrong person," Hallin said, this time without the ironic tone she had begun to get accustomed to.

Sandra was unsure whether it was a threat or yet another attempt at denial.

"I can always speak to your wife," she said. "I assume she takes the same view as I do that men should take responsibility for their children."

"Don't even try it, sweetheart. My wife and I don't keep secrets from each other, so that's a nonstarter."

Well, of course. It seemed highly probable that Hallin had gone straight home after raping a young woman and told the missus about the day's big news . . .

"I take it you would prefer me to contact the authorities about the matter?" Sandra said provocatively.

"What the hell is it you want?" Hallin snarled in a way that suggested pent-up rage.

"I had a package deal in mind," Sandra said. "In return for a one-off fee, you will never hear about the kid again, you will not hear from the authorities, and you won't hear from me."

"What sort of sum are we talking about?" he said angrily. "I'm asking out of curiosity, not because I have any intention of even considering your so-called offer. Since I don't have a fucking clue what you're talking about."

"Patchy memory? Doesn't surprise me given how drunk you were. I thought three thousand kronor per month for nineteen years would be about right. A total of six hundred and eighty-four thousand kronor."

"Six hundred and eighty-four thousand? You're having a laugh."

"I would say it's a very generous offer. You won't have to buy Christmas presents or birthday presents. We can set up an instalment plan if you like—in that case it'll be three thousand seven hundred and seventeen kronor per month up to and including December 2033, assuming you start payments immediately."

"So you're a gold digger trying her hand at extortion are you?" Hallin said in a tone completely devoid of human warmth.

"I consider it a comfortable way out for you, without all the bother of involving the authorities. Police, prosecutors, social services—well, you know. And as for my son and me, we avoid being associated with a slimeball who has to rape to get some."

"Way out? Ha ha. Call it what you want. But let me tell you that things didn't work out well for the last person who tried to blackmail me, so don't count your chickens."

"I'll text you my account details," Sandra said coolly. "Thanks for your time."

"Crazy bitch," Hallin said and hung up.

27

Jeanette

THE NEXT TIME Jeanette and Nanna had a heart-to-heart, it was chance that saw them end up together. Nanna was on the periphery of the group on the outermost bench near Östertorg, which was where Jeanette had cast off her rucksack. Now she needed to root through it looking for her rain gear—threatening clouds were looming above the city wall to the northwest. Nanna, who had already layered up, had her hood up and was awaiting the storm. It was blowing in gusts and the wind brought the first few drops of rain.

"She walked by again," said Nanna. "Perhaps she works down on Adelsgatan somewhere."

Jeanette sat down next to her to pull on her waterproof trousers over her jeans. She didn't need to ask—for some reason she already knew who Nanna meant.

"What a shame I didn't see her," Jeanette said casually. "Then I could have explained who crumpled the sheets in her bedroom when she was at work."

Nanna gazed at her inscrutably.

"You blame me," said Jeanette, sticking out her lower lip.

She did so despite knowing that simple statements like that had no impact on Nanna. Nanna took a swig from a plastic bottle, contents unknown, without dropping her gaze.

"Pfft, I'm full of shit," said Jeanette. "Obviously, I've never been in her house."

No comment. Jeanette felt ill at ease, and as though she had behaved disrespectfully. As if that woman with the long ponytail had deserved what had happened to her.

"I didn't get to grieve," she said anyway. "But it was such a damn pity about that blonde and their cute kids."

Nanna raised her eyebrow and took another swallow.

"It *was* a pity," said Jeanette, her tone gentler. "But, you know . . . You're only human. I needed comforting too. Her life would still have been smashed to pieces, she just didn't know. He would have left her for me, if . . ."

She stopped herself. She was on thin ice again—she didn't want to go there.

"Can I have a sip of that?" she asked to divert attention.

Nanna passed her the bottle but wasn't taken in.

"If . . . ?" she said encouragingly.

"If whatever it was that got in the way hadn't," Jeanette replied, hoping for a smile at least.

She didn't get one. Jeanette drank, the spirit creating a pleasant warm feeling inside her chest. She took care to drink a little more before returning the bottle.

"Hotel or what?" Nanna said.

Jeanette didn't understand what she meant at first. She shook two cigarettes out of the pack and offered one to Nanna. She lit them both. Then the penny dropped.

"Oh right—no. We couldn't afford it. And it was too risky. Someone would have recognised us and drawn uncomfortable conclusions."

Then she leant forward and cupped her hand around her mouth to stop anyone overhearing, even though no one was nearby.

"We fucked in the boot of the car," she said in a low voice.

Nanna pursed her lips and nodded. She squinted at the rain as it increased in intensity. Jeanette wanted follow-up questions. Having ended up here with Nanna by chance, *she* wanted to talk.

"In Peter's car," she clarified—as if it mattered.

But it had been a wonderful time, hadn't it? Now that she came to think about it without being melancholy. She picked up her own bottle from the rucksack, not wanting to take further advantage of Nanna.

"We would head out into the countryside in the afternoons. Anywhere, really. Somewhere different each time. We would stop on small tracks in the forest where no one went in winter. Tractor tracks—a strip of grass running up the middle, you know. We once stopped on the drive outside an abandoned cabin—an old man turned up with a shotgun and knocked on the window. Jesus, what a fright! That was the only time anyone discovered us; otherwise we were very discreet."

Words poured out. It was a day for that—and it was a good day. It was Nanna who had started this conversation and Jeanette might as well babble on since no one else was talking and the subject clearly interested her benchmate.

"There was a blanket in the back," she recollected. "For outings. It was covered in burrs that wouldn't come off—probably hundreds of them. Or rather, you *could* pick them off, but who has the patience to remove hundreds of mini burrs from an old blanket? We wrapped it around us with the burrs on the outside, folded down the back seat, and put some slow jams on the stereo. On a low volume so that we would hear if anyone was coming. And we rocked the car with our shagging."

Jeanette grinned from ear to ear. Nanna concentrated on her cigarette, blowing smoke rings that sailed into the air and were pulled apart by the squall of rain that was now beginning to dissipate. Jeanette felt that she had lost interest and wondered whether she was even listening.

But it didn't matter; Jeanette wanted to linger among her memories for a little while longer.

"He was a fantastic person," she continued. "Much tougher than me. He always saw the bright side in things, saw the opportunities where I saw the risks. But I wasn't so sentimental back then either. I dared to spread my wings, dared to be young again and to taste love again. Do you think I'm a bad person, Nanna? Do you?"

Nanna blew smoke out of the corner of her mouth. She flicked the stub onto the wet asphalt and saw it extinguished by the rain. Then she crossed her arms with her hands in her armpits and curled up. Without looking at Jeanette, she shook her head.

"You think that yourself, and surely that's enough? You're judging yourself too harshly."

Jeanette was unsure what she was getting at.

"What do you mean?" she asked hesitantly.

"You wanted to tell us," said Nanna. "Right now it's just me here. Who am I to judge?"

"Wanted to tell you what? When?"

"At your place. When the police turned up."

"But . . . You weren't there, how . . . ?"

"I was there. I wouldn't let you go home with two pissed blokes."

The rain pattered on the hood and formed puddles on the ground in front of them. Jeanette pulled the bottle from her rucksack and took a swig and then another, before concealing the bottle inside her anorak. Of course Nanna could have been there at home—Jeanette's field of vision had been limited to the bed, where Lubbi and Jimmy were. And she was unlikely to forget anytime soon how Lubbi had persuaded her to tell that awful story in the first place. How she had almost looked forward to it being over—of course they would hate her, but it would still be better than carrying the burden alone. And now she was here, one-on-one with Nanna, who would never say anything, never judge or reject her. An opportunity had emerged for Jeanette to simply eject the poison, and perhaps—just maybe—the burden would be less onerous.

Common sense pricked her consciousness: it would *never* be a good idea to tell this story—not to anyone. The last time she had got out of the trap at the last moment—this time there was no rescue in sight. Did she really know what she was getting herself into?

Her emotions also made themselves known. She was already there, in Peter's arms, and that was where she wanted to stay. She was in a good mood, talkative, blunt, and unsentimental. This was offering her the chance to offload what was weighing her down—she wouldn't have the same chance in the same favourable circumstances again.

"You'll hate me," said Jeanette.

"Hate is a strong word," said Nanna.

Jeanette took a deep breath, and felt the urge to light a cigarette, but the chances of success in this rain weren't good.

"It was in January," she began. "The last time I would see Peter—although I didn't know that at the time. We were heading into the forest somewhere, neither of us really knew where, but we never did. We talked about the future—our shared future. Danced around the subject without either of us saying anything plainly. Were we prepared to sacrifice everything we had built for this passionate infatuation that might be nothing more than that? I had a lot of gloomy thoughts. Felt dirty—so filled with lust for a man who belonged to someone else. Lying and deceitful towards my husband. I know that you can and perhaps even should let yourself feel that strongly about someone else—to do what I did. But the betrayal . . . and it was the small one in the context."

Nanna listened without comment, leaning forward slightly to shelter her face from the rain. Jeanette decided to try lighting a cigarette—she could also lean forward and protect the glowing tip with the palm of her hand and her body.

"It was freezing, so we decided not to go all that far from town. We stopped at the first good spot and ended up on a tiny road—for forestry work perhaps—next to a bigger road. We parked as far in as possible, which wasn't that far from the road—thirty metres perhaps—but we were well concealed behind the trees. When he touched me, when he undressed me, I forgot about the daily grind and all the greyness. Everything I was questioning about the relationship and our future was forgotten. I was in the here and now, in his arms, and that was what I lived for. I was convinced that applied to him too. Peter."

Jeanette handed the cigarette over to Nanna. She thought they could share it—they were about to share even more. Or perhaps it was the final time they were going to share anything.

"But we were interrupted. There was a deafening noise that broke the silence around us. We sat up, but couldn't see anything from where we were. I hauled on my trousers and jumper and got out of one of the rear doors. I pulled on my boots that were outside and dragged my coat with me as I ran towards the main road. The noise had stopped, but when I came through the trees I saw what had happened. A car had come off the icy road and was at the bottom of a deep ravine. It was completely crushed—like a scrunched-up piece of paper. The engine had stopped, but there was still smoke coming from it. I assumed that no one could survive a crash like that. Then I raised my gaze and spotted another car—a blue Audi a little farther up the road. It reversed back to the spot where the car had left the road so the driver could look down into the ravine—that was my interpretation. So I got my mobile out of my pocket and photographed it. And I was probably right, because after standing there for a minute or so without the door opening, it drove off. The driver didn't even bother to get out and see what they had done before they left the scene of the accident."

Nanna nodded thoughtfully and took a final drag before handing the cigarette back to Jeanette. She still hadn't given up faith in her. But it was probably just a matter of time. Jeanette finished the cigarette, flicked the stub into the rain and took a deep breath in preparation for the final and most frightening part of the story. The bit that kept her awake at night and tortured her, day in day out.

The bit about the big betrayal. The *two* big betrayals, to be precise.

28

Sandra

ONE EVENING WHEN Sandra had gone to bed, but still hadn't fallen asleep, she heard footsteps on the porch. It happened fairly often when you lived in the country, and sometimes she would catch the intruder red-handed, sometimes she would see the tracks the morning after. In the summer they had no such needs, but during the rest of the year wild animals weren't bothered by stairs if it was something edible they were after. A pot filled with wilting summer plants for instance, or like now: spring bulbs that were almost over.

The sound of the uninvited guest made her more alert, and the light May evening didn't make it any easier for her drift off. Instead, her thoughts began to whir, and for better or worse it was Hallin who dominated them.

It had been a week and she hadn't heard from him. She wondered what his reasoning was—she tried to put herself in the shoes of someone like him in a threatening situation like this.

The denial was hardly sincere on his part. In all likelihood, he remembered the event. That was unless he had raped so many women that he couldn't keep count, but this was highly unlikely since Sandra hadn't heard any suggestion of there being a serial rapist on Gotland. It hurt her a little to think that others who had been affected behaved more soundly than she had, and actually reported the attacks.

Nevertheless, Hallin was probably thinking about it right now, speculating which direction the devilment that had hit him might take.

The easiest thing would simply be to cough up and be done with it. But perhaps he couldn't do that without his wife getting curious and starting to ask questions, and that was possibly a fate worse than death for him. It might also be that he couldn't afford it—however improbable that sounded for a man of his age and stature in society. Three thousand seven hundred kronor a month ought to be manageable for most people in his situation.

The other option was to let Sandra report the case to the social services, whereupon he would still be forced to pay support at parity with Sandra's fairly generous offer once there had been a paternity test. Which wouldn't enable him to keep it from his wife either. There was also the risk here that Sandra would report the rape—something he must be scared to death about. But perhaps he thought the risk was minimal that Sandra would have the energy to start a process like that after so many years, and that she would lose if she did. Perhaps he was also fostering some hope that he wasn't the father of the child and he therefore had no intention of putting a penny in her account until she had managed to prove it.

A third possibility was obviously to stick his head in the sand and hope the threat went away by itself. He had tried that tactic the last time someone had tried to extort money from him four years ago, and it had succeeded.

There was naturally another scenario—even if Sandra dismissed it as unrealistic. He could always try to scare the so-called gold digger into silence.

THE MORNING AFTER, when Erik and Sandra were going out to the car, she discovered something that had to be a bouquet of flowers dropped on the floor outside the front door. They weren't wrapped in the usual paper from a florist's but were in newspaper.

She let Erik wait outside while she picked off the tape, took out the flowers from their original wrapping, and put them in a vase on the kitchen table. They were beautiful, but there was no card—nothing to reveal where they had come from.

Time was scarce at this hour in the morning, so Sandra didn't give it another thought; she simply dropped off Erik at kindergarten before heading to work. In the evening they had dinner at her parents' and it was only when she got home and had put Erik to bed that she took the time to think about the flowers.

She didn't have any admirers so far as she knew. There was nothing particular to celebrate, no birthdays, no lottery wins, no pay rises, nor even her name day. Hang on—wasn't it Erik's name day sometime in May? Today, in fact, she discovered when she glanced at the calendar. But it wasn't something they celebrated, and who wasted money on flowers for a three-year-old? With no card to boot—something he would probably have appreciated more than the flowers.

Botany wasn't Sandra's strong suit, but she thought the white flowers might be some kind of lily, with their splendid stamens and pollen that she knew left a hell of a stain. She recognised the other flowers, but she had no clue what kind they were. After googling for a while she had the answer. Calla lilies: she knew of these, but it was the colour that confused her. Sandra thought she had seen calla lilies that were mostly red, but probably other colours too. She hadn't seen this dark purple kind, however, which were almost black.

White lilies and black calla lilies, she thought, a feeling of unease creeping in. It wasn't hard to guess what the colours black and white might mean in some contexts, but what about the flowers themselves—did they have any symbolic value in the world of floristry?

Yes, lilies were a symbol of innocence. The Virgin Mary was often depicted with a lily, Sandra discovered, as an allusion to the immaculate conception. According to some sources, it could also symbolise conceitedness. The calla lily didn't seem to mean anything in particular, except that it was often used in funeral displays. Like the regular lily.

Perhaps Sandra was supposed to be struck down by fear and nail shut all the windows and leave mines in the garden. She could have thrown out the flowers so she never had to see them again.

Instead, she got angry. And the flowers were very beautiful—carefully sculpted by nature's own hand in some rainforest on the other side of the planet. So she left them in their full splendour on the dining table in silent protest and as a reminder of the contempt she felt towards that man.

Hallin's venture was frankly infantile: insinuations about virgin birth and conceit delivered in newspaper on Erik's name day with a clear reference to death and burial. It was clearly intended to arouse fear in her. To frighten her into withdrawing her demand and make her leave him alone.

Or what? Death and burial?

With the best will in the world, a bunch of flowers could hardly be considered a death threat in the eyes of the law—so getting the police involved would be the same as disgracing herself. What was more, she didn't take the threat seriously. It was a final, clumsy gesture from a floundering man who already considered the battle lost.

On the whole, death and innocence packaged in newspaper was an inspiring thought. A plan was beginning to form in her mind. Her fists clenched, she contemplated the magnificent flowers and realised that life would never be the same again.

STILL NO TRACE OF MISSING 41-YEAR-OLD

It has been more than two weeks since 41-year-old Peter went missing in central Visby. Despite extensive search efforts, including assistance provided by the Swedish Home Guard, the man has still not been found.

The man was last seen on the fourth of February. He reportedly left his place of work around lunchtime and disappeared without a trace. His car was found in the car park adjacent to his workplace. His mobile phone was last active in the same location. The search is now being de-intensified.

The man is described as being 5ft10, 12 stone and with short, dark hair. He is thought to have been wearing a black jacket, light shirt, and a pair of dark trousers when he disappeared.

GOTLANDS ALLEHANDA

JANUARY– FEBRUARY 2014

29

Karl-Erik

HE HAD SLEPT for a while on the ferry from the mainland, so he felt fairly rested as he sat in the car heading home. It was freezing on Gotland—it hadn't been yesterday morning when he had left the island. Temperatures were in free fall and it was already at the freezing point. He had to be careful, because a hazardous layer of frozen slush was forming a crust on the road.

But there wasn't far to go. Soon he would be home in the warmth, where Kerstin would hopefully be waiting with some little surprise for him. He assumed she would after all these years of waiting. At this very moment, he felt that it might still have been worth it. He wouldn't repeat it—definitely not—and if he got to relive the last thirty years of his life he would make different choices. But as of now they had a future ahead of them that wouldn't have been possible if the last thirty years hadn't happened, and he had to see that as being worth something. The fact that he, they—Kerstin too, of course—were worth it. Otherwise everything was a waste, and he didn't want to look back on his life like that.

He realised he had forgotten to call her. He had promised to give her a ring when he came ashore so that she could prepare whatever it was she was going to prepare. He smiled at the thought of it—Kerstin was a rock. In the kitchen and in every other way. She put up with him—that in itself was noteworthy. And she had been patient and waited for him all these years instead of finding a new man. Which he, against his better judgment—although he was a good-natured soul—had suggested to her at an early stage. But it had never been in the picture. For some completely incomprehensible reason she apparently loved him.

"My dove!" he bellowed when she answered.

She laughed, used to his theatrical expressions of affection.

"I forgot to call—sorry."

"I realised," said Kerstin. "But I knew when the ferry was due. Has it gone well?"

"I'm on Gotland. I've got enough petrol. There's air in the tires. I'm wearing my seat belt. I can't see any cars in my rearview mirror and the road is devoid of any hazardous objects. What can possibly go wrong?"

"Knock on wood. Where are you?"

"I just passed that crossroads where it says 'Sarve' something to the left and 'Lilla' something else to the right."

"You sound like a mainlander," Kerstin said with a laugh. "Havdsarve and Lilla Lärs. How hard can it be?"

"I've lived here for two years! You've been here for ten. They use such strange names everywhere on this island. What are we having?"

"I've made a whiskey sour—that much I can tell you. But I thought we might start with a glass of champagne."

"Oh my—she's brought out the big guns, has my beloved wife."

"Wasn't she meant to?"

"Naturally. This is the first day of the rest of our lives. What about food?"

"In that matter, you will have to be patient. Drive carefully—I expect it's getting really slippery."

"Yep. Love you, baby!"

"Love you too. Kiss kiss."

How far did he have to go? Twenty-five kilometres, perhaps? Forty-five minutes in these conditions. He drove with exaggerated care. Nothing could go wrong. Not this time—not when there was so much at stake. When he entered the bend by the old limestone quarry he slowed down even more, thinking about the horse farm they would get and about Kerstin in welly boots and a posh oilskin jacket. Then he noticed they had taken down the barrier between the road and ravine, and he thought that January seemed an exceptionally poorly chosen time to do so.

It was at that moment that he caught sight of the oncoming car as it appeared around the next corner. It was on the wrong side of the road, travelling at a speed that a child could have worked out was inappropriate in this kind of place and in these conditions. The Audi did nothing to avoid a collision, so it was up to Karl-Erik to take control and brake, potentially moving onto the wrong side of the road. Potentially, since there was still a possibility that the Audi would move back to its side of the road and brake to avoid a head-on collision. But the Audi just drove on at breakneck speed, and it was doubtful whether it slowed down at all. At the last moment, Karl-Erik realised he would have to act—he would have to swerve. So he did, and regretted it in the same moment, because he could feel that the tires had no grip on the asphalt. The car slid almost sideways across the road before hurtling off the edge and through the air, tipping backward in an improbable way that could never, never, never end well.

The first time he regained consciousness, he didn't open his eyes. Instead, he lingered on the image of Kerstin in her Barbour jacket, now holding a whiskey sour. But he was having difficulty breathing, so he let himself drift off. The next time he came to he had a horrible hangover, a thumping headache and a mouth as dry as a Bedouin in a sandstorm. Kerstin made her drinks too strong—she always had. The third time he saw a woman who he first thought was Kerstin, but when he realised he was mistaken, he closed his eyes again because he would never betray her, not Kerstin. After that he didn't want to open his eyes again, because he could see what he wanted to see inside his eyelids—good people in beautiful places where there was freedom and air to breathe and no pain.

30

Jeanette

ONCE THE AUDI had disappeared, she instinctively set off down the slope without giving a thought to the fact that she was hardly dressed for that kind of escapade. It wasn't far in terms of distance, but it was steep and the terrain inaccessible. She climbed and slithered down, occasionally setting stones rolling that caused her to slip and end up on her behind—but she didn't care, simply getting up and struggling on. She had to get down there as quickly as possible—even if the price was a twisted ankle or torn coat.

Peter was slower off the mark, but he had stronger legs and caught up with her when she was almost at the bottom. While Jeanette ploughed her way through brush and scrub to the driver's side of the car, he stopped.

"I don't think I can," he said. "You look first."

"It doesn't look good," said Jeanette when she reached the car. "It looks dreadful."

She wanted to cry—scream in fact. An awful scene lay before her: the car looked like an accordion, and the driver was squashed between the steering wheel and the rest of the crushed car. He was presumably dead, because his face was covered in blood, and he had a deep, unpleasant gash on his forehead and a large shard of glass in his throat. It was a scene from a horror film—this couldn't be happening.

"Is anyone in the car alive?" Peter asked from a distance.

He had moved round to the back of the car now.

"I don't think so," said Jeanette. "I can only see the driver, and he seems to be alone. We have to try and get him out."

She didn't really feel up to it, and thought she might faint at any moment, but she had to contain her own emotions and needs and do what she could. Only then did the obvious occur to her: they had to call for help. That should have been the first thing she did, but she hadn't been thinking—just tearing down the slope without switching on her brain.

"Call emergency services, Peter," she said. "I'll open the door and try to pull him out."

Would she even manage to open the door? Probably not, because it was so dented and damaged that it would take a crowbar to open it, and even that might not be enough. A blowtorch? Panic took hold of her. She wanted to throw up and cry and faint, or just wake up from this nightmare of wounded flesh and blood and glass and crushed metal. Why on earth had she come down here? It would have been better to call the emergency services and let the professionals do their job.

"Call emergency services, Peter!" she shouted—why wasn't he answering?

She pulled and tugged at the door, but it was stuck fast.

"Come here for a moment," Peter said eventually.

"We need to raise the alarm, Peter. Call them!"

Expending great effort, she put a heel on the centre of the door hoping to shift something into a new position, but it did nothing.

"I want to show you something first," said Peter. "Come here."

She kicked once more, tugging at the handle, doing it again and again—but nothing happened. She kicked the door one final time, but mostly in resignation rather than hope.

Reluctantly, Jeanette took her eyes off the victim, who still hadn't shown any signs of life. She struggled over a stone and through bushes to the back of the wreck where Peter was standing.

"Look at this," he said.

The boot, opened by the crash, was wide open—she had seen that from the road. What she hadn't noticed was what the boot contained—a small suitcase and two sports holdalls. Both open—she assumed that Peter had for some reason unzipped them.

At first, Jeanette didn't understand. She couldn't understand why the contents of the bags mattered here and now in the middle of this devastation, or how one person could have so much money.

"Is he alive?" Peter asked again.

"I don't know for sure. But it looks really bad. He's probably cracked his skull, and has a . . . I don't think he can breathe at all."

"With this money we can build a future together."

It was a strange thing to say—the money wasn't theirs.

"He's dead, right?" he said, reassuring himself.

"I assume so," Jeanette replied, a sob in her throat. "But we still need to call . . . why aren't you calling?"

"Where do you think he got the money, Jeanette? This is cash—he's hardly earned it or won it at the bookie's. It won't be missed, believe you me."

"It belongs to someone," Jeanette replied, feeling bewildered by the situation.

"This man has somehow come across this money. Illegally—I guarantee it. He's dead and we're here. Are we stupid or what?"

"I don't know," Jeanette answered hesitantly. "Can't we just call emergency services?"

"Why don't we leave that to someone else? It's already too late, and we didn't cause this swindler's death. This is the chance of our lives. You and me, Jeanette. We can buy a nice place to live—a house. We can travel."

She heard what he was saying, and he sounded so convincing standing there and looking at her, his velvet eyes pleading with her. She didn't want to stay here any longer; her body and soul were both exhausted and she couldn't make any decisions. She wanted to get away from the brutalised body in the car wreck, away from the cold and the darkness creeping in, and she never wanted to think about this day again.

"How much money is there then?" Jeanette asked with a jumble of emotions.

"There must be a few million—three million is my best guess."

"Three million kronor?"

"Or more."

"I don't know . . . I just want to cry . . . It's all so awful."

But Peter took her in his arms and held her tight, swaying back and forth a little as if she were a child being put down to sleep.

"Let's not do anything we'll come to regret," he whispered into her hair. "This chance won't come round again."

And he was of course right. She realised that now. It felt good to be in it together now—and in it together in future. She didn't want to hold him back, didn't want to put a stop to their opportunity for a beautiful future.

So she gave in. She dried her tears and brushed off all the twigs and bark and mud that she had only now noticed on her coat. For safety's sake, she did a lap of the car to check that all hope for the man was gone—that the decision not to call the emergency services was correct. And it had to be. The man hadn't moved an inch and his eyes were still shut, his mouth half-open. For reasons she couldn't explain to herself, she got out her mobile and took a photo of what was visible of the wounded body through the side window. Then she returned to the boot, slung one of the bags over her shoulder and started climbing. She stopped further along the road and took a photo of the wreck diagonally from above. She noticed that Peter still hadn't started climbing.

"Peter, what are you doing?" she called out. "Hurry up before it gets too dark."

"I was wrong," he shouted back. "There must be twice as much. Can you hear me? Six fucking million!"

She waited for him. It didn't take long—he caught up quickly and passed her. Once they were almost at the top, she took another photo of the wrecked car at the bottom—she didn't know why. Perhaps it was out of respect for the deceased. Someone had to document the end of his life—everyone deserved an epitaph.

AS THEY LEFT it had begun to snow heavily. Darkness fell quickly, and the snowflakes whirling in the headlights created a dramatic contrast to the safety and warmth of the car. After a long period of contemplative silence they approached the burning issue—the future.

"What should we do with all the money?" Jeanette dared to ask.

"House, car, yacht," Peter said with a smile.

"I mean right now," said Jeanette. "Where should we put it?"

"I'll deal with that. It'll be fine in the boot for now. Only I drive this car, and no one steals a car with a company logo on it. But I think I have an idea about where we can keep it for a while."

"Okay," was all she said.

Peter mostly kept his eyes on the road, but every now and then he looked at her with concern. Eventually, he took her hand.

"Sweetheart," he said softly. "Don't let's regret this. What's done is done, and we did it for us. When we're lying on our sun loungers

CARIN GERHARDSEN

in the Bahamas holding a drink with an umbrella in it, we'll thank ourselves. Don't ruin this."

"I'm not going to tell anyone about this, if that's what you're worried about," said Jeanette. "I don't want to go to prison."

"We've not committed any crime," said Peter, emphasizing each word.

At the same time, he held out his hand in a way that seemed to suggest that this wasn't the first time he was explaining it.

"We've stolen someone's money," Jeanette pointed out.

"Yes, but whose? Some bank has lost a hell of a lot of money, but what does that matter? They'll print more, for god's sake. And it wasn't us who robbed the bank."

Jeanette had a very strong feeling that they had committed another—far worse—sin too, but she let it lie. Primarily because she couldn't bear to think about it, but also because she didn't want to mar what tied them together properly. The thing that guaranteed that the future was actually theirs—together. So she capitulated.

"You're right," she said, stroking the top of his hand with her other hand. "I shouldn't be such a gloomy Gus."

"It was a traumatic event," said Peter. "Let's put this behind us and look forward instead. Okay?"

"Let's do that," said Jeanette, squeezing his hand before letting it go.

They drove for a while in silence, Jeanette looking straight ahead. She thought about the next time they would see each other—how would it feel? More intimate? More relaxed? More joyful?

Or less?

No, it couldn't be like that—then everything they had gone through would have been for nothing. Everything hinged on Jeanette—this insight hit her. If she retreated into herself, like she had done at home when it had all gone wrong, this relationship would end before it had even begun—with or without the millions. She promised herself not to be so anxious, to keep up her spirits and think positive—just like Peter always did. The future was bright—how could she have thought otherwise?

"I love you," slipped out of her.

"There it is!" said Peter, beaming like sunshine. "I've been waiting for so long!"

Jeanette hoped he would respond. It took a while, but then it came.

"Worried?" he said without looking away from the road.

Jeanette didn't answer, but she saw the playful look in his eyes and around his mouth and knew to expect more.

"Just wanted to keep you on tenterhooks," he eventually said with a smile. "I love you too—isn't it obvious?"

Then he caressed her cheek, running his fingers through her hair like a comb and gently pinching her neck before putting his hand back on the wheel.

"This wasn't much of a rendezvous," he said. "But I think we'll have to lie low for a while. You realise that?"

Jeanette did. Not because it would really make much difference, but it felt like a sensible approach.

"We'll have to exchange coded messages at work," she said with a smile.

"Back slang?"

"Morse code."

"Only until the dust has settled," said Peter. "Two weeks or so."

"I think we can manage that."

"Really?"

Jeanette sighed.

"With great difficulty," she admitted.

"The same here. But a man's gotta do what he's gotta do."

This time he dropped her off a fair distance from work, in an area with apartments where neither of them had any connections.

She would have to walk a couple of kilometres, but they couldn't risk being seen together in case their respective absences were connected—something that was more important today than ever.

They hugged for a long time, kissed briefly, and parted ways. Jeanette stood still watching the car drive off. Now she was alone with the memories of all the bad things that had happened, and it made it all the more frightening. She didn't know how she would survive two long weeks without him.

Little did she know that those weeks would become years.

31

Kerstin

ONCE THEY HAD ended the call, she applied the finishing touches to the canapés. Champagne and fancy finger food weren't normally part of her diet, but today she was making a splash. After years of waiting, here was her reward. The recompense for the heavy consequences of what had been both illegal and foolish acts for which Karl-Erik had been held accountable, all by himself.

There had been four of them in on it: a series of robberies against small- and medium-sized branches of banks and post offices outside of the big cities. Karl-Erik had taken the fall, while the others had been acquitted. He had served eight years in a string of prisons, and Kerstin had been alone for the same period. She had moved to Gotland when he had gone inside. She wanted to leave the old life behind her, including the destructive company that came with it. Start afresh somewhere no one knew who she was—and Gotland was the optimal refuge.

Two years ago, Karl-Erik had been released, and since then they had lived in the countryside—far from the hubbub of Visby and the annual invasion of tourists. During those years, they had almost certainly been under police surveillance, but they had been patient and waited for the right opportunity. Out of the total spoils of around twelve million kronor, half was going to Karl-Erik as a consolation prize and to demonstrate his accomplices' gratitude. The money had been laundered over the last ten years, so Karl-Erik had nothing to worry about, so long as he stayed on the straight and narrow and didn't throw money around.

Today was the day the money was coming home. When the dream of the horse farm was going to come true. Hence the grand celebrations.

When an hour had elapsed since his call, she poured a glass of wine for herself. Everything was ready and laid out, the candles were lit and the whole house smelled of festivity. Surely it was only a matter of minutes by now, but it was good that he was driving carefully—the temperature was just below zero, it was pitch black out there, and the snow was coming down heavily. Kerstin paced back and forth beside the window, constantly throwing glances out to the driveway.

Once she had finished her wine twenty minutes later, she really began to worry. She sent him a text message and called several times, but only got his voicemail. Had his mobile run out of charge without him noticing? Had he got a puncture, meaning that he was crouching in the cold and dark while changing a tire on the car? She put the tray of canapés in the fridge, sat down on the very edge of the sofa, and couldn't decide what to do. Around an hour later she was still there in the same position, her hands entwined in a viselike grip and her thoughts flitting between various scenarios as she imagined the worst.

No road was in that big a coverage black spot. No punctured tire took that long to change. He should have been in touch if nothing serious had happened.

Had he had the police on his tail after all? Was it possible that after all this time they had eyes on Karl-Erik at every moment, that they'd known exactly where he was—and the loot for that matter—and they had pounced on him with his boot full of cash? On Gotland as well . . . Why not do it in Stockholm? Was that possible?

Was it possible that his accomplices had taken him out? Perhaps they weren't quite as loyal as they had pretended to be—had they overpowered him in a dark and desolate spot and taken his life? Or tied his hands behind his back and chucked him in the boot of the car? Which was tantamount to murder, given it was far from certain that anyone would actually find the abandoned car before daybreak—he would freeze to death during the night. Or had other criminals caught wind of the whole thing and done something like that themselves?

The risk was there, of course. But murder . . . ? The probability of this having happened—and so close to the end of the journey—was, in Kerstin's view, almost nonexistent.

They only had one car, so Kerstin had no prospect of heading out to search for him, which would have been a foolhardy act with no likelihood of success in any case. The most probable thing was that he had been in an accident in the awful weather and had been taken to hospital.

Her heart pounding, she called the emergency room at Visby Hospital. The very fact that she had to do so felt dreadful, but the news that they hadn't admitted any patients matching Karl-Erik's description or with his name didn't exactly offer her any degree of reassurance.

Any sane person would naturally have called the police. Kerstin talked it over with herself, weighing the pros and cons against each other before eventually deciding that there was more to lose than there was to gain. Karl-Erik might have good cause to keep out of the way for a while—for Kerstin's sake, if nothing else. What did she know about who or what he had come into contact with since their call? If she sent the police after him, it wouldn't make anyone happier—on the contrary, it would ruin everything they had struggled so long to get.

It wasn't yet late enough for all traffic to be off the roads. Even if most people tried to remain indoors given the conditions, someone would have reported it by now if an accident had taken place. The police would already have been on the scene, and if Karl-Erik had been arrested on the basis of the contents of his boot, she would be informed soon enough.

In summary, there was nothing Kerstin could do. She would just have to bide her time. Sooner or later, she would get an answer to all her questions. And no news was good news—wasn't that the saying? At least, that's what she told herself when she finally blew out all the candles and crept under the duvet to try and sleep.

In the days that followed, her hopes of a happy ending fell to pieces. Kerstin felt absolutely dreadful, and couldn't bring herself to do anything other than occasionally get on the bus to go somewhere along the route that Karl-Erik should have driven. Then she would take long, draining walks in the piercing wind without making any progress. She would spend her nights in a state of spiritual darkness that she had never come close to during her eight long years of waiting. Time came to a standstill; four days of uncertainty felt like more than had eight years with a defined end point.

But eventually the sun came back, and with it a return to temperatures above zero that made the snow melt away. This was the explanation offered by the two police officers who knocked on her door one afternoon, faces grave and caps in hand, asking to come inside. They said that was why the badly smashed-up car hadn't been spotted from the road until now.

"The car was recovered from the ravine at Madvar," the more talkative one of the duo said. "And it must have been completely covered in snow. Do you know where that is?"

Kerstin did. Karl-Erik had almost been at Madvar when he had called, but she was in no state to say anything about that. She felt the blood draining from her face, and she allowed herself to be conducted—almost carried—to the living room sofa. When she had regained her senses somewhat, a small number of technicalities were presented that were intended to help her form a better understanding of the accident. Slippery, dark, snowfall, no other cars involved—all words and phrases that would in no way ease the processing of the trauma. Then the obvious questions that she couldn't answer.

"When were you expecting him back home?"

"I don't know."

"Didn't you talk to each other?"

"Perhaps he wanted to surprise me."

"So you're saying you have no idea whether he was supposed to come home last Thursday or today or sometime next week?"

Kerstin shrugged her shoulders and shook her head—playing dumber than she was.

"Why didn't you report him missing?"

"I didn't know he was missing."

Kerstin continued to feed them unclear and strange answers that could easily be punctured with phone records in the event of any suspected irregularities. Which there didn't seem to be, given that the wrecked car had been emptied of all personal possessions, which were now handed over to Kerstin in an emotionally wary manner.

A wheeled cabin bag was put in front of her on the coffee table. Judging by their looks, she was expected to open it in front of them, but it contained nothing more exciting than clothes and toiletries. They were Karl-Erik's things, which meant they were of significance to Kerstin. But not to the two police officers, who awaited her reactions while she rooted through the bag. She looked from one to the other, her eyes filled with tears, while they averted their gazes as they handed over some tools, a first aid kit, and a couple of CDs that had miraculously survived the accident.

"That's everything," said one of them.

They were completely absent of the vigilance that would have been present if there had been anything else found in the car—anything more interesting that Kerstin might have been aware of. She didn't ask either—it was obvious that someone had got their hands on the cash before the police had arrived on the scene.

IN FACT, BEFORE, the car had been blanketed in snow. That much became clear the next day. Accompanied by one of the officers who had come to the house, she was shown the body.

"I'd like to see the pictures you took at the scene of the accident," Kerstin requested afterward.

Despite the shocking news and the grief and the loss that had already firmly taken hold of her, she wanted to bring clarity to exactly what had happened. How Karl-Erik had spent his final moments on earth.

"I don't think that's a very good idea," the policeman said. "They're very distressing photos."

"I understand that," Kerstin said. "But I really need to see them—no matter how painful they may be. It's a way for me to feel closure."

Reluctantly, he allowed himself to be persuaded into taking her to his office to show her the terrible photos from the scene of the accident, guiding her through the event that had turned her life upside down.

It was then she found out that it hadn't been a case of seconds but hours. The smashed face and the wound on the forehead were upsetting enough, but the shard of glass in his throat and its excruciating consequences were probably what hit her hardest. According to the doctor who had examined the body, it had probably been the direct cause of death. No autopsy had been carried out—and wouldn't be—given there was really nothing to prove. Karl-Erik was dead. Sentenced to death from the very beginning since the accident was self-inflicted, since it had been dark and the snow had fallen so heavily that before long the car had been blanketed. The examination of the scene had uncovered that the accident had taken place just before or during the onset of the heavy snowfall, which had coincided with the fall of darkness. It had lasted all night—but no longer than that.

In a few of the photos, the little suitcase was visible in the boot, covered in a thick layer of snow like the ground around it and the roof of the car. There was no sign of the holdalls, which must have been spirited away before the snowfall on Thursday night, rather than upon the discovery of the wreck on Monday.

This was Kerstin's own analysis, and it was not one that she sought to share with the accommodating policeman. The gist of it was, however, that someone had been close to Karl-Erik just before the snow began to fall—which meant immediately after the accident. Someone who had clearly grabbed the cash and left the scene without doing anything to save his life or shorten his protracted suffering.

Was this crash involving no other cars actually a hit-and-run? It was difficult to condemn the theft itself, given the money had been stolen in the first place, but the cynicism and emotional coolness of robbing someone of six million kronor without being kind enough to call emergency services were indefensible.

But what could Kerstin do about it?

Nothing, as there was no physical evidence of anything except a single-vehicle incident. The theft of stolen goods couldn't be reported without a long shadow falling on her, since she clearly was aware of and had likely intended to use the stolen money. That was likely to be a crime in itself—something that might put her behind bars, which was an inconceivable future prospect.

So Kerstin remained silent.

32

Jeanette

JUST AS SHE had feared, the days dragged while she awaited her reunion with Peter. During the daytime, she wandered around like a zombie, simply longing for the working day to be over despite the nights being even worse. She would lie there sleeplessly, tossing and turning, her guilty conscience taking a stranglehold on her and refusing to let go.

Six million kronor—was it really worth it? To slip along the walls like a shadow, the bags under her eyes growing darker and darker by the day, afraid of herself and what she was capable of, afraid of her potentially uncontrollable reactions if she were to bump into her forbidden love, her co-conspirator, at the shop or outside.

It wasn't worth it. She knew now that it wasn't worth six *billion* kronor either. If she were faced with the same choice again, if she were able to rewind the tape and experience that confounded afternoon again, she would act differently. She would be awkward, convince Peter that one of the consequences of deeply immoral acts was that you could no longer bear to live with yourself. She would summon the police and paramedics to the scene of the accident right away, and she wouldn't even see the money.

The damage was already done—she had to adopt a constructive approach to what she had done. There was no shadow cast on Peter—he would have to take responsibility for his own decisions. She *had* to do something about her completely unsustainable situation.

But what?

She couldn't very well go to the police. In that case, she would ruin not only her own but also Peter's and their joint future. And it was for the sake of that future that she had made this sacrifice, as she now tended to regard the whole thing. Since the almost unbearable aftereffects had taken over her life.

She was basically unable to do anything. Her hands and feet were tied out of loyalty to Peter and the promises she had made to him. The relationship with Peter had given her new insights, new hope of a joyous life—even after Charlotte. She didn't want to deprive herself of those future prospects, although she also wanted to vindicate her existence after the terrible thing she had done to another person. She had to compensate. She just couldn't work out how.

The only thing that was currently bringing any light at all to her existence was the dreamy warmth of Peter's embrace on the horizon. With his untroubled manner and his unshakable optimism, he would set her on a happier train of thought, suck the poison from her veins, and help her to forgive herself. All her hopes were invested in this, and that was something. But there still remained many days of suffering in solitude ahead.

Like when the article about the car accident appeared in the local paper. Anxiety dug its sharp claws into her, and this time it wasn't just the increasingly familiar guilty conscience making its presence known. Something downright physical plunged her into a state of dizziness that almost tipped her off her chair. Her stomach was turning but, leaning on the kitchen counter, she was able to stagger to the sink to throw up the little food she had eaten.

He had been down there in the ravine for four days—four days trapped in a wrecked car, invisible to passersby under the thick blanket of snow. The article didn't say whether death had been instant, but the whole thing was just awful. For his loved ones, it must have been four days of horrific torture, without any clue as to what had happened—whether he was alive and suffering or had already been torn away from them. And then, when it was over, the burden of the knowledge that a loved one had spent day after day in the cold and darkness without any chance of rescue. Even if he had perished immediately, it was shameful, inhuman for a dead person to spend days on end squashed inside a car covered in snow.

And Jeanette could have alleviated their suffering. Jeanette could have made life easier for his loved ones—in fact, she could have ensured he was saved. She had difficulty taking in the latter point; she didn't want to believe it, couldn't let herself believe it. But the thought was there, and she formulated the words, even if they wouldn't take hold. The man *was* dead—beyond rescue. He must have been—that was her lifeline, because otherwise she didn't want to live with herself any longer.

Then a few more days without any improvement, with even worse remorse. The loneliness was monumental, and she brushed up against the idea of suicide. She was exhausted, and her hopes of being able to climb out of this even with Peter's help were fading away. And a future with Peter felt more and more remote as the days passed. She never saw him—was he still there? Or was he an unattainable dream that would never come true? A figment of her imagination that she could cling to until she went under?

One day she caught sight of the death notice in the newspaper. Unobtrusive but gripping, signed by just one person: his wife. The name of the victim wasn't familiar to Jeanette, but she had been glancing through the deaths in all the local papers every day since the accident without finding anyone of the right age and with the right death day. But now she was convinced—it had to be him.

No children, no mourning parents or siblings, just a life partner. She could barely imagine what those four days of uncertainty had been like for her—for Kerstin, that was her name. Or what her life looked like now, as a recent widow in the middle of her life.

Jeanette would have liked to do something for her, to say sorry and perhaps somehow make good on what she had done. But the woman might very well go to the police, and regardless of how they classified the crime, Jeanette knew that they would both be in real trouble—she and Peter. The affair would get out, and everything would have been in vain.

She could at least have given the widow the money—anonymously. Left it outside the door, rung the bell and run away before Kerstin had time to open up. But Peter would never go along with it. She had no idea where he was keeping the cash, and she didn't want to know—the thought of the money just got her worked up. And the widow probably knew nothing about the money. The kind of crime that earned millions of kronor was very much a man's sport. She might simply have called the police, who would catch them, and no one would be any happier for that.

But there was something that Jeanette could do. Anonymously. She could give the widow the answers she needed to heal. Jeanette knew from experience that something people needed when they were grief-stricken was the knowledge of the hitherto unknown: concrete facts to hold fast to, to structure existence around.

The widow didn't know how the accident had happened; she was living under the delusion that her husband had been careless and that his terrible fate had been self-inflicted. But there was a perpetrator responsible for his death: another motorist who had left the scene without checking what the fall-out had been or raising the alarm. When considering why, it was fair to assume that the underlying reasons, if not alcohol-related, were surely at least related to recklessness. In short, a negligent, selfish hit-and-run.

That was knowledge that Jeanette could impart to the grieving wife. The photographs she had taken at the scene of the accident were still saved on her mobile. In a gesture of respect, she had documented not just the crash site but also the other driver's car. And the deceased's upper body and face—but she didn't think that was something that would make the widow feel any better.

So she printed three of the photos and put them in an envelope. Then she found out where the bereaved wife lived, addressed the letter accordingly, applied a stamp, and posted it. Without any other message—the pictures told their own story, and for that matter, who was Jeanette to moralise about others? The widow would have to interpret the pictures herself and do whatever she wanted with that information.

It wasn't much, but in some small way, this unselfish act made Jeanette feel better. At least for the time being.

33
Jan

A FEW DAYS after he had seen Speedy Gonzales's death notice in the local paper, a handwritten envelope dropped into the letter box. It was unusual, and might indicate some form of celebration was imminent. In other words, some stimulation. Something he really needed right now. That car accident had done something to Jan. He couldn't shake off the melancholy that had descended on him.

He had a widow—the man in the oncoming vehicle. Jan had noted that with a lump in his throat. Knowing full well that it could easily have been his own death notice, with Gunilla and the kids listed as the bereaved persons. No, he was never going to put himself in that position again. He would have to consider it a lesson learned. Which didn't change the fact that he felt glum, but simultaneously unable to do anything about it by himself. That was why he had a sliver of hope for diversion as he opened the envelope in the kitchen just before dinner time.

It wasn't to be. It contained a key, but it didn't say what it was for. Inside the envelope were three pretty grainy photographs that depicted something he was at first unable to comprehend. But before he had managed to take in the motif in the pictures, he was overcome by horror. Perhaps it was the light, the long shadows of the impending dusk, the ominous feeling of what were otherwise pretty clumsy compositions. It took just a couple of seconds for him to be right back there, at the scene of the accident.

He broke out into a cold sweat and had to sit down on a kitchen chair. Gunilla glanced over at him quizzically, but then resumed her dinner preparations. He hoped she hadn't attached any importance to his reaction—at least she hadn't commented on it.

Who the hell had taken these pictures? One of them showed the crashed car from an angle slightly above it. Another—taken from the same angle but closer up—showed the wreck, with the victim clearly visible. He hadn't seen that before. He had tried to form an impression from up on the road, but it had been too dark, the angle too awkward, and the distance too far. At the time, he had been forced to face facts: the driver was dead. Had to be. But now this unfocused yet morbid photo of the dead man was being thrown in his face and it was shocking.

What was worse was that the third photograph was of his car. There was no question about it: it was his blue Audi parked above the wreck as he took in what had happened and considered how to respond to the situation. On the wrong side of the road, to top it all, which seemed more than ominous.

Inside the envelope there was also a handwritten note, which he now discovered. He mopped the sweat from his brow and tugged the small slip of paper out.

Leave six million kronor in locker number 67 at the ferry terminal in Visby. No later than 10th February at 12:00 P.M.

That was what it said, and it left him completely stunned. Six million kronor—where was he supposed to find that? He had ten days, which was fairly generous, but he wouldn't be able to pull together six million in ten *months*. Not even once. Unless he was forced out of house and home and sold both the car and the SUV. And he couldn't do that.

On the other hand, he couldn't go to prison either. For that was surely what awaited him if this came to the attention of the police. That he had been at the scene of the accident before the snowfall—in direct connection with the accident itself. That he had been on the wrong side of the road just after the bend, which suggested—even if it didn't prove it—that he had caused the tragedy. That he had been on the scene when the accident happened, but had failed to call an ambulance or tell the police. They would ask why this was, and dig up old receipts from his visits to the Lindgården Inn. And maybe even an old case about a rape nearby, if such a police report existed and had stumped the investigators.

Fucking hell! That was what he wanted to shout. But he didn't, because Jan was a problem solver and the only one who kept his calm when everyone else was running around like a headless chicken. It had to be possible to get himself out of this tight corner. All it demanded was a little imagination and a dash of luck.

The question remained: who had taken those bloody photos?

Thanks to the impending heavy snow, there had been hardly any traffic out on the roads at the time of the accident—especially not on that country lane out in the wilds where there was probably never much traffic at any time. Was there someone other than the driver in the crashed vehicle? Someone who had been thrown clear of the car as it plunged downward, or had managed to climb the steep slope before Jan had been able to bring his own car to a halt and reverse?

Not likely. That person would have called emergency services, or at least the widow, and wouldn't have left the body there like an icicle for four days.

Someone else must have been on the road without Jan noticing. That was entirely possible, given that he was fully occupied by his own problems and those of the victim. He hadn't checked his rearview mirror. If the witness had approached on foot, Jan would also not have heard anything.

"Dinner in a minute!" Gunilla shouted to him as he got up and left the kitchen.

"Be right back," he said, taking the photographs into the study.

He spread them out in front of him on the desk, switched on the desk lamp, and pulled the magnifying glass out of one of the drawers. He couldn't stop himself from glancing at the deceased first—and it wasn't a pretty sight. It really wasn't, even though the picture was unfocused. A shudder passed through his body; he felt sick and he had to take several deep gulps.

He moved the lens to his own car and noted that he was not personally visible in the photo, but unfortunately his rear registration plate was perfectly clear. There was no mistaking that it was Jan's car. But from what angle had the picture actually been taken? Not directly from behind, which would have been the case if the photographer had approached from the same bend in the road as he had. No, slightly diagonally to the right, as if the witness was peering out of the woods on the ravine side.

Wasn't there some nondescript track leading off there for forestry workers and the like? Now it occurred to him. One of those roads that was nothing more than two tire tracks with weeds in between them? Yes, he was pretty certain. And not only that—out of the mists of his memories of that unfortunate afternoon, a memory of the journey in the opposite direction emerged. A very hasty reflection of his made on the way home with the girl with all her bargain buys from the sales. She had been gritting her teeth for the last few kilometres—clearly anxious, he had noted with mild amusement, given there was nothing to worry about. That meant he had been concentrating more on driving and her reactions than on what had been rushing by on the side of the road. But just up there in the woods on the small track he had seen something fleetingly. He had noticed a car among the bare trees and wondered whether they had engine trouble or something. Something he would most respectfully not have given a shit about, given he had recognised the yellow car and its decal as belonging to a guy in the same hunting club as him. Norling was his name, and he was a self-righteous idiot. Jan couldn't have cared less about any problems that guy might have.

How much time had he spent at the house of the whisky girl—half an hour, perhaps? If Norling had run out of petrol and had been waiting for help, he might very well still have been in the car when the accident happened.

In all likelihood, that bastard was behind the blackmail attempt. Was he in dire straits financially? Six million wasn't exactly chicken feed, but was pretty much exactly what Jan *could* scrape together if he sold everything he owned.

Which he had no intention of doing. This would have to be solved by other means, he thought to himself as he put the photographs back in the envelope. He heard steps behind him and turned to face his wife with a forced smile.

"Just coming, darling," he said, shutting the unpleasant correspondence in his desk drawer.

34

Jeanette

SHE WAS STANDING waiting, amid concrete, corrugated metal, cars covered in the grime of winter roads and wet asphalt. In the rain and wind and February chill, still expectant. The weeks of eternity without Peter were finally over.

Jeanette had received a text message from an untraceable number. Maybe he had a secret number, or maybe he'd picked up a burner. The message was crystal clear: he was heading south and would pick her up outside the Bilcity store, just before the roundabout leading onto Toftavägen. On the day exactly two weeks after the accident.

Jeanette interpreted this to mean that he felt the same eagerness she did. During this difficult time, she had been worrying, among so many other things, that he would delay the whole thing. That he would extend the waiting period by several weeks—maybe even months—just to be on the safe side. And that in the meantime, interest on his part would cool off. That she would eventually give up before they had a chance to talk.

When she had received the message, there had been four days left till the meeting. Four never-endingly long days going through the now-familiar torments: sleeplessness and feeling like she was sleep-walking, shame, guilt, anaemia, nervousness, lost appetite, and basically the loss of her will to live. However, the assurance that Peter would be taking care of her in just a few days' time had helped her to get back on an even keel—it was a light in the pitch darkness. The assurance that he would touch her.

And now she was standing here, unaffected by the grim environment around her, the awful weather, and the cold wind. Nothing could possibly be worse than what she had experienced in the last few weeks, and the memories of them had been compartmentalised into some hidden corner of her consciousness. The beginning of what was to come next awaited, and that meant everything to her.

At a quarter past—hadn't he said four o'clock?—Jeanette did a lap of the large, half-empty car park. Maybe he was somewhere she couldn't see him? No.

He must have run into something—maybe they needed him at work a little longer. But she could wait; she didn't have anything better to be doing. It was half past four—was he waiting for her out on the road, even though he had expressly said the car park? Not there either, she noted, before returning to the car park. Had he gone inside to get warm? No, and the car was definitely not in the car park, so he wasn't here. Unless he had changed cars, that was. But that seemed unlikely, because he could hardly have left his job since she last saw him. The car might have broken down, of course, meaning that he'd come in a borrowed or rented car—but that would be even greater cause to show himself to her.

Bilprovningen! It hit her. He had written Bilcity, but had obviously meant Bilprovningen next door. But he wasn't there either, and it was now five o'clock. If he had written four but had meant five, then it was probable that he would turn up eventually.

She hurried back to the agreed meeting place outside the car dealership, pacing back and forth before doing the last hour all over again. Without success: he was nowhere to be seen. There was no word from him on her mobile either.

It had got dark, and when hope began to run out, she plucked up the courage to send him a text message at the untraceable number. Had she misunderstood—hadn't they agreed to meet? But she didn't get an answer, and she didn't dare be more assertive than that. He would either get in touch or he wouldn't. He knew she was waiting and that bad news was better than no news at all.

Six o'clock came, then seven, but she still hadn't given up all hope. It wasn't possible that he had tricked her into coming here only to fail to show up—he wasn't like that. But could she be sure of that? They didn't actually know each other that well . . . Well, now they did. She tried to convince herself. They were connected for life, whether they wanted it or not. Exactly two weeks ago, something had happened that neither of them would forget, and from Peter's perspective in particular it was best to keep their relationship friendly at least. And why had there been all those tokens of affection in that solitary message if he hadn't meant anything by them? Why express his love and his longing if they were merely empty words?

She prowled among the uninspiring barracks, stamped her way through industrial sites to stay warm, and let herself get splattered by stressed-out rush hour motorists on the busy roads around the roundabout—all while the clock kept ticking, minute after minute, hour after hour.

Eventually, she realised that the resilience driving her wasn't motivated by strength and patience, but by desperation and madness. Somehow, she had to get home and pull the wool over her husband's eyes with some story about how she had spent the evening. Then she would cry in silence in the darkness of the bedroom.

35

Jan

TEN DAYS HAD crawled by, and a further ten had been added to them. Only when he had made it to fourteen days over time did Jan feel like he could relax: the threat wasn't going to be realised. He celebrated in silence, albeit surrounded by people, perched on a bar stool at G:a Masters on the way home from work. The police still hadn't come to knock on his door, none of his acquaintances in the force had shot glances at him when they thought he wasn't looking. That was, without doubt, worth both a beer and a whisky.

Norling's disappearance had given rise to several articles and items on the news—not just locally but in the national media. According to sources, the police were taking the case very seriously, but despite that, they were said not to have a clue about where he might have gone, how he might have left or why. The whole thing was an enigma to almost everyone—but there was always someone who knew the truth. That was the one thing you could always be sure of, Jan thought smiling to himself before draining his whisky glass in one go.

"Another?" said the bartender attentively.

Jan nodded. The car would have to stay where it was overnight—nowadays he had stopped getting behind the wheel if he had had so much as a beer.

"Weird story, that thing with Peter Norling . . ." said the bartender while pouring the whisky into a fresh glass. "Disappearing into thin air like that."

Out of everyone, he seemed to be talking to Jan in particular—as if he had read his thoughts. The surprise must have been visible on Jan's face, because the bartender clearly felt encouraged to explain his statement.

"I seem to remember you were in the same hunting club?"

"Yes, that's right," Jan confirmed with relief. "Absolutely. Yes, the whole thing is bloody messed up."

"Tragic," said the bartender, placing the glass in front of him. "Especially for the family, regardless of what's happened."

Jan nodded. Naturally, he personally felt neither sorrow nor consternation. Instead, he revelled in the fact that the deeply unpleasant blackmail story was history.

It was *theoretically* possible that Jan had got the wrong end of the stick, and that the company car that Norling pootled about in had left the scene before the accident. Jan really had no idea, given that he had approached from the wrong direction on his way back, and hadn't been able to see up that forest track. And in that case he had been wrong when he had aimed his suspicions at Norling, and should have followed a different line of inquiry. Which was not doable since he hadn't seen a soul out there in the woods by the ravine, and he could hardly start guessing which one of the fifty-seven thousand inhabitants on this island had silently witnessed the fatal accident and then documented it.

But competent people were lucky, he affirmed to himself with a humour he hadn't felt for a month. The accident and its tragic consequences had fallen into oblivion in Jan's consciousness. Lately, the photographs from the scene of the accident had cast their shadow over his existence. But now Norling was gone, and since then the blackmail threat had not been renewed or executed. The problem was gone from the world, and Jan could look ahead with confidence.

"Cheers," he said with a smile at the bartender, appearing friendly, but not overly happy now that the subject of Norling's tragic disappearance had been brought up. Then he drained the new whisky, downed the rest of the beer, paid his tab and left, lighter of heart than he had been in a long time.

36

Jeanette

JEANETTE WAS SITTING in the car park outside work. Her place of work—that was why her car was here. But it was Peter's place of work too, and that was also why she was here. Her tongue was dry in her mouth; she really needed something to drink, but she didn't have anything. Visiting his workplace went directly against everything they had agreed on, and it didn't sit well with her. But it was the best thing she could come up with—significantly better than going to his home, which was completely unthinkable. Peter would not tolerate that, and she couldn't bear the thought of even glimpsing his wife and children. It was as if her self-confidence had been blown away, and in order to postpone the unpleasant but unavoidable visit ahead of her, she evaluated the situation yet again.

It had been yesterday, during the long afternoon and evening outside the car dealership, and during the night, that she had realised what the new component in her spiritual misery was: that absence of self-confidence. It had slowly begun to dawn on Jeanette that she could no longer be loved, and nor did she deserve to be.

There had been two practicable ways to tackle the situation at the ravine. On the one hand they could have taken the money and sneaked away from the scene, celebrating their good fortune, with a positive outlook on life and looking ahead to the future with obvious joy. On the other hand, they could have followed their consciences, flat out said no to the whole idea, and left carrying their heads high.

Jeanette had chosen the coward's option. Vacillating, she had stood there shifting from one foot to the other, listening with half an ear to the voice of her heart, while at the same time she had allowed herself to be convinced—while in a decidedly uncritical state—to do something that went against everything she believed in. By someone she barely knew.

What a silly cow she was—a milksop without her own will. A turncoat.

He got cold feet right there in the car as they had driven away from the scene of the accident. He had realised what she brought to the table—that she was not someone whose hand he wanted to hold when the wind picked up. And that she had nothing to offer even when it wasn't windy.

It was under the weight of this newfound insight that she finally got out of the car and went to the shop that was adjacent to the garage where Peter worked. With a final, tremendous effort, she plucked up her courage and stepped through the door, accompanied by a plinging sound.

"I was here about a week ago and talked to a guy about a problem with my car," she began. "I don't remember his name, but he had dark, pretty short hair, and . . ."

"It doesn't matter," said the man behind the counter. "Perhaps I can help you instead?"

He was around thirty, burly, with a bushy ginger beard and a shaved head, and he exchanged a glance that was difficult to interpret with a colleague who had just had his back to them while fiddling with the shelves.

"It's quite complicated," said Jeanette. "I'm not sure I can explain it all again. Isn't he in? The dark-haired guy?"

New looks were exchanged—did they suspect something? Had they caught sight of them together, or had Peter told them something in confidence that he oughtn't have?

"No," said the man, leaning forward with the palms of his hands spread wide on the counter.

He almost looked threatening standing there and looking at her, seemingly waiting for the next move, as if he knew she wasn't telling the truth.

"Do you know when he's expected back?" Jeanette continued obstinately.

"No," said the man again, without letting her out of his gaze.

Maybe he was offended that she wouldn't confide her mechanical issues to him?

"He's on holiday," the other one interrupted—an older man who didn't look like he had long left until retirement. "He'll probably be gone for a couple of weeks at least."

Another mysterious look was exchanged between the two men, and Jeanette was overcome by the feeling that not a single word of truth had been said during this peculiar conversation.

"Okay, then I'll try again in a few weeks," she said with a smile and a forced lightness of tone. "Bye for now!"

Then she turned on her heel and left the garage. She heard the door close behind her with another quiet *pling* from the bell there to notify the staff of new customers.

In a seemingly nonchalant way, she strolled past the window of the unit. Then she went and got back into her own car. She thought again. Tried to interpret the situation. Concluded that Peter was potentially at the garage, but had asked his colleagues not to reveal it if anyone asked after him. Such as a blonde in fashionable clothing pretending not to know him. Or maybe he really *was* on holiday. Maybe for two weeks, maybe for longer. And he hadn't told her this.

Regardless of which was true, it all seemed to bode ill. He didn't want anything to do with her any longer.

JEANETTE WAS SITTING at the breakfast table turning the pages of the newspaper, distractedly and mostly for appearance's sake, since her husband was also at the table. If she wasn't reading, she would be expected to talk to him, and she had increasingly little to discuss with her husband. The news didn't interest her either—the thoughts turning over in her head now overshadowed everything else.

More than two weeks had passed since the nonmeeting, and Jeanette's problems had only got worse. Now she no longer dared to hope for a reunion with Peter. After scrutinising every element of the drama that had taken place, it seemed more and more obvious that he no longer wanted her with him on his voyage into a brighter future. But there were a few details that bothered her and kept her hopes alive, and no matter how much she puzzled over it, she was unable to make sense of his reasoning.

How could he be so certain that she wouldn't have a breakdown, give herself up and therefore by extension him too? That risk had been looming large since the very beginning, and he ought not to feel confident in her loyalty as a result. What was more, if he had lied to her, holding out the prospect of a meeting, and then he had crept away from all of it without so much as a peep, then the situation as far as he was concerned was even more serious. Surely he grasped that this was no longer just about loyalty to him, but quite simply a matter of her own well-being? Jeanette was free to do as she wished, and if she was in the process of succumbing to remorse then the next step of contacting the police wasn't far off.

And why had he let her believe until the very end that he loved her and was missing her? The words in that final text message were beautiful, and it had clearly been a very effective method of keep her warm, as it were. But instead of proposing a meeting, he could have postponed. A week at a time, or a month. For their safety. He could have laid it out like that and she would have walked straight into the trap. Right until the day it became apparent to her that the relationship was never going to happen. By then so much time would have passed that nothing could be done, everything would drain away into the sand, and life would return to normal. If it hadn't already done so.

Her gaze fell upon an article covering a large spread describing the mysterious disappearance of a forty-one-year-old man. She read it several times and examined the picture with a rising sense of dread. Then she rushed into the bathroom to be on her own with her uncontrollable shaking and her overheating brain.

She popped a few pills that she gulped down as best as she could with water cupped in her trembling hands. Then she sat down on the toilet seat and tried to gather her thoughts while waiting for the physical reaction to dissipate.

Missing? What did that mean? And without the car?

There were suspicions that something serious had happened, and two days before their planned meeting at that. He had already been missing when she had been trudging around in cold and slush outside the car dealership. That explained why he had no-showed, and it also explained why he hadn't been in touch or replied to her message. What was more, it explained the secretive behaviour and suspicious demeanour of the two mechanics when she had turned up asking for Peter. Clearly they knew he was the subject of a search. The police had obviously been there and questioned them, sworn them to silence, and they had tried to deal with the unusual circumstances as best as they could. They hadn't wanted to give away too much, but they must have been curious about who was asking for Peter.

Did that make her a person of interest for the inquiry? It should have done, naturally. But she had probably played her role well—that of an untroubled, innocent customer who didn't know the name of the person she was asking for. Even if that was in no way a reflection of the truth. On the other hand, her lack of knowledge of Peter's unexpected absence had been entirely genuine. In conclusion, there was probably no cause for Peter's colleagues to tell the police about Jeanette's visit.

Which was good, because she definitely didn't want to get mixed up in this. Didn't want there to be any visible points of contact between her and Peter. When he came back, they could start from scratch—no one could be allowed to think this relationship was any older than that.

If he came back. It hit her, and a knot grew in her stomach. According to the police, something serious might have happened—what did that mean? A heart attack somewhere out of the way? An accident, or a homicide? What did she really know about Peter? About his health or even his propensity for getting into dangerous situations? Nothing. She had thought she knew him better before all this terrible stuff had happened. Before the theft of the money.

The money. The six million he had coveted with such avarice after he—actually, the two of them, she corrected herself—had almost literally stepped across a corpse to get to it.

Jeanette felt the trembling increasing, and was overcome by nausea. She didn't want to throw up; she wanted to keep the tablets down so that they could begin to take effect before they got out of her system. Instead, she lay down on the bathroom mat with a towel over her. Couldn't she be allowed to sleep? Just drift off from it all and never wake up again?

But the new thought refused to leave her. She was shaking so much that she was jolting about as she lay on the floor. Her teeth were chattering. And here came the tears too. She cried into the towel so that it wouldn't be audible, but she couldn't stop the tears. Not once had she realised the great betrayal.

Peter had convinced her it was reasonable to leave a man who had been in a serious accident to die. He had *convinced* her to do it—against her own instincts. Because *he* wanted to steal two hold-alls filled with cash. Jeanette hadn't been and still wasn't interested in the money. But she had done what Peter had told her to do, for his sake and for love and for the sake of their mutual future. She was his accomplice and just as guilty, with the difference that she felt much worse about what they had done. The only thing that had kept her going was the dream of Peter—the dream of a life together with him.

And now he was gone. Taking all the money with him. She didn't care about that, but it was just as much hers. Peter hadn't been able to withstand temptation—for him, money clearly meant more than love, and Jeanette had just been an obstacle in his path.

He had disappeared into thin air, wearing the clothes and shoes he had been wearing that day, leaving the car, his passport, his toothbrush and suitcase at home—all of them things that could be obtained elsewhere with money. He had created an unsolvable mystery around his disappearance, broken hearts, and left behind fatherless children.

That was why he had kept her hopes up with his loving promise that they would soon meet. Because he knew that by the time of the meeting, he would already be gone and after that it wouldn't matter what Jeanette did. Her loyalty made no difference to him—she could go to the police and confess if she wanted, but it wouldn't affect him. Only her.

Cynical, ruthless—the betrayal was enormous. How would she manage to go on living after this?

37

Kerstin

NOW SHE WAS truly alone. She had her work as a child minder at a kindergarten in Fårösund, and she got along well with the children and staff alike, but she didn't have any real friends there. And right now she wasn't fit for work—and wouldn't be for a while, since she was struggling to eat and sleep.

She didn't have any neighbours in immediate proximity either, although she maintained a polite but distant and impersonal relationship with those who were closest. A flock of chickens and two cats were the flesh and blood that were closest to her—at least while she was signed off sick following Karl-Erik's death. Otherwise, her current company consisted exclusively of fictitious characters in the books that she read.

Kerstin was truly alone, for real this time. It was hard to take in, but that was how it was. That was how it was going to be—possibly forever. When Karl-Erik had been inside, she hadn't felt as abandoned: even if it had felt distant for many years, there had still been an end to the torment. They had talked on the phone several times a week, and she had visited him monthly. Soon enough he had his weekends on partial release, which hinted that his full release was approaching.

Now there was nothing to anchor herself to, and the absolute loneliness loomed large over her. They had no children, Kerstin's father had overdosed many years before, and her mother hadn't wanted to have anything to do with Kerstin since it had become clear that she mixed in criminal circles. Circles that she had left behind long ago, but that had had no impact on her mother's decision. She had pulled her hand away from her only child once and for all.

Moving back to Stockholm and her old friends was out of the question—that time was behind her. And she couldn't stay out here in the countryside. She couldn't afford it, now that she was going to be the sole provider for her needs. What was more, it was far too desolate, too antisocial. Kerstin was essentially a companionable person, even if that wasn't the initial impression she gave. She thrived among people and would undoubtedly get cabin fever if she had to stay on her own in a little cottage in the country.

That was why she decided to move into Visby, where she could live in a cheap rented flat. She would find it easiest to find a job there, and she would be able to get involved in clubs in order to meet people. What kinds of clubs or people she had no idea, but surely there had to be something she could get into? Some people who could take an interest in her, even if she had stigmatising tattoos that lengthened the odds against her?

Body Found in Woods

A body has been found in a wooded area close to the Digerrojr barrow in Alskogen in the south of Gotland. Emergency services were contacted on Wednesday by a member of the public.

It has still not been possible to determine the identity or age of the deceased, but the remains are thought to be male. It has also been established that the body was in this location for a relatively long period prior to its discovery.

The circumstances around the man's death remain very unclear, and the matter is now in the hands of the police.

"Whether a crime has been committed in connection with this death is not clear at present," said the pretrial investigator. He believes it is also possible that the individual got lost, given that the body was found in a location not usually frequented by people.

Thus far, there are no firm suspicions, but the police have cordoned off the scene and the man's remains have been sent to the National Board of Forensic Medicine.

"It's not yet possible to say whether this is the 41-year-old male who has been missing since 2014," said the pretrial investigator. "An autopsy is due to be carried out on the body and we hope to identify the body at that stage. However, we have notified the man's next of kin that it may be him. We do not know at present when identification will be complete," he added.

GOTLANDS ALLEHANDA

JUNE
2018

38

Sandra

IT HAD BEEN more than a month since Kerstin had last called, and that worried Sandra. Kerstin seemed so burdened by her worries and the loneliness she was experiencing that she might be in the danger zone for ending it all. But Sandra persuaded herself that Kerstin would never take that step without contacting Friends-on-call and Sandra first. It simply couldn't be any other way. She was attached to Kerstin, inspired by their conversations and the detective work they were doing together. What was more, she needed to talk to Kerstin. Their conversations were therapeutic for Sandra too, and there were questions she needed to ask.

Kerstin wasn't the only person keeping their head down. There had been no sign of life from Hallin since that fateful bouquet of flowers had turned up on the porch. Above all, the child support payment she had demanded hadn't shown up in her bank account, which was unacceptable.

He'd had a month or so to gather his thoughts and make a sensible decision. To respond by sending a threatening message via the flowers, in practice basically ignoring the problem, wasn't just thoughtless but was sheer lunacy given that he was risking a rape accusation being pinned on him. Hallin must surely have understood that was the risk he faced if he didn't do the right thing.

And Sandra had no intention of giving up. Now that she knew who he was, it was impossible to let him scurry away. Sandra didn't want to be a weak parent who couldn't stand up for her child anymore. Even if it wouldn't be long before Erik understood that he was the result of a rape, both he and the world around them would understand that made him an even more welcomed child. He was assurance personified and would never have to doubt for a moment how loved he was. She intended to fight out this war for her son and for herself. For financial reasons, of course, but also in order to force Hallin to do the right thing, somehow—to admit what he did and suffer for it. And the threats she had issued were ones she could really implement. If she wanted, she could report the rape, even if she wasn't sure she felt up to taking things that far. But she could indubitably pull herself together and demand a paternity test that would force him to pay her the just level of support. The choice was his to make—would this matter take place in the public eye or not? It was high time she turned the screws a bit more.

She turned on her mobile and checked that the "Hide my number" option was activated. He obviously already knew who she was and where she lived, but since the rape she had got a new, secret number because she wasn't cut out for dealing with terror by phone. This time she wasn't especially nervous—in fact, she could feel the adrenaline pumping through her. Sandra knew that she was better at conversations by phone than face to face, that her uncertainty disappeared when she didn't have to display her less than appealing outer self. She took a couple of deep breaths and then dialled the number of the Hallin family landline.

"Hallin," said a man's voice.

"I'd like to speak to Gunilla," said Sandra.

"I'm sure that can be arranged. Who should I say is calling?"

"You can tell her it's Sandra. You know, the mother of your child."

There was silence on the line. Sandra imagined the frustration growing on the other end as her words sunk in.

"What the fuck are you playing at?" he hissed with rage, his voice low now.

So he kept some secrets from his wife then, despite his denials when they had last spoken.

"Thanks for the flowers by the way," said Sandra. "Aren't you worried I'll report you to the police?"

"Not really, you know. Aren't you worried about what the consequences of this kind of blackmail might be for *you*?"

"It's not blackmail—just a request for what corresponds to the regular, statutory level of child support. And to answer your question, I figure that the consequence of this is quite simply that you'll agree to my demand and deposit the sum I asked for into my bank account. It won't be any worse than that, and I'm struggling to understand why you're so dismissive."

"Oh really? You are? Then let me inform you that it's because I don't appreciate it when some little gold digger barges into my life like this to grab a fuckload of cash."

"In that case, allow *me* to inform *you* that it's significantly less than half of what I spend on the boy," Sandra said combatively. "And it's not exactly like I asked for this pregnancy."

"I definitely didn't either," Hallin growled. "It would have been easiest for all concerned if you had got rid of the child."

"The easiest thing—beyond doubt—would have been if you had done your thinking with the head that you've got up there sitting on your neck. You know, instead of the other one."

"You're out of your fucking mind."

"Seriously?" Sandra laughed contemptuously. "It's *me* who is crazy when it's *you* who runs around raping women?"

There were a few moments of silence before he spoke again, this time in a more controlled tone.

"Look, let me put it to you like this. That thing that you're referring to—it was a bit uncalled for. I admit that. I might have misjudged the situation, and if I did then I'm sorry for that. But child support? I'm not interested in some stupid brat. And you had every opportunity to get rid of it, right? Especially if you can't afford to look after it. But you chose not to. That was your choice, and I respect that. But don't get me mixed up in this—I wasn't asked."

Sandra was taken by surprise by the change in tone. It was easier to respond to arrogance and bitterness, that much she now realised. But just because he had toned down his indignation didn't mean Sandra had to do the same.

"*I* wasn't asked whether I wanted to have sex with you," she countered. "Which I pretty clearly showed I *didn't* want. Wouldn't it just be easiest if you transferred that money and then the matter will be settled and you'll be rid of me for good? And no one will ever need to find out about any of this."

"No one is going to find out anything anyway."

"What do you mean by that? Is that some sort of threat?"

"You won't report that so-called rape. You would have done so long ago if you were going to. And there's no proof of anything like that either."

"A paternity test certainly proves something. And reporting a rape would stir things up a bit I should think."

"He said, she said—and like I said, there's no evidence. You'll never pin anything on me."

"Very possibly, but it'll damage your reputation, and I think that's something you'd like to avoid. Just pay and the problem will go away. Otherwise I'll have to take steps that you won't like."

"*That* sounds like a threat. You have no idea who you're dealing with."

"I have a pretty good idea of that, actually," Sandra said truthfully. "I know much more about you than you think."

"I think it's about time we wrapped up this call," Hallin said with an edge to his voice. "Drop this. Now. That's my genuine advice to you."

"No chance," Sandra said coolly. "Now can I speak to your dear wife?"

"You ugly, fat, fucking slut," Hallin said as a parting shot, and Sandra could hear him frothing at the mouth as he spat out the words.

Then he slammed the phone down. But judging by the description, at least he still remembered her, Sandra noted with a sad smile.

39

Jeanette

IT WAS HOT and sunny, and there were a lot of people out and about today—the tourists had already started to stream onto the island. Midsummer was approaching and it was obvious that the posh schools in the fancier parts of Stockholm had closed their doors for the season.

Jeanette was sitting between Lubbi and Kat, watching people rushing past. Everyone seemed to be in such a hurry—they seemed to have important things they needed to do before the next important thing they needed to do. The Stockholmers brought the urgency and stress of the subway with them all the way to Gotland. It was only as Medieval Week approached that they usually began to calm down somewhat, just as their holiday was almost over.

"The nine-to-fivers, the nine-to-fivers are funny to observe," Lubbi sang, to the tune of *Små Grodorna*.

Kat laughed loudly. Jeanette gave a tepid smile, but at least she recognised the reference, which she was pretty sure Kat didn't. She was too young to remember Stefan Jarl's old documentaries about Swedish society and customs.

Jeanette felt a bit depressed at the thought that she was no longer one of the nine-to-fivers, but one of the misfits, as they were known. When she thought about it, there was a hint of approval in the very words. A certain degree of respect for the people who had chosen an alternative lifestyle, as it could also be termed. Despite it not being something you chose, but a state that you ended up in because you lacked the capacity to make thought-through choices that were good for you in the long-term.

"Those mainlanders are so stressed they'll go to an early grave," Jeanette said.

"There'll be a lot of herring needing pickled just now," Lubbi posited. "A lot of salmon to be cured and bottles and bottles of the hard stuff to be bought. Cheers."

Then he raised his plastic bottle and knocked back a couple of gulps of some moonshine he had found and mixed with coke. Jeanette was about to get her own bottle out of her rucksack when she caught sight of two police officers who had changed tack and were heading straight towards them.

"Look out Lubbi, s'the fuzz," she said in warning, pulling a cigarette out instead and lighting it.

Lubbi rapidly put away his bottle and was also in the process of sparking up when they began speaking to him.

"Are you drinking hooch straight from the bottle, Lubbi?" one of them asked—a fundamentally kind woman, but with a stern expression.

Lubbi leaned back nonchalantly with his cigarette between his lips.

"What's a man supposed to do?" he said, holding out his hands. "Riedel glassware has got so damn expensive. Haven't you got anything better to do than lurk around here harassing sunbathers?"

"Apparently not," said the policewoman. "You be careful you don't burn yourself, Lubbi. You're already starting to look a bit rosy."

"Thanks for thinking of me," said Lubbi, crossing his arms over his chest. "But shouldn't you focus a bit more on that murder and a bit less on the factor of my sun cream?"

Her male colleague smiled, but the grim policewoman wasn't to be deterred.

"Try to be discreet, guys. You don't need to advertise what you're up to. And you don't actually *own* these benches—there may be other people who want to use them too."

"I'd like to see them try!" said Lubbi with feigned indignation.

"Exactly my point. They won't. Maybe you could try out some different benches some time? Or settle down on a blanket in the woods somewhere?"

"We'll give it some consideration," said Lubbi, exhaling smoke through tight lips.

The two officers left them and Jeanette resumed her hunt for the bottle in her rucksack. She took a good long slug from it and then put the bottle away again—it seemed unnecessary to tempt fate.

"They're not half annoying, those cops," Kat said.

"Meh, they're just doing their job," said Lubbi.

"What does it matter if we're sitting here?"

As usual, Kat struggled to see the obvious.

"Just like they said, we sit here all day so no one else gets a chance to use these benches. They could have driven us away loads of times, but they don't. They see that we're drinking, but let us stay even though the consumption of alcohol is illegal in public space. They could have arrested the lot of us, put us in the van and driven us away, but they don't because they're all right."

"I think they've got a nerve ticketing cars and harassing sunbathers instead of catching murderers."

"Kat," Lubbi sighed, which resulted in a cloud of smoke. "Firstly, it was a joke—the thing I said about harassing sunbathers. They're not doing that. They're kindly pointing out that we're not meant to be sitting here getting pissed with everyone else around. Secondly, the police don't issue parking tickets—that's the parking wardens employed by Region Gotland. Meter maids—have you heard the term? They're not police. Thirdly, there are different kinds of police. Those ones were beat cops—they're not the ones who investigate murders. That's up to CID."

Kat rolled her eyes and made a movement with her head that seemed to express her pain at being surrounded by idiots. Then she cracked open a beer can with a hissing sound.

"What murder are you talking about?" Jeanette asked.

"Haven't you heard?" Kat said excitedly.

"It's in no way certain that it's a murder," Lubbi said, stubbing out his cigarette with the sole of his shoe. "But they're 'not ruling out the possibility a crime has been committed,' as they so beautifully put it. Likely as not, someone got lost in the woods or had a stroke or something."

"Which woods?" Jeanette asked.

"Somewhere down south. Garde."

"But it was ages ago," said Kat.

"Ages ago?" Jeanette repeated, who did not feel at all relieved by that information.

She sought out more answers in Lubbi's eyes, and something must have been going on in her own, because suddenly his face changed.

"Let's drop it," he said apologetically.

"No, why?" said Kat, whose ability to read the mood left something to be desired. "I think it's pretty fucking exciting. What if it's him!"

"Him?" said Jeanette, swallowing. "Do they know who it is?"

"Kat, let's change the subject," Lubbi said, looking unhappily at Jeanette.

"They suspect it's a guy who went missing ages ago," Kat continued, a glint in her eye. "And that he was murdered."

Now Lubbi took Jeanette's hand and squeezed it hard.

"No, Kat," he said sternly. "*The journalist* speculated that might be the case. The police haven't said anything like that—they're waiting for the man's autopsy so they can identify him."

This was a final, desperate attempt to silence her, but the damage had already been done. Jeanette wanted to hear what Kat had to say, even though Kat just had a craving for sensation, and even though the conversation was making Jeanette's stomach do somersaults.

"Of course it's him," said Kat. "Has anyone else on the island gone missing?"

"Who?" said Jeanette in a faint voice.

Lubbi screwed his eyes shut and looked like he wanted the earth to swallow him up. But he didn't let go of her hand, so she was still able to cling on to it tightly.

"The forty-one-year-old," Kat said triumphantly. "Don't you remember? He was in all the papers."

"Do you know what, Kat?" said Lubbi. "Jen knew him, so she probably won't be thrilled to hear this coming from you like that."

"Well, sorry," said Kat with a shrug of her shoulders. "But it's in the paper, you know. So it's not like I came up with it all by myself or anything."

Then she got up and slouched away with a slight look of being wronged. Her seat was taken by Nanna, who had appeared from nowhere behind the bench. Lubbi pulled Jeanette close and tucked a wisp of hair behind her ear. Without really being able to explain it, tears welled up in her eyes.

"Sorry, Jen," he said. "I *should* have told you, one way or another. I didn't put two and two together with it and that story of yours. Until it was, you know, too late. Sorry."

Jeanette said nothing, absorbed in her own confused thoughts with her head against Lubbi's shoulder. She was unable to make head or tail of any of it. She had no idea how she was supposed to react to this news. How it affected her—did it even affect her at all?

"Did you hear that, Nanna?" Lubbi asked shamefacedly.

"Yes, I heard," Nanna confirmed, and gently stroked Jeanette's cheek.

"What an idiot I am," Lubbi said with a sigh.

"There's no need to drown our sorrows in advance," Nanna suggested. "Let's agree to postpone our grief until we know there's something to grieve about."

That sounded more or less doable, and the respite gave Jeanette a few days to prepare herself for the worst. Even if she did so with sinking hopes and a growing sense of panic.

40

Sandra

IT WAS THE morning of Midsummer's Eve, and ahead of the day's festivities they had spent the night at her parents'. Erik and his grandparents were already well under way with preparations ahead of the invasion of guests, while Sandra was still sitting outside enjoying her breakfast and the chance to read the newspaper from cover to cover without any interruptions.

Of course she had heard about the case, but it was only now that her interest was properly piqued about this man in early middle age who had been missing without a trace for more than four years. He had been found by a member of the public in southern Gotland, in a wooded area with few people around, which wasn't remarkable in itself, given that he had been buried, and buried corpses weren't usually left in places where just any old person would find them. That was the whole point of burying a body—to make sure it wasn't found for the foreseeable future.

The fact that a crime had been committed was clear beyond all reasonable doubt—corpses hardly buried themselves. The cause of death was blunt trauma to the head, and the murder weapon was in the grave beside the body: the spade that it had to be assumed had been used to dig the grave.

To Sandra's ears, it sounded like an execution—had the victim dug his own grave? Peter Norling was his name and prior to his disappearance he had never "been of interest to the police," as they put it. That didn't surprise Sandra. He looked nice in the photo—if you could judge a dog by its breed, which you usually could in the case of mafia-style executions, whether you were evaluating the victim or the executioner.

Norling owned a company that repaired cars. His own car—a company car—had been abandoned outside his place of work, where he had last been seen. It was featured in one of the photos in the article, and looked a bit tragic—almost rejected out there in the car park in the slush and grey, surrounded by police tape and with a big gap between it and all the other cars. The company logo was blurry in the photo—almost unreadable. But to her surprise, Sandra could picture the design of the logo and the name of the company. Why? she asked herself. She had never had any dealings with the company, and didn't even know where their garage was. And it didn't say where anywhere in the article either.

It was a terrible story. After spending the morning at the garage, he had popped out at lunchtime, never to be seen again. He left behind his wife and children, house and debts, but no life insurance policy had paid out since there was nothing to suggest he was dead. Or alive, for that matter—but the insurance companies were more inclined towards the former. The disappearance had been in early February 2014, so the family had lived with the uncertainty of what had happened to their father and husband for more than four years.

Four years and four months to be exact. Almost exactly the same amount of time she had lived in ignorance about who the father of her son actually was. But that was a deeply unfair comparison. Sandra's life had got better—she had got happier. The Norling family's lives had been smashed to pieces. Back then, when it had happened, and now again. It was inhuman. The rape was something she had got over. All that lingered was the contempt for the perpetrator.

As happened often, her thoughts ended up back in that Audi. His voice droning on about this and that, the scent of an expensive car, leather mixed with the smell of booze from lunchtime, black ice forming on the road and the speed of the car that seemed to increase in step with her knuckles turning white. His borderline sadistic approach to driving, which she knew was a direct response to her fear. How instead of slowing down he sped up when they reached the bend before the ravine. If they had met an oncoming car there, it could have been Sandra who had been trapped in a wrecked car covered in snow for four days. But they hadn't—in fact, they were fortunate enough not to meet a single car during the final miles of their crazed journey.

Actually, wait a minute . . . Just before the bend after the ravine—hadn't there been a car parked up in the woods? Yes, she remembered now: there had been a car in among the trees. And hadn't a question flickered through her head at the time—what on earth was it doing there? In the middle of winter, in that awful weather—no cars ever drove up there and the road led nowhere. But she hadn't had time to bring the thought to a conclusion, given that she had been fully occupied with fearing for her life, concerned about what they would encounter around the next bend. And now she could see it clearly—it must have been the grainy photo in the newspaper that had crystallised her thoughts. It was that car. The yellow company car featured in the newspaper, with its illegible logo—but at the ravine the logo had been fully visible. PN Auto. Her memory had stashed it away somewhere at the back of her mind, enabling her to retrieve it at some point in the future when she needed it.

Now.

Was that what had happened when Kerstin's husband had come round the corner before the ravine? Had Peter Norling decided to pull out onto the road in his company car at that very moment? Had he been careless, thoughtless, maybe lost control of his vehicle and forced the oncoming car off the road and down the precipice? Had he then reversed back onto the forest track to avoid being as visible, photographed the blue Audi that had passed by shortly after and stopped and then left the scene, before then climbing down to the wreck and photographing it and leaving without raising the alarm? Whereupon he had sent the photos to Kerstin to direct suspicion in a different direction.

That must have been what had happened. Hallin was innocent, at least when it came to the hit-and-run. That was why he was able to ignore the blackmail attempt without any scruples. Peter Norling had caused the catastrophe.

Two weeks later he had been dead—murdered. The question was why, but it seemed likely it was connected to the accident. Which in turn suggested that Kerstin was responsible for the murder. But it seemed highly unlikely, given that nothing in their nightly calls had hinted that Kerstin had known enough at the time of Norling's disappearance to undertake such drastic measures. She couldn't reasonably have known about Peter Norling's role in the whole thing. And Kerstin simply didn't seem to be a brutal person—quite the opposite, in fact.

MIDSUMMER LUNCH WAS served in her parents' garden with friends and family invited. After plates had been cleared of herring and new potatoes, and beers and schnapps drained, they cycled in a pack to Fridhem where the traditional celebrations were being held. There was dancing around the maypole, childish games, and fishing for the little ones.

The rather large party had spread out their blankets on the edge of the site, right beside a copse of trees. Late in the afternoon, just before they were due to cycle home again and prepare the evening barbecue, Erik wandered off into the woods with a couple of the older children. Sebastian and Fredrika were both nine years old, and they promised to keep an eye on Erik.

They returned twenty minutes later, each one of them carrying a bouquet of flowers assembled with childlike artlessness. Large, sprouting weeds drowning out the flowers that ought to have been the gems in each bouquet. Nevertheless, there were seven different kinds of flowers to place under their pillows on Midsummer's night, just as the tradition dictated. The purpose of this was to ensure that one's dreams provided a premonition of one's future life partner—something that seemed pretty far-fetched for the three-year-old and nine-year-olds alike. A distant prospect, at any rate. But the kids were exhilarated, and that was the main thing.

Like the other adults, Sandra showed only a passing interest in the children's bouquets. She barely looked at them, wrapped up as she was in a conversation with one of her cousins and his wife. It was only a few minutes later when they began to prepare to leave and packed up their picnic baskets that she actually *saw* Erik's bouquet. Among the thistles, chicory, and dandelions with long roots, there were also a white lily and a black calla lily hiding.

She quickly got up and scanned the thinning crowd, looking towards the woods. Nowhere was there anyone who might be Hallin, and in among the trees there wasn't a soul to be seen. She swept her gaze across the meadow and its surroundings once more, but if he was there he was staying well concealed. He had presumably slunk away as soon as he had completed his task.

But what sort of nonsense was this—a grown man behaving like some kind of bloody psychopath in a horror movie? It must have been by chance—a lucky coincidence—that Erik had ended up being drawn to one side, and while picking flowers at that. But if it hadn't happened today then it would probably have happened some other day, by some other means.

Sandra wasn't afraid; she was angry. But she kept her calm, firmly determined to keep her parents and everyone else out of this. Seemingly unaffected, she crouched in front of Erik and spoke to him in a kind voice.

"Aren't these lovely flowers that you've picked, sweetheart? Where did you find them?"

"In the woods over there," Erik said, pointing.

"Including these ones?" Sandra asked, prodding the clearly shop-bought flowers in the bouquet.

"Yep!"

Erik's face lit up like the sun.

"Were they really growing in the ground like the other flowers?" Sandra coaxed him.

"Yes, they were. But not as hard!"

"No, because you can see that someone had cut the stalk here, and you've not got a knife, have you?"

"No, I haven't."

Erik looked troubled and seemed to feel that he wasn't being believed.

"You weren't given them by anyone then?"

"No, I picked them all by myself."

"You did a really good job, Erik. They're beautiful. Did you meet anyone in the woods, or was it just you and Fredrika and Sebastian there?"

"There were other people, but we didn't talk to anyone."

"No one that you particularly remember?"

"No, we didn't talk to anyone."

"Okay," said Sandra, ruffling his hair. "You're going to have sweet dreams tonight!"

Erik laughed and scooted away to the other kids.

Sandra remained standing there, watching him, lost in her own thoughts. She could understand that Hallin wasn't all that keen on coughing up half a million in child support for a kid he didn't want to acknowledge. She knew that. It was enough that he had stated it. And it didn't even need saying; she understood it anyway. But this—what was this supposed to mean? A veiled threat in the form of funeral flowers—it was just downright stupid. And this was the second time—the first lot hadn't had any impact.

But there was one significant difference: Erik had been personally involved. Was the subtext that a three-year-old boy was going to die and be buried? Because Hallin, despite having the means, had *no desire* to pay child support? It was horrible.

However, the step from sending flowers to killing was a big one, and Sandra had no intention of being scared off from pursuing the matter further. Her convictions were only strengthened: Jan Hallin was tearing towards his own demise in leaps and bounds. And Sandra had every intention of helping him along.

Time was tight; she needed some time alone at the computer. She couldn't get her parents or anyone else involved—people who would be guaranteed to object and probably bring the whole enterprise tumbling down. And she needed to get back in touch with Kerstin. Really soon.

41

Jeanette

TO BEGIN WITH, she had followed Nanna's recommendation to the best of her abilities, and had prepared as much as she could. She had turned herself inside out in an attempt to decide how she saw Peter after everything that had happened, and how that would change if it turned out that it was his body that had been found in the Alskogen woods. But it was draining rooting through a past that she preferred to forget, and placing it into some sort of future perspective that didn't exactly look promising.

Just as usual, one thing led to another. Despite her friends' support, she felt incredibly lonely in this endeavour, and the only cure she knew for the all-too-familiar anxiety was alcohol. In copious amounts. Which left her numb in a way that partly suppressed the issue, but the result was that she wasn't especially well prepared when the news came.

That happened on Midsummer's Eve itself. Jeanette was still in bed when she found out from a news site on her mobile. The body that had been found close to Digerrojr was that of the forty-one-year-old who had been missing since 4 February 2014: Peter Norling. He left behind a wife and two children.

Instead of breaking down immediately, which was what she had hazily expected she would do, she managed in some strange way to push all emotions to one side. This left space for a relatively clear-headed analysis.

Was *Jeanette* grieving?

If this news had arrived at the beginning of February 2014, she would without hesitation have considered herself to be grieving. At the time, she hadn't yet realised the extent of the presumed betrayal, and if she had, then she would in all probability have reconsidered. She would have realised she had got the wrong end of the stick, and that the feelings he had said he had for her had probably been genuine. Peter's death would have finished her off in her state of mind at the time, but then so had what she had mistaken for betrayal—so it made little difference.

But now? Was she in shock? Was she experiencing grief now that news had reached her of her lover's death?

It had been a long time since he had been her lover. On the other hand, it had been just as long since he'd been a father or husband, but *they* were grieving—of course they were, aside from what it said in the newspaper. Consequently, Jeanette was grieving too. When Peter had died, Jeanette had been his lover. He had loved her, she had loved him unhesitatingly. The natural thing to do now—in light of what had happened—would be to transport herself back to the situation she had been in then. To forget all the erroneous blame she had cast over his memory, to erase those four years of hatred and bitterness and forgive him. To quite simply resume her original position.

But it probably couldn't be done. Grief is grief—perhaps she had finished grieving for him.

Murdered, she thought to herself. Peter hadn't just died—someone had taken his life. Smashed his head with something solid and heavy, before chucking him in a grave so deep that he hadn't turned up until more than four years later, when the foxes had caught wind of his remains.

It was dreadful. Someone had done that to the man she loved. But why? How had he managed to fall out with someone to such an extent that it resulted in his death? Peter? It was incomprehensible.

Might it be to do with all that money? Had he run off at the mouth? Bragged? No. He had pinned his future—their future—on the six million. He wouldn't risk it all—not to mention his freedom—by being indiscreet . . .

Over these four years, Jeanette hadn't thought about the fact that Peter might not be alive. She *knew* he had left her and legged it with the cash. She had thought so many evil things about him, she had ascribed so many unpleasant qualities to him. Oh, how she had hated him, wishing all the pain in the world on him.

That tormented her now. The worst possible thing had happened to him, and instead of being grateful for all the joy and pleasure he had brought her, and remembering him with the respect and sorrow that he deserved as the upstanding person he had been, she had felt sorry for herself and thrown her life away.

It was when that insight hit her that the grief washed over her. The pure, unadulterated emotion, that reminded her of joy, despite the tears streaming down her cheeks. And it had been a long time since Jeanette had been happy. She was thinking that to herself as she got out of bed and went to the bathroom cabinet.

42

Sandra

THE REST OF Midsummer's Eve passed without incident, and Sandra and Erik spent the night at her parents' once again. Erik was going to spend the whole weekend there while Sandra was working. That was the excuse she had used. She blamed the fact that lots of her colleagues were on holiday over the Midsummer weekend, which was partially true but not the whole truth. Granted, she had accepted a temporary management position until the end of July at the expense of some holiday, but that didn't mean she had to work night and day for another five weeks. Sandra had other things to fill her time with, but her parents didn't need to know about that.

Hallin wasn't going to get away with his clumsy attempts to scare her into silence. Eventually, he would be forced to pay the child support that enraged him so much—there was no doubt about that—but first she wanted to give him a chance to admit his crime by doing the right thing without getting the authorities involved. In other words, she wanted to frighten Hallin into obedience at the same time that he was trying to scare her into silence. It was certainly an interesting form of limbo they had ended up in. And the provocative spate of veiled threats merely spurred her on.

Now she had the phone in her hand and was going to exchange a few words with Mrs. Hallin for the first time. Sandra was utterly convinced that a move like that would be frightening enough—she wouldn't need to go any further than that in her first step. If Hallin picked up then she would fake a wrong number. It turned out not to be necessary.

"Gunilla Hallin," said the voice on the other end of the line.

"Hi, my name is Sandra. I'm currently in discussions with your husband about child support payments for a little boy who is living in very modest circumstances."

"That's interesting," Gunilla Hallin said. "And pretty typical of Jan, as well!"

Really, Sandra thought to herself. For Jan Hallin, charity work was as typical as the craze for gender equality was for Captain Dress—the county chief of police who had been on the barricades when he was on the clock and had raped little girls when he was off.

"Yes, I've understood that he's very committed to charity work of various kinds," said Sandra. "Especially when it comes to children in need."

"That's right. Do you want me to give him a shout?"

"Yes please," said Sandra, thinking to herself that it was pretty obvious.

She caught herself letting her contempt for Jan Hallin stain his wife, and there was no justice in that. The woman sounded pleasant, and actually a little bit proud of her husband, a great quality to have in a life partner. And she was after all a victim herself, even if she didn't know it. Who wanted to be married to a rapist? Or even a womaniser? Because it was surely not the only time he had been unfaithful, even if one hoped and presumed that he didn't usually compel others into sex through the use of violence.

Now she heard soft voices in the background and a door closing. Before long, she heard Hallin's hissing voice.

"It's high time you put a stop to this. I'm not going to have this conversation."

"I just wanted to give you one final chance to come to your senses," said Sandra coolly. "You don't scare me."

"*You're* scaring the living daylights out of *me*, I have to say."

"You know how a lioness is with her cub."

"I'd appreciate it if you avoided bringing my wife into this."

Hallin spoke in a low voice, almost a whisper, but he sounded quite tired. More resigned than angry.

"All you have to do is pay what you owe," Sandra said matter-of-factly.

"You don't just blow six hundred whatever-the-fuck-you-said thousand out of your nose."

"Just as I said, I'm fine to take it in instalments."

"You're a stubborn cow."

"You've already got the account number, and you can double the amount for the first transfer since you missed May, unless I'm mistaken."

Hallin sighed audibly.

"Okay, I'll pay," he said eventually.

"I'll take that as a confession," said Sandra, the sweet taste of triumph spreading through her body.

"Never contact me again," said Hallin.

"Not if you manage your financial obligations properly."

But Hallin had already hung up. Sandra glanced at the time and noted that the conversation had taken just a minute or so.

A little too quick, perhaps? What if he just wanted to protract the entire thing?

But Sandra shook that feeling off—she was satisfied with her efforts thus far and wanted to believe that she had exhausted him. That she had got her confession, even if it didn't exactly contain an apology. It seemed as if she were going to get her rightful support after all—that was admission enough.

She decided she would give him a week. If the money wasn't in her account by then she would take further steps, but she hoped she wouldn't have to. She had other, more important things to do.

43

Jeanette

WHEN SHE OPENED her eyes, she was in hospital. It was a sober observation, and Jeanette didn't want to be sober. She didn't want to be awake either, or in hospital. She had planned to be somewhere else by now, so she shut her eyes and took her leave again.

The next time she woke up, her gaze fell on Lubbi and Nanna who were each sitting in a chair by the bed, talking in low voices. As soon as he spotted that she was conscious, Lubbi leaned forward and took her hand.

"We're here, sweetheart," he said softly. "No need to be afraid."

Jeanette sighed and switched her gaze to an undefined spot up on the ceiling. She had nothing to say. Why couldn't everything just stop? That would have been an adequate end to the whole thing.

"Do you believe in God and heaven and all that?" Lubbi asked.

Jeanette shook her head without looking at him.

"Then I suggest you stay down here with us. We're here for you—you know that. And we're not going to let go of you that easily."

"How . . . ?" Jeanette whispered.

But she couldn't bring herself to finish her sentence—she wasn't really that interested in the answer.

"How did we know?" said Lubbi. "We probably saw the same thing you did, I guess. It was Nanna who . . . We tried to call, but you weren't picking up. So we went round to yours. Knocked on the street door, shouted and made a fuss until the neighbours came out and asked what was going on. But you still weren't answering. It felt bad."

"I'm a deep sleeper," Jeanette said quietly.

She thought to herself that it was a real spectacle she had caused, given that she had tried to be anonymous in that block of flats where suspicious looks followed her whenever she came and went. Couldn't a person be left in peace?

"The bottle was empty, Jeanette. Don't lie—not to us. I thought you'd quit that shit?"

"I just needed . . . to calm down a bit."

Lubbi shook his head, let go of her hand, and leaned back in his chair. He looked horrified, and Nanna was next to him watching her with an inscrutable expression. Jeanette didn't even have it in her to cry. She felt like everyone was staring at her, and all she wanted was to disappear from here.

"How exactly did you get inside?" she asked, trying to summon something else in those watchful eyes except pity.

"We broke in," said Lubbi. "After some persuading, we got one of your neighbours to give us a crowbar, so we forced the door. We were almost done when the police showed up, so they actually let us finish the job. Can you picture that . . . the police standing there cheering me on as I break into a flat? Fuck me, there's a first time for everything."

Jeanette's lips twitched into a smile. It seemed to infect her two observers, who both perked up a little. Lubbi bent over her and brushed his lips against her forehead before sitting back down on his chair.

"Come on, girl," he said, gently punching her bicep. "Don't do this to us again. You're hurting us, don't you understand that?"

No, perhaps she didn't. As usual, she was mostly thinking about herself. She hadn't realised that her actions affected others. Or that there were people to whom she actually meant something. Despite the fact that they didn't really mean much to her. Other than providing her with daily distraction.

The people who were important to Jeanette were all gone.

44

Sandra

WHEN THE MIDSUMMER weekend reached its end, Sandra picked up Erik from her parents' place ahead of the last normal week before the summer holidays. Sandra wouldn't have any holidays for a while, but Erik's summer would initially be spent with his grandparents. They would be on holiday as of the next weekend, and when they went back to work four weeks later, it would be Sandra's turn to take time off. There was a lot of piecing things together to make sure life worked for Sandra and her little boy, and even though she felt a little ashamed, she was grateful to her parents. Glad that their spending time with their grandchild was just as much for their own enjoyment as it was about making things easier for her by taking over some of her responsibilities.

Despite her current heavy commitments elsewhere, Sandra hadn't taken any time off from Friends-on-call. Ellen was still calling almost every weekday, and she was the highlight now that Kerstin had pulled back. Otherwise it was just the usual calls about fears and loneliness, anxiety about the future and worries about the past. Rewarding and interesting for both parties, she hoped. For her own part, Sandra felt satisfied that she was able to offer some small assistance to people who needed someone to talk to.

The evenings passed by quickly these days. The time when she had lain on the sofa idly watching TV between the infrequent calls was gone. Now she filled her time in other ways, and jumped every time the phone vibrated next to her on the kitchen table. It was the same now, and when she glanced at the clock on the wall she realised it was just gone midnight, which meant she ought to have gone to bed if she was to deal with the challenges of the next day. In other words, it was downright lucky that the call got through.

"Kerstin! I'm so glad you've called! I've been really worried."

"Worried?" said Kerstin. "Why?"

"Oh, you know. You've got your troubles, and I don't know how well you deal with them on a day-to-day basis."

"You mean whether I'm predisposed to suicide?" said Kerstin, getting straight to the point. "I'm not, so no need to worry on that account. On the other hand . . ."

She interrupted herself, which made Sandra curious.

"On the other hand what?"

"Oh, I'm getting there. Something has happened that I'd like to discuss with you."

"Nothing serious, I hope?"

"In a way," said Kerstin. "But not in the way that you think."

Sandra didn't know what she was supposed to think, so she was presumably going to be surprised by whatever followed. She often was during her conversations with Kerstin.

"Okay," she said. "I'm listening."

"I've met someone I hate," Kerstin said gloomily. "That's why I haven't called in a while. I had to think about how to deal with it."

The target of Kerstin's hatred was something that Sandra was more than familiar with. The only thing was that since their last call, Sandra had discovered that the hit-and-run-driver-slash-photographer was no longer alive. Kerstin *couldn't* have met him.

"Met?" Sandra said, uncomprehending.

"Or . . . Not met. That's the wrong word," Kerstin corrected herself.

Good. Hatred was a big thing, not to be used recklessly.

"I've known her for several years. Socialised with her."

"Her?" said Sandra in confusion, thinking that Kerstin must be on the wrong track.

"It's a pretty long story," Kerstin said apologetically with a sigh. "I think I have to start from the beginning. If you've got time?"

"We've got all night," said Sandra, who suddenly felt no need at all to regain her strength ahead of work the next day.

And then Kerstin told her the tale.

Of her past life of crime and her lover the bank robber who had been caught. About the departure from the destructive setting in Stockholm and the move to the countryside in Gotland, about the release and the laundered cash. Kerstin skipped the details about the crash, but described the days she spent waiting for her husband who never turned up and the time after she found out about the death: the grief, the loneliness, and how she was received when she moved to Visby. She explained how hard it had been to find a job, to find meaning in life, how she had come down in the world and eventually ended up with the social outcasts by the East Gate. Just to get out, to satisfy her need for people around her. How her name and personality had resulted in her nickname: Barbamama. She had chosen not to see it as a taunt, but thought it was meant with affection. Before long, it had been shortened to Nanna—as everyone in her surroundings now called her. A shoulder to cry on and an ear to listen.

Kerstin painted the picture of the whole thing with tenderness and unobtrusive suffering. Sandra couldn't hold back her tears. But it wasn't over yet, because what Sandra had heard thus far was merely the framework for a story that was far more important to Kerstin. That much Sandra grasped, but she also knew that Kerstin didn't yet know how important the story about the fatal accident was to Sandra too.

"I'm sorry," said Sandra, when Kerstin paused to light a cigarette. "I'm very sorry for everything you've had to go through. But I'm glad you've got friends."

"Jeanette," Kerstin said, resuming the conversation. "One of the girls on the bench. She tried to commit suicide on Midsummer's Eve. They found a body down in Garde a while ago, but it was only on Friday that the papers reported who it was."

"Peter Norling?" said Sandra, who realised they were approaching something important—something she might have missed.

"Yes," Kerstin confirmed. "I knew that Jeanette wouldn't take it very well. You see, Peter Norling was her lover."

"At the time of the disappearance?"

"At the time of the disappearance."

Sandra still wasn't entirely clear what significance this held, but she had a strong feeling that it was important.

"His car was at the scene of the accident," she felt compelled to say.

Now it was Kerstin's turn to be surprised.

"How can you know that?" she asked.

"I passed the ravine just before it happened," said Sandra. "I've realised that with your help. And when I read about the body being found, when I saw the picture of Norling's car, I remembered that I happened to see that very car in the trees that afternoon. It might have been him who caused the accident. And took the photos."

"No," said Kerstin. "It was Jan Hallin who forced Karl-Erik off the road. And then did a runner."

Sandra stopped breathing. Had it been the rapist who had thundered round the bend on the wrong side of the road while pissed after all? And met another car without giving an inch? Just like they had first believed, just like she had truly, truly *wanted* to believe. Before those photographs had messed it up for them, and got them to see a conspiracy instead of the obvious.

"It was Jeanette who took the photos and sent them to me," Kerstin said. "Both she and Peter Norling were in that car. They didn't cause the accident, but they left without telling anyone too. Without lifting a finger to save Karl-Erik's life."

"The shadow," Sandra thought aloud. "It's the shadow of Peter Norling that you can see in that photo. Not Hallin or anyone else."

"Exactly," said Kerstin.

"But why?" Sandra asked in agitation. "What drives a person—*two* people—to do something like that?"

"Greed," Kerstin said with emphasis.

And then she repeated the part of the story about forbidden love and avarice, remorse, anxiety and longing, betrayal, hatred, and a death wish.

Jeanette's story, in short. And she presented it without any subjectivity whatsoever. Honestly, plainly, and with the same feeling that she had told her own story.

"Does Jeanette know who you are?" Sandra asked carefully.

"No, she doesn't know my real name—to her I'm just Nanna. And I haven't revealed my identity. Not sure I'm going to, either. It depends."

"On how you should approach this? And Jeanette?"

"Among other things," Kerstin said thoughtfully. "I'm still thinking about it."

"I'm not going to give you any advice," said Sandra. "You'll find the answer inside yourself somewhere."

Kerstin said nothing in response to that, instead pointing out something that had already been occupying Sandra's thoughts for some time.

"Jeanette was tormented by a guilty conscience and sent the photos to me. I sent them to Hallin with an implied threat that I would go to the police with what I knew. If he didn't give me the money that I erroneously assumed he had stolen. Hallin didn't have the money, but he was terrified that the police would catch wind of this—so what was he meant to do?"

"We thought he buried his head in the sand and hoped it would go away," Sandra said contemplatively.

"Which it did," Kerstin added. "Given that I didn't dare remind him of the threat or put it into practice. But perhaps he interpreted it in another way."

Sandra felt something take a deepening grip of her throat.

"If the root of the problem could be removed from the world . . ." she said, developing Kerstin's reasoning. "Peter Norling."

"My thoughts exactly," said Kerstin. "It seems like too much of a coincidence that Peter Norling was murdered so soon after the hit-and-run that he witnessed. The only question is how Hallin was able to find out that Norling was there when the accident happened."

"For the same reason that I did," Sandra said slowly. "He passed the scene not long before the accident and noticed the car."

Kerstin said nothing for a while, probably hoping that Sandra would finish what she had begun.

"Can you expand on that?" she eventually said.

Sandra thought the time might be right. That she and Kerstin had so much in common in this matter that they might as well tackle it together. For better or worse.

"I was in Hallin's car when he passed the ravine the first time," Sandra admitted resignedly. "I didn't know him, had never met him before. But he offered me a lift home and I accepted. He was driving like a car thief, and seemed to be under the influence. And when he dropped me off, he drank more booze. And . . ."

"And . . . ?" Kerstin said encouragingly.

"He raped me. Left me on the floor like a wet rag and left."

"I'm . . . I'm truly sorry," Kerstin said.

"It was only when you and I began talking that it dawned on me . . . what else he might have done that afternoon. Before you said that, I didn't know who he was."

"That was why you were so convinced he was the one who was responsible," Kerstin said with a note of understanding. "You knew he was drunk and what he was capable of."

"I knew that he left my house a few hundred metres from the scene of the accident at half past three with no passengers. So there's the answer to your question. Finally."

"I'm so sorry," Kerstin repeated.

"You're the only person other than Hallin who knows this, so I'd be grateful if this could remain between us."

"Of course, don't worry about it."

"There's a lot more to tell about this," Sandra concluded. "But let's do that another time. If you want. We're not supposed to talk about me, after all."

"Of course I'm interested," Kerstin said enthusiastically. "We're in this together now. He'd just raped a woman, was driving drunk, and caused the death of a person. It's not all that surprising that a guy like that didn't call an ambulance. Because that would have meant the police turning up too. He dodged a lot of years in prison that afternoon."

"If he's responsible for the murder of Peter Norling, then there will be a fair few more on top of that," Sandra said, by way of reminder. She was struggling to let go of the thought.

"Somehow, we need to make sure that bastard gets put away," Kerstin said with emphasis.

"We're going to do it," Sandra said. "But for now, I wonder whether you could help me out with something?"

"Help you?" Kerstin said in surprise.

"Consider it a job offer. I've got a couple of questions I need answers to as well."

45

Kerstin

THE CONVERSATION WITH Sandra had brought Kerstin new hope in her otherwise rather grim situation, but her daily existence remained the same. Jeanette was back on the bench outside the city wall by the East Gate, and people from all over were attentively checking in on her. People were sensitive enough not to mention what had happened, but it still permeated the atmosphere. The tenderness she was being shown was pretty conspicuous, and warmed Kerstin's stony heart as she sat there watching it all.

It wasn't the only feeling she was experiencing. Of course she was happy on the one hand about the unalloyed empathy in her friends' behaviour, but on the other hand she was slightly affronted by Jeanette's way of taking it for granted, and her inability to show gratitude.

But Jeanette was depressed, she reminded herself. Just a few days ago, she had made a serious attempt to take her own life, and it was down to pure chance that she hadn't succeeded. Kerstin's intuition, to be specific. No one else knew as much about Jeanette as Kerstin did, and it hadn't occurred to any of the others that things were so bad.

It was nothing but base instinct that had made her wake Lubbi from his beauty sleep and drag him to the neighbourhood where Jeanette lived in her small rented flat. Kerstin had had misgivings ever since she had first heard about the body that had been found, and she had set her alarm clock early in the morning to ensure that—if possible—she heard the news before Jeanette did. That way, she could deliver it personally and catch Jeanette if she fell.

Why she had done this for Jeanette's sake Kerstin didn't really know. Jeanette had been—if one believed her account—a reluctant participant in the theft and everything that it involved, which was a form of mitigation. But she had allowed herself to be persuaded into leaving Karl-Erik to die, and she could have chosen differently. It didn't seem to have been all that hard to persuade her either—blinded by love as she had been. Kerstin's own interpretation was that Jeanette had lost her senses because of her need to be loved. And by an unscrupulous individual who only thought about himself, at that.

So Kerstin was of two minds. Jeanette was a human being made of flesh and blood who served as proof of humankind's weaknesses. And who wasn't weak? But there were still some limits. Jeanette probably had some fundamental values that were sensible, but unfortunately they were ones with very shallow roots. They had been torn out of the ground in a flash, along with Kerstin's entire existence.

Just like Jeanette's. Yet another mitigating circumstance. The question, however, was whether Karl-Erik's death or the loss of her lover had caused Jeanette the most harm. The answer was pretty obvious. Which meant that loathing for Jeanette and her thoughtless self-absorption once again washed over Kerstin.

That was the course of her thoughts, ebbing and flowing between extremes. One moment she felt sympathy for Jeanette, the next out-right hatred.

Nevertheless, Jeanette was surrounded by friends for the time being, so Kerstin didn't have to engage. Instead, she studied her from a distance, while thoughts gnawed away inside her head.

After the conversation with Sandra, the picture had become even clearer. Jeanette was really only a minor character in the whole thing, but still an important one who could have changed the outcome of everything. Jeanette had been there when the opportunity had been presented not only to save Karl-Erik's life, but also to put Jan Hallin behind bars for rape, drunk driving, manslaughter, and committing a hit-and-run. Which in the long term would have saved her lover's life. When it came to that, Kerstin also felt a pang of guilty conscience, given that the murder of Peter Norling wouldn't have happened if she hadn't tried to blackmail Hallin. He was the natural enemy in the whole affair. His crimes were so grave that they could put him away for many years—maybe even life. And even though she had known so much about him for such a long time, it was Sandra—someone she had never met and didn't even know the age of—who had come up with the plan that would finally see him caught.

That was what they were hoping, anyway, even if they would doubtless encounter a number of tricky obstacles along the way: the burden of proof, a lack of witnesses, the ravages of time, and Hallin's good reputation and wide network of contacts, to name but a few. The project made Kerstin feel quite exhilarated, and although she had something to lose, she was all in.

The compliancy that had characterised everything that had followed that fateful afternoon in January 2014 was regrettable. Jeanette, who hadn't dared to say no, call an ambulance, or contact the police; Sandra, who hadn't dared to report the rape to the police; and Kerstin herself, who hadn't had the courage to get the police involved when her husband had disappeared on a well-marked stretch of road.

But better late than never: it was time to let the axe fall.

46

Sandra

IT WAS THE first day after Midsummer, and Sandra put Erik in the back seat to drive him to day care in Visby before she went on to work. The call with Kerstin had continued well into the small hours. Sandra felt tired and worn-out. Above all she was afraid.

The pieces of the jigsaw had slowly fallen into place, and together Kerstin and Sandra had managed to create a complete picture of what had happened that January afternoon four years ago, as well as what had followed. Of course they could have gone to the police with it, and of course the police would have been forced to take the accusations seriously and start an investigation. This would probably have shaken Hallin up a fair bit, but it would have been enough for him to deny everything completely and the investigation would have collapsed like a house of cards. Plus there was the fact that they would never persuade Jeanette to join them on that approach, and she was the only one who could testify as a witness to the accident. Everything that Kerstin knew or thought she knew was hearsay, apart from the grainy photos that possibly indicated something, but didn't actually prove anything. Not even the money was around to support the theories that they could have championed without Jeanette's help.

In summary, filing a police report wouldn't be of any great use, but there were other ways. And now she had Kerstin with her on the journey, and that was a tremendous relief. Not least because Kerstin had filled in the gaps in Sandra's reasoning and corrected the errors, lending far more weight to their future plans for Hallin.

So far, everything was under control, but the same errors had made her think that she would be able to corner Hallin at no risk to herself. With that kind of attitude, she might have met the same fate as Peter Norling, and that was a frightening prospect for the future, to put it mildly.

She had brushed aside those lilies as a form of minor, crude encouragement to withdraw her demands for support payments, but Hallin had succeeded with his ridiculous scare tactics. Sandra was beginning to feel really frightened, almost terrified. Hallin was clearly not a man to be toyed with, and Sandra had pushed it too far. She had a small child to care for—nothing could be allowed to happen to her.

That was what filled Sandra's thoughts as she shifted down a gear to third; Erik was singing in the back seat and she eased her foot off the accelerator as she entered the bend by the ravine. Coming towards her from the other end was a lorry, so she braked slightly to be on the safe side.

What the hell? It seemed like her brakes weren't working properly. Oh well, no harm done—she was already going slow enough that nobody would be in danger. She had her right foot on the brake pedal, which meant that her speed wasn't increasing at any rate. The two vehicles passed each other without difficulty and the lorry vanished in her rearview mirror. Erik finished Little Ida's Summer Song and moved on to Pippi Longstocking. Both were fixtures in the rather unoriginal singing repertoire of the beautifully voiced children at the final assembly before the kindergarten's summer holidays a couple of weeks ago.

When Sandra exited the second bend, there was a short straight lying ahead of her before a long downhill section. She tried again—several times—but the brakes really were not working. And now she had reached the crest of the hill, and her speed was guaranteed to pick up on the run downhill—she had no idea how much, but it was clear to her that she would be going faster than she felt comfortable with.

And that was exactly how it was: the speedometer crept up from 30 to 40 to 50 mph. "And all the sweet mosquitoes, I want them too," Erik sang while panic took hold of Sandra. Over and over, she pushed the pedal to the floor without the brakes responding. What the hell was she meant to do?

When she reached the bottom of the hill she was doing well over fifty, and that was much too fast because she was about to reach the crossroads where there was a stop sign, and where she could already see that there were cars approaching from left and right. She needed to bring the car to a halt—how was she going to do that?

She vainly pumped on the brake pedal, but the brake system did nothing—it was definitely not working. Erik's song drowned out her own thoughts and panic took hold. There was one thing she could do to avoid a crash up at the crossroads. Granted, it meant putting her and Erik in danger, but it wasn't as serious as the alternative. She had to leave the road. It was lined by ditches that weren't all that deep. It would be okay. It had to be.

But doing over fifty—would it definitely be okay? She imagined wrecking the car and having to call for roadside assistance and take an ambulance and arrive late for work. Erik continued to screech away unconcernedly about tanned legs and freckles, while unintelligible thoughts rushed through Sandra's head. She swore silently and struck the palms of her hands against the wheel.

And then she thought of it. It was so obvious . . . Fear had paralysed her and indecision had almost sent her into the crossroads with

Erik sitting innocently in the back seat. She was such an idiot, she thought to herself as she pressed the clutch and shifted down to first so that the engine brake kicked in.

Then she drove the car calmly and in a controlled manner into the ditch, without causing any injury to life or property.

47

Kerstin

THE SUN SET slowly behind the wall, making the ancient stones on top look red hot. The wind had dropped and the flags were slack. The shops in the Östercentrum shopping centre were shuttered for the day and the people crisscrossing the square since the morning had dissipated. The plants in the beds between the benches emitted stronger scents at this time of day, and if she ignored the jabbering of her friends then Kerstin could clearly make out the low humming of the insects in the flowerboxes.

Now that the dust had settled following Jeanette's suicide attempt, and Kerstin had managed to gather her thoughts after Sandra's unexpected proposal, she realised that there was one thread she hadn't followed up on properly. Something that seemed less important than people's lives, and that she had not focussed on for that reason. But since they had found Peter Norling's remains the question had become far more pertinent: where on earth had the money gone?

It had to be somewhere, and it was unlikely to be in a bank account, given that the money laundering laws these days didn't let banks accept big sums like that without meticulous paperwork documenting its legitimate source. And there wasn't any. Even if the cash had been laundered, it would be tough for anyone to justify a deposit of that size. Or an acquisition. The money had to be spent with restraint in limited amounts.

But where could it be? According to Jeanette, Norling had taken care of it and hidden it somewhere no one would find it. That sounded promising as far as Kerstin was concerned, as it was likely no one else would have stumbled across it. But it might also mean it was so well hidden that Kerstin wouldn't be able to find it either, despite the fact that she—unlike almost everyone else—knew that it existed. As far as she understood, it was enough to fill two sports holdalls, and must weigh a fair bit. That wasn't exactly the kind of thing you hid behind the books in your bookcase.

When it was time to head home, Kerstin fell into step with Jeanette.

"You're not thinking about . . . doing that again, are you?" she asked cautiously.

Jeanette shrugged her shoulders as if it barely mattered to anyone else, let alone herself.

"Not today, if that's what you're wondering," she said.

Naturally it wasn't. But Jeanette's answer was clear enough.

"You're still young, Jeanette. Don't do this to yourself. There's help out there."

"Oh really? Some fucking shrink that I have to feed lies to—I bet that'll help. Or I could tell the truth and end up in jail."

Kerstin shook her head in resignation and sighed.

"You know you can talk to us at least. Do that next time you feel you can't bear it any longer. Promise me that?"

Then she put a hand on Jeanette's shoulder—a rather unusual gesture for Kerstin, who wasn't exactly the biggest fan of physical touching.

"Okay," Jeanette said without looking her in the eye.

"I lie awake at night worrying about how you feel. I don't want to find you in the same state that I did on Midsummer's Eve again. Or worse. Do you hear what I'm saying?"

"I promise I'll do it in the middle of day next time," Jeanette said dismissively. "So that I don't ruin your night's sleep."

Full of herself, as usual, Kerstin thought to herself. And evil too. Kerstin took back her hand in an unobtrusive movement.

They continued to stroll in silence. After a while, Jeanette stopped and looked at her with an expression filled with regret.

"Sorry," she said. "I didn't mean to hurt you."

"Good," Kerstin said. "Consider it forgotten."

You don't even understand the meaning of the word "hurt," she thought to herself. *If only you knew what you have done to me.*

"I was thinking about something," she said softly, in order to avoid seeming too keen. "About something we might do together—to divert our thoughts elsewhere, as it were."

"Get pissed?" Jeanette said, with the smallest grain of humour.

At least Kerstin thought so, but Jeanette didn't move her lips.

"Always," Kerstin said with a smile. "But I had something else in mind. Are you up for listening?"

"Why not?"

"I was thinking about the money you mentioned—the six million. Now that Peter is gone, it casts a somewhat different light on the matter, doesn't it?"

"How do you mean?" Jeanette asked, not seeming to respond with any surprise to the choice of subject, despite it being about Peter.

"You always thought that Peter had done a runner with the cash, but now it turns out that can't have been the case."

"And . . . ?"

"I just mean it has to be somewhere," Kerstin explained. "You said he took care of it. Where do you think he might have hidden it?"

"I don't know, and I don't care."

"It's six million kronor," Kerstin emphasised. "It might be very useful."

"I didn't care about the money then, and I care even less now," Jeanette said. "It's caused nothing but misery."

"That may be so, but an amount like that could be useful and a source of happiness. It seems unnecessary to leave it lying wherever it is. And it'll soon be worthless anyway."

"It probably already is."

"Why would that be?"

"Because we stole it from some goddamn bank robber."

Jeanette had no idea how right she was.

"Bank robber?" said Kerstin. "Where did you get that idea from?"

"Who else do you think drives around with six million in cash in their boot?"

"You think the notes are traceable? That you and Peter sacrificed it all for a pile of useless cash?"

"Pretty much that," Jeanette said laconically.

Kerstin thought for a while about how to tackle this. Jeanette wasn't thick, and she'd had plenty of time to reach this conclusion after the event. It just so happened that Kerstin knew her to be wrong, but this was something she naturally couldn't divulge.

"It may well be," she said. "But it seems unnecessary to assume the worst. We might as well start by locating it. Then we can figure out what to do next if we find it. I suggest you have a think about where he might have hidden the money, and then we can join forces to find it. It might be really good to get away a bit—just you and me. It's only the two of us who know about the money."

The last bit was a lie, but a white lie—Kerstin convinced herself of that much. She saw no reason to get Sandra mixed up in this.

"Sure," said Jeanette. "If you think it might lead somewhere."

48

Sandra

THERE WASN'T a single scratch to the car, nor to Erik either. He seemed to have found the incident most entertaining. The taxi ride to kindergarten alone was an adventure in itself. He didn't get a chance to see the tow truck, but the thought that it had come and fetched the car and towed it to the garage was fascinating in itself. The fact that his mother had driven into a ditch was something he repeated over and over again to anyone who would listen—largely children and some of the staff at the kindergarten, and naturally his grandparents, whom they were moving in with until further notice.

It didn't feel safe for the two of them to live alone in the countryside in a house with no intruder alarm or burglarproof doors and windows. They were usually more than welcome to stay with her parents, and it seemed unlikely that a solitary man would try to get into a house containing three adults.

Just as Sandra feared, it transpired that the car had been sabotaged. Someone had cut the brake lines under the car—a simple intervention for anyone with the requisite knowledge and the right tools—and it was perfectly clear that it wasn't to make her drive gently into a ditch with no injury to life or limb. The sabotage must have taken place under cover of night—between midnight and a couple of hours later—when Sandra had been on the phone with Kerstin just a few metres away.

The thought of that panicky journey ending with going into the ditch made her feel dizzy. The ravine—what if she had been going faster when she had driven round the bend? The long downhill after that when the speedometer had been moving up at an alarming pace that she couldn't influence, and the busy crossroads that had come towards her at a rapid pace . . . They had been lucky beyond comprehension, and that wasn't something she could count on in future.

Sandra said nothing to her parents about the true reason behind the accident. They would only get worked up about it, and that wouldn't help the situation in the slightest. On the other hand, she did report the entire thing to the police, somewhat against her better judgment. She reluctantly acknowledged to herself that everything was going off the rails and that couldn't be allowed to go on without the police being made aware that something was off from the beginning. At the same time, she also notified them that she had felt under threat for some time: that on several occasions she had received funeral flowers sent to her anonymously.

On the other hand, informing the police who was behind the threats and the malicious tampering with her car would be moronic. Not to mention pointless, given that he would deny the accusations, and it would be impossible to find any evidence. Plus it would make Hallin furious, which might drive him to do even worse things. The fact that he was *definitely* going to punish her was the only thing she was certain of.

At least the police now knew that something was going on, and that might give her a slight advantage in what was to come.

She now needed to seek out Hallin's wife. It wasn't something Sandra *wanted* to do—most of all, she wanted to pull out of it all and have nothing more to do with him. But the more she thought about it, the more viable she saw that route was. It was no longer intended as a threat or designed to harm Hallin. It was a plea to the only person who—in the best-case scenario—could put a stop to this harassment.

Thanks to a phone call made to Hallin's place of work, she had made sure he wasn't at home because she definitely didn't want to see the guy again, and above all she lacked the courage to confront him. Discounting a future trial, of course—when she would probably be in the witness box.

And now here she was, standing outside Hallin's front door ringing the bell, her mouth bone dry with nerves and her hands trembling so much that she had to put them in her trouser pockets in order to disguise it. She knew that Gunilla Hallin was at home because she had glimpsed her inside, passing the windows several times.

The door opened and there was a woman in her fifties standing there smiling at her. She had an open face with laughter lines at the corners of her eyes, and she didn't look too dangerous.

Sandra cleared her throat and swallowed.

"Hello," she said. "I'm Sandra."

"I recognise that name—wasn't it you who called the other day? About some kid that Jan had promised to sponsor?"

"Yes," Sandra acknowledged. "That was me."

"I'm afraid he's not at home, but . . ."

"I was actually looking to speak to you," Sandra interrupted her.

The woman took on an expression of confusion that seemed to demand an explanation.

"You won't like what I have to say," said Sandra. "But I'm doing it because I don't see any other way out."

"That sounds worrying," said Mrs. Hallin, frowning.

"I wasn't entirely truthful the last time we spoke. I tried to show you some consideration, and I hoped it would be resolved without involving you."

"What is it you're trying to say?"

The initial friendliness was dissipating; the woman was preparing herself for bad news and didn't want to string out the torment for any longer than was necessary. What Sandra had to say was provocative in itself, but the way she said it might soften the blow. She had already made up her mind to wrap up her words so that they didn't seem too aggressive.

"I've got nothing to do with your relationship whatsoever, which is why . . ."

"That's something we can agree on," the woman interrupted. She had begun to look irritated. "Get to the point."

"Jan is the father of my child," Sandra stated.

Gunilla Hallin looked at her wide-eyed—she seemed to have stopped breathing. Sandra waited for the message to sink in, predicting a torrent of accusations in return. But when the woman finally managed to control her breathing, she gave a deep sigh, crossed her arms over her chest as if to protect herself from some outer danger, and stared down at her feet. She sighed again and gave Sandra a teary-eyed look.

"And now you want money?" she said, swallowing.

"It was a one-time thing," Sandra explained, still just as compassionately. "It was only recently that I found out that it was your husband who is the father. The boy is three and a half now."

Gunilla Hallin looked crushed, but Sandra needed to get out what she had come to say, and with empathy and tenderness at that.

"Jan is the father of the child whether he likes it or not," she said. "He doesn't want anything to do with the boy, and that suits me just fine. So in order to avoid involving social services, I suggested a private arrangement—which isn't unreasonable anyway. On the contrary, I think my demands are more reasonable for him than if we got the authorities involved."

"But . . ." the woman said, unable to grasp it. "Why involve Jan? It must have been your decision to keep the child?"

She didn't level it as an accusation, she said it more as a reasoned thought. She was tempted to put up an opposition and explain what had actually happened, but Sandra preferred not to start a war around this. She wanted to end one.

"I'm not here for the money," she said truthfully. "I've been threatened several times. To begin with, it didn't really scare me, but my car was sabotaged today—and it's not fun anymore. Both my son and I could have been hurt. Naturally, I could have gone to the police and told them what your husband was up to, but I don't want to rile him up anymore. And since I can't communicate with him, I've come to you instead. I thought you, as a woman, might have some understanding for my situation as a single parent. But, as I just said, I'm not here for the money—I'm here to plead with you for help. The harassment needs to stop. Otherwise I'll be *forced* to report it to the police—for the sake of my own safety and my little boy's."

Mrs. Hallin looked caught off her guard. She shook her head several times without saying anything, but her eyes were fixed on Sandra's. Sandra felt incredibly sorry for the woman, who had done nothing to deserve what she was suffering now.

"Jan . . ." Mrs. Hallin stuttered. "He would never . . . I've known him for almost thirty years, and he's not capable of . . . How could he possibly stage a car crash to hurt you? He can't even clip someone around the ear. The whole thing sounds preposterous."

Sandra was ashamed and almost regretted involving the innocent wife in this feud. At once she felt both selfish and inconsiderate, and shrunk a little inside herself. She hoped it wasn't visible on the outside—she needed all the presence she could summon to lead the conversation where she wanted it to go.

"I understand this is far from good news for you, but I'm just presenting the facts," Sandra said apologetically.

Not that she needed to apologise for being raped, threatened, and subjected to something that was suspiciously like attempted murder. But at the same time, she understood Hallin's wife too. It was clear that she had difficulty reconciling herself with such grave allegations against the man she had chosen to spend her life with.

"I don't know what to say," she said. "I find it very hard to believe . . . A police report would break him."

"I don't *want* to report him to the police," Sandra explained. "And I'm not *going* to report him to the police. So long as he stops these awful threats and the danger he's putting me and my son in. That's all I ask."

"And the money?"

"I just wanted to engage in sensible dialogue about the support payments for my child that I'm legally entitled to from the father. That was my sole intention before the whole thing degenerated like this. And I'm truly sorry that I've had to put you through this—I fully understand how you must feel about me right now. But I would ask you one more time: please make sure he stops harassing me."

The woman gave her an incredulous look, letting it wander from her head to her feet and back again. She said nothing, but Sandra reckoned she could read her thoughts.

Was it really likely that her husband had been with this creature?

Gunilla Hallin looked like she was about to say something, but she stopped herself. Instead, she shook her head sadly, took a step back into the hallway, and shut the door.

49

Jan

GUNILLA WAS IN a state of utter misery when he got home. She was sitting at the dining room table quietly crying, and she didn't even look up when he came through the door. She rarely cried—almost never—but when she did it was serious. Jan was overcome with dread.

Why wasn't she looking at him, why wasn't she seeking comfort in his eyes like she usually did?

He pulled out the chair next to her and sat down, taking her hand. It was slack and unresponsive in his, and she didn't react to his caresses.

"What's happened, sweetheart?" he asked softly.

He had to, but he could tell where it was going to lead. It was *he* who had made her upset—otherwise she would have met him at the door, burrowed herself into his embrace, and cried against his chest.

She didn't answer and carried on staring down at the table while crying her ominously quiet tears. How long would they have to sit there like that until it all kicked off? He felt powerless in a way he rarely experienced. He was usually the one who had solutions to everything. But this time he wouldn't be able to help her—he could feel it.

"She's just a kid, Jan," Gunilla said quietly, without looking up.

She? Did she mean Sandra? So Sandra had been here, marching into his territory and upsetting his wife. Rage welled up inside him. That greedy fucking slut certainly wasn't afraid to make good on her threats. Now she had dragged Gunilla into the mess—and that was disgraceful. Gunilla had nothing to do with it—this was a struggle between the two of them, between Jan and Sandra. But Sandra didn't understand the rules of the game. She was setting herself on innocent parties and meting out punishments.

Jan didn't know what to say, so he said nothing and simply squeezed Gunilla's hand a little more tightly to show that he was there for her. That he was upset too. What an idiot he was—how could he carry on in a situation like this?

"What were you thinking?" said Gunilla, still without looking at him.

He had asked himself the same thing and he had no answer.

"I wasn't thinking at all," he said, looking down despite the fact that she wasn't looking at him. "I'd have to blame the booze."

That hardly merited comment—he knew what she thought. And he essentially agreed with her. If he couldn't handle his alcohol then he shouldn't be drinking. Or at least he should be drinking less.

"How do you think it would look if we suddenly had a little boy in the house every other weekend?" said Gunilla. "What do you think people would say about that? And the kids especially?"

Where had she got that from? Sandra would never suggest anything like that—that was the only thing he was certain of.

"That's not in the cards," he said truthfully. "She is absolutely certain that she doesn't want me involved in raising that youngster."

"And you believe that?" said Gunilla, looking him in the eye for the first time. "She's a young girl and probably has a job to go to. Of course she needs some respite."

"Gunilla, I don't know anything about that person, but . . ."

"Don't call her that. She has a name and she's the mother of your child. Show her some respect."

Gunilla was in tears, but she was talking to him now—in a low voice, with reasoned arguments. Anything was better than that suffocating silence.

"What I wanted to say," said Jan, "was that I barely know anything about . . . Sandra. However, what I do know is that she *doesn't* want me around while the lad grows up. But money—that's something she does want."

Gunilla shook her head with a look of regret in her eyes and came to Sandra's defence, using the same deadly quiet tone of voice.

"Of course she needs money, Jan. She can't be more than thirty, and whatever line of work she's in, she won't have reached a salary that's worth mentioning. She's the sole carer for a little boy—kids aren't cheap to look after. Of course she wants the child's father to pay child support."

"There's nothing to say that I'm the child's father," Jan blurted out.

"Yes, Jan. There is," said Gunilla.

And of course there was. Gunilla was right, and that made him even angrier at Sandra.

"So you actually think that I *should* pay support to that little whore?" he exclaimed.

He regretted it the very same moment. The tone of voice was inappropriate for the situation. Gunilla shuddered and looked at him with an expression of distaste.

"Why are you talking about her like that?" she asked. "Surely that makes you a lech? She's just a young girl who was unlucky."

That one hit home. He probably deserved it. But it was hard to strike the right balance when comforting one's distraught wife while also boiling with internalised rage.

"Unlucky?" he said. "She had every opportunity to get an abortion, but chose not to. I've no wish to pay the bill for a financially unsound decision that I wasn't involved in."

Gunilla was silent. But she had calmed down now and was no longer crying.

"What did you say to her?" Jan asked.

Gunilla wiped the end of her nose and her eyes with a crumpled handkerchief that had been concealed in her hand.

"She caught me by surprise, and my spontaneous response was to defend you. She seemed like such a kind and sweet girl, but I shut the door in her face. I wish I had dealt with the situation differently."

Sweet? That was just about the last thing she was. Sandra was inconsiderate in her approach, and now she had managed to dupe his wife too. Were the police next? Jan could feel the sweat forming on his brow.

"Surely you don't think I should go along with her demands?" he repeated.

"I don't think anything," said Gunilla. "This has actually nothing to do with me."

"You're involved with the family's finances, surely?" Jan muttered.

"Your child, your decision," Gunilla sighed.

"Then I guess I'll put six hundred and eighty-four thousand in that . . . in Sandra's account," said Jan.

He was well aware that this wouldn't fall on fertile ground with his wife. But he wanted them to make the decision together, so that he wouldn't end up dealing with the backlash later on. After all, he had no plans whatsoever to pay a penny of bloody support for a child he didn't know with any certainty was his. Considering there were several compelling reasons why he *didn't* want to be the father of it. Agreeing to pay child support would be the same as admitting something that could lead to further and more serious allegations, and that couldn't be allowed to happen.

"It'll be at the expense of the kids' inheritance then," said Gunilla sadly.

Jan smiled to himself. That was exactly where he wanted her.

"Yes, and that doesn't feel right," he said. "I think we should let the matter rest. I think it'll probably come to nothing."

Gunilla pursed her lips and shook her head in resignation, an introspective look on her face. But she wouldn't be able to complain later.

50

Kerstin

SHE DIDN'T WANT to seem too eager, so she didn't mention the prospective stash of money again—instead she waited patiently for Jeanette to take the initiative herself. She had almost given up hope when on Thursday Jeanette came and sat next to her on the bench, and said she was willing to head out on a treasure hunt.

"There's a summer house," she said. "There might be something?"

Jeanette had been in a slightly better mood over the last few days, and hopefully that boded well. At the same time, she was shit-faced most of the time, so it was hard to know exactly where she was. Including now, as she sat there swaying back and forth in a way that obliged Kerstin to grab hold of her on several occasions so that she wouldn't tumble off the bench. Jeanette didn't even notice, or she didn't care. It was hard to tell which.

"Absolutely," said Kerstin. "Do you know where it is?"

"Tofta beach," Jeanette said. "Or somewhere nearby."

She was slurring so much it was barely possible to hear what she was saying.

"Tofta beach?" Kerstin replied, wanting to be sure.

Jeanette nodded.

"Do you know where?"

"No idea," said Jeanette. "But he used to call it Meadow Hill."

"Good work," said Kerstin. "How about we take an outing there tomorrow?"

"Sure. We going to nick a car or what?"

"We'll bike there," Kerstin said with a smile. "There's a bike lane all the way. Do you have a bike?"

"Yes, but I'm not sure there's any air in the tires."

"We'll sort that. I'll make a packed lunch and come to yours around eight o'clock. You make sure you're sober, otherwise I'll go without you. Okay?"

"Yeah, yeah," said Jeanette, trying to roll her eyes—but it mostly looked like she was gazing up at the sky.

THE NEXT DAY it was cloudy and quite windy, but the weather was meant to stay dry. Jeanette had shaken off the last few days of misery and was sober, or at least she seemed to be. She was able to cycle at any rate, despite the occasionally strong headwinds.

The plan—which hadn't been that well thought through, Kerstin acknowledged that—was to ask around. There must be hundreds of houses in Tofta, but perhaps not that many that were next to something that might be considered a meadow. She had hung a couple of buckets over the handlebars, containing some clothes and cleaning fluid, rubber gloves, and some black bin liners. Her idea was that they could pretend to be cleaners and ask around. She hadn't got any further than that in her thoughts, but the project still had an air of adventure to it. Jeanette seemed to be in a good mood and some fresh sea air never did anyone any harm.

The ride there took around an hour, after which they spent two hours and twenty minutes asking people for directions to Meadow Hill and the Norling family summer house before they got a bite. It took another half hour for them to get into the house, and, disregarding the forty-five-minute lunch break in the garden, it took them five hours to turn the place upside down and inside out before putting it all back the way they had found it. Then they cycled the twelve or thirteen miles back to Visby, a job well done.

Not completely, if they were going to be picky, because they now knew at any rate that the money wasn't *there*. But they'd had a pleasant if somewhat strenuous day. And Kerstin had been able to spend time alone with the object of her darkest fantasies. She had studied Jeanette in a different setting than her usual one, weighing her good and bad qualities against each other. Only to realise that she was none the wiser as a result.

Jeanette was a complex being, and if she was in a good mood then she was easy to like. If she wasn't, then she awakened other emotions, but it was hard to build up a grudge against someone who was suicidal. It was in the middle ground of her emotions that one found Jeanette's most unsympathetic characteristics: her insatiable need for affirmation, her self-absorption and indifference towards other people, and her inability to take command of the situation and put her back into anything. In other words, she was someone who could easily be described as both unenterprising and lazy, and perhaps it was these rather ordinary qualities that made her weak in circumstances that required a bit of fighting spirit.

Guilty or innocent? Kerstin still hadn't the foggiest, but sooner or later she was likely to beat her to a pulp if the chance arose and the stars aligned. But no matter how strange it seemed, the memory of Karl-Erik and what had happened to him had become more distant as she had got closer to the truth of the disaster. Perhaps talking about it was healing in itself—the constant presence of such terrible, life-changing events made them less devastating. The conversation had the effect of taking the edge off. Just like alcohol, but its impact was less pernicious.

They had, however, learned a few things during the course of the day. In particular, that Jeanette—with her unspoilt exterior—found it easier to make contact with people. Kerstin, with her deeply furrowed face, hoarse voice, and tattoos, scared people away. Jeanette had to handle the chat, while Kerstin hovered in the background and pretended she didn't speak Swedish. If they were going to make any more outings, then Kerstin needed to make sure she wore sunglasses and long sleeves. A toolkit wouldn't do any harm either, and a towel so that they could jump in the sea afterwards.

51

Sandra

IT WAS FRIDAY and she had almost reached the deadline that she had mentally set for Hallin to start paying the bloody support. It had been on Midsummer's Day that he had unexpectedly given in when she had called him, but just as she had suspected, this had simply been a delaying tactic. He had needed time to prepare the next phase of his vendetta: sabotaging her car. That had clearly shown her who she was up against. The only thing she had been able to do was plead with his wife to ask him to stop his persecution, and perhaps it had worked. Four days had passed without any threats, and Sandra could only hope that it was over.

Personally, she had absolutely no intention of taking the matter any further—not in light of what she now considered to be a death threat hanging over her. Sandra had explained clearly to his wife that she didn't care about the money—all she wanted was to get out of this with her health intact. If they communicated with each other at all, then the news had surely reached Hallin.

That was why she was hopeful, but she also regretted not being warier back when the bunch of flowers had turned up on her porch. Then she would have avoided the fear, as well as the logistical hassle involved in having her life in one place and living in another.

Despite all the negativity, the thought of the bollocking that Hallin must have got from his wife after Sandra's visit was very entertaining. Even if the intention at the time hadn't been to cause trouble for Hallin, she had still given him a real kick in the balls, metaphorically.

Despite her budding optimism, the fear wouldn't go away entirely. It wasn't just any old person she was dealing with—she occasionally had to remind herself that the guy was literally capable of murder. Peter Norling had been lured to a secluded spot before being brutally beaten to death. Despite his presumed innocence. After all, he hadn't taken those photographs, let alone sent them to Hallin. Hallin was ruthless, stopping at nothing to conceal his mistakes. Which were only mounting up.

And he was the father of Sandra's child.

But she refused to see it like that. Erik was *her* son. He had no father, and if he were ever to get one in future, it wouldn't be Hallin. He was more than welcome to pay child support—in fact, he was *going* to—but she didn't view it as child support. Thus far, she had managed just fine to cover the expense of food, clothing, toys, housing, and childcare. Erik got what he needed. This was money for Sandra—damages. For the pain and suffering, the sick leave, the anxiety, and all the harrowing memories. An unwanted pregnancy that she had initially been uncertain how to deal with. And a tenacious fear of men in general, and intimate relationships as a whole.

THE FIRST TIME it rang, she was at work standing in a circle with her colleagues issuing instructions to them on how to structure the rest of the afternoon and evening. She glanced at the display while continuing to talk, noting that it was the kindergarten calling. She rejected the call, meaning to call them back straight after the meeting. Less than a minute later, she had another call from the same number and realised that something might have happened. Maybe Erik had come down with a fever or started throwing up; in that sort of situation the staff were usually keener than the parents were to have the child picked up quickly. So she rejected that call too, although her anxiety was rising. When they rang again immediately afterwards, she excused herself and went into an adjacent room where she could shut the door.

"Erik is missing," said the head.

"Missing?" Sandra said, dumbfounded.

"We were in the woods at Furulundsskogen on an outing and suddenly he was gone."

Sandra pulled out a chair and sat down while thoughts whirled around her head. She concluded that if the head of school was compelled to contact a parent on such a sensitive matter, then it had presumably been a while since the child had gone missing.

"When did this happen?" she asked.

"Around two o'clock. We've looked everywhere, but we can't find him. I'm sorry—I never thought I'd have to impart news like this."

Sandra looked at the time and noted that it was ten past three. "Hasn't he just gone home?" Sandra suggested. "To his grandparents, that is." She didn't want to believe that it was anything worse than Erik falling out with someone and deciding to leave. Little Igor, she thought to herself. That little bully had probably done something bad to Erik—made him angry and upset, made him feel unfairly treated so that he ran away, offended.

"One of the staff has driven over, and he wasn't there or anywhere on the way."

"He's three years old, he probably doesn't know the way," Sandra said.

Then she realised that this was not an exchange of words that either of them had to win. She couldn't stand the head of school, but this wasn't about their personal chemistry—it was about collaborating.

"Have you called the police?" she inquired.

"I'm going to do that now, if you'll let me."

"Do it," said Sandra. "I'll be there as soon as I can. Furulundsskogen, did you say?"

"We'll keep searching. See you at Gråbo."

"Whereabouts?"

"In the free car park behind Träffpunkt Gråbo. Outside the youth club."

Only now did the penny really drop. Erik was missing and the situation was serious enough that Sandra had been called and the police were going to be brought in. The picture of the future being painted before her eyes looked extremely ominous—a life without Erik was unbearable, unthinkable, and couldn't be allowed to become reality. This was a warning shot that was shaking her into action, a hint about how things might go if she didn't take good enough care of what gave her life meaning.

It was in a state of rising panic that she got into the car and drove over to the woods at Furulundsskogen.

TEN MINUTES LATER, she arrived on the scene. A couple of her colleagues from work had come with her, and her father also appeared. Her mother was waiting at home in case Erik—in spite of everything—managed to find his way there, somehow. There was an ambulance in the car park, and Sandra got it into her head that it was for Erik. Had he climbed into a tree, fallen out, and lost consciousness? Broken his arms, legs, neck? Had he cut himself on something sharp or been bitten by a dog? A snake? Had he had a bad reaction to a wasp sting?

The Furulundsskogen woods comprised a charming but compact area consisting of delightful beech trees with dense canopies in places, while elsewhere there were a variety of trees including a sprinkling of pine. The chirping of birds and the dancing sunlight filled the treetops, while the ivy struggled to make its way up towards the sky. The ground was covered in goutweed and moss, soft and bewitching. There were a thousand shades of green, each one the source of a unique scent. A great place to take kindergarten kids on an outing. No water, no obvious dangers. On the other hand, it was surrounded on all sides by houses and roads. Houses with people living in them who might take it into their heads to take a kid home, roads that led to bigger roads, bigger forests, and the sea, which was everywhere.

The world grew around Sandra, while at the same time her field of vision shrank.

Children and grown-ups were tugging at her—they had things to tell her and questions to ask. That made the gravity of the situation even more palpable. Maybe this wasn't a warning sign—maybe Erik was gone for real? Forever? The police had a thousand questions, were talking about mobilising search parties and inquiring about Erik's habits and things he didn't do, his appearance, his build, medical issues, clothing, and interests. Did the child have a father? Any threats?

Were there? What was she supposed to say? If there was no child then there was no father—that was the nature of the threat. But yes, she had already reported threats to the police. And yes, there was a father—not a nice one. Concentrate on him, do it now, but be discreet, and don't make yourselves known. Follow his every movement and sooner or later you'll find Erik. Unless he's dead already—then we won't find him for a long time.

Over and over, she had tried to get the policeman to understand this vital point. It was only when he pointed out that he had got the message long ago that she fell silent. He promised that they wouldn't prioritise police procedure over Erik's health and well-being. And that they would immediately put Hallin under surveillance.

She had irrevocably taken matters to the extreme, created desperation of a calibre that had put her own child in mortal peril. Had she really not grasped until now that she was facing something that might already be fact? But—she had to remind herself—it might not be.

Contacting Hallin was out of the question—terrified as she was of riling him up. Driving by his house to look for traces of Erik would be both futile and dangerous. An approach from the police would be even worse. If Erik was unharmed, Sandra's and the police's actions couldn't be allowed to change that.

All she really wanted to do was set off and search, but there were more important things to do and others were doing the searching. It ended with her being sent home—not to her parents' house but back to her own. Since Erik knew his own address, perhaps he might have asked someone for a lift home? It was just for the night, then she could be reunited with her parents, enveloped in the warmth, share her despair with them.

So Sandra spent the night alone in her desolate house. She had rejected all offers of company from friends and family. Her father was roving through the woods with hundreds of others, searching, while her mother watched over her house and Sandra over hers.

She worked. With raging ferocity. But when her thoughts began to wander, she allowed herself to be distracted by the summer night outside. Then she crept out of the open door, taking in the dew-heavy scents and wandering around the garden. Searching for sounds and shadows, shouting and crying.

She sat down at the computer again. Now things were urgent. More urgent than ever before. She thought and pondered, turning everything that had happened inside out. Her brain was overflowing with thoughts, but that kept her going and on her toes.

Hadn't she expressed herself clearly enough—was there any doubt when it came to the financial demands? Hadn't she said that yes, she wanted to withdraw her claims, but that the threats had to stop?

Please, I don't care about the money—just make sure he doesn't hurt us. Surely that had gotten through?

Or was the problem that she had done just that—pleaded? Was the kidnapping retribution for humiliating herself in front of his wife? Because she had got his wife *involved*?

Or, to go one step further—had the visited been misinterpreted as Sandra putting her threats into action? Might it have been seen as the first step being taken—his wife had been informed that *something* had happened that afternoon, that forbidden and immoral relations had occurred? Had he interpreted it as meaning that she was about to take the next step—the one that could not be taken at any cost—informing the police about the rape?

Was it one of these elements, or all of them in combination, that had driven the man who had raped Sandra to steal away her son? If there was no child, then there was no father. The child was the only thing that could support loosely created theories about rape and drunk driving, which might in turn lead to accusations of manslaughter, hit-and-run, and even murder. A kidnapping added to the charge sheet hardly mattered.

Or another murder.

Perhaps it might make the difference between the longest time-specific sentence that could be handed out and a life sentence—if the murder of Peter Norling and all the other stuff wasn't worth a life sentence, then a child murder would be. But for Hallin, it probably didn't make much difference. He didn't want to be deprived of his liberty, full stop, and he was clearly prepared to do whatever it took to avoid it.

Perhaps even killing a child.

Sandra entertained little hope that the police surveillance on Hallin would lead anywhere. Assuming they had even taken her misgivings seriously. He had killed Peter Norling with a heavy shovel—it couldn't have taken more than a few seconds. If the intention was for Erik to die, then he was already dead and buried by now.

Sandra tried to keep that incomprehensible thought away from herself. She alternated between padding back and forth by the window with a sob in her throat and working, biting her lip so hard that she tasted blood. She didn't sleep a wink that night—there was no time.

THREE-YEAR-OLD MISSING AFTER KINDERGARTEN OUTING TO WOODS

During an outing to the Furulundsskogen woods on Friday afternoon, staff realised that the boy was missing. It has not yet been determined how he disappeared, but according to sources the children were bird-watching when the boy ran away.

Shortly after the alarm was raised, police initiated a massive search effort. In addition to multiple police patrols, search-and-rescue dogs and helicopters were also deployed. Around one hundred volunteers also joined the search, which has continued throughout the night.

"At present, we do not suspect that any crime has been committed, but we are working without any preconceptions," said the officer in charge of the search. "We would urge anyone who may have seen or heard anything of interest to contact the police."

The boy has short blond hair and is around 90 centimetres tall. At the time of his disappearance, he was wearing blue jeans, a red sweatshirt, and green boots, according to the police.

GOTLANDS ALLEHANDA

JULY
2018

52

Kerstin

JEANETTE WAS BACK to her heavy boozing, and Kerstin was sitting next to her, watching. Taking in the way she curled up like a kitten in Lubbi's arms and sucked up the attention she generated around her whenever she was in that kind of mood. *There she is*, Kerstin thought to herself. The woman who left Kerstin's great love to suffer and die for her own gain. The one who wasn't interested in the money, but still let him die because her *own* great love thought it was a good idea.

At certain moments, Kerstin managed to summon the energy needed to put herself in this unforgiving state, but for the most part she didn't. More often, she saw Jeanette as a woman who had lost her child and then lost her footing. In the same way that she, Kerstin, had when she had lost her husband. For the most part, she remained fairly neutral, observing Jeanette with cool interest—just like anyone else who moved around the fringes of the woman's consciousness. She supposed that was where she had ended up in her ponderings—somewhere in between, in the harsh landscape of indifference.

It was the first day of the political festival known as Almedalen Week and political aficionados had begun to stream in from all directions. They flooded the town for a week, parking thousands of bicycles by the East Gate. But they were fun to watch. They were nothing like the average tourist; they represented other values. As a rule, they were happy and enthusiastic, and surprisingly well-behaved given the amount of rosé they tipped back. More often than not, they were engaged in lively conversations with each other.

Kerstin was glad that she now had Sandra to talk to, and that they also had a joint project to focus on. Kerstin had already carried out some tasks, and Sandra had been very happy. Now it looked like Kerstin was going to let her down when it came to the money, because Jeanette had no other worthwhile ideas up her sleeve. A break-in at the Norling family's house while they were on holiday didn't seem constructive. Partly because Kerstin no longer engaged in criminal activities—disregarding the break-in at the summer house, of course, which had been for a good cause and had not led to anything being destroyed or stolen. Partly because the money would have been found long ago if it was at the Norlings' house—by the police, if nobody else, since they had probably turned the house upside down in their hunt for the truth behind the disappearance. The same was likely to apply to the garage he had worked at.

No, Jeanette seemed to have completely lost interest, and Kerstin had no ideas of her own. How was she supposed to come up with anything? Norling had probably got in his car and gone into the woods and buried the bags somewhere. Sooner or later, someone would stumble onto them, and it wouldn't be Kerstin. What was more, it would be too late—the clock was ticking quickly now.

Kerstin decided she would call Sandra that evening and explain the situation. Apologise that neither Jeanette nor she had any more ideas about where Norling might have hidden the cash, but emphasise clearly how eager she was to help in all other ways imaginable.

Jeanette was shouting to her from the grass a small distance away, merrily running away with some of the younger boys chasing her. Kerstin didn't care about her—that exhilaration might at any moment be transformed into depression and tears, or a thirst for battle and virulence. She was hammered too; there was probably a tear to her clothing or a twisted ankle in her near future.

But Jeanette shouted again. At the same time she was choking with laughter as one of the young guys—Jimmy—wrapped his arms around her from behind and pulled her down into the grass.

". . . hunting . . . !" Jeanette shouted indistinctly.

Yes, I suppose he is hunting you. Big deal, Kerstin thought to herself.

"A hunting tower or something!" Jeanette tried again, and now the penny dropped.

She was talking about Peter Norling—she was taking advantage of feeling light and happy to think. Kerstin's heart softened again, and she reflected that Jeanette was fighting things her own way, and that she had underestimated her.

A hunting tower, Kerstin thought to herself. Surely it wasn't possible to hide something in a place used by many people . . . But a hunting cabin? That sounded more promising. Not that she knew what that was exactly—a cabin for spending time in before and after the hunt, maybe? With a shed where they could hang up the dead animals, perhaps . . . Did they skin them? Or was that an outdoor activity? There might be bunks too, if the hunt lasted for several days.

A hunting cabin was surely not all that different to a summer house, except that it would be out in the middle of the forest somewhere. In other words, a suitable hiding place. But where? In which forest? And even if Jeanette could answer that question, she wouldn't know the address. If hunting cabins had addresses, that was. Consequently, asking around would not be an option on this occasion.

Then it occurred to her that there had to be a way of finding out which properties someone owned. Maybe you had to go to court, she thought to herself. Wasn't there a population registry office? That sounded familiar. She got out her mobile and searched using the keywords. She found the property registration database on the Swedish mapping agency's website. She clicked on "Order information about a property," but it all looked very complicated. It seemed she needed to represent a company, and she might only be able to find out about one property, rather than seeing which properties someone owned.

But she was going to get to the bottom of this, rather than skipping over it because it might be hard. On Monday, during business hours, she would call their customer service line and ask how it worked—but first she would ask Sandra. She probably knew how to do it. She might even be able to access the information they needed quicker than that. Why hadn't she thought of that straight away? It might have saved them the trouble of wandering around Tofta disguised as confused cleaners.

Sandra and Kerstin had exchanged phone numbers now so that they could reach each other at any time. Sandra was no longer just a voice in the night but also a friend she could call whenever she liked. And vice versa. Kerstin was very reluctant to abuse that trust, but this was about the six million kronor, which was important to their joint project. And it was urgent. So she stepped to one side and called Sandra, who picked up straight away.

"I'm so glad I caught you," Kerstin said. "And sorry to bother you like this on a Sunday afternoon. But I wonder whether you'd be able to make use of your contacts to find out which properties Peter Norling owned? Or owns—he must still be in the system."

Sandra was silent for a few seconds before replying.

"I should be able to do that. But not until I get to work, and I'm not sure when that will be. Is this about the stolen money?"

"It is," Kerstin confirmed. "We found a summer house that we turned upside down, but with no joy. There may be a hunting cabin too, but if there is then we have no idea where it is. There might be more—I hope you can find that out?"

"As soon as possible. I'm a bit tied up right now."

"Then I'll get out of your hair," said Kerstin.

"I'll be in touch," said Sandra, and she ended the call.

She sounded unusually curt. Kerstin hoped she hadn't transgressed some invisible boundary by calling her on a Sunday.

53

Sandra

THE HOPE THAT Erik would knock on the door had dissipated, so on Saturday Sandra had moved back into her parents' place. It was now Sunday evening and Erik had been missing for more than forty-eight hours. The shared worry characterised the movements and tones of voice of all three of them, but none of them allowed themselves to lose their grip. Each one of them was processing their emotions in their own way and was preparing for what was to come.

Her mother was working in the kitchen, filling the fridge and freezer so that no one had to go hungry either now or when they became exhausted.

Her father had been out searching all weekend together with the police, dogs, helicopters, and hundreds of volunteers. Despite heavy rain and thunder, more people than expected had participated in the search—or perhaps that was why. But there was no trace to be found of Erik, no clue as to where he might have gone.

Sandra had reluctantly realised there was nothing she could do to streamline or speed up the search; there were already plenty of people out there and her presence would not add anything to that. Everyone was working their hardest at their assigned task. The best thing she could do was to assiduously continue her work on the thing that would hopefully make at least some small difference to a few of them. The thing that she had spent almost all her free time on since Erik's name day when the first threat had materialised.

Even if her parents didn't waste words expressing their anxiety about what had happened to Erik, they spoke quite plainly when it came to Sandra's sleep habits and the frenetic way in which she continued to work on whatever it was she was doing. Sandra was secretive and didn't initiate them into the project she was carrying out behind a door that was both closed and locked. On the other hand, she fully agreed with what they had to say about her all-too-brief nighttime slumbers, though she didn't do anything about it. She worked until she fell into bed at night, and got up a few hours later to do it all over again.

There was the occasional break when she stopped by work for a while, mostly to check that everything was proceeding as it was supposed to, despite her absence. It seemed to be, and she delegated the responsibilities she would normally have covered to a couple of her closest colleagues. Everyone was sorry about what had happened and expressed their conviction that it would all turn out for the best. This was something Sandra doubted more and more, but she refused to give up hope.

In her thoughts, she was with Erik, talking with him, calming and comforting him. The fact that she couldn't physically share whatever he was experiencing with him made her feel like an inadequate parent. But the fictitious conversations brought him to life and that was what she needed to keep her spirits up. She felt his presence throughout her entire being, and while she was aware deep down that the feeling wasn't anchored in reality, she continued to tell herself that it was.

On Sunday evening, they received visitors in the form of the policeman Sandra had spoken to at Gråbo, just after Erik's disappearance. Sandra caught sight of him through the window and met him out in the street.

"My parents need to be kept out of this," she said in a low voice. "They're not aware of Jan Hallin."

"No problem," said the policeman.

"You absolutely mustn't contact him. Do you understand?"

"Absolutely. We've made that decision ourselves. We generally try to avoid precipitating rash responses from desperate people."

"It could be disastrous. At least wait another few days."

"That's what we're going to do," the policeman reassured her. "Sooner or later, we'll obviously have to question him, but at the current time we don't want to take any risks. If subjecting him to questioning would put Erik's safety at risk, then obviously we'll stick to watching Hallin from a distance."

"And you've been doing that?" Sandra wanted confirmation.

"We've had our eyes on Hallin for forty-eight hours now, but nothing suspicious has taken place."

Which was unfortunately more or less what Sandra had expected. If Hallin had had anything to do with the disappearance, she would probably have heard about it almost straightaway. At the same time she was grateful that the police had listened and had taken what she had said seriously enough that they had put Hallin under surveillance, so the knowledge that it hadn't paid dividends was crushing. He wasn't keeping Erik captive anywhere with the intention of handing him back if certain conditions were met or once enough time had passed—what he had done had already reached its conclusion. That was what common sense told her, but everything inside her was in tumult and she desperately wanted to believe something else.

The rest of the conversation took place with her parents in the kitchen, but nothing emerged that provided any relief. There was no trace of Erik, and despite the huge search effort they were none the wiser. Sandra was tempted to give in to her emotions and just scream, but that would have been letting go and giving up, and she couldn't allow herself to do that, even for one moment.

And now she was forced—despite all her promises and intentions—to contact Jan Hallin anyway. It was still too soon to drop him in it with the police completely, but she had to try and get hold of him. What else was she supposed to do? After all, doing the opposite would hardly help . . . Sandra knew that he was behind the threats, the sabotage, and Erik's disappearance. She couldn't just sit there and let something unthinkable take place. Unless it already had.

It was a desperate measure, but her tone of voice couldn't be allowed to divulge her desperation. She had to show despondency, but not rage. That was why she initiated the call in a controlled voice.

"I'd like to apologise for calling on your wife. It was stupid of me, and I'm genuinely sorry if it's caused any problems."

"Yes, you can be sure it has. Do you think you'll get any richer by getting my wife involved? Or do you think apologising will do it?"

"I don't want any money," said Sandra. "I've withdrawn my demands. You'll never hear about my son and never hear from me again."

There was a few seconds' silence, then sarcasm dripping in venom.

"That sounds just super. And not a moment too soon."

"On the condition that Erik shows up again, of course," Sandra said. "Alive."

"Erik?" said Hallin. "Who the fuck is that?"

Sandra didn't reply. She was perfectly sure he already knew the answer to that question.

"Oh, the son?" he said with clearly feigned surprise. "That sounds dramatic. Has he gone missing?"

Sandra could have sworn she could hear a smile in his voice. He was toying with her, but she didn't plan to give him the satisfaction of hearing her despair. She had to keep her cool and provide a calm and collected version of herself.

"It's about time we called a day on this," she said. "Just make sure he comes home."

Hallin laughed out loud.

"You're blaming me for the kidnapping?"

"Not at all. I'd just appreciate it that if you happened to bump into him you would please make sure he gets home safely."

Sandra took great care not to level any accusations. If he felt in the slightest bit threatened, there would be no incentive to cooperate. On the other hand, if he wasn't expressly identified then there was always a chance that Erik might simply turn up somewhere. Without the police necessarily having to suspect a crime. That was what she was gambling on right now. She was pursuing a secret agreement of sorts in which nothing was spelled out, but where both parties knew what was expected of them.

"I promise," said Hallin. "If I run into the boy, I'll put him on the first bus home."

His tone was one of gentle amusement, and that was frightening in itself. His wording suggested he had no specific plans to meet the three-year-old, which could mean it was all over. But Sandra couldn't give up this easily. This was her chance to influence the outcome, and she couldn't waste it.

"I swear I'll never bother you again," she said. "Or your wife. I'll never demand a paternity test, never demand child support, and never get the police involved in what happened four years ago. I haven't done so far, so why would I now? If the boy is found, then things will be for the best for everyone involved and the matter will be forgotten."

"Well, that's marvellous news," said Hallin with a warmth that felt anything other than genuine. "Then let me wish you and the boy the best of luck."

And with that the call was over.

The question was whether they had reached the desired arrangement, or whether he had simply put off the evil hour in his usual way. Unfortunately, it felt like the latter was the more probable of the two.

54

Jan

SINCE GUNILLA WORKED on Monday evenings, Jan had to eat dinner alone. That meant the menu was a little plainer than usual—instant mashed potato and tinned Pilsner sausages weren't what his beloved wife usually laid out on the table. Nevertheless, it tasted good and it took less than ten minutes to make. While he was eating, the phone call from Sandra resurfaced in his thoughts.

He couldn't have cared less about her accusations—they were just something she had reeled off for the sake of it. She had no idea what had happened to the boy, and the question was whether she ever would. According to the papers, the police had nothing to go on, and despite hundreds of volunteers joining the search they hadn't come even a millimetre closer to a resolution. And now seventy-two hours had elapsed, so it was no bloody surprise she was desperate.

She had been unable to hide her desperation, and even though she had tried to sound cool and businesslike, he could practically hear her heart beating like a piston hammer down the phone line when she withdrew her demands for child support. It must have hurt, given how infernally pigheaded she had been about that money. The fact that she had now given up that battle was yet another confirmation of how scared she was. An observation that he made with a degree of schadenfreude, he had to admit.

When it came to the boy, there had been a small degree of uncertainty at the very beginning. It had been possible that Sandra might lose her head entirely and tell the press and the police and anyone else who would listen how the boy had been conceived through rape, as she chose to describe it. But that kind of behaviour had still seemed unlikely, because—just as she herself had put it on the phone—why would she bring it up now when she had kept quiet for so long? And who the hell wanted to publicise that their firstborn son had been conceived through rape, as she put it? That he was unwanted? It would have been almost the same as saying that it didn't matter all that much if he didn't come back, and that would have been blown out of all proportion by the media.

Jan had shaken off pretty quickly his misgivings that the boy's disappearance would set those particular hares running. For good reason, it had turned out, given that the question of the boy's conception—there was only an outside chance of anyone considering that—hadn't been touched. There was nothing to worry about; on the contrary, most things were going Jan's way. Three days had already passed, and it was probably only the boy's nearest and dearest who hadn't given up all hope. And as far as Jan was concerned, a dead boy had two good qualities: he didn't need any child support and he didn't need a father. Two birds with one stone.

On the other hand, there was something else which had cropped up that—no matter how silly it seemed—concerned him just a little. At least it awakened his curiosity in a not altogether positive way. The ladies at work—who would gossip like mad as soon as they got a chance, usually by the coffee maker—had had a standing topic of conversation as of about a week ago whenever they were in the kitchenette. Since Jan, due to a lack of interest, hadn't been involved from the beginning, he wasn't completely up to speed about what was being discussed, but it seemed they all watched the same TV show or something. Jan didn't waste his time on that kind of thing; he was more interested in news and sports, especially right now, given the football World Cup was on.

They had been yakking on about this for a while, and everyone was super into it: which was most immoral . . . doing this or doing that? Did such and such place really exist? Have we ever heard of anything like that event? Did it work out in the end? Where did *he* go then? Might it be her, the dark-haired one? Do we know anyone called that—what if it's him? But was it *actually* a true story?—no, surely it must just be fiction?

And it had carried on gnawing away like that, every single day. "Ravine" was a frequently reoccurring word, but he hadn't paid much heed to it. He had also encountered the occasional "drunk driving" and "hit-and-run," but nothing more than that. When "rape" had become increasingly common in their conversations a few days later, he had begun to wonder what it was that had captured their interest so intensely. But he hadn't wanted to ask; he had hoped he'd figure it out by himself without anyone discovering that he too had begun to take an interest in this. Whatever it might be. But he hadn't been able to ascertain what, and soon enough he had become both impatient and a little bit worried.

Over the weekend he had therefore dug out the TV guide for the previous week and had scrutinised each and every channel every day all week—but nowhere had he been able to find anything that was even reminiscent of what he had overheard during the eager conversations in people's coffee breaks at work.

But then the chance had presented itself. Probably because for once he hadn't been standing to one side with his back turned, but was standing with them during their conversation and looked engaged. The engagement had been genuine, but the reason why was different than the one they might have expected—at least he had hoped so.

"You're following it, aren't you, Jan?" one of the girls had said, a craving for sensation shining in her eyes.

Jan had shaken his head a little hesitantly and looked quizzical.

"It's set here, among us," she had explained. "It's really fascinating, because it leads to so much speculation and so many questions."

"Here?" Jan had said. "On Gotland?"

She had confirmed that, which didn't feel one hundred percent okay, but he had maintained his mask.

"I guess this must be some TV series that you're all discussing so much?" he had said.

"No, it's a book," several people had said.

A book? Then surely it must have an ending? Or were they members of the same book club—maybe they were only allowed to read one chapter at a time or something?

"You *follow* a book?" he had said in confusion.

"We're talking about the summer serial, Jan."

He had remembered something from the summers of his childhood.

"On the radio, you mean?"

"No, in *Gotlands Allehanda*."

"Aha," he had said, stirring his coffee cup to ensure the feeling of discomfort gnawing at him wasn't visible. "Should I be reading it then?"

Everyone in the kitchenette had agreed that he should.

As soon as dinner was over, Jan locked himself in the study and found the first part of the serial online. The author was called Sting, who to Jan's knowledge was a British pop star. When he did a search on it, he didn't find any authors with that name, so he concluded it must be a pseudonym. Not exactly something that set his mind at ease.

Jan didn't normally read works of fiction, so it took him a while to get going. But once he got started, he was pretty quickly wrapped up in a description of a car accident that felt very familiar. It was depicted from several people's perspectives. One of which seemed reminiscent of his own.

It wasn't as bad as he had feared, and it was really time for him to go to bed now. But something kept him up. Where exactly was this going? Who were all these people that the reader got to follow? And what was it about this story that captured his colleagues to the extent that they couldn't stop talking about it?

So he downloaded more issues of the newspaper and read more chapters. The person who seemed a bit like him was no longer part of the plot, but it had to be assumed that it was he who had died in the crash. Instead, a lot of it was about some alky and her friends. Jan was truly sorry about the outcasts of society and their difficult situation, but he didn't know whether he was up to reading a whole book about their welfare.

So he brought his reading project to a close for the day, and, in Gunilla's absence, he spread out in their double bed.

55

Sandra

ON TUESDAY, the fourth day after Erik's disappearance, Sandra was so hyped up that she struggled to sit still. Her body protested—it needed to rest when it was awake, and above all else it needed to sleep at night. But she knew that if she stopped this work, if she allowed herself to sleep, she wouldn't be able to get up again. In that case she might as well lie down in bed and await the final news, and that would be akin to giving up.

She thought about Kerstin, who had also had to wait four days for something that would later turn out to be news of a death. Those days must have been unbearably long and comfortless, and Kerstin had been completely alone. Like Jeanette in a way, abandoned by the one she had otherwise shared her troubled times with. She had waited for days and weeks, experienced loving and longing, which then transformed into hatred; she had felt her body and soul breaking down, before finding out more than four years later that everything she had thought and felt had been wrong.

At least Sandra was surrounded by people who loved and cared for her, even if each and every one of them had their own suffering to contend with.

After having spent the best part of the night writing, she had to get some exercise and breathe some fresh air. It was raining again, but that didn't matter—the gloomy weather reflected her state of mind. Everything had gone to hell, and she only had herself to blame. The knowledge that it was her own stupid ideas and conclusion, her own naive approach that had put them all in this situation was a dreadful thing to live with.

She couldn't even bring herself to speculate how Erik was doing. Either he was alive or he wasn't—she didn't allow herself to go any deeper than that. Not right now, when she might run into someone else at any moment. She wanted to be alone in the dark when she unleashed that particular worry.

She pulled on her anorak and walked to work. It was very early in the morning, but there was always someone in the newsroom, no matter what time it was. The odd time of day meant she didn't risk running into more than one or two of her colleagues, which meant she would avoid having to endure all her colleagues' apologetic looks aimed at her at once.

It was just the head of news who was in, and he was tactful enough not to inquire after her emotional state. He settled for asking whether there was anything he could do, or anything new to report, but there wasn't. She glanced through the day's headlines and reviewed the pieces about Erik. She made sure that the serial was running as it was supposed to, and that it was being given the prominence it needed. Her eye settled on Kerstin's name, which reminded her that Kerstin had asked her a favour.

She couldn't remember what it was. Kerstin had rung at some point over the weekend, and she should probably have dealt with whatever it was sooner. But the days had merged into one, and nothing seemed all that important any longer. Oh yes, she reminded herself—the serial *was* important. Whatever the outcome of the awful thing that was happening just now, the book would avenge Erik. It would get redress for her, too, as well as for Kerstin and Karl-Erik. Jeanette and Peter Norling deserved to have their story told; not everything was black and white.

Peter Norling—that was it. Sandra had promised to find out whether he owned any properties, and that was no more difficult than checking up on him in the InfoTorg database. The head of news was already at his computer, so she asked him to do it for her. It was quick to accomplish—Sandra took a photo of the page of results and forwarded it to Kerstin. Then she set off home again to carry on writing.

She changed her mind en route however and decided that she wanted to see whether Hallin was really under surveillance with her own eyes. Maybe that policeman had never believed her, and had only been playing along to calm her down. Maybe they didn't have the necessary resources. And maybe they had called off the operation when the surveillance had turned up nothing. Or because there was no longer any hope of Erik being found alive.

Four hours, Sandra thought to herself. It was something she was sure she had heard in these situations. If the child wasn't found within four hours, the chances of doing so before it was too late minimised drastically.

It had been almost four days.

There were no cars on the street outside Hallin's house that might contain surveillance officers. Sandra preferred not to think that the policeman had lied straight to her face, but perhaps that was the way they dealt with unstable family members. Or perhaps they were busy curtain-twitching somewhere nearby, so well concealed that not even Sandra—who knew what she was looking for—could manage to spot them.

Then she remembered that what he had actually said was that they'd had eyes on Hallin for forty-eight hours without spotting anything suspicious. That didn't necessarily mean that they would incur the expense of another forty-eight hours of man-marking. They had probably done their jobs, but now the Hallin-trail had gone cold, and inquiries had been directed elsewhere.

Sandra felt winded, and she sat down on the kerb. She knew that it was Hallin who had staged the disappearance, but her theories didn't have enough credibility for the police to put everything else to one side. She knew that, and it was in a way understandable that they weren't listening too much to single points of view, but were instead justifying their methods on the basis of their experience. And if you thought about it, it might even be the right approach in this case, given that if Hallin hadn't behaved suspiciously then Erik was either dead or something else, entirely different from what Sandra imagined, had befallen him. The top priority was finding him, and Hallin didn't seem to have any plans to lead them to the right place.

That was what was going through Sandra's head as she sat there despairing, watching raindrops splatter onto the asphalt, creating trickles of water that combined to form torrenting streams gushing down the street. She felt a hand on her shoulder and looked up, thinking that it might be a police officer who had caught sight of her and was going to ask her to leave.

To Sandra's surprise, it was Hallin's wife, standing there in her dressing gown beneath an open umbrella.

"You shouldn't be sitting out here in the rain," she said. "Come inside and warm up over a cup of coffee."

"No," Sandra said in horror, standing up. "That's out of the question."

She had obviously seemed to be angling for it, sitting here in the pouring rain looking vulnerable. It wasn't even six o'clock yet—she'd not given a thought to the fact that someone might spot her from inside the house.

"I insist," the woman said with a smile, although at their last meeting she had not been particularly accommodating.

"Absolutely not," Sandra said firmly. "I was just leaving."

"But why did you come here? If you haven't got anything particular to do, I mean?"

"I . . ." Sandra began.

She couldn't think how she was going to get out of this. What on earth had she been thinking when she had sat down outside Hallin's house, of all places?

"I understand," said Gunilla Hallin. "You want to see Jan."

"No," Sandra countered. "I was just out and . . ."

That sentence didn't have a predetermined end to it either, but fortunately she was interrupted.

"I'm sorry for my behaviour last time we met. For slamming the door in your face. It was unnecessary. I don't have anything against *you* as such. It's Jan I ought to be angry with. *Am* angry with."

Sandra nodded with gritted teeth, mostly feeling self-conscious. She had no desire to even brush up against that subject, let alone discuss the presumed extramarital affair with the rapist's wife. The time when Sandra had thought that she could reach Hallin through his wife was over. The last—and only—attempt had resulted in disastrous consequences.

"I promised I would never look him up again," said Sandra. "And I intend to keep that promise, so I'll go now. I don't know how . . . I don't know why I ended up here. I'm sorry."

She nodded in farewell and started to walk away.

"I'm sorry about the thing with the boy," the woman called out behind her. "I hope it works out."

Sandra half-turned around to avoid seeming too obviously rude.

"Thanks," she said, half-jogging away from the embarrassing situation.

But something good might have come out of the unplanned meeting anyway, she thought to herself. Gunilla Hallin had received the message loud and clear that Sandra wasn't going to bother them again. Even if what had just happened wasn't the most successful example of Sandra's intentions in that regard. She could hardly have missed Sandra's despair as she sat there, either—staring emptily into space in the rain. That was something that in all certainty would reach her husband, with an implied wish that the boy would be released.

Just as long as it wasn't too late.

Four days of this suffering was an inconceivable period of time. Sandra didn't know how much longer she could cope. At the same time, she had brought this on herself. All she could do was stand there and take it, she thought to herself as the rain whipped her face. She had to hold fast until she died in battle.

56

Kerstin

KERSTIN WAS WOKEN by the sound of a text message arriving on her phone, which was lying on the nightstand. And she found to her delight that it was Sandra, who had pulled up the address of what had to be Peter Norling's hunting cabin. Other than his home and the summer house, it was the only property he owned—while he had been alive. Now it was probably considered Mrs. Norling's property.

She examined a couple of different maps and satellite images on her mobile and noted that the location was in the woods over towards Slite. It was some distance away, but there were buses going there. If they took their bikes with them on the bus, it looked like they'd be able to get pretty close to their target without having to trek an inordinate distance through the forest. She couldn't see any neighbouring properties, so it seemed in every regard the optimal place for housebreakers to work undisturbed. And they could leave their cleaning gear at home.

She called Jeanette and got her out of bed. She seemed to have scant interest, but that would sort itself out. They'd had a really nice time on the last occasion, even though Jeanette had taken it very badly in the few instances where something had reminded her too much of Peter.

And although they'd had to put their backs into it at times, Jeanette had largely remained in good spirits.

Kerstin guessed that there would be less work this time. Fewer knick-knacks, fewer household items—less stuff in general, given that the cabin was for hunters. She was picturing the odd hunting trophy on the walls, stuffed animals and birds, some majestic roebuck horns. Meagre supplies in the fridge and larder—just enough for hungry hunters to cook a bite to eat in a convivial setting. She imagined that beer tankards and schnapps glasses might have their own dedicated shelf.

It was probably a retreat just for men, it now occurred to her. That wasn't necessarily true, but she was pretty certain that efforts to achieve equality for women hadn't yet reached the point where they were represented to the same extent as men in hunting clubs around the country. And if looked at through cynical eyes, that might mean that Mrs. Norling rarely or never set foot there. This in turn led to the conclusion that it was a suitable location for a man needing to stash away six million stolen kronor intended for use by himself and his lover.

The odds were thus pretty good, although she would have to disregard the clouds heavy with rain that hung low over Gotland and had been there for several days.

THEY GOT OFF the bus just before ten o'clock and then used their bikes and Kerstin's mapping apps to make their way along increasingly narrow tracks in the forest. It transpired that they could have driven all the way up to the cabin—at least if they had had a car. They abandoned their bikes a little way into the woods, where the overgrown forest track leading to the cabin began. In order to be on the safe side, they left them behind the roots of a fallen tree and covered them in pine branches. In the unlikely event that anyone passed by, at least the bikes wouldn't give them away.

The fact that it was a hunting cabin and nothing else was unmistakable. It was a proper log cabin and at the gable end above the door there were half a dozen or so roebuck horns on shields made from a very dark wood. The house was set on a wild plot where just enough brush had been cleared to ensure that trees and bushes didn't completely take over, and to enable free access to the two smaller buildings also standing there. But it had to be years since anyone had done anything—probably more than four, at a guess.

After searching for barely a minute, they found the door key on top of a ledge and entered the house. The cabin itself was bigger than Kerstin had expected, including a small kitchen, a large common area with a dining table and chairs for eight, and a sofa suite around an open fireplace. On either side of the fire there was a door, behind each of which there was a bedroom with bunk beds for four people. Apart from the size, there wasn't much that differed from how Kerstin had pictured a hunting cabin. The hunting trophies were there, and there were a few candleholders—the decorative approach was otherwise not especially impressive.

It was dark and drab, and there was little in the way of natural light. The house appeared to be connected to the power grid, but Kerstin was wary about turning on the electricity. Against the odds, someone might catch sight of the light and wonder what was going on, and neither of them was in a position to deal with the consequences of being discovered. However, what they were searching for was so large in volume that they could hardly miss it due to poor lighting.

Even though they were in Peter's house, it didn't really contain anything that could be associated with him. No photos, no clothing, no handwritten notes, no nothing. In short, the house was impersonal, and that was probably a contributing factor to Jeanette's buoyant mood. The entire enterprise seemed exciting, and the rain pattering on the roof enhanced the thrilling sensation and created a new sense of relaxed intimacy between them.

They talked. About this and that and nothing in particular. Not like social misfits and addicts. Not like deadly enemies or people with suicidal tendencies. Just like two completely normal people. It was liberating.

Kerstin looked in the fridge, just to confirm her suspicions. No one had stayed here for several years—all that was to be found in the fridge was beer with a best before date more than three years ago. While Kerstin turned the kitchen upside down, Jeanette worked on the common space. Neither of them found what they were looking for, or anything else of interest. Not even in the chimney.

Then they tackled the bedrooms, the halls, the porch, and the veranda, and they even put a ladder up outside in the pouring rain so that they could check the loft in the roof, which had to be accessed from the outside. But nowhere did they find what they were looking for.

At around two o'clock they stopped for lunch and sat on the covered decking, shivering as the heavy rain drenched the forest around them.

57

Sandra

SANDRA WAS SITTING in her old childhood bedroom under the eaves, with her gaze fixed on a faded Spice Girls poster with greasy stains left by Blu Tack in the corners. It was three o'clock, and in a few hours' time the afternoon would turn to evening and then night. The fourth day would soon be at an end, and what would happen then? How much time had been assigned to the major police operation, how long would the volunteers keep up the search before their motivation began to falter?

Sandra realised that within the not-too-distant future, there would be no one searching any longer, and the investigation would end up in a box under someone's desk, awaiting new leads that would never emerge.

But they hadn't reached that point yet, she had to remind herself. It was the middle of summer and light practically 24/7, not counting the almost-black clouds darkening the sky and the persistent rain threatening to drown the whole island. To date, the conditions hadn't deterred the hundreds of remarkable people who had still gone out into the woods and countryside to search for Sandra's son. If *they* hadn't given up yet, then Sandra couldn't either—that went without saying.

And she had caught up. She had spent six weeks slaving over the book, writing in all her spare time, and now she had reached the present day. All that remained was to write what hadn't happened yet. Or hadn't become clear. The work she faced would demand less effort—a normal, fully achievable level of work—which she would pursue during her free time.

Tomorrow she would return to the office. She made that decision on the spur of the moment—she could no longer sit here doing nothing. She was needed at the newspaper, and she needed distraction from the never-ending wait for something that might never come. In the event that something happened during the day, she could note it in the evening—the book project would proceed as a diary project. For her own sake, and for Erik's.

The serial, however, would need to be drawn to a close before the summer ended. She needed to tie up the story somehow, so that any followers weren't disappointed. But there was plenty of time to work out how—the readers had only just passed midsummer in the story.

Sandra fell to thinking about Kerstin. Despite the fact that four days had passed since Erik's disappearance, Sandra hadn't informed her about what had happened. Partly because she didn't feel up to talking about it, but mostly because she felt in two minds about it all. On the one hand, they barely knew each other. She and Kerstin had never met. On the other hand, Kerstin knew more about Sandra—in some regards—than anyone else. Kerstin had been initiated into the project, and was helping with the fact-checking and other elements. Like finding the cash from the robbery.

Sandra was in a situation where she didn't need to take anyone else into account, but she still had pangs of guilt when it came to Kerstin. She felt disloyal. Kerstin had nudged the door to her innermost self ajar, and was now letting Sandra write about it in the newspaper—possibly with legal consequences for Kerstin. During their calls, Sandra had been driven to explain that she had been raped and by whom. But that was it.

Their original relationship was built on unilateral trust, but it had developed into so much more. They were pursuing a project together, working towards the same goal. And Kerstin's contribution was so great. If anyone had earned the right to her trust, it was Kerstin—Sandra owed her the full story, not just the crime report.

While Sandra was at home feeling depressed, Kerstin was out and about—together with her worst enemy—on the hunt for evidence for the investigation that would hopefully follow this entire episode. Completely ignorant of why Sandra hadn't gotten in touch or why she was dismissive and curt when she had.

Sandra felt that she could no longer keep Kerstin in the dark about this. It hadn't been a conscious choice from the beginning, and there was no particular reason to tell her now either, other than it being the right thing to do. And rather than sending a simplistic and unnuanced text message, she opted for the more personal approach: a phone call.

"How's it going?" she asked. "Have you found anything?"

"No," said Kerstin. "Not yet. But I have a good feeling about this place."

"There's something I ought to have told you," said Sandra. "A long time ago, actually. But it . . . I never did."

"Okay . . ." Kerstin said encouragingly.

"My son," said Sandra. "He's the result of the rape."

"I know that," Kerstin replied. "I read the papers just like everyone else."

Naturally. Kerstin didn't just read the parts of the text that Sandra had passed to her—she was reading all of it.

"Then you also know that when I found out who the rapist was thanks to your help, I made a less sensible decision," Sandra continued. "I contacted him and demanded he pay child support. On the quiet—I figured no one needed to know."

"Yes," said Kerstin. "But that was before we truly understood what he was capable of."

"Yes. And by then it was too late. He had already begun to threaten me, and now he's taken Erik."

"Erik?" Kerstin said with horror in her voice. "You mean it's your boy that . . . ?"

"Exactly," said Sandra. "I'm sorry I didn't tell you sooner, but things have been pretty turbulent. Obviously I should have told you at once."

"I'm so sorry, Sandra. I don't know what to say."

"You don't have to say anything—I just wanted you to know. Good luck with the search."

"We're just about to . . ." Kerstin said, but she didn't finish her sentence.

She was silent for a few seconds while collecting her thoughts.

"I was out searching for him over the weekend. Your Erik. Saturday and half of Sunday. I just thought you'd want to know that. Take care."

"Thanks," Sandra said, at a loss. But Kerstin was already gone.

The volunteers had a face now. Or a voice at least, Sandra thought to herself as tears formed in her eyes. Kerstin was there for her, even when she didn't know about it. Together with hundreds of other faceless people.

The world wasn't entirely ugly.

58

Jan

DURING THE SUMMER holidays, people were free to come and go from work more or less as they pleased without it causing any trouble, and Jan made sure that he took advantage of this on the odd occasion. Today was just such a day, since Sweden's knockout match against Switzerland was due to kick off at four o'clock. He didn't want to miss the prematch studio buildup, which was scheduled to start two hours before the game. And given there was barely anything to do at work there was little point in him sitting there twiddling his thumbs between lunch and the match. He stopped for his lunch break at half past eleven and headed home.

Gunilla was at the hospital, so he was able to settle down in peace and quiet at the computer and continue reading the summer serial while eating his sandwich. To begin with, he read without concentrating while his thoughts drifted off in all sorts of directions, but after just a few minutes he snapped to attention. There was something very familiar about the events being described. Jan decided to read it all again from the beginning.

This time he paid greater attention, and his sandwich lay untouched. Jan sweated profusely. It couldn't be true. Someone had written a book that was being serialised in *Gotlands Allehanda*, in which a person who bore a distinct resemblance to Jan Hallin was depicted as a rapist. What was more, it was done with such credibility that as he read it he instinctively took the side of the other party.

But that was just the beginning.

It transpired that immediately after the rape, the car crash, which he had read about the day before, had happened. The serious accident in which the driver in one car died after great and prolonged suffering. And the other car, which had avoided any harm, was being driven by the rapist. Who—given the fact he had just raped a woman nearby—decided to leave the scene.

All these similarities with Jan's own experience had to be coincidence. Yet his mouth was completely dry. Someone had woven together a believable and exciting story based on equal parts fact and fiction. There had been some details about the car accident in the local press, and the rape . . . Surely rapes took place on an almost daily basis? It didn't take much in the way of imagination to cook up a tale like that.

This was a story, he persuaded himself. With certain themes that happened to have things in common with something he himself had experienced. There was a lot that was wrong about the character that was reminiscent of him: name, places, car make, profession, to name but a few. That was probably true of all the other characters too, so what was there to say that *anything* at all was really factual in this account?

Nothing, of course. It was nothing but pure fiction. A socio-realistic figment of the imagination. But he still had to admit that some parts of this serial were awfully close to the truth.

He had to go into the kitchen and drink a glass of water. And another. He splashed some water on his face too—it was so bloody hot in here. Then he went back into the study and sat down at the computer again. He took a deep breath and continued reading.

Large swathes of the text—including the passages about the alky scum on the benches—didn't especially interest him, so he hastily skimmed through those. But there were other parts that engaged him far more, which he read with his heart in his mouth. No matter how much he wanted to, he couldn't stop reading. Jan downloaded issue after issue of the paper as he saw the story unfold on the screen in front of him with a rising sense of horror.

It turned out she was pregnant—the woman who had been raped. And she kept the child. Very soon, the man—the rapist, the hit-and-run driver—received a blackmail threat. A demand for the astonishing sum of six million kronor by way of support payments. How many people had received a letter like that? It didn't exactly feel like the amount had been plucked out of thin air.

A knot formed in his stomach and it felt as though the air in the room had run out. He had to go to the window and open it wide. Breathe air into his lungs. Convince himself that any correlations between that bloody serial and real life were just coincidence. After a few minutes, he felt strong enough to withdraw from the window and sit back down at the desk.

He didn't remain there for long—when he reached the bit about the hit-and-run driver realising that it was a passing acquaintance, a mechanic from his hunting club, who had witnessed the accident and therefore had to be the person who was blackmailing him for money, he was forced to rush into the kitchen and splash more water on his face.

And when shortly afterwards the hit-and-run driver cheerfully noted that the witness-slash-blackmailer had vanished from the face of the earth, it all got too much for Jan. He didn't need to read any more to realise that the book was a crucifixion of himself. He was not only being identified as a rapist, a drunk driver, and guilty of a hit-and-run, which was bad enough, but also as a murderer.

The writer had even got inside his head and knew his reasoning. It seemed so improbable, but there was no room for doubt that someone out there had knowledge of all these details pertaining to Jan and his actions that day and in the period afterwards. How on earth that was possible was a mystery, but there was no doubt as to who she was. The mere thought of her left him furious.

Judging by his colleagues' enthusiasm, this story had a lot of readers, and it would soon have even more. Because sooner or later someone was going to pick out Jan as the guilty man, and it was pretty likely the police would be brought in at the same time. But that hadn't happened yet, and the serial hadn't reached its conclusion.

He still had some time to get out of this. The football would have to wait.

59

Kerstin

SHE FELT PARALYSED after the call. Jeanette looked at her anxiously, hesitating whether to ask her what was wrong. But Kerstin forestalled her and explained with a sob in her throat that the missing boy everyone had been talking about was the son of a friend. Jeanette looked even more dumbfounded—she probably wondered what friends Kerstin had that she, Jeanette, wasn't aware of.

It had been four days since Erik's disappearance—four days of inconsolable waiting for Sandra. Kerstin knew what that was like and regretted the fact that she had disturbed Sandra with her phone call on Sunday. She had been able to tell from her voice that something was up. The money no longer seemed important now that a life was at stake. Kerstin knew that better than anyone. Six million was a small price for a human life. Whether it was Karl-Erik's, Peter Norling's, or Erik's.

Kerstin decided that she would rejoin the search party if it was still going the next day. It felt right to show her support to his loved ones—to show that there were still people who hadn't given up hope.

But the boy was three and a half . . . Even if it were possible to find him then he was probably dead.

It probably wouldn't be possible to find him. Peter Norling had been so well hidden that it had taken four years for him to turn up. A little child was even easier to hide.

She needed to push away the thoughts around this. They had gone to the trouble of coming all the way out here, and they weren't going to leave without having done their best. And Kerstin had a positive feeling in her gut. Not in terms of Erik, but in relation to the cash. If Norling hadn't got rid of the money the bags would be here. She just knew it.

As they were done with the house, they needed to tackle the outbuildings, despite the dreadful weather. They peered inside the larger of the two to start with. It turned out to be a slaughterhouse, with a water supply, hooks on the ceiling, a large stainless steel counter, and an impressive slicing machine. Kerstin left Jeanette in the slaughterhouse and went to the smaller of the two buildings, which seemed somewhat less comfortable to search. It was effectively a shed with an odour that Kerstin classified as fairly typical for a poorly maintained outbuilding. No one had been there in years.

Kerstin jerked open one of the two doors, behind which a wood store was concealed. The wood was stacked from floor to ceiling, and it was most certainly not a dream job to unload the logs to see whether anything had been hidden underneath them or behind them. However, it had to be done. First she wanted to see where the other door led.

She could have guessed: an outdoor privy. Which reminded her that rather than crouching in the pouring rain, she could use the loo. There was toilet paper too, so she would be sitting pretty, even if the smell in these kinds of places wasn't especially appealing.

That was what she thought to herself, but before she'd had time to pull down her trousers, it occurred to her what an ingenious hiding place an outhouse like this would be. Who on earth wanted to dig through human poo?

Only someone who knew what she was looking for, which Kerstin did. She promptly shelved her plans to relieve herself and instead went out into the rain to find a shovel. A broom. Anything that ensured she wouldn't have to go overboard in her enthusiasm to dig through excrement.

A floor scraper was what she eventually found, in the slaughterhouse with Jeanette. Plus a pair of gloves that would come in handy. She started by lifting away the bench containing the toilet seat, so that she had a better view of the two latrine tanks. She shone her mobile phone torch into both of them, but all she was able to conclude was that neither had been emptied in a long time. And that any holdalls there might be were not immediately obvious to the eye, which was hardly unexpected.

All she had to do was start digging. Or more precisely, rooting around in the tanks. Pressing the shaft of the scraper down into the shit. And there . . . Wasn't that something offering some resistance at the bottom, something of the wrong consistency that was elevated above the bottom of the tank? Despite the less than agreeable circumstances, she couldn't stop the smile that spread across her face.

But what was she supposed to do now? Lift up the entire tank and drag it into the woods to empty it? Or try to reach one of the handles of the bag—if that was what it was—and try to prise it out of there somehow?

She decided to go for the latter. Partly because it felt less hands-on and less disgusting in some way if she didn't have to grasp the tank, partly because it felt more respectful to the plot and its owner if she didn't empty a lot of shit onto the land.

However, it turned out to be more difficult than expected. The scraper itself was fairly weak, and threatened to break if she wasn't careful. What was more, all sorts of things splashed up out of the tank, making her realise that she had a solid task ahead of her. And it still ended with her having to stick her gloved hands into the excrement, before searching for a handhold and pulling the bag out by hand.

It was definitely a bag. Carefully wrapped in a black bin liner. Whether it was the right bag was something she would find out when she was outside and could get rid of the gloves. She opened the door with her foot and threw the package out into the rain.

Since it seemed unnecessary to make a mess twice, she thought she might just as well do the same thing with the next tank. Shortly thereafter, she heaved out another black bin liner with something inside it that definitely felt like a holdall, which she also threw outside.

She reached for the floor scraper, threw it outside as well and shouted for Jeanette.

"Jen!" she cried out. "Come here, I think I've found the cash!"

Then she turned around and went back inside, sinking to her knees while she attempted to get the bench back into position. Even though she was filled with anticipation about the contents of the two black packages, she took her time restoring order while she was still wearing the gloves. The bench was awkward—it had been easier to get it off than it was to put it back—but eventually she managed to fit it in between the walls and apply pressure so that it levelled out.

Odd, she thought to herself as she stood up. Why hadn't Jeanette answered? Why hadn't she come running? Kerstin shoved the door with her shoulder, ready to tackle the bags and then finally throw the gloves onto the grass.

60

Jeanette

JEANETTE HAD GOT her hands really dirty, and felt the need to get the worst of it off, so that she didn't leave conspicuous handprints on everything she touched. Unfortunately, she discovered that the water supply in the slaughterhouse was off, and decided to go outside to get clean. There was hardly a water shortage in the great outdoors.

She had been planning to rub herself clean in the wet grass outside the door but then she caught sight of a rainwater barrel by the wall of the hunting cabin, so she ran over to it at a crouch. Just as she put her hands in the water, she heard Nanna shout from over by the loo.

"Jen!" she cried. "Come here, I think I've found the cash!"

Was it that simple? Jeanette thought to herself. Some half-baked ideas about where the money might be, a couple of days' searching, and they were safely into port. And with what, exactly? What was going to happen to the money? And to Jeanette?

But it had been pretty good fun while it lasted, she told herself as she dried her hands on her trousers. The search. Now it was over and everything would go back to the same old misery.

She didn't get any further than that in her thoughts before she stopped mid-movement. She had taken one step towards the privy before spotting the headlights over by the drive up to the cabin. Then she heard the rumbling of the car engine through the din of the rain.

It was impossible. A car in the middle of the woods in this weather. At a hunting cabin no one had set foot in for ages. And just when they were engaged in what could only be described as a burglary, even if the intended loot wouldn't be missed by anyone.

Jeanette had no intention of being discovered, so she took a step back and curled up behind the rainwater barrel. Things looked less good for Nanna, who had just cried out in joy over all the money she had found. It had to be assumed she didn't want to go to prison either.

But there was still the hope that the driver of the car hadn't heard Nanna's joyous outburst through the noise of the rain on their windscreen and the engine—and maybe the air vents on full blast too. What seemed more troubling was that Nanna would wonder why Jeanette wasn't answering, why she hadn't come to her, and that she might come marching straight out of the privy with the two bags in her hands.

Which was tantamount to stepping straight into the spotlight cast by the car while holding six million kronor that could hardly be considered hers.

61

Kerstin

SHE MANAGED TO close the door just as quickly as she had opened it. With her disgusting gloves on, but still.

There was a car coming up the drive to the hunting cabin.

Given the speed with which she vanished back into the out-building, Kerstin didn't manage to see the driver's face behind the rain-spattered windscreen with its frenetic wipers working away. She hadn't had time to think; all she had known was that this encounter was not allowed to happen.

Was that why Jeanette hadn't replied when she had shouted for her? Because she had seen or heard the car? Kerstin hoped that was the case and that she had managed to take cover without being seen. Anything else would be a disaster. Jeanette would be unable to deal with a meeting with a stranger in these circumstances. She was barely capable of taking care of herself, let alone acting instinctively and intelligently in a rapidly unfolding situation like this one. She would break down and give the wrong answer to all the questions.

If there were even any questions to be asked.

Because who had any business being right here, right now, having come down those small, winding, remote tracks in the pouring rain? Certainly not Peter Norling's widow. She hadn't taken the trouble in over four years, so it was hardly likely she would choose today of all days to have a clear out and get the place sorted.

No, it was to do with the money—it had to be. And here was Kerstin hidden away in the outdoor privy at Peter Norling's hunting cabin, with shit up to her elbows and two big bags neatly packaged in black plastic lying on the grass outside.

Would she have time to get away? Not with the money, that was for sure—but would she have time to run into the woods without it? She carefully nudged the door open a crack once again. No, it wouldn't work. The driver was opening the car door. They stepped into the rain. Directed their steps straight towards Kerstin. Straight towards the two filthy pieces of luggage she had heaved out of their hiding places.

It was a matter of seconds before the door would be thrown open and it would all be over. Several people had already died for the sake of this cursed money—Kerstin would be no exception.

She pulled her mobile out of her trouser pocket and did the only thing she could do.

62

Jan

JAN GOT OUT into the rain and looked around anxiously. Clearly no sane person would be out in this weather. But the realisation that he was now the man on everyone's lips had driven him to look over his shoulder, even if most of his fellow human beings hadn't realised it yet. It was only a matter of time. How had things gone this far?

It was a very painful discovery. Especially the thought of what was to come when his friends, neighbours, and colleagues found out about the disaster that he had caused for everyone involved. Not least his own children, who would definitely pull away from him. He had brought shame and disgrace to his family. The children didn't know that yet, but they would suffer too. Who wanted a father who had gone from being a successful environmental expert to a criminal in the space of an afternoon?

And who wanted a husband like that? Gunilla had already dealt with her own shared misery but had fortunately still not given up all hope in him. They had far too much in common, too many memories that would always be theirs, no matter how this turned out. That was why she was sticking it out—he had known that for a long time.

His shoes squelched and he could feel the water penetrating through the stitching, but he didn't care. Instead, he remembered how Gunilla had looked at him on that terrible January afternoon in 2014 when he had come home unhappy and anxious. She knew him and could tell how he was feeling. The days had passed and she had become happier, keeping pace with him becoming happier. Until that newspaper article had been published about the man who had died in the awful single-vehicle accident. Jan hadn't quite been able to conceal his reaction when he had read it, and Gunilla had probably guessed what was going on in his head. But had she held him accountable? No. She had most likely asked herself what he had been doing in such a remote place at such an odd time. A woman, obviously. It wouldn't have been the first time. But there were no questions, no accusations. She respected and loved him for the man he was, despite his faults and shortcomings.

A few days later, she was just a few metres away from him in the kitchen when he had opened that letter. He had thought it looked like an invitation to a party, but quickly discovered that the contents were far from what he had expected. He had begun to sweat and sank onto a chair. It hadn't passed her by, but she had returned to her household chores without comment. Jan had weighed up the situation and then withdrawn to the study where he had examined the photographs with a magnifying glass. This had led to an underdeveloped idea about who had witnessed the accident and was now blackmailing him for money. When dinner was ready, Gunilla had appeared in the study. She had obviously been aware that he wasn't himself and had asked about the letter. Caught off guard, he had been unable to do anything but seek help in her eyes. That was what you did if you loved someone that much—you looked to each other for support and you got it.

A normal man in a normal relationship would have denied all knowledge of those pictures from the scene of the accident until he was blue in the face. He would have claimed they were faked or taken out of context. But not Jan. He had been candid with his wife.

That girl he had given a lift home from XL-Bygg, he had said. He had even helped her carry all her things inside, even though it was late and he really needed to get back to work. She had tried to pay for his petrol, which was adorable in a childish sort of way—as if he needed financial compensation for going a little out of his way into the countryside to help a fellow human being. So, naturally, he had declined. Instead, she had suggested a cup of coffee and a snifter of something stronger.

A snifter was perhaps not what he had been expecting—young people these days were so proper and health conscious. They went to the gym and did yoga and cycled to work and did bootcamps and played padel tennis, or whatever the hell it was called. But she had got out the whisky bottle, which was in itself scarcely a surprise given that she was quite clearly boycotting the health craze. She had insisted on topping him up once and then twice—granted, just a few drops each time, but still—and he had accepted out of pure courtesy. When all was said and done it didn't matter anyway, given that the modest intake from lunch was long gone from his system.

Completely unexpectedly, she had launched a passionate charm offensive, suggesting that she ought to thank him properly for the lift. It wasn't exactly how he had pictured this side excursion panning out, but given his fondness for the flesh, he had fallen into the trap.

Then she had suddenly changed strategy and played hard to get. She had said no, all the while smiling and flirting in that tender voice. It had quickly transpired that what she was really after was a firmer touch, to full-on indulge in that Stone Age instinct some girls had—the inclination to be dragged back into the cave by their hair to succumb to a wild beast of a man. One thing had led to another, and there was no doubt that she had liked it. Without a shadow of a doubt, this woman had a powerful sex drive—nymphomaniac was not too strong a word to use in this context.

And then when he had left to go back to work, the road had been as slippery as an ice rink. He had driven carefully, just as he usually did—even more carefully than usual in fact, precisely because he knew there might be people out on the roads who were less practised drivers using worse tires. This had turned out to be true sooner rather than later. A minute or so after that he had encountered a madman driving straight towards him, who—in an insane attempt to avoid a head-on collision—had put his foot on the brakes, skidding on his worn-out tires. You hardly needed a Nobel Prize to predict that. And he had plunged straight over the edge into the ravine.

"I saw the wreck and knew the driver was dead," Jan had said, by way of excuse. "Was I meant to climb down into the ravine to check something I already knew?"

"It wouldn't have changed anything," Gunilla had agreed.

"I should have called emergency services. Anonymously, if nothing else."

"Of course you should have, but he would have died anyway."

"He wouldn't have spent hours there suffering before he did," Jan had noted unhappily.

"I doubt he suffered, sweetheart. He probably lost consciousness on impact."

Jan had been distraught, but Gunilla had stroked his back and relieved him of his burden of guilt. She appreciated his honesty, and was big enough to accept that people—even Jan—were rarely infallible.

And it had all settled down, Jan noted as he lumbered forward in the rain. The agitation had levelled out, thanks to the rock in his life that was Gunilla. Since that occasion she had never mentioned one word about the trying experience that he—both of them really—had been through. No stray words, no insidious looks, no bitter reproach, and no self-pity. She had taken him for the person that he was, forgiven him and moved on.

For four long years. Until this spring when that girl—Sandra—had turned up out of nowhere and stirred up old emotions. Called Jan a "rapist" and claimed that he was the father of her child. A child he would never get to meet—whom he truly had no desire to meet—but that she still wanted him to pay child support for. She had threatened to involve the authorities and the police, which he regarded as a veiled threat to file a report about the rape. For what it was worth, he strongly doubted she would be able to get over the finishing line with that, given the time that had passed, but he really did not want to draw the police's attention to where he had been at the time of that confounded car accident.

As some kind of initial first step in her terror campaign, she had been planning to tell his wife about that brief and transient moment of infidelity. He had told her from the start that this would be no use—since Jan and his wife kept no secrets from each other. It was the truth, albeit modified, but Gunilla undeniably knew most of what had happened that afternoon with Sandra.

What was worse was that in the heat of the moment, he had also dropped some comment along the lines that things hadn't gone well for the last person who had tried to blackmail him. It seemed stupidly premeditated now that the bitch was writing a book in which he was accused of murder. As a guy who murdered blackmailers, to be precise.

But that statement hadn't had the intended effect either—soon enough this Sandra had made good on her threat to get his wife involved. The sexual act itself hadn't been news to Gunilla, but the fact that it had resulted in a child was something she hadn't taken as well as Jan had hoped she would. She had been very upset, and even though she hadn't had the slightest desire to serve up almost seven hundred thousand kronor, she had stepped up to defend Sandra and made Jan feel ashamed.

So much so that he had been forced to admit to himself that he actually wanted the boy gone from the face of the earth. So that he didn't have to deal with paternity tests, demands for child support payments, and rape reports, and all that this involved. And all the other misery that as sure as fate would come along too.

But now, with something akin to an answer key in her hands, it was the mother of the brat who seemed to be the biggest threat. Who would have guessed she would write a book about what had happened more than four years ago? That she would have such an improbable amount of knowledge about what had happened even after the so-called rape that she could write a whole fucking book about it? A book that was being serialised in *Gotlands Allehanda*? And all while she was still nagging at him for the bloody child support, threatening him with this and that. When the worst that could happen was already happening—he was being dragged through the mud in public, being pilloried before all of Gotland.

The very fact that she had the stomach to do it—it made him feel sick just thinking about it. He wished so hard that he had spotted that serial while it was still in its infancy.

The widespread public interest in the publication would probably get the odd police officer and prosecutor to raise their eyebrows, and soon enough the circus would be in full flow. Which would inevitably result in a personal catastrophe for Jan.

What he wanted most of all right now was for anyone who had read even just one instalment of that serial to be hit by anthrax. For the *Gotlands Allehanda* offices to be blown to kingdom come, for the printers to burn down to the ground. But above all, he wanted the person who was responsible for all these dreadful attacks, the one behind the slanderous campaign and its unpredictable consequences, to die. She needed to die a slow, painful death.

In short, he wanted Sandra dead, Jan thought to himself, rain running down his face as he pulled back the bolt on the cellar door.

63

Jeanette

JEANETTE HARDLY DARED breathe as she sat there squashed behind the rainwater barrel with her arms tightly wrapped around her legs. She listened intently for any sound, but all she could hear was the incessant thud of the rain on the ground and the trees, water forming into trickles running into the soil, gushing down the drainpipe, and making the barrel overflow. Beyond that, what she was expecting to hear were other sounds from over by the privy: voices and the door slamming.

But she didn't. Since the car door had been slammed shut, there had been silence from that direction. The driver didn't seem to have spotted Nanna, who in turn must have spotted the car in time to shut the door and her mouth. The driver's business wasn't in the outhouse, but somewhere else on the plot—probably inside the cabin itself.

But if that was true then wouldn't she have heard *that* door slam? Had they locked up behind themselves? she thought to herself. Had they hidden their belongings and the leftovers from the packed lunches they had eaten on the veranda? No, of course they hadn't. They weren't finished here and they had been planning to tidy up and shut everything up as the last step before leaving.

At least the front door *was* shut, and that was some small comfort if all the driver was doing was quickly inspecting the exterior. Perhaps the hunting cabin was going to be sold, now that Peter was out of the picture? Perhaps it was a stranger who had come to visit, an outsider who wanted to check out the plot and the buildings ahead of a viewing of the interior, and didn't care a jot about unwelcome visitors or the two bags filled with cash.

Now she could make out the sound of someone moving across the sodden grass with squelching but determined footsteps. It was clear that they were heading away from Nanna and towards Jeanette. She hardly dared to look, let alone lean out to catch a glimpse of the mysterious visitor.

What if she needed to sneeze? Cough? She couldn't, quite simply. Not now. Why was she even thinking like that? It would only become a self-fulfilling prophecy—and now she suddenly felt the urge to cough even though she hadn't at any point during the day.

A smoke, she thought to herself instead. She was dying for a drag. Now. Surely no one would notice if she sparked up in this weather?

Nanna would go round the twist if she knew what Jeanette was up to, how nuts she was, and how little self-control she had.

She spotted a movement between the rainwater barrel and the wall. Somewhere further off on the plot, beyond the crack. All she could see through that gap was part of the back of the slaughterhouse unless she bent forward from behind the barrel, which would give her away to anyone paying attention.

What on earth was going on? There was something behind the slaughterhouse, something at ground level that seemed to capture the interest of the visitor. Of course—it was a root cellar that she and Nanna would have checked last of all. Bolted from the outside but without a lock. It was probably full of garden spiders and other nasties that liked being in the darkness.

Jeanette didn't seem to be alone in those thoughts. After sliding back the bolt and standing there as if in contemplation for about half a minute without pushing the door open, it was apparently time for the visitor to leave the root cellar behind. And the place as a whole. Less than a minute after the squelching steps had once again passed by Jeanette's water barrel, the car door slammed again. Then the engine was started up and the car left.

Without anything much at all having happened.

64

Kerstin

KERSTIN HELD HER breath as she stood there, counting the seconds, but the door to the privy never opened. After a while, she realised that the visitor must have turned right in front of the car, changed course from one that appeared to be heading straight towards her, and instead headed into the yard between the cabin and the out-buildings. Shortly afterwards, when she dared to nudge the door ajar, her suspicions were confirmed. There was no one to be seen between the car and herself.

If it hadn't been raining, she might have been able to hear something and form an understanding of what the visit was for. Given the situation, she could only be grateful that she hadn't been discovered, hope for the best on behalf of Jeanette, and dutifully wait in the darkness until the visitor had left again. Preferably without taking any interest in the two stinking packages outside the privy door.

Her prayers were answered, and faster than she dared hope. Just a few minutes after the visitor's arrival, Kerstin, who was significantly more attentive now, heard the engine start back up, before the car reversed into the yard to turn around, and then the sound grew ever more distant. Only then did she open the door and step into the rain.

She glanced at the two plastic-wrapped bundles that were begging for attention, reached for the floor scraper and turned them over with the intention of letting the rain play its part before she got to grips with them. Then she tore off her gloves, dropped them on the grass and headed over to the slaughterhouse, calling out for Jeanette—who made herself known when she peeked up from behind a barrel brimming over with rainwater.

Kerstin struggled to contain her laughter when she caught sight of her. Jeanette looked as though she had taken a dip in the barrel without permission and been caught in the act.

"Oh my sweetheart," Kerstin exclaimed compassionately. "Did you end up hidden round the end of the house?"

Jeanette nodded and looked like she was about to burst into tears.

"And the water was overflowing and I was about to sneeze and cough and it was just terrible," said Jeanette. "I thought I was going to give us away."

"But you didn't," said Kerstin, rinsing herself off in the water barrel. "You did a great job. Come on, let's get you into some dry clothes. Then we'll take a closer look at those bags."

"We need to check the root cellar first," said Jeanette. "It was so weird . . . The only thing that person did was to slide back the bolt on the door."

"Without opening it?" said Kerstin.

"Without opening it. They hesitated for a while, then went back to the car. That was all I could see through the crack between the wall and the water barrel."

"What a bizarre thing to do," Kerstin said thoughtfully. "Coming all the way out here just to undo a bolt."

"Without even noticing our leftovers on the veranda," Jeanette pointed out.

That was something that hadn't occurred to Kerstin in her minutes of horror spent in the outhouse. They had left truly obvious evidence of their presence. Under normal circumstances those would have disclosed the presence of intruders on the property. But the circumstances were anything but ordinary, she noted to herself. The visitor hadn't noticed their cups or backpacks on the veranda, or the black bin liners outside the privy. They weren't really in the here and now, and had been focusing on something else entirely. They had headed towards the root cellar, undid the bolt, and then departed without doing anything else.

What a weird thing to do, Kerstin muttered to herself. And then she was struck by a peculiar and almost panicky feeling in her chest that made her set off at a run towards the root cellar door without any clearly formulated thoughts or words. Jeanette was on her tail, and together they raised the heavy hatches and threw them to one side. Kerstin pulled out her mobile, turned on the torch and descended the steps into the subterranean space. She shone the light around the chamber. It was bare and uninviting, and lined with rickety shelves without any sign of any food. It was raw and damp down here, water trickling down the walls to form large puddles on the floor.

But there, at the far end in the darkness by the wall there was something lying on the floor that didn't look like it belonged there. She moved closer to it and gasped when she realised what she was looking at.

A little boy in blue jeans, a red sweatshirt, and green boots.

"It's Erik!" Kerstin cried out at once, throwing herself forward to gather him up in her arms.

He was cold, wet, and loose-limbed. It was impossible to tell whether there was any life left in the boy, but Kerstin just ran. Up the steps and into the light and rain. Jeanette proved herself to be unusually efficient in the situation and ran ahead towards the house, tearing open the door and wedging it wide open, before rushing inside with her muddy boots on. She went over to the sofa where she spread out a blanket.

"Lay him down there," she ordered Kerstin. "Take his clothes off and I'll fetch more blankets."

Kerstin did as she was told: she removed his boots, trousers, jumper, and underclothes with furious speed. Everything was cold and wet.

"Lie down with the boy in your arms," Jeanette said. "I'll wrap you up in blankets. If he's alive then he needs your body heat."

Kerstin had no medical knowledge and no clue what she was supposed to do, but now that she was lying with the naked, cold little body close to her own she could feel that he was breathing. It was fast and shallow, but he was breathing. While Jeanette wrapped them in the blankets, Kerstin massaged him as best as she could, kneading his small limbs and the little back with her rough hands, exhaling warm air onto his face and his throat.

"He's alive," said Kerstin. "Call emergency services."

Jeanette made the call and explained the gravity of the situation, explaining that it was probably the missing boy. With Kerstin providing prompts, she described where the hunting cabin was and the easiest way to get there. She asked for instructions, but was directed simply to keep the child warm and to get him to drink fluids if it were possible.

Once the call was over, Jeanette went to fetch water. She bathed the boy's lips and then forced one drop of water after another into his mouth as best she could. To her relief, Kerstin felt the temperature rising in the small child's body, his breathing becoming deeper and slower.

"He must be famished," Jeanette said. "But they'll put him on a drip as soon as they arrive. It'll be okay—we saved him."

A small smile appeared on her face, and it was infectious. They—Kerstin and Jeanette—had done something together. They had saved the life of a small child—how would Kerstin be able to see Jeanette as an enemy after this?

Four days, she thought to herself. Didn't they say that a fully grown adult could manage three days without water? And Erik—a little kid—had managed four. Four days of constant rain.

"If it hadn't been raining so persistently over the last few days, he wouldn't have made it," she said. "The kidnapper didn't count on all that water leaking into the root cellar. Erik was wet and cold, but he didn't go thirsty, and that's what kept him alive."

Rage germinated inside her. Only now did she have the opportunity to think through what had actually happened. Someone—and she reckoned she knew who—had spirited away a three-year-old and locked him up in a cold, dark root cellar without any food or water. With the intent that he would die—of thirst and hunger. A little kid! What kind of monster were you if you subjected another person—a very small person—to something like that?

"The kidnapper?" said Jeanette.

"What do you think the purpose of undoing the bolt was?" said Kerstin.

"You mean . . . Do you actually think someone intentionally locked him in there four days ago so that he would die?" Tears began to form in Jeanette's eyes.

"And now they came back to undo the bolt in the belief that it was all over and people would think he had wandered in there by himself," Kerstin said with a nod.

The thought that the kidnapper hadn't even dared to see for himself the misery he had caused—he had simply left without glancing into the cellar—left her raging. But she contained the agitated emotions within her, pursed her lips, and kneaded the boy's body with almost manic eagerness.

"There are a few things you need to do, Jeanette. Before the ambulance gets here. And probably the police too."

"Yes?"

"I want you to tidy up after us. Close doors, remove any visible traces that we were ever here. I should have done it myself, but it would be good if you could wipe up a bit inside the privy. The door, the bench, the floor, the walls—well, you'll see what I mean. Use the gloves. But first of all, you need to drag those bags down to our bikes. Leave them in the plastic, but put them there and hide them well. You can take the branches that are covering the bikes—we don't need to hide those any longer."

"Respectfully, I don't give a shit about the money," said Jeanette.

"I know that, Jen. But it'll come in handy very soon, and if the police find it here with us, then things won't work out the way we planned. Believe me."

Jeanette looked at her incredulously but shrugged her shoulders in resignation. She glanced tenderly at the boy, who was moving slightly in Kerstin's embrace. Perhaps he was resurfacing from unconsciousness.

Kerstin extracted her mobile from her pocket, thinking to herself that she should call Sandra and tell her that they had found Erik—if the news hadn't reached her yet. But she had no signal.

"Emergency calls only," said Jeanette.

"It worked an hour ago," Kerstin objected. "I received a call."

"But now it's emergency calls only. Same for me. You've got to be grateful for the little things."

"Little things?" Kerstin said with a smile. "The only thing that matters at all, if you ask me."

Jeanette nodded and smiled back at her, before resuming a serious expression.

"What exactly are we doing here?" she asked.

At first, Kerstin didn't understand what she meant. She dipped her fingers in the glass of water on the table and tried to get the boy to suck at them. Jeanette had her arms crossed and was looking at her lying there with anxious eyes that were imploring. Now she realised what the question meant.

"We're on a bike ride," Kerstin replied. "We stumbled on this seemingly abandoned place, sought shelter from the rain and decided to eat our lunch out on the covered veranda. I needed a shit, and I took the chance to use the outdoor privy. Then we saw a car turn up and you hid behind the end of the house. And so on. After that, we'll stick to the truth. Okay?"

"Okay. I'll get on then. How is he doing?"

"He's breathing, and his temperature is rising. He'll be okay. Thanks to you, Jen."

"Thanks to me?"

"It was you who noticed the weird thing happening over by the root cellar."

Jeanette pursed her lips and something flashed through her eyes. Then she left the house, walking more lightly than she had done in a long time. Perhaps this was the opportunity she had been waiting for, over the course of more than four years. An opportunity to do something right, once and for all. To compensate for everything she had done that had been so very wrong.

Kerstin smiled to herself and made the decision she had been tussling with for such a long time.

Jeanette was forgiven.

65

Sandra

AN HOUR LATER, she was still sitting there with her eyes glued to the faded picture of her childhood idols. She was unable to move, incapable of forming coherent thoughts, and she didn't have it in her to face her parents. She wanted to be left alone with her torments, wanted to be able to turn on the waterworks at any time without an audience. But she wasn't even capable of crying. She was sitting there seemingly paralysed into silence—all she could hear were the seconds dragging by on her wristwatch.

Until the quiet was disturbed by the rattle of her mobile on the nightstand.

Then a stream of elusive events that she would never remember clearly or be able to return to. Sandra answering out of habit in a flat, indifferent voice. The kind voice telling her that Erik had been found and was alive—he was on his way to Visby General Hospital. Sandra, unable to assimilate any further information, already on her feet before the call was over, grabbing things that might be needed during the coming night. She tore through the house, brought her sorrow-stricken parents back to life, and suddenly the house was filled with light and sound and movement. And joy that knew no bounds, that could no longer be contained out of fear for the consequences and aftermath. Because what was the point in worrying about the future when the miracle was happening here and now?

66

Kerstin

EVENTUALLY, THE AMBULANCE arrived. There was nothing wrong with their directions, it turned out. Apparently, they had opted for an air ambulance, realised it was impossible to land anywhere nearby and instead dispatched an ordinary vehicle all the way from Visby. It took forty minutes from their call until the paramedics arrived and took over.

Kerstin explained that the boy had been cold when they had found him, but that the temperature in the small body had since risen, and that his breathing now seemed substantially more stable. She also explained that they had managed to get him to take fluids drop by drop, but that he had probably been drinking rainwater over the preceding days and that hunger would probably be the bigger issue. The ambulance crew listened with great interest, and both women were treated respectfully in light of their actions.

That quickly changed with the arrival of the police. They had their routine down pat and knew who was upstanding and who wasn't—perhaps they actually recognised the two women from less flattering circumstances. Kerstin in particular—but also Jeanette to some extent—was met with nothing but suspicious looks.

Their statements were questioned, as were their motives for being at the scene at all. Which was entirely justified, it had to be added, given that their original purpose for visiting was decidedly dubious. But they stood their ground and told the story about the mysterious visitor several times without once getting the impression that what they had to say was being noted.

How had they got into the cabin? They had found the key on the ledge above the door. Just like that? Yes, the law of necessity—the break-in itself was surely excusable given that they had saved the life of a child. Someone had clearly locked the kid into the root cellar and had then come out here just to undo the bolt? Yes, that was how it seemed. And this someone was driving a car? Yes, a blue car—an Audi at a guess. What about the driver—man or woman? Impossible to say; they had both been squirreled away in their hiding places and had seen almost nothing. Why had they hidden if they had nothing to hide? Well, they did have something to hide since they had trespassed on someone else's property and didn't want to be discovered.

Not even the fuzzy picture that Kerstin had managed to take of what she wanted to believe was a blue Audi and its driver was taken seriously by the police. Pulling the wool over their eyes, they said—and why on earth had she even taken the picture? Had she already had a feeling that something wasn't right before everything else happened? And wasn't it actually the case that they themselves had held the boy captive, and had now at long last decided to release him? No, no, and no again. Then they would hardly have done what they had done, and they would definitely have abandoned the scene before the ambulance arrived.

No one wanted to hear that angle. Kerstin did what she could to defend her own and Jeanette's behaviour. Everything they said was received with scepticism, but then they were navigating through a thicket of half-truths and lies. And their own appearance counted against them. Kerstin was marked forever by the life she had led, Jeanette not so much—but the glassy-eyed uncertainty in her appearance and the fact that she was in the company of Kerstin told its own, clear story. Neither of them could be taken seriously, no matter how great a role they had played in the recovery and rescue of the boy.

However, eventually they were allowed to go, under strict instructions that they should stay at home while they were the subject of further inquiries. Two chastened castaways trotted downheartedly towards their bikes in the woods. They pulled away the branches, tore off the plastic and threw it to one side. They checked the contents of the two holdalls and their eyes met in a smile, before they each slung a bag over their shoulders and cycled away from what had become a crime scene. Six million kronor richer.

IT WAS ONLY once they were on the bus with their hands clasped around the bags that Kerstin noticed that the expression on Jeanette's face had changed. Despite the harassment from the police, there had been an air of exhilaration about her entire being since they had found the boy—a feather-lightness to her movements. Kerstin interpreted it as a form of redress—that Jeanette had been vindicated in her own self-perception. She had contributed to a big, important event: a child's life had been saved, and Jeanette had been involved. Not all children died in her arms—this time she had been *able* to do something and she had done it, too. And with remarkable decisiveness and command.

But now the darkness had crept back over her—the hollowness in her gaze had returned and Kerstin didn't understand why. She tried to read her facial expressions and patterns of movement to discover what was going on inside her, but Jeanette turned her back to her and directed her gaze out of the window. Kerstin was tempted to put her hand onto Jeanette's and ask how she was feeling, but she thought that could wait until she shifted position and wasn't making it quite so clear that she wanted to be left in peace with her thoughts.

Around ten minutes passed, and Kerstin could feel the anxiety spreading through her body. Now and then, she glanced at Jeanette but without getting the response she was looking for. Judging by her breathing, she was still awake, yet she didn't make the slightest motion to seek contact. They were a duo now—they had surpassed themselves and not only found the money but also saved Erik's life—what had gone awry? The thoughts continued to grind away in Kerstin's head, and the situation began to feel unbearable.

She followed the contours of Jeanette with her gaze, her finely shaped ear and the hair, which, despite being wet and tangled, still fell so beautifully around her face. Her slender arm in the anorak, the bend at the elbow, and the forearm resting on the big bag. The small white hand peeping out from the sleeve and the vicelike grip on . . . Well, on what exactly?

The luggage tag on the bag. On one of the holdalls that Karl-Erik had taken from home when he had gone to the mainland to collect the loot from the robbery.

She quickly examined her own bag and noticed it was missing a tag. Surely it couldn't be that . . . ? What if it was clear from the name tag Jeanette was clutching who the bag had once belonged to? It couldn't be that—not now that everything was going so well for Jeanette, now that they had managed to do something absolutely incredible together, and everything had been forgiven and almost forgotten.

She carefully took Jeanette's hand between her own. It was limp and didn't move. Jeanette didn't react to being touched. Kerstin prised the name tag from her hand and detached it from the bag. She examined the business card behind the plastic window—the one that belonged to a child minder called Kerstin Barbenius, which included not only her contact details but also a photograph of her in profile. She sighed deeply and sank back resignedly in her seat.

She had to handle this in a balanced and carefully considered way. She had to set aside all her hurtful thoughts—all the bitterness and intolerance. What she was going to offer was tolerance for human weakness, understanding, and the power of forgiveness. And surely that couldn't be so hard, given that was all she had left?

"Jen," she said cautiously. "It's okay."

"No, it isn't," Jeanette said. "It's anything but okay. Now I know where the name Barbamama comes from. Nanna. If only I'd checked up on that sooner, we wouldn't have ended up here. We wouldn't have had to deal with each other at all."

"It didn't cross my mind that there would be a name tag on the bag with a photo of me on it. You have to believe me. I really didn't want you . . ."

"Me to know? Me to find out who you are?"

For a moment, it crossed her mind that Jeanette might actually be upset at having been hoodwinked—that she had been tricked into telling her life story to Kerstin in particular, the only person who definitely couldn't be allowed to find out. But she dismissed those thoughts and continued to pursue her soft approach.

"No, actually, I didn't. I wanted to spare you that. I didn't consciously keep my real name a secret from you, but today wasn't exactly . . ."

"Spare me?" Jeanette interrupted, turning to Kerstin with shiny eyes. "Me? You must hate me."

"Why?" Kerstin asked.

"When I told you about my own part in that accident—you must have wanted to kill me there and then."

"I'm not inclined that way," Kerstin said truthfully.

"But why didn't you say anything?"

"What was I supposed to say?" said Kerstin. "I was taken completely off guard. I had to gather my thoughts and decide how to act around you."

"And what was your conclusion?" Jeanette asked.

"That both of us are only human. That you didn't take on your role in that saga on purpose, that you were a victim of circumstance—even if you should have taken greater responsibility in the situation. And that you have regretted it every moment since it happened. That's good enough for me."

Jeanette looked at her mistrustfully. Her eyes were brimming with tears.

"Sorry," she said reaching out with her hand and placing it in Kerstin's. "I'm so sorry."

"I know," said Kerstin. "But I want you to be happy now. I thought you were going to be once we had found Erik. That you were on the way to reconciling yourself with it. And that made *me* very happy. I don't want all of that to crumble just because there happened to be a name tag with my photo attached to one of the bags."

"But what I've done to you," said Jeanette. "It's dreadful. How am I supposed to live with that?"

"Look at it the other way around," Kerstin suggested. "Accept that fate brought us together and that it was the best thing that could have happened. Now you've had the chance to explain yourself and apologise, and I've realised how what happened could have come to pass, I've processed my trauma and forgiven you."

Jeanette looked at her, eyes filled with tears.

"Have you really?" she said. "Forgiven me?"

Kerstin nodded and squeezed Jeanette's hand.

"How is that even possible?"

Kerstin shrugged her shoulders.

"You have to make the best of the situation," she said. "What's done is done and can't be changed. You feeling like shit doesn't make me feel better—quite the opposite, in fact. You're my friend, a person I care about. And you've punished yourself harder than I ever could have. Or would have wanted to. It's for the best—I'd like us to put it behind us."

Jeanette scrutinised her through her tears. She didn't seem entirely able to take in Kerstin's words.

"We're the heroes of the hour, you and me," Kerstin said with a smile. "I could tell you were proud of yourself—for the first time ever, I think. Satisfied with what you had achieved. It was great to see. Can't you hold on to that feeling? Accept that all the terrible things that happened four years ago are over, turn the page, and look forward to a new future?"

Kerstin thought she glimpsed a tiny smile in Jeanette's eyes—at least she wanted to believe that was what she could see. Jeanette took a deep breath and shut her eyes. They sat in silence for the remainder of the journey.

LATER ON WHEN they dropped the bags off at Kerstin's flat, she asked Jeanette whether she wanted to stay for a while so that they could talk, drink, eat, or anything else—celebrate, quite simply. But Jeanette declined.

"Don't do this to me," Kerstin begged. "Don't take away my one cause for rejoicing in this life."

"*Your* cause for rejoicing?" Jeanette said, dumbfounded.

"I've reconciled myself with the thought of what happened. You should too—I'm asking you to. Don't let an old business card ruin both our lives, now that things are shaping up so nicely."

Jeanette looked at her for a long time. Her eyes were vacant—the gaze contained nothing that gave away what was going on inside. Jeanette had shut herself off, and Kerstin wasn't welcome inside.

"How I feel has nothing to do with you," Jeanette said coolly.

Kerstin, who didn't want to burden Jeanette with any more guilt, still felt compelled to refer backwards. She had to say *something*.

"If your mental well-being depends on my name and my picture being on that baggage tag, then surely it's got something to do with me? *I* say that what happened four years ago is in the past. *I* say you're forgiven, that your actions today have atoned for the bad choices you made then. Don't you see how lucky you are to know me—you've had the chance to explain yourself and apologise and be forgiven?"

Jeanette studied her with her blank gaze and inscrutable expression. Kerstin felt hopelessly excluded from Jeanette's thoughts, and somewhat desperate for acknowledgment. Not so much for her own sake as for Jeanette's—she needed to get her to see the person Kerstin. Not the phenomenon—the widow, the heartrending cry from the past. Sisters of misfortune, as it were. Only then could she help her out of the abyss where she seemed to find herself at present.

"Doesn't that mean something?" Kerstin battled on. "Would you have preferred to carry on being depressed on your own, looking for penance on your side without it ever doing the victim any good?"

Jeanette didn't drop her eyes from Kerstin, but she didn't answer either. There was something about her demeanour that made Kerstin think she was on her way out.

"We've done something big today, Jen. You and me, together. Stay and we'll celebrate. We've earned it."

"What are you going to do with the money?" Jeanette asked, seemingly altogether uninterested in everything Kerstin had said.

"Give it to the police," Kerstin replied.

"Why didn't we do that out at the hunting cabin then?"

"It would have been taken the wrong way—we would have fallen under suspicion."

"Oh really," Jeanette said indifferently.

"You're pushing me away, Jen. Why can't we talk?"

No visible reaction—in Jeanette's world there was only room for Jeanette.

"I'm going now," she said.

"Do you really have to? You could sleep over."

But Jeanette shook her head and began to go down the stairs.

"I'll walk you home," Kerstin said.

"No, you won't. Don't be so bloody clingy."

That hurt. Wounded her. Clingy—that wasn't a good thing to be. Almost anything was better than that.

"Okay," said Kerstin, swallowing hard. "Take care of yourself, sweetheart. And I'll see you tomorrow."

Jeanette raised her hand without looking her in the eye and vanished round the corner as she went down the stairs. Kerstin continued to stand there until she heard the street door slam.

67

Sandra

MANY HOURS LATER, when darkness descended on the town and those activities that didn't stop altogether took on more cautious and low-key modes of expression, she found herself sitting in the darkened hospital room with Erik's hand held in hers. They were alone together for the first time, and he was sleeping deeply and peacefully while a solution of nutrients and antibiotics was fed straight into his small body through an insertion in the crook of his arm.

Everything was going to be okay. They had promised her that: there were no physical injuries, the malnutrition would soon be dealt with, and any infections had been nipped in the bud. He was warm and safe, no longer subject to thirst or hunger. He would see a psychologist, but given his young age, poor grasp of time, and the diffuse memories he had expressed, the whole thing would hopefully vanish into a blurry haze. He had woken up from a nightmare, but so long as no one dug too deeply and reinforced those impressions, he would forget about it all soon enough.

All Erik could remember was that he had been sitting in a cold and dark room, that he had been hungry and so thirsty that he'd had to drink the dirty water from puddles on the ground. Nothing about being abducted, nothing about his rescue. There was nothing but darkness, thirst, and hunger to build his nightmares around, and who didn't have nightmares about darkness? Thirst and hunger were passing feelings, acute needs in the moment, but hard to relate to when not being experienced. The horrifying nights and days would shrink in his consciousness, seem unreal, and be forgotten. That could only be good for his mental well-being in the future, even if it was a little strange that he didn't remember being separated from his kindergarten group and then being transported somehow from the woods at Furulundsskogen. Had he been drugged? Surely he had to have been—who would have been able to trick him into coming with them otherwise without him remembering it?

The police still hadn't been in touch—she had to assume that they were leaving her in peace with her son for the first night out of respect. Sandra didn't have anything to offer the investigation either. She had already shared her suspicions, and in that regard nothing had changed. They also had a crime scene to investigate—the chamber where Erik had been held was cordoned off. She hadn't seen the clothes he had been wearing when he had disappeared; they were presumably already safely in the custody of the forensic specialists. Somewhere there had to be a trace of Hallin, if only a strand of hair.

Sandra hadn't understood much about what had happened when Erik had been found, but apparently a member of the public had raised the alarm. Someone had happened to open a door by chance and had found the boy, realised that it was Erik, and done what was needed. Sandra had wanted to hear more about that, but was also grateful that the police were leaving her alone for the time being. She would find out the details soon enough, and she would have the opportunity to express her gratitude to those involved.

Her mobile vibrated in her pocket. She pulled it out and noted that it was a picture message. From Kerstin. A very blurry photo of something that she couldn't initially identify. And there was no explanatory text either. The subject was so compressed that it looked like the picture had been taken through a crack between two planks of wood or something. Upon closer examination, she thought she could make out parts of a car—possibly a blue one, or grey. And perhaps a person, too. If so, they were walking alongside the car, coming towards the photographer. But it was hard to make out, because there seemed to be water pouring down between the photographer and the subject of the picture. And no matter how much she zoomed in, the picture got no clearer nor any more comprehensible. Sandra concluded that Kerstin must have pressed a button and sent the message by mistake. She turned off her screen, put the mobile back in her pocket, and directed her attention back at her sleeping son.

As far as the book was concerned, the story was beginning to reach its end, and Sandra decided the time was ripe to rewrite her own experiences during the day. What had happened when Erik had been found would have to wait until the morning, but she could still portray everything she had seen from her own perspective.

The hospital staff had been kind enough to let her spend the night in the room, so she snuggled down with her laptop in the visitor's bed and began to write.

AFTER SEVERAL HOURS of intense work, she was disturbed by a vibration from her pocket. She pulled out her mobile and saw that Kerstin had sent her a message. "Want to talk?" it said. Sandra glanced at the clock on the wall and saw it was just after eleven. She went over to Erik, who was sleeping deeply in his bed. His ribcage rose and fell, the connections from the two bags on the drip stand producing small shiny drops of fluid that fell down their drip chambers at a stately pace, making a sound akin to crystal being tapped. Everything looked fine, but she still felt ill at ease. She sat back down on her bed and rang Kerstin.

"Hi Sandra," said Kerstin. "I'm so happy for you."

"Oh, is word out already?" Sandra said with a smile.

"It may well be," Kerstin replied. "How is he?"

A nurse stepped into the room, crossed the short distance to Sandra, and proffered a tray with glasses on it. Sandra picked bilberry soup, something she never drank these days, but that she had loved as a child. She had a long night ahead of her, and even though she wasn't all that thirsty she took the opportunity to help herself to a glass of apple juice as well. She needed energy both to write and to watch over Erik. Maybe she was overreacting, but if his condition changed at all, she wanted to know straight away. The nurse smiled benevolently at her from behind a pair of oversized spectacles with thick rims that didn't seem to belong in this millennium.

"Given the circumstances, he's well," said Sandra. "He was cold, dehydrated, and malnourished, but he'll recover quickly. And his memories are pretty hazy, so I think that if we handle this situation right he'll be okay mentally too."

"That's good," said Kerstin.

Sandra placed the glasses on the bedside table and thanked the nurse, who disappeared back into the corridor with her tray.

"How did things go with the cash?" she asked Kerstin.

"It went well."

"You found the money?" Sandra said with a laugh. "You really did?"

"We did. I said I had a good feeling about this."

"That's wonderful, Kerstin. Well done, really!"

"It was more luck than anything else, but we had to work hard. The bags were in the tanks under the outdoor privy, covered by . . . Well, you can probably imagine that yourself."

"How on earth did you think to look there?"

"Well it was exactly that which gave me the idea," Kerstin replied. "The fact that no one would think of looking there."

"Impressive," said Sandra, and she really meant it. "Where is it now?"

"At my flat," said Kerstin. "You can pick it up when you've got time."

The door opened and another two nurses appeared. One was pushing a trolley in front of her.

"I have to go," said Sandra. "Let's talk again tomorrow?"

"Sure," said Kerstin. "Good luck with it all."

Sandra ended the call and looked up at the nurses.

"My name's Maria and I'm the night nurse tonight," said one of them. "I just wanted to introduce myself. Branca here is an assistant nurse and is going to check your little one's blood pressure and temperature. Do you have any questions?"

Sandra thought about this while the assistant nurse raised the bed and stuck the thermometer in Erik's ear.

"Thirty-seven point two," she said, wrapping the blood pressure sleeve around Erik's arm and attaching a clamp to his finger. "It's beginning to normalise."

Erik wasn't disturbed in his sleep; he had no idea that he was the subject of a range of medical checks.

"Ninety-five over sixty," said Branca. "Saturation ninety-seven percent, pulse eighty-nine."

"Those are excellent figures," Maria explained. "Erik is definitely on the mend, so you can sleep soundly tonight."

Then they vanished with the trolley, leaving Sandra with a number of questions spinning around her head despite their best intentions. One of them related to security at the hospital. Could she really sleep soundly tonight? For some reason, she didn't feel convinced.

There was barely a sound to be heard from the corridor, and the town outside the window was calm too. Erik looked peaceful lying there on his back in the adjustable bed, which was still propped up following the checks. The soft glow of the night-light cast secretive shadows over his face. What exactly had happened to him? Would she ever find out?

Right now, it didn't matter. Erik had been restored to life; he was in safety and under the watchful eye of hordes of uniformed health personnel with sound skills and kind voices. All eyes on Gotland were looking towards Erik; it was unthinkable that anything would happen.

Yet there was something inside her that kicked back. Sandra didn't go in for premonitions and omens very much, so she didn't allow herself to take the ominous feeling so seriously that she did anything tangible to prevent what she imagined might happen. She didn't make a hysterical call to the police to demand police protection, nor did she ask her parents to keep her company during the night.

Her only plan was to stay awake all through the night and to press the alarm button if necessary. After everything that had happened, she was just overwrought. The worst that could happen had already happened, and it wouldn't happen again.

She shook off the baseless unease, settled down in bed with the laptop on her knee, took a deep breath, and began to write again.

68

Kerstin

SEVERAL HOURS AFTER Jeanette had left her, Kerstin was pacing back and forth in the flat with a really bad feeling in her body. The feeling that she wasn't good enough, the feeling of having all the dials turned up, of being too much. Clingy, as Jeanette had put it. It was downright painful. Like a bad conscience, it was impossible to wriggle free from it, impossible to push it to one side and take a breather.

Kerstin tried to read, watched some TV, cooked, ate, played games on her mobile—but it wouldn't go away. She couldn't concentrate on anything. The joy at the day's exploits was unable to penetrate through the din of negative and irrelevant emotions. What did it matter how Jeanette dealt with the knowledge that it was Kerstin's husband she had left to die in the car wreck once upon a time? How could it ever be Kerstin's problem to arrange a soft landing for Jeanette after she found that out? If Jeanette wanted to torture herself, then let her. She could just as well let the curses whistle past her if that was the way she wanted it.

Kerstin tried to persuade herself. But she wasn't disposed that way. She wanted the people around her to feel good, and it was most unsatisfying that she personally had some responsibility for Jeanette's emotional about-turn. She knew full well that the problem was founded upon Jeanette's obstinacy rather than Kerstin herself. But if anyone had it in them to break the deadlock inside Jeanette, it was Kerstin. Perhaps it was presumptuous to think like that, especially given Jeanette's harsh parting words, but Kerstin needed to rise above that kind of thing. Despite the fact that Jeanette was an arch-egoist, incapable of pulling herself together even though Kerstin had been magnanimous and had forgiven her, it was probably best for now to put Jeanette first and deprioritise her own emotional needs—such as not wanting to be seen as excessively pushy.

It was around midnight when she decided to stroll over to Jeanette's flat, force her way in, and refuse to climb down in the face of harsh words and outright insults. She was going to stay with Jeanette until she had softened and become more reasonable. She would prevent her from continuing in her downward spiral and from harming herself, if it was really going that far.

That was why she put on her shoes, pulled on her thin padded jacket, and stole out into the summer night. It was a magnificent, starry night, the moon making little fuss as it made its shy retreat. Nature was giving off the scents of saturation, and the deluge of water that had fallen from the sky to Erik's benefit over the last few days had already been sucked up into the natural circulatory system. Everything was beautiful: the grass, trees, and bushes shimmered in various shades of green and immediately put her in a better mood.

She considered what there was to be happy about—not least for Jeanette. The fact that Kerstin and Jeanette had managed to get their hopeless project across the finishing line—despite their limited resources in every respect—and that they had managed to find the money was frankly verging on miraculous. The fact that they had also saved the life of Sandra's three-year-old was even more worthy of celebration, even if it wasn't really a proper celebration since they had simply been lucky to be in the right place at the right time. And they'd had the presence of mind to take the necessary action demanded in that situation, just as anyone else would have done.

Kerstin saw Jeanette before her, radiating with joy when Kerstin had praised her for the initiative she had demonstrated in rescuing the boy from the cellar. She remembered the roguish look in her eyes when they had managed to wriggle free from the grasp of the police, when they had retrieved those two bags and cycled away from the hunting cabin with three million kronor each slung over their shoulders. Together, the two of them had managed to do all this, and while they had been doing it they had become closer than ever before.

Kerstin had finally decided to forget old injustices—putting it mildly, of course, but effectively offering forgiveness. She would put all the infected memories behind her and look ahead. This was a day when life had smiled broadly at both of them; Jeanette and Kerstin had every reason to be happy together. Yet, their day together had ended in emotional catastrophe—a teary darkness from which Jeanette seemed unwilling and unable to extricate herself.

But she reminded herself of all the beautiful things around her: the sky, the dazzling scents, and colours of nature. She wanted to believe that Jeanette could appreciate all that too. That the fresh night air and all it carried on its currents would make her feel more lighthearted too. Kerstin would try to get her into a better state of mind, and despite what awaited her she was convinced she was doing the right thing.

There was a pling on her mobile, but that wasn't going to change anything.

69

Sandra

IT WAS ALREADY past midnight and Sandra had finished jotting down the day's events, or at least what she knew had happened during the day. Since the police had not yet been to see her, and she hadn't contacted them, there was a lot she didn't know about how Erik had been found and in what circumstances he had spent the last four days. On the other hand, what she did know was what her own day had been like, how she had been cast from extremity to extremity before finally ending up in a bed at Visby General Hospital. And that was only the start, since all aspects needed to be depicted, including her own. Now, however, there was nothing more to write about—she would have to wait for the morning and try to stay awake by other means.

She had no intention of sleeping. She was going to watch by Erik's side, making sure that his condition didn't take a turn for the worse and that no one other than the night staff visited the room. Of course it was possible that Erik had left the kindergarten group and the woods at Furulundsskogen under his own steam. But given the subsequent search efforts, the idea that he could have succeeded in disappearing without anyone seeing him was unthinkable. In short, he must have been helped, and in view of the timing and the threats that Sandra had received, the idea that it was anyone other than Hallin behind the disappearance seemed impossible. He had everything to gain from Erik not being found alive, and it must have upset his plans that the boy had eventually been found against all the odds.

So what would he do about it? And when? Sense told her that he ought to avoid being seen anywhere near Sandra and Erik, but emotionally she couldn't relax. All the effort that must have lain behind everything that had happened to them lately! But it had been of no use to Hallin, since Erik was still his son. Since Erik was still alive.

A child's life seemed so fragile. Erik was so small and vulnerable that it seemed as if he wasn't built for survival, and yet he clearly had been. The death of such a small person felt like an impossibility, yet at the same time the exact opposite did too. The fear of what might happen if she let herself fall asleep overwhelmed Sandra in waves as she sat there, hugging her anxiety in the soft night-light.

She achieved no great success in her efforts to ward off imagining the worst. Just about anybody could pass through a Swedish hospital completely unnoticed at any time of day. They could easily enter a room and reconfigure or disconnect some tubes without anyone noticing.

It was crazy really that she hadn't already contacted the police to find out what they had to say, to find out what their view was on Hallin's role in the disappearance, and to request police protection at the hospital. After all, the kidnapper had not been fully successful in his endeavours thus far. At the same time, it seemed somehow pointless—assigning the three-year-old and thereby herself such importance that uniformed police officers had to guard the room they were in, as if they were in some Hollywood movie.

Of course Hallin wouldn't try anything here and now. It would draw too much attention and create too much commotion in relation to himself. He had to assume that Sandra would make sure that all spotlights were aimed at him in particular. So when all things were considered, Sandra had nothing to fear, but she was still sitting there throwing suspicious glances around and jumping at the slightest sound from outside the ward. It was just a feeling she had—it might be illogical but it was still very tangible. Somehow, she felt exposed, and the darkness and stillness around her did nothing to improve matters. Right now, the morning seemed a very distant prospect.

She browsed on her phone a bit to see whether she had missed anything. She had read somewhere that using your mobile was the last thing you should do if you wanted to try and sleep. The flickering light, or the sound, or whatever it was, triggered all the wrong receptors in the nervous system, and postponed sleep by several hours. Splendid, Sandra thought to herself. She rediscovered the message she had received earlier that evening from Kerstin. She decided to give it another look in the absence of anything else to do, and she sent the photo to her laptop via Bluetooth.

She imported the blurry photo to her image application, but realised before she had even got started that she lacked the resources and skills necessary to deal with it. Instead, she sent it over to one of the editors at the newspaper who she knew was working tonight and asked him get someone with the right expertise to do their very best to enhance the photo quality. Then she did what she could on her own: she enlarged it, auto corrected, modified the exposure and contrast and anything else she could think of without being able to make head or tail of what was in the photo. Other than it being a car in the rain, and possibly a person.

It was probably irrelevant—Kerstin hadn't mentioned the picture message when they had spoken an hour or so earlier, after all. And there had been no writing in the message, which suggested Kerstin hadn't sent it intentionally. Or even taken it intentionally. And now

Sandra was reluctant to disturb her again with a question about a missent picture message that was only being asked because she was struggling to pass the time during the night shift.

The door opened and the nurse looked in again—the one with the old-fashioned spectacles. She gave Sandra a sunny smile, nodded without saying anything, and withdrew back into the corridor, as if they were communicating in some shared code where a nod meant everything was under control.

She realised that she had completely forgotten about the bilberry soup that she had been given earlier in the evening. It was standing together with the apple juice slightly concealed behind her toilet bag on the nightstand. She reached for the glass and took a big gulp. It tasted just like she remembered: sweet, but not *too* sweet. It was tasty, with a distinct bilberry flavour minus that natural acidity, and with lovely small seeds that lingered on your tongue. She downed the lot in just a few short gulps, and immediately regretted not having taken two glasses when she'd had the opportunity. She didn't feel like apple juice right now, so she didn't touch it.

She cast another disillusioned glance at the incomprehensible picture on her computer, felt impatient, and thought that she could at least ask Kerstin whether she was awake. She fired off a text message and got an answer straight back saying it was fine to call. So she did.

"Aren't you sleeping?" she asked.

"No, I'm actually out for a walk," Kerstin replied. "I thought I'd look in on Jeanette."

"Why?" Sandra said with concern. "Don't you trust her?"

"No, I wouldn't put it like that. She found my business card with a photo of me on it attached to one of the bags. Then she realised that it was my husband who died in the ravine, and you might say she didn't take it very well. Your real name doesn't really matter in our circles, so she's always thought of me as Nanna. And after it dawned on me who she was, I wasn't exactly eager to open her eyes to the truth either."

"Gosh. And you . . ."

"I've forgiven her, Sandra. And she knows that. She refuses to accept it. She can't forgive herself."

Sandra sighed. It felt as though Kerstin had more important things to do than answer questions that Sandra wanted to ask to pass the time.

"What was it you wanted to talk about?" said Kerstin.

"It occurred to me that I never got an explanation for that picture message you sent earlier this evening," Sandra explained.

There was silence on the other end of the line for a moment.

"I'm not sure I'm with you," said Kerstin uncertainly.

"I thought as much," said Sandra. "That you didn't mean to send it. It was a picture of something pretty hard to make out—might have been a car or something, seen through a crack."

"Ah, now I'm with you," said Kerstin. "I sent that this afternoon—around four o'clock. But I lost coverage out there after you and I spoke on the phone. The message must have got stuck in cyberspace somehow and only been sent once I returned to civilisation."

"No writing and terrible picture quality," Sandra laughed. "What exactly were you trying to say?"

"I wouldn't say it was a cry for help," Kerstin said. "But it was meant to be a clue as to what had happened. If we didn't come back."

"What are you telling me, Kerstin? Did someone turn up at the hunting cabin who scared you so much that you weren't sure you were going to leave there?"

There was silence at the other end of the line. Sandra could hear Kerstin's breathing as she walked, her footsteps on the asphalt.

"Hello?" she said. "What's going on?"

"So you don't know?" said Kerstin.

"That's becoming increasingly apparent. Tell me now."

So Kestin did as she was asked.

"I had found the bags and chucked them out onto the grass when a car showed up," she explained. "I caught sight of it at the last moment, and I was totally convinced that I had been spotted and that the driver was on their way over to where I was hiding in the privy. I thought I'd reached the end of the line, and I realised I could take a photo through the crack in the door and send it to you."

"But nothing happened?" Sandra said, encouraging her to go on.

"Something happened," said Kerstin. "But the visit had nothing to do with the money, which was obviously what I was worrying about."

"So what was the purpose of the visit?" Sandra asked.

"To undo the bolt on the door to the root cellar," Kerstin replied.

"That's all?" Sandra said in confusion. "They came to undo a bolt?"

"Exactly."

"But why?" Sandra demanded.

She had a strong feeling that she was being told something very important right now, but she couldn't for the life of her understand what it was all about.

"Because it had to seem as if the boy being held captive in the cellar had wandered in there by himself," Kerstin said.

Sandra couldn't understand what she was hearing—she was unable to file the words into the right compartment of her brain.

"The boy?" she said, dumbfounded.

"Erik," Kerstin clarified.

Sandra felt her pulse quicken and her cheeks flush. What was going on?

"Are you saying that Erik was being held captive at the hunting cabin? And that a car showed up to release him?"

"I'm saying that the car showed up to fabricate the suggestion that Erik had made his own way into the root cellar and then been unable to get out."

Thoughts whirled around Sandra's head. Erik—what on earth did he have to do with the treasure hunt at the cabin?

"Was . . . Was he locked in?" Sandra stammered.

"He was locked in without any food or drink," Kerstin confirmed. "The kidnapper had probably been counting on him having died after such a long time, but the heavy rain meant he was able to drink rainwater."

"And of all people it was *you* who rescued him?"

It was incomprehensible. Sandra couldn't understand how it all fit together.

"It was Jeanette and me who *found* him," Kerstin clarified. "And if you think about it, it's not entirely illogical. Hallin didn't know anything about the money, but he knew that Peter Norling's hunting cabin was empty, and probably knew about the cellar too."

Sandra let Kerstin's words sink in. The questions she wanted answers to were countless, her gratitude to Kerstin knew no bounds, and yet she had talked to her earlier that evening without the subject being raised. And without Sandra saying a single word of thanks.

"I'm absolutely speechless, Kerstin. I had no idea . . . Thank you. What can I say?"

"We just did what anyone else would have done," Kerstin said dismissively.

"Tell me," said Sandra. "I want to hear every detail."

So Kerstin told her. She accounted in depth for every moment after she spotted the car on the drive leading up to the cabin. When she was finished, there were still questions that were unanswered.

"Your blurry photo is actually evidence against Erik's kidnapper?" Sandra said. "Do the police know about it?"

"The way I look goes against me," Kerstin admitted. "They didn't take anything we said seriously, and I think it would have suited them best if it had been *us* who had held Erik captive. I showed them the photo, but they just waved me away."

"And who is in the photo?" Sandra asked.

"Hallin, of course," Kerstin said with conviction. "But since it was bucketing down and we were both hiding, neither of us got a good look at him. With regard to the car, I'm pretty sure, even if cars aren't my specialty. I would say it was a blue Audi. But with the right tools, a pro must be able to improve the photo, right?"

"I've put a colleague to work on it," Sandra said.

"You need to send the police in the right direction too. There must be tire tracks at the cabin, and maybe footprints as well. There might be traces of the perpetrator in the cellar too. I mentioned all this to the police, but in their eyes I seem to lack credibility."

Kerstin laughed as she said it. A little sadly, perhaps, but she laughed. Regardless of what she herself called it, she and Jeanette had saved Erik's life, and the police had dismissed them as if they knew nothing.

"Awful," said Sandra.

"Pardon?"

"The police response to you and Jeanette is awful," said Sandra.

"I didn't catch that," said Kerstin. "It sounds like you're slurring your words. Is your coverage bad?"

Sandra checked the bars at the top of her mobile display—four of them. Was she really slurring her words?

"I've got perfect coverage," Sandra said.

Well, perhaps the words weren't tumbling out of her mouth with the same directness they usually did. And Kerstin hadn't said anything either. What was happening?

"Get onto the police as soon as you can, first thing in the morning," said Kerstin. "That should give them time to intervene before Hallin leaves the country. He must feel the trap closing on him. And make sure you get the rest of that serial published as soon as possible."

"I'll do that," said Sandra. She could hear now that she didn't sound at all well. "Am I still slurring?"

"Sounds like you are to me," Kerstin confirmed. "Call the doctor."

"Could you come here?" Sandra asked.

"I can't hear what you're saying, and I have to go now," Kerstin said. "I'm at Jeanette's flat."

"Come here!" Sandra commanded.

It wasn't intended as an order, more a way of ensuring she got her message across in as few, easily decipherable words as possible.

"You're in a hospital, Sandra. Press the alarm button. I'll check on Jeanette, and I'm going to stay there for the night. Okay?"

"Okay," Sandra mumbled, well aware that what was coming out of her mouth bore little similarity to what she was trying to say.

She wished Kerstin luck, but doubted her words were clear. She ended the call and tried without success to push her mobile back into her pocket. Instead, she laid it beside her on the bed and reached for the alarm button that was dangling on a string from the triangular handle above the bed. That didn't work either—it was as if her body wouldn't obey her as she sat there gesticulating in the air. She shut one eye in the vain hope that it would clarify her focus, but the opposite happened. All her senses were degenerating completely, and she could feel that if she tried to get out of bed to summon help, she would collapse onto the floor.

As a security measure, she shut the laptop and pushed it under the duvet at the foot of her bed. She was afraid she might otherwise end up pushing it onto the floor, and that couldn't be allowed to happen. The next task was to attempt to take the few steps to the wall behind the bed where there was another alarm button. She could hold on to the nightstand—the problem was that it was on wheels, so it might roll away if she supported herself on it. She would have to try and walk without support, or possibly slip to the floor and crawl there.

She didn't get any further than that in her planning before the door opened and a long shadow was cast over the floor. She squinted and tried to fix her gaze on the visitor's face. He shut the door behind him and looked around—probably to ensure that they were alone in the room. Then he picked up a visitor's chair that was leaning against the wall and unfolded it. He stepped forward to where Sandra was sitting on the bed, positioned the chair in front of her and sat down. Only now did she manage to get her eyes to focus on the visitor's face, and the realisation of who it was hardly helped set her at ease.

The disaster had come to pass. She was completely defenceless—drugged, probably poisoned. That had to be what had happened. Her senses had suddenly weakened, and several key bodily functions had collapsed at the same time, although her brain was still capable of thinking clearly. And the man who appeared at the very moment she was attempting to contact the outside world in a final desperate measure seeking rescue from her hopeless situation was none other than Jan Hallin.

70

Kerstin

SHE ENDED UP standing there with the phone in her hand. What was happening to Sandra? Had she been having a stroke while they were talking? Kerstin sincerely hoped that wasn't the case, but in the unlikely event that it was, then it could hardly happen in a better place than Visby General Hospital. She tried to persuade herself of that.

Provided, that was, someone was informed of the unfolding situation. As she had already told Sandra, all she had to do was summon the doctor. The alarm button was never further away than any old wrinkly with poor mobility could reach.

Nevertheless, she felt unsettled. This was Sandra. Sandra, the woman in the middle of exposing a rapist, hit-and-run driver, murderer, and kidnapper to the vast majority of the public on the island of Gotland. Sandra, the woman whose son had been the subject of attempted murder and had been a hair's breadth from death. Was it that far-fetched to imagine that the two of them were still in the danger zone, that Sandra had been incapacitated with drugs, or even given an overdose? Considering the boy was still alive, and the serial wasn't so far gone that it couldn't be stopped without any definitive answers being provided to the many questions the eager readers had . . .

No, not really. But Sandra was still in a hospital and was in good enough condition to raise the alarm with the staff. While Kerstin was far away and could hardly do anything for Sandra that the doctors and nurses couldn't do themselves.

On the other hand, Jeanette had no button to press if the situation felt untenable. Jeanette only had one lifeline, and that was Kerstin, who had volunteered against both her friend's will and her own better judgment. And Kerstin had misgivings. This unyielding side to Jeanette was one she had seen before—this indifference towards others. That was why she made the decision to set aside her concerns for Sandra's welfare for the time being and instead concentrate on Jeanette.

For some reason, she tried the door before ringing the bell. It was unlocked, and that was very alarming.

71

Jan

EARLIER IN THE EVENING when his mobile had pinged and a news flash had informed him that the missing boy had been found, Jan had made a decision. When he considered what his life would be like, the looming scandal and the subsequent prison sentence, he decided he needed to leave this sinking ship. He would take the cheap overnight ferry to the mainland, stay beneath the radar as best he could, and eventually make his way to a country without an extradition treaty with Sweden and start over there. That was the plan, and Gunilla, who had read selected excerpts of the serial on Jan's advice, agreed with him fully.

The serial was a form of revenge—Jan understood that much. It wasn't a very fair approach, since it circumvented the justice system and described what had happened from the supposed victim's perspective before then condemning and smearing the reputation of the supposed perpetrator without any trial. A desperate, but also understandable, action for someone who considered herself to be a victim of a crime, one for which she had little chance of securing legal redress so long after the fact.

But if what was left of the serial wasn't published, then the whole thing would be cast in an entirely different light. There would be no trial, no prison sentence, and no accusations of murder or kidnapping. The Hallin name wouldn't be dragged through the mud, and Jan wouldn't have to flee.

That was the straw to which he was clutching when, just after midnight, with the biggest suitcase he had been able to find in the basement, he stepped into the hospital lobby and headed towards the lifts.

The fact that Sandra felt that what she had been subjected to was straightforward rape was pretty clear, and Jan would have to compromise—admit that he was a rapist. It didn't sound good; in fact it had a bad sound to it, when in reality it was just a single encounter that had gone off the rails. Jan didn't consider himself a rapist, but he agreed that he had raped. *Once*. To lend credibility to his denials.

The author also seemed to think that the poor sod in the ravine had been the victim of a crime. Jan didn't agree. Two cars had encountered each other on a road covered in black ice, and one of them had crashed into a ravine. The idea that it was solely Jan's fault was impossible to prove now, and it wouldn't have been possible to prove it at the time either. But Jan hadn't been sober, Jan had left the scene, and Jan had failed to call emergency services. *Those* constituted his crimes—not that he had caused the death of another person. His guilt was down to the distorted legal system—for the accident itself he bore no guilt.

Sandra was reeling off unfair and misleading accusations against Jan, and he couldn't allow that. This was the reason why he shortly thereafter stepped into the room where he had found out she and the boy were. He put the suitcase down outside the door, which he closed behind him. Then he sat down on a visitor's chair that he positioned provocatively close to her curled-up body on the bed.

72

Sandra

"I'LL BE BRIEF," said Hallin. "I don't want you to publish any more of that serial."

It came as no surprise that Jan Hallin didn't want his crimes to be described in a form that got people seriously engaged, got them to empathise with the victim's suffering and condemn the actions of the perpetrator. Sandra dared not and could not answer—she lay there trembling on the bed waiting for his next statement.

"You're probably well aware of that," he said. "But I still want to make it clear that I'm being publicly hung out to dry just because it suits you. Rapists and hit-and-run drivers aren't normally identified in the press, so I would say you're abusing your authority."

Hallin certainly had a point there, but it was about more serious crimes than that, crimes that would remain unsolved if Sandra didn't prove that they were all connected in this way. Something the police would never have pulled off on their own. What was more, she hadn't given Hallin away, since there was no crucial detail relating to him personally. Funnily enough, he seemed to be reading her thoughts.

"I know you haven't named me or anyone else involved. And I guess you probably consider the book to be an extensive, detailed police report. Smart move—and you're generating a lot of interest around the case too. The cases, I should say. People will follow as it unfolds and find out who's who on their own. I'll be particularly harshly condemned in the eyes of the public since you've given them so much understanding of those events that you describe. That's why I'm begging you, Sandra. Please let me set things right, but don't ruin my life."

"You've done that all by yourself," Sandra couldn't help herself from saying.

She said it slowly and with emphasis on every word, hoping that the message would get through, even though she was talking as if she had a mouth filled with porridge. Hallin frowned and looked at her with suspicion.

"I admit the rape," he said unexpectedly. "I'm sorry—it was a terrible thing to do and I'm ashamed. I'm prepared to pay the child support that you've asked for and stay away from the boy, if that's how you want it. But stop that serial now, give it an ending that people like, but that has nothing to do with reality. I'll admit to the hit-and-run, if that's important to you—but don't force me to be pilloried as a rapist when it was just a one-time step over the line, an isolated incident. At least give me some humanity."

He said the last bit while bending forward with his eyes fixed on hers, and with a tap on the laptop at the foot of the bed with his clenched fist. Despite the fact that she had hidden it under the covers, he had still figured out where it was. Sandra opened her eyes wide in horror and shook her head in protest at what he had demonstrated he was capable of and what he presumably intended to do.

"For the love of God, give me some humanity," he begged again. "For what it's worth, I also think you ought to consider very carefully whether you really want to publish this, for your own sake. Given you've got the wrong end of the stick in a lot of places. Especially on some of the more important stuff, I'd say. Your credibility will be gone if you pursue that line."

"Which line?" Sandra asked, and this time she was met with an almost scared look.

"That I supposedly murdered Peter Norling. And buried his body. That I sent funeral flowers and sabotaged the brakes on your car. That I kidnapped a child. Was he meant to die? Without knowing any of the details, I would guess so. Would I attempt the murder of a three-year-old? My own son? I can tell you in all certainty, Sandra, that's out of the question."

"Who else could it be?" said Sandra with an attempt at a sneer.

"Sorry, I didn't catch what you said," Hallin said.

"Who?" Sandra said unambiguously.

"Who did if I didn't?" Hallin interpreted suspiciously. "You should have had the decency to find that out *before* you wrote your fucking serial."

Darkness was descending before Sandra's eyes—she was unsure whether it was the poison or the horror of what this man intended to do to her.

"Who's guilty?" Sandra persevered. She could no longer see who she was talking to.

"What are you saying? What's wrong with your speech?"

Her balance was failing. She collapsed back on the bed, no longer able to keep playing along.

"What's wrong with you, Sandra?" Hallin cried out. He stood up and grabbed her shoulders. "What the hell is going on?"

Sandra was no longer capable of communicating, but that didn't matter either. She wasn't in a state to protect either her son or herself from external dangers, and she would never see the computer again. If she ever woke up, which didn't seem all that likely.

She closed her eyes and glided into the darkness.

73

Kerstin

JEANETTE WAS LYING in bed looking strangely peaceful, almost happy. Perhaps convinced that she was going to succeed this time, that she had scared off Kerstin well enough that the night was hers to die in. Jeanette had been wrong, but Kerstin had allowed herself to be affected by Jeanette's harsh words, and the bitter aftertaste had lingered for a long time. That was why she was now standing here contemplating the earthly remains of her best friend, her worst enemy, with tears streaming down her cheeks.

Of course she could have stopped this if she had been thicker skinned, less sensitive about how she was perceived, more analytical in her perspectives on those closest to her. At the time, this had been Jeanette's wish—to cease to be—and perhaps it ought to be respected. Jeanette no longer owed anybody anything, she no longer had any family or any loved ones that she had moral obligations to. Kerstin and the other friends on the benches were extras in Jeanette's life. She was the maker of her own happiness, and a dreadful one at that; in her heart and soul she was incapable of being part of a community or feeling genuine joy. Jeanette's causes for rejoicing lay in the past, and she didn't want it to be any other way.

Kerstin caressed Jeanette's cheek and wiped away one of her own tears that had landed on her face. She lifted the covers slightly. Jeanette was beautiful. She had changed clothes since their last meeting a few hours ago, and she was wearing white jeans and a blue and white striped sleeveless blouse. The room around her was tidy, and Kerstin was grateful that Jeanette had chosen to end her life sleeping in bed, rather than dangling from a hook on the ceiling or submerged in a bathtub filled with water. That would have been much more demanding of the person who discovered the tragedy.

Kerstin ran her fingers through Jeanette's fringe, adjusted the covers, and left the bedroom. What she really wanted to do was sink to the floor and let all the sobs out of her body. Instead she swallowed a few times, wiped her nose, and stepped into the kitchen with a disconsolate and very heavy sigh. Jeanette was gone, and with her a whole era had drawn to a close.

Kerstin's clouded gaze stopped at the table, where Jeanette had left her mobile. Beside it there was an envelope with the words "To Kerstin Barbenius" on it. Her first impulse was to pocket it to read later, but after some consideration she concluded that this was not something to delay. She rubbed her eyes with her hands, opened the envelope using her thumb, and pulled out the handwritten letter.

Nanna,

I'm guessing you're first on the scene—sorry this is what you found. Today felt like a good day to take this step. Just like you pointed out, I've been very lucky to get to know you and get the opportunity to explain myself and apologise for the indefensible things I did in the past. You say you've forgiven me, and that's almost certainly true. I'm grateful for that, but as you know, I'm unable to forgive myself. Maybe I can't, maybe I don't want to, but there's one thing I do know—I don't want to be alive here and now. I want Charlotte in my life, and perhaps Peter too.

The truth is that I'm too lazy to go on living. I don't have it in me to build new, close relationships, and I don't have the strength to believe that any opportunities like that would come along in the future.

Love.

Hope.

The joy of life.

No, you can hear for yourself how alien those words sound when they come from me. But that's what I wish for, for those of you who never gave up hope in me. You, Nanna. And Lubbi, Jimmy, Micki, Kat, and the others. You probably see yourselves as my friends, but I don't have any friends and I am friend to no one.

Thanks for trying.

Sorry that I didn't.

Don't grieve, I don't love anyone.

Best wishes, Jeanette.

PS. The mobile is for you. There are photos on it that I took after the hit-and-run. Take good care of them.

The letter was peculiarly absent of any statements of tenderness, honest in its nakedness. Jeanette had wanted to say thank you and sorry—she hadn't wanted them to believe they had meant anything to her. A loveless and therefore meaningless existence was what she had left, and at least her suffering was over.

Kerstin tore off a sheet of the kitchen roll on the counter and wiped away her tears before dialling emergency services.

74

Jan

HE STOOD THERE looking at his unconscious antagonist, weighing up how to respond to the situation. This was very much match point, and all Jan had to do was take the computer and leave. That would mean all his problems would be gone and life would be able to return to normal—which had been the intention of this visit from the beginning.

It was not without bitterness that he recalled Sandra had accused him of kidnapping a child and attempted murder. What was so awful was that Jan actually had something to gain from Sandra's boy ceasing to exist. He would evade the paternity issue, the demands for child support, the rape accusations, and the suspected involvement in the hit-and-run by the ravine. If there was no child, then none of the rest existed either—and Sandra could sit there with her serial and her accusations without there being any evidence to back them up.

But now the boy had been found, and it seemed to be Sandra's own life that was suddenly at stake. This actually suited Jan even better than her computer just disappearing from the face of the earth. That meant the police would never get interested in Sandra's story, and Jan would never be investigated. The beautiful façade that the Hallin family had maintained for so long would continue to stand, just like the good reputation of Jan and his wife. The family wouldn't have to suffer, and there would be no derision at what had gone on behind the scenes.

There was a sound from the foot of the bed and Jan was roused from his contemplation. He lifted the covers, picked up the computer, and opened it. Of course, it was the book manuscript that he was interested in rather than the email that had just arrived, but he still clicked on the email out of reflex. There were a number of pictures on the computer screen of a car, a body, and a face.

But not just any face.

The email had been sent by someone at *Gotlands Allehanda* and contained a question: "Is this to do with Erik's kidnapping?" Jan gasped for breath, turning to ice on the spot. Of course, he said to himself. How had he managed to avoid seeing it?

The face was Gunilla's.

And here was Sandra, lying there completely knocked out—perhaps dying—right in front of him, while he held her laptop in his hands.

How was he supposed to deal with this?

75

Sandra

WHEN SHE CAME to, the room was in semidarkness, but some daylight was filtering in from somewhere. She was tucked in bed, and she felt around the foot of the bed with her feet. The bastard had taken advantage of the situation, stolen the computer, and got out of there. Hallin's campaign of persuasion hadn't succeeded, so all that remained was to commit further crimes—in the classic style—to protect himself from accusations relating to the earlier ones.

She closed her eyes again and tried to recollect how the conversation had progressed and how it had ended. But the only thing that seemed to have stuck in her brain was how eager he had been to silence her, how he had insinuated that he had every opportunity to seize the computer and get his hands on the writing that was upsetting him so much.

Slowly, the awareness that something else—something much worse—had happened during the night began to dawn on her. Had she been somehow unwell? Why else was she in bed in the middle of the day? Had he drugged her so he could take the laptop? Tried to kill her? Was that the real reason for his visit?

She couldn't remember a disturbance. Instead, she remembered the bilberry soup she had been given, and how it had brought back childhood memories. She remembered Erik's deep sleep, the calm he had radiated and his rhythmic breathing.

Erik! She suddenly remembered. Was he all right? Had Hallin harmed him again? She sat up in bed and looked around in horror. The room looked different. There were several other people asleep in the room, but Erik wasn't there. Where was Erik? Instinctively, she reached for the red alarm button and pressed it. She noted that she had tubes and wires connected to her and that her condition was being monitored by machines. She let her head rest back on her pillow and tried to marshal her complicated thoughts into order.

She remembered Hallin's shaken look when he had seen her. How he had grabbed her upper arms and shouted things. Maybe in his desperation he had attacked both her and Erik? Tears welled up in her eyes, but before anyone had time to respond to the alarm, she had drifted back into unconsciousness.

76

Jan

WHEN THE SUN came up, Jan still hadn't slept a wink. The anger and confusion following the shocking discovery made his pulse thunder at his temples, and he felt like the stress wouldn't ever dissipate. He paced back and forth, trying to sort through the thousand thoughts streaming through his brain.

The boy, he thought to himself. The fact that Erik had been found didn't help Jan, but he didn't seriously want a small child dead. The threat to Sandra's health—seemingly from poison—was beneficial for Jan and also his wife, for whom the charming façade and the excellent reputation were even more important than they were for him. Earlier that day she had comforted him on the phone and given her whole-hearted support for his idea of fleeing from the anticipated spread of rumours and disappearing from Gotland—indeed, from Sweden. Jan going underground would almost certainly be taken as a confession, which indeed it was, but not of murder and kidnapping. A move like that would definitely shift focus away from the person who was responsible for the truly terrible crimes here.

The person saving her own skin when the suspicions began to pile up against Jan. The one who had imperceptibly manipulated him ever since the beginning of this story. She had seemed supportive, but had in practice had her eye on one thing only: the family's honour. And alongside that, the well-to-do life they had led.

It wasn't for Jan's sake that she had so ruthlessly removed obstacles to their shared well-being. At first glance, it might seem like that, but it became clearer and clearer to him that the woman he had chosen to share his life with was prepared to do anything to appear in a good light and to live in financial comfort. She had literally stepped across bodies. After all these years he was seeing his wife for the first time, in a new and less flattering light.

Gunilla had convinced him that he had done the right thing in not climbing down into the ravine. Jan had interpreted it as meaning that rather than finding fault, she supported him in a decision that was irreversible. But when it came to the punch, it must have suited her better that he had left the scene of the accident without raising the alarm. Personally, he had almost immediately reached the opposite conclusion due to his conscience, but there was no going back.

When the blackmail letter had turned up on the kitchen counter one dinner time, Gunilla hadn't confronted him straightaway, despite the fact that his reaction awakened suspicions, judging by her expression. She had let him withdraw to his study with the letter before she checked up on him, at the expense of the food getting cold on the stove. She had seen him fumbling through the photos on the sly and demanded an explanation from him. It turned out that she had already drawn certain conclusions about what had happened that day, and now that Jan had come clean about everything that had happened, she had been set on solving the problem rather than showering him with reproach. "Think," she had insisted. "If it was impossible for the girl to take those photos then someone else must have done it. Think." But Jan had managed that all by himself, just before Gunilla had showed up. He had told her about the memory of Peter Norling's company car up there on the narrow forest track above the ravine. How he had realised that Norling had in all likelihood been the person behind the blackmail attempt against him. He had to be the one who was threatening to go to the police with the photos and report Jan for at least the hit-and-run. If he didn't get six million kronor.

Now it transpired—at least if Sandra's serial was to be believed—that Peter Norling had been by the ravine and had witnessed the accident, but that he was innocent of the blackmail attempt. Nevertheless, he had vanished after a few days, and with him the threat. This had been very fortuitous for Jan, who hadn't come up with a better plan than hoping for the best while awaiting catastrophe in a state of perplexity. As far as Gunilla was concerned, that kind of approach was alien—and Jan ought to have understood that back then. Naively, he had never regarded it as Gunilla's concern that *he* would end up in prison for rape, a hit-and-run, and so on. He had seen that as his own problem.

Only now could he look past his own perception of Gunilla—the perception of the world at large too. He could see clearly how she emerged from the shadows in the car park outside PN Auto. The irresistible Gunilla, who had seen Norling coming out of the garage for his lunchbreak and persuaded him to get into her car. He had accompanied her south to where her broken-down SUV was, the one that had been lent to their son, who had a house not far from there. Charming Gunilla, who despite the cheeky imposition and the time it had taken, had kept him sweet all the way down to Digerrojr, and had somehow managed to switch off his mobile. Or destroy it. Inexorable Gunilla, who had lured him to his future burial site in the woods, where the pit had already been dug and the supposedly broken-down SUV might have been, or perhaps not, even if it was the pretext for getting him there. Hard-boiled Gunilla, who had whacked him with a shovel when he was least expecting it, who had mobilised all her strength and repeated the movement as many times as required for her life to continue as normal. Whereupon Peter Norling had fallen or been helped into the pre-dug grave and had thus disappeared.

It was terrible. The fact that Jan's wife of more than twenty-five years was capable of such acts was a complete surprise to him. It transpired that he didn't know her at all, while for her part Gunilla knew him better than he knew himself. She had duped him without him noticing and deceived him into thinking and believing only the things she had wanted him to think and believe.

What they had recently read in the newspaper while at the breakfast table about Peter Norling's body being found hadn't particularly bothered Jan. The man had been missing for a long time and Jan hadn't liked him much when he had been alive—why put on a show now? On the other hand, Gunilla had been very agitated. She had expressed the view that the blackmail attempt didn't show his best side, but that she wouldn't wish the fate that had befallen Peter Norling on her worst enemy. Not to mention the situation faced by his loved ones. A premeditated and most brutal murder—on the island of Gotland of all places. What was the world coming to?

Following Sandra's unannounced visit, Gunilla had cried in disappointment over the misery that Jan had drawn down upon them—she had reproached him for speaking about Sandra in derogatory terms, for not treating her with enough respect. The impression that Gunilla had given at the time was that in spite of the act of infidelity, she empathised with Sandra. It was now clear to him, however, that she was even more coldhearted towards her than Jan was. Even more derisive and damning. This was because Sandra was throwing a wrench in the works for Gunilla, and that wasn't allowed to happen.

Disgrace was not to be drawn down on the Hallin family, and major and unforeseen expenses were not welcome additions to the budget either. On that topic, Mr. and Mrs. Hallin were most certainly in agreement, but when it came to how to achieve this goal, they seemed to have diametrically opposed views. On the whole, Jan had shied away from the problem, hoping that everything would resolve itself if he simply bellowed his refusal and expressed his contempt for beggars and gold diggers and other belittling terms for people like Sandra with sufficient emphasis.

While Gunilla, for her part, had kidnapped a three-year-old. To what end? he asked himself. The ultimate aim must have been to get rid of the boy. Gunilla must have had roughly the same thoughts he had, but with the not insignificant difference that she had tangibly grappled with the task of ridding herself of the child.

It must have been so much easier for a woman than a man to leave the woods with a child in her arms. What was more, if the child had been sleeping then it was doubtful whether any outsiders would even have noticed it. Erik must have got separated from the kindergarten group, and that had left Gunilla just enough scope to do what she needed to do. A quick injection of anaesthetic or whatever it might be—something that a nurse with an imagination would be able to lay her hands on without much difficulty. Then she must have driven him away unnoticed, and what she had subjected him to after that wasn't even worth speculating about. With one miscalculation on her part: the boy had been found again. "Exhausted, but alive," as the media had put it—what did that mean? Had the boy miraculously survived a murder attempt? Floated ashore on a beach? Jumped out of a burning building? Escaped from captivity or recovered from an overdose of some narcotic concoction?

The latter had undeniably been close at hand—even if in Gunilla's case this might have directed suspicion towards someone working in healthcare, and thereby potentially herself. On the other hand, no one would have suspected Gunilla, who was highly regarded in all settings that she moved in. And if there had been any traces of Erik in the car or on other Hallin family possessions then it would have been Jan who was fingered. Including by Gunilla, it had to be assumed—even if she would have done it in a highly practised and barely perceptible manner. Superficially, she would have fought tooth and nail to clear her husband of such preposterous accusations, but under cover she would have worked for the opposite outcome. If it was too late and the family succumbed to scandal, Gunilla had no intention of being pulled down with it. His planned flight was something she had naturally supported on the sole basis that given the current situation it played into her hands.

In short, Gunilla was undoubtedly highly resourceful, and that was a personality trait that he recognised in her. However, what surprised him was her propensity to take risks. The entire procedure of abducting the boy had encompassed a major and imminent risk of discovery. Merely stealing pharmaceuticals from work involved serious risk, but Gunilla had probably made sure to direct suspicions elsewhere or had given patients common salt solutions or nothing at all while keeping their prescriptions.

She had caught Peter Norling in the car park outside his place of work and had been lucky enough not to be seen. Nor had anyone paid any attention to them as they had made their way out of town in her car—her and Jan's car—and driven all the way down to Garde. She could have been seen. The car could have been seen wherever it was parked. Facts that had clearly done little to frighten her.

Jan had apparently been living with a psychopath for almost thirty years. How the hell had he missed that? But she had saved him from one sticky situation after another—he couldn't deny her that.

77

Sandra

WHEN SHE WOKE up again it was in a different kind of light and in a different room. It might be Erik's room, but she didn't have the strength to raise herself in the bed to confirm it. This was in part because she was strangely powerless, and partly because she was quailing at the prospect of discovering yet again that he was no longer there. Was it a genuine experience or something she had dreamt? Sandra didn't dare speculate. She felt totally confused and completely detached from reality. She shut her eyes again.

Someone touched her upper arm. Softly, carefully, and completely lovingly. She cautiously turned her head. At first all she saw was a pair of glasses, which made her jump—an odd reaction given that it was her mother wearing them.

"Sweetheart," she said. "Are you finally awake?"

"What are you doing here?" Sandra asked, dumbfounded. "Where's Erik?"

"Erik's with Grandpa, eating lunch in the dayroom."

"He's okay then?"

"He's absolutely fine," her mother said with a smile. "We've been more worried about you."

"But why?" Sandra said impatiently. "What's happened?"

"Somehow, you ended up with a big dose of some drug or other in your system—they're still not sure what. But it may have been Rohypnol or something like it. You lost consciousness and they had to pump your stomach. Don't you remember any of it?"

"I remember waking up in a different room from this one," Sandra said hesitantly, unsure whether it was a genuine memory.

"That was the recovery room in the intensive care ward. They had you under full observation there for hours and hours. You can't feel anything now?"

"I feel like normal, although I've got a sore throat."

"That's because of the gastric irrigation, as they call it. You've had a tube down your throat."

"I began to slur my words," Sandra remembered. "I was talking to my friend Kerstin on the phone, but she couldn't hear what I was saying."

"Someone called Kerstin came by this morning," her mother said, with a strange expression on her face. "She wanted to check that you were okay. So she said. But she didn't look . . . like she was one of your friends."

Sandra had no response to offer to that remark for several reasons, one of which was that she had never met Kerstin.

"The important thing is that you had a visitor when you lost consciousness."

"He was the one who . . ." Sandra began.

Then she stopped herself. She didn't really know anything.

"He was the one who raised the alarm," her mother said. "If it hadn't been for him, you probably wouldn't be alive."

Sandra could scarcely believe her ears. Hallin? What had he done? Apart from stealing her computer, which was one of the absolute worst things that could happen to her?

"He was apparently very overwrought, and moved heaven and earth to help you. He got nurses to come running from all over the place, and the on-duty doctor turned up after just a few minutes. He claimed that your and Erik's lives were in danger—said he was convinced you'd been poisoned, that you'd unknowingly taken an overdose of some drug or other and needed your stomach pumped straight away. He called the police and insisted the room be guarded round the clock, and that the contents of the two glasses on the nightstand be analysed. Apparently he was also the one who gave the order for your dad and me to be called and brought here."

"And . . . ?" Sandra said.

She was having great difficulty taking in what her mother had just told her. It simply didn't add up; the logic was precarious. Hallin had shot himself in the foot by *saving* rather than *taking* her life? After having liquidated Norling in cold blood and subjected Erik to attempted murder? What had she missed?

"And that's what happened," her mother summarised. "He did all that and then he disappeared. Before the police showed up and without anyone finding out who he was. But perhaps you can tell us about that?"

That needed some thought—apparently not everything was as straightforward as it seemed.

"I don't actually remember anything," she replied. Which was not all that far from the truth, when all things were considered.

"It'll come, you'll see," her mother said, smiling, running two fingers over her cheek.

"My computer . . . ?" said Sandra, who had already prepared herself for the worst.

"In the cupboard where you keep your valuables," her mother said, holding up the key. "Do you want me to get it?"

"Yes please," Sandra said, even though she had no great expectations that the manuscript would still be on it.

But she was mistaken. The large document was strangely enough exactly where it was supposed to be, and at first glance the hitherto unpublished component was seemingly untouched. With an ever-so-small addition to the end: "Check the pictures in your inbox and remember what I said. Murder and kidnapping aren't my thing. Like I said, I'd appreciate it if you humanised me. Get better soon."

The thing about humanising was something she recognised. Now it all began to come back to her slowly. Sporadic memories from the minutes before it had all gone dark: Hallin's appearance at her bedside, his unexpected confession to the rape and his promise to make good, his wish not to be described as a monster. Sandra also remembered that he had accused her of abusing her authority, while at the same time he had denied the most serious crimes in this whole affair.

Could it really be true that it was thanks to the odious Hallin that she—and perhaps Erik—were still alive? That, despite all the negative consequences it would have for him, he had refrained from making the book disappear, from making Sandra disappear? It was an unexpected ending to his role in this protracted drama, to say the least. And the question was whether he had thus managed to ward off his worst fears altogether. The night's events had allowed him to *demonstrate* that he had human, even downright self-sacrificing, traits.

Sandra left the message from Hallin in the document, closed it, and opened her email. The inbox contained several new messages, but only one from the colleague she had contacted during the night. There were a number of photos attached. First there was the original picture taken by Kerstin at Norling's hunting cabin, but in far better condition. Now the car was clearly visible—without doubt a blue Audi. There was also a person visible in the pouring rain: slender, with inclined shoulders, possibly a woman—probably not the significantly broader-shouldered Jan Hallin.

Picture number two was an enlargement of the car's licence plate. It wasn't a registration that Sandra recognised, but it provided a clear, unambiguous reference to the car's owner.

Picture number three showed the person's body close-up—now undoubtedly a woman—while the fourth picture was a detailed study of her face. It still lacked sharp contours, was still partially concealed by rainwater, but it was familiar. There was no longer any doubt about who had undone the bolt on the root cellar door where Erik had been held captive.

Jan Hallin was apparently innocent. At long last it turned out that his wife was the one who had been prepared to go the extra step to protect her social status and finely polished façade. And just as Hallin had tried to explain to her, Sandra now remembered, the wrong person was identified as the perpetrator in her "fucking serial," as he had put it.

Now Sandra also remembered who had served her that bilberry soup. If you removed the unfashionable glasses and what Sandra now realised had to be a wig, the nurse shared significant similarities with Gunilla Hallin. She was a nurse by profession—Sandra knew that. Yet she had been so short-sighted she hadn't immediately made the connection between her body's collapse and the bilberry soup, between the bespectacled nurse and Gunilla Hallin.

It had been careless, prejudiced, and not all that clever of Sandra. She could have died as a result of her narrow-mindedness and preconceived notions. Who knew what Gunilla Hallin would have managed to do, if Jan hadn't thrown his weight around noisily and taken direct action in a way others might not have? What would have happened if Sandra had knocked back the apple juice too? The plan must have been to get rid of Sandra. Or Erik. Or both of them. Perhaps it had been a final attempt to clean up all the loose ends—this time in one fell swoop.

The thought made her feel dizzy. Sandra had had some forewarning, although despite all the drama that had preceded the incident, she hadn't taken her own anxiety sufficiently seriously. But she had been lucky. She had received help from an unexpected quarter. And she had learned some important lessons about not putting the well-being of herself and those closest to her in the hands of fate: in the future she shouldn't take obvious warning signs so lightly; she ought to avoid putting herself in risky situations.

That was what Sandra promised herself as the door opened and a three-year-old's expectant little face cracked into a sunny smile before he ran to the bed and climbed into his mother's arms. The joy couldn't have been greater in either of them.

78

Kerstin

SANDRA HAD CALLED ahead and warned that she was on the way round to Kerstin's flat in Bingeby. Kerstin was worried about what Sandra would make of the neighbourhood dominated by blocks of flats and looking so tired in the depths of July; it was a far cry from the roses and ruins of historic Visby and the slightly mad week dominated by visiting politicians taking place within the old walls. Kerstin had thus far been no more than a voice to Sandra. A voice and an assortment of life experiences. She hoped that Sandra wouldn't be too disappointed, that she wouldn't have to cope with the same mistrust in Sandra's eyes that had materialised in her parents'.

Her worries turned out to be unfounded. Sandra was beaming when she turned up, and embraced her without any prior examination. Kerstin concluded that it could be one of three things: Sandra had already checked her out at a distance to prepare for their first meeting, Sandra had been prepared for the worst after what had passed between them in their calls, or Sandra didn't care about Kerstin's appearance since she knew who she was. Kerstin hoped it was the last.

"It's so good to finally meet you, Kerstin."

"Sorry," Kerstin said awkwardly for the third or fourth time.

"I'm sorry for your loss," said Sandra. "And there's really no need to apologise for being unable to be in two places at once. You prioritised your friend, and you were right to do it. Unlike me, she wasn't surrounded by medical staff, and she couldn't help herself. I'm so sorry about what happened to Jeanette."

"It was what she wanted," said Kerstin. "That's some comfort to me."

Sandra nodded and looked around the small flat.

"This is a really lovely place," she said. "You've got so many books—I like that."

"Thanks," said Kerstin. "I've got a hell of a lot of money too."

Sandra strolled over to the bags and slung one over her shoulder with some effort.

"And you cycled with these?" she said, laughing. "Quite a job, I have to say."

Then she looked at the spot where a tag had clearly been removed from the holdall she had picked. She looked up and caught Kerstin's eye.

"You know that was just the final straw, right?" she said. "The one that broke the camel's back."

Kerstin wasn't so convinced. She shrugged her shoulders and pursed her lips.

"If Jeanette hadn't found that tag, some other last straw."

It was possible that Sandra was right. Kerstin wanted to believe she was, but she felt far from certain. However, there was comfort in the fact that Jeanette had made the choice herself, and that even in death she had looked satisfied with the choice she had made.

"Come on, Kerstin. You'll have to take the other bag."

"But I can't . . ."

"Nonsense, of course you can. We're going to end this together."

It wasn't what they had agreed to, but Sandra was so persuasive that Kerstin was unable to resist. And perhaps it was about time to get a new, healthier relationship with the long arm of the law.

HALF AN HOUR LATER, they were standing at a desk in an open plan office at Visby police station. Sandra had specifically asked to speak to the same investigator she had been assigned as a liaison while Erik had been missing, but Kerstin also knew him. He was one of the two officers who had brought her the news of Karl-Erik's death after he had gone missing—the one who had been there when she had identified the body.

"This bag contains three million kronor," said Sandra, heaving the holdall onto the table with a loud thud. "The proceeds of multiple robberies years ago."

Following Sandra's cue, Kerstin did the same thing. Several other officers had already stood up at their desks and joined the trio with ill-concealed curiosity.

"This bag contains another three million kronor," said Kerstin.

"Consider this cash as evidence," said Sandra. "As the background to a sequence of dramatic events. You'll have to decide yourselves how to respond to them. They're all described in this document, which also contains the as-yet unpublished conclusion to the summer serial in *Gotlands Allehanda*."

Now she let the manuscript drop onto the table: a printed copy of all the words and sentences that comprised the story of the fateful events forever binding together Sandra, Kerstin, and the destinies of several others. The police around them—ten or so by this point—exchanged looks, unclear whether to be taken aback at the workload or to look forward to getting stuck into the thick bundle of prose.

"Here's the mobile that has photos from the hit-and-run at the ravine in Madvar," Sandra continued. "That's evidence too. And here's a document that sets out the real details that I've disguised in the serial. It includes names, ages, years, dates, times, weather, places, car brands, professions, modus operandi, and so on. You'll find everything that you need to proceed all set out nicely."

There was a murmur spreading among the police now, which gradually rose and became an expectant hubbub while the mobile was examined, the bags opened, and the manuscript thumbed through.

It suddenly felt very good to see the police officers' reactions to the handover, and it was no use denying that Kerstin felt a certain pride at having been involved in the work that had gone into that thick document. She had obtained redress of sorts for Karl-Erik, and perhaps even for herself. Despite what it had cost her. And what it might cost her in the future.

INGENIOUS UNMASKING OF MURDERER AND KIDNAPPER WITH A STARRING ROLE FOR *GOTLANDS ALLEHANDA*

A 52-year-old woman has been arrested on suspicion of abduction, attempted murder, and murder. The kidnapping of three-year-old Erik has been resolved thanks to the popular summer serial "Black Ice." The author is anonymous, but is responsible for a number of revelations that eventually led the police to the guilty party.

The boy went missing without a trace on the last Friday of June during a kindergarten outing to the idyllic Furulundsskogen woods just outside Visby. The woman, who works in the healthcare sector, is thought to have seized the boy in an unguarded moment, drugged him, and transported him to a property in the east of Gotland. He is thought to have been held captive there for a period of four days in a subterranean space, and this is now being classified as attempted murder.

Thanks to thorough groundwork by the author of the serial and the woman who eventually found the missing boy, the police have been handed photographic evidence uncovering the woman's guilt in the kidnapping drama.

The 52-year-old is also a suspect in the much-written-about murder of 41-year-old Peter Norling, who had been missing for more than four years before he was found in southern Gotland earlier this summer. In that case, the woman's husband has assisted with evidence, as the victim's blood was found on an SUV owned by the couple that the 41-year-old car mechanic was thought to have been tasked with repairing prior to his disappearance.

The 52-year-old nurse was arrested without any drama at her place of work, but denies all involvement in the crimes and blames her husband instead. The arrested woman claims her husband confessed to the crimes before leaving Gotland and going underground. In reality, he remains on the island and has cooperated with police to enable the arrest of the suspected murderer and kidnapper.

There have been a significant number of accidents and crimes of varying gravities presented by the author and *Gotlands Allehanda* to its readers, and according to the police they have managed to tie the 52-year-old woman to the most serious of them all.

"We are both surprised and grateful for all the help we have received from unexpected sources," said a police spokesman.

For his part, the deputy chief prosecutor states that he is convinced that the evidence and witness testimony gathered so far will be enough to secure a conviction.

"Given the planning involved and the ruthless nature of these crimes, I will be seeking a life sentence," he said.

GOTLANDS ALLEHANDA

Acknowledgements

NOW YOU HAVE READ the almost-true story about what a mess a little snow and cold can cause, and how the consequences can be beyond all proportion for a small number of people. I know the story has met with great interest and that many of you have sought to identify similarities between the characters and actual people, as well as connections between what happens to them and true events. As I just mentioned, the story is almost but not entirely true, so these correlations are hard to find, which has been my intention all along. I'd therefore like to take this opportunity to thank you, the reader, for your attention and tremendous engagement.

Thanks also to Jeanette Wretberg for being such an important person to my good friend Kerstin, for opening up your heart to her and sharing your tragic story that formed the basis of this one. My gratitude in relation to your rescue of Erik together with Kerstin knows no bounds. You will always be in my thoughts now that you have, at last, found peace.

Peter Norling and Karl-Erik Barbenius: your roles were decisive in this story. You were already gone when I began to take an interest in the events that tie us all together. This means that sadly, I have not been able to depict you in a way that is entirely true to life. I regret some of your choices, but I am genuinely sorry for all that you have been subjected to. No person deserves that. I would like to think I have brought you justice, and I hope you rest in peace.

Jan Hallin: you set the ball rolling; you sowed the seed for all that I have depicted, which is deeply unfortunate. You are a better person than that, which you were given the opportunity to demonstrate. You are repentant, and instead of fleeing from your responsibilities, you chose to stay in the country and cooperate with the police. For reasons I'm sure you'll understand, I don't intend to thank you for giving me a son, despite this being one of the greatest of gifts there is. But you also have many fine qualities—human traits, if you like—that I hope to see in Erik too. Last but not least, I want to thank you for putting my life above your own future. It was a heroic gesture, and I will always hold you in high esteem for it.

Above all, I want to thank my very dear friend Kerstin Barbenius. Without you, this book would never have been written. Without you, I would also have lost the light of my life—my son, Erik. Your sincerity and your big heart gave rise to this story, and I'm deeply thankful for your substantial input in terms of fact-checking. I cannot find words to express my feelings in relation to your and Jeanette's resourcefulness—and tenderness—when you found my son, but you will always be a significant person to me and I hope you will be a presence in our lives.

Yours sincerely,
Sandra Christoffersson.